LADY APPRENTICE

A Serving Magic Book – Volume One

TONI CABELL

Linden plunked herself down at the breakfast table, dropping her book bag next to her chair. She ignored the storm clouds on her mother's brow and smiled as Mille poured tea and served her a heaping portion of thick bacon, fried eggs, and fresh-baked scones with melted butter on top.

Linden picked up a strip of bacon between her fingers and took a noisy bite. Her mother huffed in annoyance but wouldn't say anything in front of the servants. Linden took another bite, crunching loudly.

Her father waited until Mille withdrew from the room. Pulling a crumpled piece of parchment out of his pocket, he smoothed it on the table—her report card, which she'd tossed out. Linden put the bacon down on her plate and wiped her fingers on a linen napkin, wishing she'd taken the time to burn her report card.

He tapped the parchment and cleared his throat, stalling for time. Linden knew her father had led Royal Marines into battle, but he hated disciplining her. "This is disappointing and—"

"Totally unacceptable," interrupted her mother. "I don't know what's worse, the report card itself or that you lied about it." Her mother's voice hitched, and Linden felt the familiar roiling pit in her stomach that only her mother could produce.

"I know, I'm a big disappointment, and an embarrassment to both of you. And our family." Linden pushed her chair back, but her father reached out a hand, motioning her to stay.

"You're not a disappointment, but your grades are," he said.

"You're failing nearly everything, even magic handling. This doesn't make any sense," said her mother.

"Especially magic handling, you mean," Linden mumbled. She came from a long line of mages, skilled practitioners of Serving magic. To fail at magic handling was an unthinkable breach of family tradition.

"You're not focusing enough. Perhaps we need to hire another tutor—"

"It won't matter, Mother, how many you hire for me. I can't focus! Every time I do, bad things happen."

"You're exaggerating again."

"And you're not listening again!" Linden grabbed her book bag, slung it over her shoulder, and stormed out of the house, slamming the front door behind her. She paused on the front porch to button her blue wool cardigan against the early spring chill. Glancing up at the gray clouds scuttling across the sky, she debated returning for an umbrella but thought better of it.

Hiking up her calf-length skirt, woven from blue and green nubby yarn, she jogged down the driveway without looking back. She often wished she could wear pants to school, but girls were required to wear skirts, even during exercise classes. If she ever had a say in the matter, she'd make sure girls could wear whatever they wanted. At least she didn't have to wear a formal uniform like her brother at his military school in the capital. She could choose her own outfits each morning.

Linden zigzagged through alleys and fields to avoid running

into any of her mother's large extended family on the way to school. She couldn't avoid them entirely since several of her cousins worked at the school. Her relatives meant well but drove her crazy, always asking what was wrong, or how they could help, or suggesting she should visit the newest healer in town. Then her aunties would cluck their tongues and tell her not to worry, she'd be fine. Her gifts were simply a little late forming. These things sometimes happened in magically gifted families, they'd assure her. She wasn't the black sheep, at least not yet.

Linden sprinted the last fifty yards to the ivy-covered brick school building that occupied a large tract of land at the outskirts of town. The school's four interior hallways surrounded an open courtyard in the center, an impractical feature given the number of rainy and snowy days in Quorne, a border town that sat at the westernmost edge of Valerra.

She made it past the frowning headmaster with seconds to spare before the late bell rang. Linden trotted to her first period class in the gymnasium, located behind the courtyard at the back of the school. As she entered, she smelled the familiar scent of perspiring students and the lemon oil used to clean the gym's wooden floors.

She'd forgotten that her fencing class was hosting an exhibition match with a school from the neighboring town. Students from the two schools lined up on opposing sides of the gym, either sprawling on bleachers or taking a few practice lunges as they impatiently waited their turn. Linden dashed into the girl's locker room, threw her sweater and book bag into an empty locker, and reached down into her book bag to withdraw a hair tie. She pulled her long wavy hair, the color of coal with streaks of blue, into a sloppy ponytail. Linden grabbed her padded fencing jacket and mask off a hook by the door and paused just long enough to select a dull gray practice sword from the storage trunk before re-entering the gym.

"You're late," grumbled Heidl, her fencing master. "And you're up next." Linden donned her padded jacket and walked over to her opponent, a broad young man who towered over her. They shook hands, put on their masks, and squared off. She glanced down at her long skirt and stiff knee-high boots, wishing once again for a pair of slacks and shorter boots like the boys wore. *Boys have such an advantage in the wardrobe department,* she thought, *especially during a fencing match.*

"On guard!" yelled the student referee. Her opponent immediately charged, thrusting his sword at Linden's left side. She parried and riposted, which he deftly blocked. He was an experienced swordsman, and despite the difference in their size, they were well matched. Linden concentrated on each thrust of his sword, trying to anticipate his next move.

They alternately lunged, parried, blocked, and counter-attacked for several long minutes. She backed away and danced around the young man, forcing him to come to her. She had the energy and discipline to bide her time until the end of the five-minute match. Linden sensed her opponent was tiring—his size was a detriment in terms of his endurance, although his strokes were powerful.

She began to enjoy herself and relaxed ever so slightly. That's when she noticed her dull gray sword pulsing with glowing green hieroglyphs. *Not again,* she thought, her sword wobbling slightly in her hand. This was the third time green hieroglyphs had danced across her practice sword during a fencing match, breaking her concentration every time.

She knew what happened to mages—or mage apprentices—who started seeing things that weren't there. Linden sometimes visited Auntie Oonie, who lived in the special wing of the sanatorium reserved for mages who'd lost their way. Oonie now spent her days talking to invisible beasts and conjuring cakes from lavender and clay. Linden vowed she'd never become another Gloomy Oonie, her brother's nickname for their great-aunt who often made doom-filled pronouncements.

Linden gripped her sword harder, trying to focus, until she heard the sound of hobnailed boots tramping directly behind her. She heard something else too. A snuffling, snarling animal sound. She whipped her head around—letting her guard down as she tried to figure out where the sounds were coming from —but she saw no animals or hobnailed footwear in the gym. Just a bunch of students hanging around, and her coach shaking her head.

Linden's opponent slipped his sword under her right arm and made a swift stroke from sternum to navel. If they'd been using real swords, she'd be dead. He stepped back and brought his sword up to his mask in a salute to her. She did the same, and then pulled off her mask. Linden walked stiffly over to the sideline, all the adrenaline from the match drained out of her, leaving her feeling weak and slightly nauseous.

Heidl pulled her aside. "What happened out there? You were winning and then froze up again!" Heidl tapped the side of her own head, and then the center of her chest. "Your head and your heart need to be moving in the same direction—with one you focus, with the other you feel. If they're not in sync, you're not going to be able to win."

Linden nodded wordlessly and headed to the locker room. Her father had been so proud when she'd won the regional fencing championship last year, and now she couldn't pull off even a simple intermural match.

"Maybe Uncle Ric can give you some extra tips," Heidl called out. Linden ignored her cousin. She knew why she'd lost three straight matches. Each time, flashy green hieroglyphs had sprouted along her sword. This was the first time she heard noises, though. Since magic and the sight (which included hearing things) didn't mix well together—and she was exhibit number one in why they didn't mix—she'd have to figure something out, and fast. Maybe she *should* listen to her aunties and visit that new healer, anonymously of course. She didn't want to wind up in a sanatorium if anyone found out about her visions.

Magic handling lab, which used to be her favorite class, occupied a double period after lunch. Linden dropped into her seat at the lab table she shared with Jayna Buri, her best friend. Jayna, who told her last week that she'd be moving to Bellaryss at the end of the school term, was the one person she trusted above everyone else. And even though Linden could visit her, or send her letters, or even use her mother's carrier pigeons for a quicker response, she knew things wouldn't be the same. They wouldn't get to see each other every day. Bellaryss, the capital and largest city in Valerra, was all the way on the other side of the country. Linden rubbed her forehead. She'd woken with a slight headache that morning, which had progressed into heavy throbbing at her temples.

"What's wrong with you?" Jayna asked, a small frown line creasing her smooth brown complexion. Jayna took her healing gifts seriously.

"Headache. And lost another fencing match. And my parents found my report card."

"Oh no."

"They've threatened to hire more tutors and I'm not—"

Master Mage Boreus called the class to order. "I'll be testing your shape-shifting spells and counter-spells today. Prepare your labs." Linden groaned and Boreus glared at her over his half-moon spectacles. "I've placed a shape-shifted pomegranate at each of your lab tables. Use a shape-shifting spell to revert your pomegranate back into its original fireball form, and then deploy a water-douser spell to contain the flames. Remember: Focus, Funnel, Find, Flow. Which means?"

The class recited their teacher's favorite mantra. "Focus your magic, Funnel your energy, and Find the spell's Flow."

"Excellent," said Boreus. "Now let's begin."

Linden stifled another groan. He made it sound so easy, but it wasn't. Especially if you got strange visions when you started focusing too hard. She poked at the red pomegranate on their lab table. The pomegranate rolled around inside a heavy iron bowl, deep enough to contain any fireball that might flare up. "You better start without me," she said.

"But why?" asked Jayna.

"I can't do shape-shifting spells."

"But I've seen you shift pencils into feathers into ribbons and back again. How's this any different?"

Linden took a deep breath and rubbed her head again. She didn't want to let Jayna down, and she knew shape-shifting labs worked better with two apprentices casting the spell.

"Alright, show me the lab book." The girls poured over the book for a while, until they were sure they'd memorized both shape-shifting and water-dousing spells. Once they started the incantations, it would be too late to go back and re-read the spells. They'd be committed to the magic and would have to flow with it.

Linden and Jayna placed their hands above the iron bowl and incanted the fireball shape-shifting spell in unison: "Shift from red, round fruit to flames so bright. Stop when burning true and right."

Concentrating on the pomegranate, they repeated the incantation in a continuous loop. Nothing happened during the first three repetitions. During the fourth incantation sequence, the red skin shriveled and took on an orange hue. During the sixth sequence, Linden felt warmth begin to radiate from the fruit.

Jayna smiled at Linden, who stared at their hands hovering over the bowl, too afraid to break her concentration long enough to smile. They repeated the incantation until a small flame burst out of the pomegranate's center and spread quickly, congealing the fruit into a pulpy black mess. The flame rose higher, licking the edges of their iron bowl.

"Let's start the counter spell," said Jayna. Linden barely heard her, because a small hooded man hopped around inside the flames in front of them. Linden blinked rapidly. *Did he just wave at me, like he's flagging me down?* Jayna switched to the water-douser spell. "Source of water running near, pour forth upon us from the air."

Linden intoned the words to the counter spell. She might have mixed up a few of the words but it was too late to worry about that now. Beads of sweat broke out on her forehead as she tried to focus. "Source of water running in, pour upon us from within."

The flames flickered as if someone had opened a window, but no miniature waterfall gathered above the iron bowl to drench the fire. Linden was too busy staring at the little hooded man to do more than mumble along with Jayna. *Could he be one of the fay folk? But why did he make himself so small? The fays were the same size as the rest of us. And why is he standing inside a bowl of fire?* She shook her head, fumbling the words and mixing up the two spells. "Shift from red, round fruit to fiery flame, soar above us from within."

The fire metastasized, leaping out of the bowl and spreading across their table. The hooded creature vanished in a wisp of smoke. Jayna swept their books and papers off the table in one motion and shouted the water-douser spell. Linden repeated her jumbled incantation, which made the fire spread even faster. Flames jumped onto the floor and raced over to the next lab table, where one of the students looked down and screamed. She and her partner pushed their table away, sending their fireball toppling to the floor, where it combined with the first one. Other students yelled and tripped over themselves trying to run away.

"Everyone stand back!" yelled Boreus. He raised his hands

and incanted the water-douser spell. A large waterfall opened up in the ceiling above his head, burst over the lab tables and onto the floor. Water sprayed books, papers, book bags, jackets, and food wrappers, running in rivulets down the aisles and drenching Boreus. After he was certain the fire was out, he lowered his hands. The waterfall slowed to a drizzle and petered out. A hazy curtain of smoke hovered above the classroom. Linden sneezed. The room smelled like burnt parchment, wet wood, and old rags. Boreus removed his spectacles and reached inside his soaked robe for a damp handkerchief to mop his face.

"Hari, Neds, Lon, please set the tables and chairs to rights, and then go to the headmaster's office for brooms, buckets, and the like. The rest of you, start sorting out the books and papers. Let's salvage what we can, and then everyone is on cleanup duty."

Linden and Jayna headed toward their overturned table to begin the clean up, but Boreus held his up his large hand. "We're going to have a little chat. Outside in the courtyard, ladies." The girls followed Boreus outside, where he indicated they should sit on one of the stone benches scattered about the courtyard. A lone crabapple tree not yet in bloom stood in the center of the courtyard, surrounded by a few clumps of daffodils.

"I want to know what happened in there. Start from the beginning and leave nothing out. And I mean nothing," he directed that last comment at Linden, who arched her eyebrows at him innocently. "Jayna, please go first," he said.

After Jayna finished explaining how the water-douser spell didn't work, he sent her back to the classroom to help with the cleanup. Jayna cast a sidelong glance at Linden and mouthed, "Good luck!"

"Your turn, Linden. What really happened in there?"

Linden shrugged. "It was just like Jayna told you, the spell didn't work."

"Repeat the spell please." Linden rubbed her head and blinked. Nothing. Her mind was a complete blank, except for the image of the little hooded man waving at her from inside the fire.

"Well?"

"I think I jumbled up the two spells," she said quietly.

"Even jumbling up the two spells wouldn't cause that fire to jump out of the iron bowl. No, something else is at play here."

"Like what?"

"Like you're not telling me the truth."

"But I am!" Linden wasn't going to tell him about the little hooded figure in the flames, or the glowing green hieroglyphs on her sword, or any of the other weird stuff she'd been dealing with lately. She'd almost told Jayna last week, but that was before Jayna's mother was appointed head of the Royal Healer's Guild, and Jayna had been crying about moving at the end of the school term. Linden didn't want Jayna to start worrying about her, which Jayna would, so she kept her fears to herself.

Boreus removed his spectacles and tapped them on his knee. Linden looked at the closest clump of daffodils and decided she liked the yellow ones better than the white ones. Boreus stopped tapping and shrugged. "Then you've left me no choice. I'm recommending your suspension, until you've been seen by a healer and deemed fit to return to school." He added more gently, "Something's not right with your magic, lass. We both know that."

"But what about my job?" Linden worked part-time in the after-school program three days a week and loved spending time with the younger children, who looked up to her. She felt like it was the one thing she got right.

"Sorry, Linden, but you're fired."

Linden stood up, her arms stiff at her sides, "But you can't fire me—I'm your cousin!"

"I don't care if you're Queen Ayn herself! I can't have you anywhere near the younger students in your current condition."

"What'll I tell my parents?" Linden's stomach knotted at the prospect of all the family commotion heading her way. And it wasn't just her parents that worried her. Her grandmother would be all over her, insisting on taking charge and having her seen by every master healer in the capital.

"Tell your parents what you're not telling me. The truth." Boreus stood up and nodded. "Now report to the headmaster's office. I'll be along shortly."

Linden's shoulders slumped. She shuffled across the courtyard, her mind reeling. Between her headache and queasy stomach, she wanted to curl up in bed and stay there until she could sort things out. And maybe think of a good story to explain everything away.

She'd just re-entered the school from one of the side doors when she heard the distant peal of a bell. She paused to listen. Someone was hard at work, ringing the warning bell in the watchtower at the top of the hill that overlooked the western border.

Linden darted to the front of the school and ran outside. Other bells picked up the signal. Soon every bell in Quorne, from the provincial headquarters where her parents worked to the fire brigade, rang out the emergency code for a border raid. Linden looked around at the students and teachers gathering on the front lawn, their mouths open in disbelief.

Raiders attacked at night, trampling crops, damaging property, and stealing horses. But these raiders were crossing the border on a cloudy spring day. And Linden's school sat at the edge of town, the closest building to the western perimeter —and directly in the path of whoever or whatever was heading their way.

CHAPTER 2

"**G**et inside, now! Raiders are coming!" Linden waved her arms and ran toward the younger students—many of whom she knew well from her after-school job, which she realized with a pang no longer existed. None of that mattered at the moment. She had to get them somewhere safer than the front lawn of the school.

Boreus, Heidl, and the other teachers sprang into action, ordering everyone to gather in the gymnasium. It was the only room large enough for both faculty and students, and its heavy oak doors could be bolted from the inside. But instead of lining up in age order as they'd been drilled, everyone started running at the same time. One girl tripped and skinned her knees. Two friends grabbed her by the arms and hauled her along. Some of the children started crying. A couple of older students picked them up and carried them into the building.

"Sending everyone into a single room makes us sitting ducks for the raiders," Linden said to Boreus, who was holding open one of the front doors and shooing students inside the building. "My father would never approve."

Boreus looked at Linden distractedly. "It's the most defensible position in the school."

"It'd be better if we spread out and locked ourselves in classrooms and closets and such."

"Why?"

"Harder to hit a dispersed target."

"We'll conjure a defensive shield inside the gym. Their firearms will be useless." Linden knew that active magic disabled mechanical devices, including guns. But the raiders knew that as well.

"I still think—"

Boreus nodded toward the hill. "Too late. Inside, now!"

Linden looked over her shoulder and saw what looked like an entire army unit heading their way. Usually raiders wore dark tunics, crossed into Valerra after midnight, and moved with quiet stealth. These raiders wore Glenbarran uniforms, marched in daylight, and wanted to be seen. A jolt of adrenaline-fused fear surged through her.

Boreus pushed her through the front door and threw the bolt. They joined the throng of students clogging the main hallway. Boreus directed the students to split up, sending half the students, including Linden, around the north side of the courtyard where they'd enter the gym through the left door, while the rest of the students headed in the opposite direction, toward the door on the right side of the gym.

Linden jogged behind the others, straining her ears for any sounds of breaking glass or splintering wood. Maybe the raiders would bypass their school. After all, what would an army of raiders want with a school? There was nothing of value inside, nothing they could take and resell to black market merchants across the border in Glenbarra.

As Linden rounded the corner, she thought she heard someone crying in one of the classrooms. The students ahead of her were almost through the door to the gym. Linden turned around and started opening classroom doors, calling out, "Is anyone there?" After opening half a dozen doors and finding no one, she turned to run back to the gym but heard a child crying close by. Linden crossed the hall and opened the door to the kinder-class. Delle cowered under a desk, her two chubby hands covering her ears. She looked up at Linden, her face streaked with tears.

"Bells ringing," Delle hiccupped.

"They'll stop soon enough," Linden said, reaching under the desk and taking her hand. "Come along to the gym." She stepped into the hall with Delle. She hurried the child along until they reached the gym door, sealed shut against intruders, the defensive shield already cast.

"Hey! Open up—it's Linden and Delle!" Linden yelled and pounded on the door with both her fists. Delle started crying again. Linden continued pounding and hollering until she heard a loud crash from the front of the school, followed by sounds of shouting and hobnailed boots tramping on the flagstone floor.

Linden's heart thundered as she glanced around for a good hiding place. She swung Delle into her arms and dashed into the healer's office across the hall. Linden closed the door, but the lock wouldn't latch. She put Delle on a cot and dragged a chair over to the door, wedging it under the doorknob.

Linden knelt down by Delle and whispered, "We're going to play a game. Aright?" Delle nodded. "It's like hide-and-seek, only better."

"How?" asked Delle.

"First, we have to be really quiet. Can you do that?" Delle brought a finger to her lips. "Then we have to hide and not move a muscle, no matter what happens. Are you ready?" Delle nodded again.

Linden led Delle into the healer's supply closet, where she pulled the child next to her and slid the door closed. The old door didn't fit flush to the wall, and a small shaft of light peeked through.

A loud crack rent the air, like something breaking or giving way, followed by screaming and more shouting. *Did the raiders break into the gym after all? Jayna and Heidl and Boreus would be trapped, surrounded, and then what?* Linden rubbed her temples and tried to calm her racing pulse by taking deep breaths.

That's when she heard snuffling, snarling animal sounds outside the door to the healer's office. The beast growled and started scratching the wood. One of the raiders pushed on the door but Linden had jammed it well.

"What's that?" asked Delle, forgetting their game.

"Shh!" Linden clamped her hand over Delle's mouth. The little girl's eyes widened but she didn't fidget. Linden pulled her hand away and whispered, "We're still playing the game."

Someone began ramming the office door. Linden frantically tried thinking of a spell, anything that would cast a safety net around them. She pulled Delle against her chest and closed her eyes. *Think, Linden! This time it really counts.*

A page from *Timely Spells* popped into her head. The spell was so simple even she couldn't mess it up. Linden studied the spell in her mind's eye, squeezed her eyes shut in concentration, and conjured a veil of drabness to conceal them. "Drape us in a veil of gauze, hide us from inquiring eyes."

She and Delle would be hidden in plain sight from any searchers, and even their scent should go undetected. Linden crossed her fingers and kept repeating the incantation in her head, silently moving her lips, until she was certain the veil would hold. Delle shifted in her lap but remained quiet.

The raider and his beast broke into the healer's office. Linden peered through the slit where the closet door didn't meet the wall and nearly yelped in surprise. The wolfish face of a crossbreed peered back at her, snapping the air in front of the closet with its powerful jaws. Crossbreeding programs were illegal in Valerra, but not in Glenbarra. She'd heard of crossbreeds but never encountered one before.

This creature had a bushy tail and four wolfish legs, with a pair of furry human hands for paws up front. Its forehead and eyes looked like a man's, but the snout and muzzle were all wolf. The wolf-man reared up in front of the closet, sniffing and growling. Linden's heart jumped inside her chest. "Drape us in a veil of gauze, hide us from inquiring eyes," she repeated in her head, terrified the crossbreed might have detected them with its superior sense of smell.

A grubby-looking trooper, who'd followed the creature into the office, came up behind it and looked around. Linden froze, praying Delle wouldn't squirm. The soldier reached out a hand to open the closet door. Someone shouted a muffled command from outside the office. The soldier turned away and blew on a high-pitched whistle. The crossbreed let out one more growl and then trotted after the soldier.

Linden exhaled—she hadn't realized she'd been holding her breath.

"Ugly!" whispered Delle.

"Very ugly!"

They stayed in the closet for another fifty minutes or so, long after Linden heard the last of the hobnailed boots stomping past. Delle had dozed off in her lap. Then the all-clear rang from the school bell out front, and Linden heard normal sounds again—teachers calling out instructions and students chattering in the hall, ignoring them. She roused Delle from her nap and took her hand.

Linden found Heidl near the school entrance. The fencing master clapped a hand on Linden's shoulder, a grin spreading across her face. "Found 'em!" Heidl called outside, where Boreus was questioning several students. He looked at Linden over his half-moon spectacles and heaved a sigh. Boreus came up to Delle and tousled her hair, and then he actually smiled at Linden.

"Your father would've flayed us alive if anything had happened to you, lass!"

"Is everyone safe?" she asked. They both nodded. The raiders hadn't crashed into the gym, as she'd feared, but they'd destroyed a number of classrooms, including their magic handling lab.

"The defensive shield held—but barely," Boreus admitted. "They used powerful counter spells I've never seen before."

"We'll be consulting your father on school security," said Heidl.

"Mamma!" Delle slipped her hand from Linden's and ran into the waiting arms of her mother, who'd run to the school searching for her. Linden looked past them to the school lawn, where parents were arriving by foot or horse or steam-powered locomobile, frantically searching for their children. Whoops and tears accompanied their joyful reunions. Linden said good-bye to her cousins and walked outside, scanning the crowd. Jayna ran up and threw her arms around Linden before heading home with her younger sister and mother.

Linden milled around the grounds looking for her parents. She ran up to one couple that looked like them from behind, until they turned around and called out to the boy next to her. Their reunion ratcheted up her anxiety and brought a tiny stab of pain. Her mother and father should have been here by now, unless something had gone terribly wrong.

After checking out every woman and man still standing in clusters on the lawn, Linden took off for home. She ran past aunties who'd gathered outside to ask about the school, past clusters of neighbors standing in the street, everyone talking at once. The first few raindrops from the incoming storm pelted her back as she dashed up the drive to her white two-story frame house. Linden leaned on the porch railing to catch her breath. Straightening up, she noticed the front door, painted her father's favorite shade of forest green, hanging ajar. As Linden walked up to it, she saw the door had been partially ripped from its hinges.

"Mother? Father? Mille?" she called out. "Anyone home?" She pushed the door aside and sucked in her breath.

The gilt-framed mirror in the front hall hung at an odd angle on the wall, the glass inside a spider-web of cracks. Her legs shook as she picked her way through the debris of their front parlor. Tables and bookcases were overturned, the books scattered about and their pages shredded. Sofas and chairs were slashed open, wallpaper scored, and artwork torn down.

Linden wondered whether she should go any further or wait. What if a raider were hiding inside? She returned to the front hall and grabbed an umbrella from the brass stand by the door. Not much of a weapon but it made her feel better. After she'd navigated the main floor, calling for her parents and grimacing at the extent of the destruction—someone had taken an ax to her mother's prized mahogany dining table— Linden ran upstairs but wished she hadn't. The worst damage had been inflicted on the family's bedrooms.

Raiders had busted her brother's collection of chess sets, the more valuable pieces stolen. Matteo's acceptance letter to the Royal Marine Academy in Bellaryss was stripped from its frame and stamped with a dirty boot print. Linden missed her brother right then. He could be incredibly annoying as her parents' golden boy, but she loved him despite the fact he was perfect.

Her parents' suite was thoroughly ransacked, the wardrobes turned out and clothing scattered all over the floor. Linden reached out a trembling hand, the umbrella clattering to the floor. She touched a recent family portrait hanging in her mother's sitting room. Her father, mother, and Matteo stared back at her. But her image had been cut out of the frame. Panic turned her stomach into a fistful of knots. Why would anyone want her portrait? Her parents were the famous ones around here. Her mother was the provincial governor and her father a retired war hero. She, on the other hand, was a failure at pretty much everything she tried.

Linden flung open the door to her bedroom, expecting the worst. Her dresser was lying on its back and her mattress was slit open, the stuffing tossed about the room. Draperies hung from the rods in long shreds, her books were clawed apart, and her paperweight collection smashed.

She knelt on the floor and pulled open her top dresser drawer. Pushing aside the nightgowns, her hand closed around *Timely Spells*, given to her by her grandmother on her sixteenth birthday. The book had been in her family for generations. Written in fay hieroglyphs that no one could read anymore, the book decided which set of spells to reveal, and when, translating them from the ancient fay language for the current owner. She was sure it had saved her life that day. She tucked it away in a leather pouch she'd retrieved from her wardrobe.

As far as she could tell no one was home. Linden wanted to believe this was good news, but she feared the worst. Her mother would have been in her office downtown when the raiders attacked, and her father, as chief of security, would've been nearby. Afterwards they would have rushed to the school to search for her. Not finding her there, they would have come home.

Tears coursed down her face and Linden didn't try wiping them away. Grief and guilt tore her up inside. She'd been so snarky to her parents lately and had run out of the house that morning without even saying good-bye. She couldn't remember the last time she'd said she loved them. Linden cried, beating her fists on the woolen carpet of her bedroom until her hands hurt and she was gulping for air.

She stood up shakily, trying to decide where to go next,

when she heard a noise from somewhere inside the house. Linden stepped out of her bedroom and slowly descended the stairs, a finger of fear creeping up her spine. She'd just reached the bottom step when she heard a rustling sound from the parlor.

Linden edged around the corner but saw nothing. Then she heard the noise behind her, near the front door, and her chest tightened. She pivoted on her left foot, prepared to spring at whoever was behind her. Instead she screamed as a ball of fur and wings screeched loudly and smashed into her chest.

CHAPTER 3

"Kal!" Linden's miniature griffin clicked his beak excitedly and circled around her several times. Kal had the body of a lion, with four paws and a tail, plus a pair of wings that could carry him across a field faster than a horse. A soft reddish mane fringed his eagle's face.

"Linden!" her father stood in the doorway and called behind him, "Kamden, she's here! She's fine."

Linden's mother skirted around her father and ran into the front hall. Her eyes were puffy and red, and her well-tamed chestnut brown hair had escaped from her neat bun and hung in chunks around her face.

Linden choked back a sob as she ran to her mother, at which point her mother broke down. Her father wrapped his arms around them both and closed his eyes, probably to hold any tears in check. Then everyone started talking at once, all the while Kal continued clicking his beak until Linden's mother shooed him onto the porch.

That's when her mother and father registered the mayhem all around them. "Ric look at this place! What were they after? Why destroy our home?"

Linden's father looked about him in disbelief. "I don't know why they did all this," her father waved his arm, "And targeted the school and sanatorium—the young and the disabled. This was no ordinary raid," he said that last part under his breath.

"It's worse upstairs. Our bedrooms—" Linden's voice wavered. "And they ripped my image out of our family portrait. They left Matteo's image, and yours, but took mine. Why?"

"What??" Both her parents spoke at once and then looked at each other.

"Why would they do that?" said Linden. "You're the famous ones around here, and Matteo is a star cadet at the academy. It makes no sense."

"Show me," said her father.

Linden took her parents upstairs and waited in the hall while they went into their bedroom to examine the damage. Linden didn't want to enter the bedrooms again. Something about them scared her more than staring in the face of that crossbreed. Like she'd been violated somehow.

Her mother walked out looking pale as moonlight, while her father clenched and unclenched his jaw. He took Linden by the hand and led her downstairs to the kitchen, which had escaped relatively unscathed. He nodded at the oak table and cane-bottom chairs. "Have a seat," he said to Linden, pulling out a second chair for her mother. Then he put an extra scuttle of coal inside the stove and fired it up. He filled the teakettle with water from the tap over the kitchen sink and placed it on the stove to heat. Tap water was still a relative novelty in Quorne, although Linden's grandmother had installed running water throughout her home in Bellaryss a decade earlier. It took a while for inventions to make their way from the capital to the far-flung border towns.

Linden's father fixed them steeping mugs of sweet hot tea mixed with brandy. The tea burned all the way down Linden's throat and into her stomach, but in a good way. Her father was about to speak when they heard faint knocking. He jumped up to follow the sound out of the kitchen and down the back stairs to the root cellar and winter pantry.

He walked back up the stairs with two frightened servants —Mille and her husband, Yogi. They'd hidden in the pantry when the bells started ringing, but then the lock jammed, and they'd been trapped inside. Her father gave them the rest of the week off, which they insisted they didn't need, and paid for them to stay in the inn downtown, since their rooms had been damaged as well.

Then he sat back down to his now cold tea, which he drank anyway, and stared at his mug while Linden's mother asked about the raid at school. Linden filled her in but skipped the part about being locked out of the gym and almost discovered by a creepy wolf-man. She also bypassed the other parts of her day, like losing another fencing match due to her glowing sword, starting a fire because she saw a little hooded man in the flames, and then getting suspended and fired from her after-school job. Linden hoped the raid would kind of wipe the slate clean. Although that was a lot to wipe clean, even for her.

Her father asked a few questions, but he mostly listened to her mother and Linden talk about the raid. Linden knew he took any breach of security, any danger to his family, as a personal failure.

"What happened downtown?" Linden asked when she'd finished talking about the attack at her school.

"Nothing. We heard the warning bells, locked ourselves inside our offices, and cast a defensive shield around provincial headquarters," her father said. "When the all clear sounded, we went outside and didn't see any damage, so we thought it was a false alarm."

"Until the chief constable arrived to tell us about the attacks on the school and sanatorium," added her mother. "And that's when we hurried to the school, but we couldn't find you."

"Speaking of which, I want to check on Oonie and the other patients at the sanatorium. But first I need to get you two settled at Heidl's. We can't stay here." Linden's father sent her upstairs to pack a bag, but he saw her hesitation. His eyes —the same shade of shale gray as hers—softened. He wordlessly went upstairs and packed for her and her mother.

"What about Kal? We can't leave him here," Linden asked when her father came downstairs with the luggage.

"Certainly not! He's a member of the family. And he's the one who urged us to hurry home," said Linden's mother.

"*Kal* urged you home?" Linden asked. Her mother had never really liked Kal, so Linden wondered if her mother might be suffering from shock.

"He found us—well me, actually—getting all panicky at the school when we didn't see you anywhere. And he kept clicking his little beak and circling overhead. It was your father's idea to follow him. He thought Kal was trying to give us a signal, and he was right."

When Linden had discovered Kal in an abandoned nest last year, her mother hadn't wanted Linden to keep him. She finally relented when Linden promised to take full responsibility for his care. Linden sent Kal outside in the mornings so he could hunt for his own food, and Kal returned home every day after school. Linden decided her mother's new attitude toward Kal might be the second-best thing to have happened that day. The best thing—everyone was safe.

"Kal can stay on Heidl's porch," said her father. "Why don't you carry him out to the locomobile?" Her father's sleek white locomobile was one of the newer models, with two rows of blue upholstered seats that could comfortably fit a family of six. Her mother refused to drive "that steam-powered contraption" as she called it, preferring to walk or take her horse and buggy wherever she needed to go.

Kal nibbled Linden's ear when she picked him up. "Ouch!"

Linden said, "Cut it out!" He settled down in Linden's lap and fell asleep during the short ride to Heidl's.

Heidl laid out a simple supper for them while Linden's father lugged their bags into their rooms. Linden yawned and excused herself. She dropped her clothes on the floor, donned a nightgown, and tumbled into bed, waking hours later with her heart pounding. She'd dreamt of the crossbreed staring at her through the gap where the door didn't close, only in her dream he'd then used one of his furry hands to push open the closet door and grab her by the hair. She wouldn't fall back to sleep anytime soon.

She padded down to the kitchen, planning to warm up some milk, when she found her father stirring a pan of milk on the stove. "Enough for two?" she asked.

"Always. And just in time, too." He grabbed two mugs from the cupboard and expertly poured out the milk. Then he reached into his pocket and unwrapped two squares of chocolate. He held up a square and pointed to her mug.

"Always," Linden said as her father plopped the square in her mug. It was the Arlyss version of hot cocoa.

They alternately stirred and sipped, each lost in their thoughts, until Linden remembered her father had visited the sanatorium.

"How's Auntie Oonie?"

Her father didn't answer right away. He seemed to be searching for the right words. "Traumatized. Furious. And mostly lucid, at least I think so," he stirred his milk again. "She wants to see you tomorrow. Says she has a message for your ears only."

This was the woman who'd sent her a pie filled with stinging nettles on her last birthday. Lucid? Linden doubted it, but she didn't say anything. She nodded.

"Good," he said. "Thanks." He washed his mug and leaned over to plant to a kiss on top of her head. "Coming soon?"

"In a little bit," Linden said, indicating her mug.

She found a large crocheted throw in Heidl's parlor and tossed it around her shoulders. She opened the door to the screened-in porch and pulled the throw more closely around her. Kal stirred in the corner.

"Hey buddy," she whispered. "Can you use some company?" She stretched out on the lounge chair. Kal hopped up and laid down protectively at her feet. Linden fell back to sleep, undisturbed by dreams of raiders and crossbreeds.

Linden and her father stood outside the sanatorium. Although the raiders had broken windows, hacked down shrubbery, and terrorized the residents, the single-story brick building was intact. She entered through the main door and nodded at the healer on duty, who asked after her parents. The place always smelled of ammonia and roses. They used ammonia to clean the rooms and roses to mask the pungent odor.

Linden found Oonie staring at the boarded-up window in her room. She smiled when she saw Linden, who pulled up a chair next to her. Oonie braided her long gray hair around her head like a crown.

"Did you see them?" Oonie asked without preamble. That was Oonie. Straight to the point, even if you had no idea what she was talking about.

"See who?"

"The grihms."

Linden looked confused so Oonie explained, "The wolf-men."

"Oh. Yeah, they were at my school."

"I dreamt of them months ago, although I'd never seen one until yesterday."

"You saw one here?"

Oonie nodded. "A grihm broke my window and then bared his teeth at me."

"Why wasn't there a defensive shield around the building?"

"There was, but the master disabled it."

Linden was having trouble following Oonie. "The master?"

"Aye, girl, now pay attention. The master came with the raiders, searching for something or someone."

Linden furrowed her brow. "Searching for...?"

"Well that's the question now, isn't it?"

Linden waited for Oonie to say more, but she didn't. "Who's the master?"

"He comes from up north." Oonie waved in a southerly direction, but Linden realized she was talking about Faynwood, where her father's family was from. A place she'd never visited because they'd been fighting a civil war since her father's mother was a girl. Whenever she'd ask her grandmother about growing up in Faynwood, Nari would get a far off look in her eyes and say it was a magical place, literally. Everyone could cast spells, from kitchen maids to clan chiefs. So much Serving magic swirled about the place that Faymons didn't use modern technology, like telegraphic transmitters or steam-powered locomobiles. All that magic interfered with the operation of the mechanicals.

Linden had her Faynwood relatives to thank for her distinctive shade of hair, darkest black with vivid blue highlights. According to her grandmother, all Faymons had blue highlights in their hair, whether their base shade was black, brown, ginger or blonde. Although Linden's father and brother had some bluish streaks in their dark brown hair, Linden's blue highlights were brighter and more obvious. She'd taken a lot of teasing about her hair color in school, and sometimes people still stared at her, especially on a sunny day when her blue highlights practically shimmered.

When she was six or seven, after a particularly bad day of

teasing at school, Linden had run home in tears. Her Valerran mother thought Linden was overreacting and should simply ignore the taunts. But Linden's father, who'd grown up as the son of Faymon immigrants, understood what it felt like to be singled out. He explained that the teasing and name-calling might have more to do with the unease many Valerrans felt around Faymons; after all, Faymons were more powerful mages. After her father visited the school and spoke with Linden's teacher, much of the obvious teasing had subsided.

Oonie seemed to have lost her train of thought and was pulling at a loose piece of yarn on her sweater. "Why is the master here?" Linden prompted, not sure she wanted to hear the rest of what Oonie had to say, but she'd promised her father.

"He's looking for one who can conjure and see. Like me. Like you."

The hair on the back of Linden's neck bristled. "What are you talking about?" She hadn't told anyone about her visions. They'd started weeks ago, on the day she turned sixteen-and-a half, and at first, she thought she was coming down with a fever. But she almost never got sick.

"Don't spin a tale for me, girl. I've known about you for a long time."

"Known about what?"

"You're both mage and seer. It's not an easy path. Especially if the master's after you."

The idea of winding up like Oonie roiled Linden's stomach. Her headache had lifted during the night, but she found herself rubbing her temples.

"Strange dreams. Day visions. Headaches." Oonie continued, "And your magic goes haywire. Can't focus on your spells." Oonie narrowed her eyes at Linden. "Don't deny it, girl. I've seen you."

Linden desperately wanted to leave, but her curiosity got the better of her. "Seen me? Where and when?"

"On the run. From the war. From the master himself." Linden stood up to leave. She'd heard enough from Gloomy Oonie.

Oonie called out as Linden's hand pushed open the door, "When they tell you to run, girl, be sure you run fast. Remember Auntie Oonie told you first."

Linden's father was leaning against the passenger door of their locomobile. He waited until they both got in and closed the doors before asking, "How'd it go?"

"About what I expected."

Her father paused in the middle of stomping the clutch to start the steam engine and shook his head. "I'd hoped she had something to say, something meaningful."

"What was it you always used to say? 'Hope isn't a plan and wishing isn't a mission.'"

"Pretty obnoxious, huh?"

"Nah. Just fatherly, in a commanding marine officer kind of a way." Linden smiled at her father. "What's Mother up to?"

"Organizing cleanup crews, getting quotes for repairs, and lodging a formal complaint."

"Well good. How long before our house will be livable?"

"She's taking care of *official* business right now. Your mother has a province to run—one that's just been attacked. She's going to be extremely busy for a while."

"What about our house?"

"We'll get it sorted out soon enough."

"Sorted out? It's a disaster! We can't even live there." Linden looked at her father suspiciously. "There's something you're not telling me."

Her father didn't answer her. They rode in silence for a while, and Linden leaned her head back against the plush upholstery. Only town folks had locomobiles, because they'd didn't run well over country lanes and were useless in mud or snow. But give them a gravel road, and they could keep pace with a horse. Of course, everyone that drove locomobiles also owned horses, because they still needed to travel in the country and through mud and snow. Linden liked all modes of travel, anything that let her feel a little sun on her face and whipped up her hair behind her, which was why she rolled down the window as soon as she got into the locomobile. She inhaled the fresh air, grateful to be outside, anywhere but Oonie's confining bedroom.

Quorne was a quaint town, really more of a large village, overlooking the Windrun River. Buildings constructed of red brick with slate roofs surrounded a large green in the town center. Trees lined the streets and dotted the square, their buds and leaves not yet open after the deep-freeze of winter. The shops and cottages were single story, except for provincial headquarters, the village pub, and a few of the newer frame homes at the edge of town, such as Linden's, which had an upper level.

Her father took the river road, since he knew she liked it best. They rode in companionable silence, Linden staring out the window at the crystal-clear river running below them. Farther along the riverbank was a tiny strip of beach that she and Jayna would frequent during the summer. Linden remembered Jayna would be moving at the end of the school term and sighed, wondering how she'd cope without her best friend.

They pulled up in front of provincial headquarters. Linden greeted the two friendly constables guarding the front entrance and followed her father into the building and down the short hallway to her mother's office. Her father opened the office door and said, "Family conference."

"Can't we skip the family conference for today? After all, I just visited Auntie Oonie. She's family."

"That's quite enough, Linden."

Linden hated family conferences because no one ever conferred with her. It was code for her parents making an important decision affecting the rest of her life and then telling her about it afterwards. Like when they made her move from Bellaryss to Quorne four years earlier, when her mother had been appointed governor of Valerra's western province. Linden had just started secretly dating Toz Valti, and then poof. She had to move. Of course, she and Toz hadn't been serious—they'd only been twelve at the time—but still.

She slumped in one of the overstuffed chairs in her mother's elegant office and stared at the gold-striped wallpaper. Her mother glanced at her. "Sit up honey, it's so much more becoming."

Linden slouched down further, and her mother huffed. Their truce from the previous evening was over. Not that she didn't love her mother—yesterday had reminded her just how much. But this was her future they were discussing.

Her father sat in another of the overstuffed chairs but managed to maintain perfect military posture. He cleared his throat. "Linden, your mother and I, well we want to...that is, we believe...Queen's Crown. I'm not explaining this well at all." He looked at Linden. "We can no longer keep you safe here in Quorne. We thought we could, but yesterday was a warning—a warning that came far too close for comfort."

Linden's mother got up and walked around her elegant teak desk. Wearing a long burgundy dress with little pearl buttons down the front, her hair tamed back into a businesslike bun, Kamden Arlyss looked ready to manage her province, her home, and her daughter. Leaning against the desk to face Linden, she said gently but firmly, "What we're trying to tell you is that we're sending you away, for your own good."

"Where to?"

"We're sending you to live with your grandmother."

Linden's day just went from bad to worse.

Her parents were sending her to Bellaryss—all the way on the other side of the country—to live with the highest-ranking master mage in Valerra. Nari Arlyss could see through a lie faster than Kal could spot a field mouse in the underbrush. Linden's days of keeping secrets would soon be at an end. And then what? How would her grandmother react when she found out about Linden's weird visions and failed magic?

One thing was certain, Nari would monitor Linden's friends and activities even more closely than her mother. She'd make it her business to find out why Linden's magic wasn't working, and then she'd try to "fix" it. If Linden wasn't careful, she'd wind up spending every spare second with her grandmother or one of her healer cronies.

Linden's social life was officially over.

CHAPTER 4

"**I** can't believe Matteo talked me into this," Linden muttered, smoothing out her mint-green silk ball gown with the sweetheart neckline. The full skirt flounced around her legs as she squirmed in the backseat of her uncle's chauffeured locomobile. Although she'd moved from Quorne to Bellaryss two months earlier, she hadn't quite adjusted to the formalities—and luxuries—of life at Delavan Manor, a sprawling quartz and marble complex with a grand staircase, twelve bedrooms, large rotunda, and fluted columns in the front. Linden had managed to get lost a few times trying to find her way back from the woods at the southern edge of the estate's extensive property. Even though she'd visited Nari and her Uncle Alban many times over the years, actually living at Delavan Manor took some major adjusting.

Kal, on the other hand, had adapted marvelously. The staff pampered him with homemade treats, and Goshen, the butler, had one of the gazebos enclosed for Kal's private residence. The griffin clicked happily and almost sighed when Linden sent him in there at night.

Although she used to live in Bellaryss before her family

moved to Quorne, Linden still found herself gaping at the sheer size of Valerra's capital city. Bellaryss could probably fit twelve or more Quornes inside its walls. Most of the buildings soared three or four stories in the air and were made from pink and gold marble, topped with red and green and even gold tiled roofs. Almost like an enchanted city in a storybook, the entire downtown turned golden at sunset, when the sun's rays struck the marble facades.

"Stop grumbling! It's our first military ball," said Jayna. "And we both have hot dates." The only good thing about living in Bellaryss was seeing Jayna again. She'd arrived the week before, when her mother started her new job leading the Royal Healer's Guild. Their school friends in Quorne gave Jayna a going-away party before she left, complete with gifts and promises to visit. Linden, on the other hand, had been shipped off to Bellaryss the day after the family conference. And instead of going to a new school, where she might make some new friends, her grandmother filled her days with private tutors in every academic subject imaginable. Except magic handling. Nari insisted Linden needed a break from all magic for a few months. Linden figured Boreus must have snitched to her parents and grandmother.

"Well at least one of us has a hot date." Linden knew Jayna had a not-so-secret crush on her brother. Every time Matteo had gone home to Quorne on a school break, Jayna managed to pop up for dinner or horseback riding. When Matteo asked Linden to find him and his roommate dates for the dance, she decided to play matchmaker for Jayna. But that meant she was stuck with her brother's roommate. She could only hope the evening didn't turn into a total disaster.

"I'm sure Stryker is passable. He's your brother's friend, after all."

"Uh-huh."

Jayna pulled out a small mirror to check her hair, which was the same mahogany shade as her eyes, and pursed her full lips to dab on some lipstick. She adjusted the bodice of her ivory satin gown, the color a perfect contrast to her brown skin. Jayna would be turning more than Matteo's head that night.

Linden reached out her hand for the mirror and examined her reflection. Rather than an up-do, which Jayna had opted for, Linden's hair was swept back from her forehead with a jeweled barrette, allowing her long waves to flow freely around her shoulders. It was less formal, but suited Linden far better.

Their driver pulled up to the gatehouse and presented their invitations. A marine guard waved them into the walled compound. They drove around the marine base, past barracks, offices, mess hall, and infirmary, until they reached the Royal Marine Academy, a newer building constructed from the same golden-hued stones used in the city's outer walls.

As soon as Linden got out of the locomobile, she felt immediately sticky in the hot, humid air. Summers in Bellaryss were generally cooler than in Quorne, but they were having a hot spell. Linden fanned herself with one lace-gloved hand as she and Jayna joined the throng of guests lining up, single file, at the main entrance to the academy. Jayna handed her invitation to the sergeant-at-arms. He escorted her to the top of the long staircase, the red plume in his cap fluttering as he walked. The sergeant called out the names on the printed invitation, "Miss Jayna Buri, guest of Cadet Matteo Arlyss." Linden watched as Jayna swept down the marble steps, where Matteo looked up at her, handsome in his blue dress uniform. Matteo flashed Jayna a lopsided grin and extended his right arm. She grinned back and looped her arm through his. *Matchmaking accomplished,* thought Linden.

She was next in line. Linden gathered her flouncy green skirt in her left hand and waited for the sergeant to announce her. "Miss Linden Arlyss, guest of Cadet Stryker Soto." She descended the staircase slowly, trying to figure out which one of the cadets hovering near the bottom was Stryker. She reached the last step and looked around. No one stepped up, and the sergeant's booming voice called out the next guest in line. Linden's face flushed and she felt hot and itchy under her gown. *I've been stood up! In front of hundreds of guests!*

She plastered a fake smile on her face and stalked her brother and Jayna. As soon as Matteo saw Linden's face, he cleared his throat, so like their father. "Linden, trust me, Stryker's coming. He's just a little late."

Linden crossed her arms. "But he's a marine cadet. They're not supposed to be late. Or rude. Or stand up girls wearing fussy green gowns."

"Look, the senior cadet sent him to kitchen duty again. But he'll be finished soon."

"Kitchen duty? Again? Who is this guy?" asked Linden, drawing her brows together.

"He's one of the good ones. He just gets into more trouble than most."

"You mean he's a loser."

Matteo waved behind her. "Stryker just got here." Then he leaned over and hissed in her ear, "Try to be nice. He's my friend. And he's had a tough year."

"Sure." Linden turned around and spotted a tall, broad-shouldered cadet heading their way. He waved back and smiled, his white teeth practically sparkling in his tan face. *He has a nice smile*, thought Linden. *But his dark hair is sticking up in little damp spikes, his dress pants have lost their sharp crease, and he's misplaced his regulation white gloves.*

"I'm sorry I'm late," he arrived slightly out of breath. "I'm sure I've made a terrible first impression." A scent of wood smoke and pine needles wafted towards her and Linden wondered what type of soap he used.

The orchestra struck up the Royal Quadrille, saving Linden from having to answer him. He escorted her to the dance floor and acted like he knew what he was doing, but they kept bumping into other couples that actually knew the steps.

"Do you want me to lead?" Linden asked. "I used to help Matteo practice the Quadrille."

"Oh, yes, please do." Stryker carefully followed her as they danced through the complicated sets, mimicking each of her moves and steps. *At least he doesn't have a massive male ego.*

On the last set Stryker might have gotten overconfident or maybe a bit eager to demonstrate what he'd learned. He spun her around, tripped over his scuffed-up boots, and stepped on Linden's skirt. They both heard the telltale sound of ripping fabric. And everyone else heard it too, since the orchestra had finished the first number. Linden's face flushed for the second time that evening.

She grit her teeth and asked, "Where's the women's lounge?"

"I can't believe I did that," Stryker said, gawking at the gap where her skirt had been ripped from her bodice and her undergarments peeked through.

"Stop staring! Stand in front of me and lead me straight to the women's lounge. Now!" Linden commanded. The tips of Stryker's ears turned red. He nodded, turned around, and stepped in front of her.

The attendant in the women's lounge had needle and thread and managed to patch up Linden's dress so the tear hardly showed. Linden reached into her reticule and pulled out several coins to tip her. The attendant thanked her and winked. "That young man's clumsy as an ox, but he's gorgeous to look at."

"You know Stryker Soto?"

"He's often on kitchen duty with my husband, who's one of the cooks here," she hesitated and then added, "Poor boy lost his mother last year. Spent his holidays alone."

Linden recalled how she'd felt when she thought her

parents were dead. If the worst ever happened, she knew her relatives would never let her spend even a long weekend by herself. Linden thanked the woman and left.

Stryker was leaning against the wall by the lounge and snapped to attention when he saw her. "At ease!" she said with a smile.

"You should do that more often," he said.

"Do what?"

"Smile. Transforms your whole face."

"Oh really?"

Stryker looked down at his rumpled pants and unpolished boots. He blinked. Linden noticed his long lashes and soft brown eyes for the first time. "You've probably noticed that I'm accident prone," he said.

"I've noticed. So?"

Stryker looked at her hopefully. "You don't mind?"

"Try to avoid any more rips—my dress can't take it." She shrugged and smiled again. "Do you know how to waltz?"

He shook his head. Linden reached out and took his hand. "Come on, I'll show you."

After leading Stryker through half a dozen more dances, Linden was ready to sit when the orchestra announced a break. They joined Matteo and Jayna in the candle-lit dining hall and found a table for four. The topic of conversation turned to cadet postings over the summer. As second-year cadets, Stryker and Matteo would be posted to the borderlands to observe, and if necessary, to fight alongside marine guard units.

"I've heard the Glenbarran army's using trained crossbreeds now," said Stryker.

"I've heard that too. And oddly enough, one of our aunts claims to have encountered a grihm, a wolf-man crossbreed, during the raid on Quorne," said Matteo.

"They sound hideous." said Jayna.

"They are!" Linden blurted out and immediately clamped her mouth shut, but it was too late.

"What? Have you seen one? Where?" everyone spoke at once.

Linden put up her hand. "I saw a grihm during the school raid in Quorne. Definitely a cross between a wolf and a man. Though I'd say the wolf parts won."

"But wasn't the whole school locked inside the gym? At least that's what Father told me. How'd you see one?" Matteo asked.

"The whole school was locked in the gym," said Jayna and then turned to Linden. "But come to think of it, I couldn't find you anywhere." Linden focused on enjoying her chocolate-lingonberry tart, taking small, slow bites. She refused to meet her brother's eyes.

"Where were you during the raid, Linden? How did you manage to see a crossbreed?"

Linden sighed and put her fork down. She told them how she had been locked out of the gym because she'd heard Delle crying. She'd gone to investigate, and the two of them hid in one of the offices, the grihm nearly exposing them both.

"Why didn't you tell Father and Mother about this?"

"Because I didn't want a lecture about safety, and obeying instructions, and a lot of 'what-if' scenarios."

Matteo started to say more but Jayna hastily switched to a safer subject. Linden knew her brother would drag the details out of her the next time they were alone. After Matteo and Jayna left for the dance floor, Linden asked, "Could we skip the dancing for a while? It's really getting crowded in there, and I'm not a fan of tight spaces."

Relief spread over Stryker's face. Taking her hand, he led her to the library, where gas-lit wall sconces cast a soft glow on the polished cherry wood tables. Linden dropped into a chair and removed her heels, stretching out her legs in front of her. "Much better," she sighed.

"How'd you escape from the grihm?" asked Stryker. Linden started to frown but noticed he seemed genuinely curious, so she told him about casting the veil of drabness over herself and Delle.

"And that protected you from a grihm?" asked Stryker. "That's an impressive bit of magic."

Linden snorted but quickly turned it into a cough. "Believe me, if you only knew, you'd never say that."

"If I only knew what?"

When she thought about it later, she couldn't really say why she told Stryker everything—about her disastrous shape-shifting experiment and starting the fire in school, about almost winning and then losing all her fencing matches, and even about the visions she'd been having. It felt good to tell someone else—especially someone who listened without interrupting and whose doe-brown eyes opened wide a few times in sympathy.

"So, are you a mage or a seer? Or a little bit of both? Trying to master both gifts must be really hard," he said.

"Only when I start fires and get suspended," she quipped. "Seriously, I'm not sure what I am. Or whether I'll ever become a proper Serving mage. But what about you?"

Stryker ran his hand through his hair, causing even more little black spikes to pop up. "I'm what you'd call a speaker."

"Never heard of that. What can you do?"

"Let me show you," he gestured to Linden, who slipped on her shoes and followed him into the hall. He led her outside to the parade grounds, where he asked her to stand still and cup her hands in front of her. Stryker shouted an incantation that almost sounded like a foreign tongue. Linden heard the flutter of wings and a white and gray pigeon flew into her hands and stared back at her. She smiled and arched an eyebrow.

The pigeon cooed a few times. Stryker spoke softly to the bird, and it flew over to his shoulder. He reached into his pocket, pulled out a bit of bread, and gave it to the pigeon, which accepted it and flew off.

"So, you speak to birds?"

"And squirrels, cats, dogs, horses. Pretty much any animal."

"Can you understand them, too?

Stryker hesitated and then stared down at the ground. "That's part of why I'm so accident prone. If I'm not careful, I'm overwhelmed by all the sounds around me."

Linden narrowed her eyes. "What about people? Can you hear our thoughts too?" She took a step back from him.

"Oh no, not people! Animals only." His eyes still downcast, he added softly, "I don't think I could stand it if I heard people's thoughts, too."

Linden started to reach out and touch him, but let her arm drop to her side. "That sounds really hard. I think you're the first person I've met who's worse off than I am. Magically speaking, of course."

Stryker was about to answer when they heard Matteo's voice calling out for them to hurry. Curfew for cadets was in ten minutes. They sprinted across the grounds to where the Delavan locomobile sat idling on the drive. Matteo handed Jayna into the backseat and promised to visit during his next free weekend.

Linden slid into her seat and Stryker leaned his head through the open door. "Can I write to you?"

"Are you asking whether I'll answer you?"

Stryker nodded.

"Alright. I mean, yes. Sure." Linden wondered whether Stryker's awkwardness might be contagious.

She overslept the next morning and breakfasted alone in the small dining room on the main floor of Delavan Manor. She was enjoying her second cup of tea when her uncle popped his head into the room.

"Ah, Linden, I wondered where'd you'd gone off to," said Uncle Alban, who was her father's older brother. "Didn't see you last night at dinner either." He smoothed his black hair, salted with silver and vivid blue, and waited. As Valerran Prime Minister, Alban had long ago mastered the art of waiting—a master negotiator, he could outwait anyone. In this case, though, he'd simply forgotten her weekend plans. Sometimes Linden thought he'd forgotten they even lived in the same house. While they shared occasional meals together, their lives generally diverged after breakfast and days might pass before they'd see each other again. Alban often worked well into the night, dining with supporters from the Queen's Council or conferring with members of Parliament.

"I went to the academy's year-end ball with Jayna Buri. Remember?"

Alban's black eyebrows rose, as if trying to recall an important fact, and he said, "Yes, yes, that's right. Did you young ladies enjoy yourselves?"

"Yes, thank you."

"Good, good. Well, I wanted to mention we'll be having a small dinner party tonight for the Queen's Council. Ah, please look your best, that sort of thing," he smiled and withdrew from the room.

Linden looked down at her short-sleeved brown and ivory checked dress, trimmed with brown piping, and shrugged. They must be important guests if they required formal dinner attire. She wished she could be like other girls, whose relatives were healers or farmers or teachers, anything but politicians.

Alban popped his head back inside. "Ah, one more thing. Your grandmother wants to see you. In her office. When you're ready, of course."

Linden jumped up from the table, smoothed her dress and

ran up the two flights of thickly carpeted stairs to the family's wing of bedrooms. An invitation to Nari's office generally involved magic of some kind. Linden crossed her fingers, hoping it meant her grandmother had decided she could resume her magic handling lessons.

CHAPTER 5

"Come in!" Nari answered Linden's knock. Her back was to Linden, and her silver hair, streaked through with blue, was pulled back in a tidy bun. Nari turned and Linden jumped back with a yelp. Her grandmother's dark eyes stared back at her, grotesquely enlarged.

"Oh! I'm sorry!" Nari smiled as she pulled off a pair of magnifying goggles. "Have a seat."

Linden had been in her grandmother's office a handful of times over the years, always as Nari was wrapping up. Unlike Nari's adjacent bedroom and the rest of Delavan Manor, her office was messy.

The walls were paneled in a rich dark wood, with an odd mixture of carved dragons, griffins, cherubim, and mermaids that seemed to step out from the paneling all around the room —definitely not Linden's decorating style.

There were four large tables, the kind often seen in a healer's stillroom, lining each wall. On the tables were beakers of colored liquid, test tubes, and various dried herbs scattered about. In the center of the room stood an enormous crystal globe mounted on a brass tripod, the base of which formed three scaly legs, topped off by scary-looking claws that held the crystal globe in place.

The tripod and globe were so heavy that it took three footmen to move them, which happened about once a year when Nari decided to clean underneath the globe. The globe itself was made of a swirling, milky crystal, similar to polished quartz. On the rare occasions when she visited her grandmother's office, Linden had been instructed never to touch the crystal, since it channeled the magic available in even an innocent touch. The crystal might reveal something that she didn't want to see.

Nari said, "Do you know why I've invited you here?"

"Because you've found a master mage to tutor me?" Linden couldn't keep the hopefulness out of her voice.

"In a manner of speaking, yes," Nari said. "But before your magic lessons can resume, I need you to be completely honest with me. Please tell me about your last day of school in Quorne, from your first class of the morning—fencing, I believe? —to the school raid in the afternoon. Leave nothing out."

Boreus definitely snitched me out. And maybe Heidl said something, too. Linden took a deep breath and repeated the same sanitized story she'd told before, leaving out all the parts about her seeing visions, starting a fire, and encountering a grihm during the raid.

"And that's the whole truth?"

Linden nodded vigorously.

"I see," Nari compressed her lips. "We're going to try a little experiment." Nari walked over to the crystal globe. "Please place your hands here."

"But I thought you told me never to touch it. And now it's fine?"

"With proper supervision, it's perfectly safe." Nari waited until Linden had stepped over to the globe. "I want you to clear your head of all thoughts except the day of the raid. I want to see that day through your eyes."

Little beats of sweat broke out on Linden's forehead. *This is not going to end well.* She took a deep breath and reluctantly stretched out her fingers, laying them on the smooth rounded surface of the crystal. Nari touched the crystal and chanted a truth-saying spell. "Open eyes and heart and mind, so that nothing hidden shall remain."

Linden felt the crystal pulse beneath her hands, and she was back in Quorne on the day of the raid. Images played out across the surface of the crystal globe: her argument with her mother at breakfast, the glowing green hieroglyphs on her sword, the small hooded figure waving at her in the flames, the jumbling of spells that fueled the fire, her casting a veil of drabness for protection, the grihm nearly discovering them, and her despair when she thought her parents were dead. Then she seemed to fast-forward to the next day and was in the sanatorium with Auntie Oonie, who was spouting her nonsense about mages and seers and the master.

Tears streamed down Linden's face and she grit her teeth, trying to stop the images. Nari pulled Linden's hands away from the crystal and held them in a firm grip.

"There, now you know the truth! I'm a freak!" Linden yelled. Tugging her hands free, she dashed from the room. Nari called after her, but Linden hiked up her dress and ran down the back stairs, past the kitchen, where the servants took one look at her face and closed their mouths, and outside through the servants' entrance.

Linden jogged through the formal gardens and orchards, weaving in and out of the rows of trees, sprinting until her breathing came in ragged gasps. She pressed her hand against the cramp in her side and slid to the ground. She wrapped her hands around her legs and leaned back against a large maple.

Linden's fury gradually ebbed away, leaving her drained. She wiped her face on her sleeve and tried to come up with a plan. If Nari or her parents tried sticking her in a sanatorium she'd run away, maybe head north and try to find her Faymon relatives. They lived somewhere deep in Faynwood. Except the civil war still raged there, and Nari had had no contact with her Faymon clan in years. Linden couldn't go back to Quorne and the western province, and she couldn't go any further east, unless she knew how to sail across the Pale Sea. That left the Barrens to the south. Without a guide she'd be dead in two days.

Linden heard a swoosh of wings and looked up. "Kal! Come over here!"

Kal landed gracefully and padded over to her on his large— for a miniature griffin—paws. He yawned as Linden rubbed his neck and mane. Linden yawned too and decided to close her eyes for just a few minutes.

She must have dozed for a while, with Kal lying at her side, because when she woke up it was late in the afternoon. Kal clicked his beak and poked her legs. "Ouch! Stop it!"

Kal poked her again, and she stood up. "Fine, I'm going. Time to face Nari. There's nowhere to run anyway, so I'll have to finesse my way through this."

Linden trudged back through the orchards and gardens, Kal padding alongside her until a mouse skittered across his path. As she re-entered the house, she heard voices drifting down the hall from Alban's study. One of those voices belonged to Nari. Linden glanced down at her wrinkled, grass-stained dress. She ran her fingers through her hair and pulled out a leaf. She tiptoed toward her uncle's study, hoping his dinner guests hadn't arrived early.

"...It's true, Alban."

Alban murmured something about old seers being wrong before, and Nari said, "I'm quite certain. A revelator."

She heard more mumbling from Alban and then the door

opened. Nari's face softened as she took in Linden's swollen eyes, fly-away hair, and ruined dress. "My dear girl. None of us realized—"

"What's a revelator?" Linden asked.

"It's what you are," Nari said. "A person with incredibly special gifts. Both a mage and a seer, in equal balance."

Linden drew her brows together. "You mean like Auntie Oonie?"

"Of course not! Poor Oonie is definitely *unbalanced*. You're nothing like her!"

"You're not just saying that to make me feel better, are you?" Linden raised one eyebrow.

"Certainly not," Nari said, "All you need is proper training in Serving magic—and plenty of hard work and practice—to manage two strong and competing gifts." Linden realized she'd been holding her breath since mentioning Oonie's name and exhaled in relief. She wanted to grab her grandmother and dance. *I'm not going to become another Gloomy Oonie!*

"Which is why your grandmother has decided to tutor you herself," Alban said. "Do you realize Mother hasn't taken on a new mage apprentice in years?"

She looked at Nari expectantly, and Nari nodded. Linden threw her arms around her grandmother, hugged her close, and whispered, "I'll work so hard. Anything to stop the crazy visions and magical disasters."

"I didn't say anything about stopping the visions—or the magical messes. You'll learn how to channel your gifts so you can control them, rather than being controlled by them."

Alban looked at his watch. "We have guests arriving in about half an hour. I suggest we—"

"Half an hour! I'll need at least an hour to look even remotely cute." Linden hugged her grandmother again and then ran up the stairs, calling for Yolande, her formidable lady's maid.

Linden hadn't needed a lady's maid in Quorne since her skirts and sweaters and even her undergarments were easy enough to pull on by herself. Not so in Bellaryss, where her grandmother insisted she have a whole new wardrobe, with calf-length dresses for daytime, floor-length dresses for evening wear, equestrian outfits with actual slacks for horse-back riding, and ball gowns with tight bodices for special occasions. Nari had even permitted Linden to order some tunics and leggings, made of a flexible, dark navy fabric, for her fencing lessons. Despite her frustration over having to leave Quorne without notice, Linden had to admit her new clothes were pretty amazing. However, there were so many unwritten rules about what to put on first, and how to layer each piece, especially now that she was sixteen and "a young lady," that Nari insisted she needed a lady's maid.

Yolande was crankier than usual and clucked her tongue when she saw Linden's rumpled appearance. "Really, Miss Linden. I don't know why I bother. Five minutes after I help you dress, you're already a mess!"

Linden normally enjoyed a good verbal sparring match with Yolande, but not tonight. She switched topics. "Do you know what a revelator is?"

Raised at Delavan Manor, where her mother served as Nari's personal secretary, Yolande knew a surprising amount about Serving magic. She crinkled her brow in concentration. "Let me think now." Pursing her lips, she said, "Aren't they folks who're both seers and mages? But they're exceedingly rare, and most of 'em go bonkers."

Linden scowled. "Well, Nari just told me I'm a revelator. And that I'm definitely not going to go bonkers."

Yolande put her hands on her generous hips. "That so? Well then, perhaps you could see just a wee bit into the future each morning and let me know when you'll be trudging through grass and mud. Then I'll know to pull out one of your old dresses from Quorne and not bother with your hair. I'd be much obliged."

Linden crossed her arms during Yolande's little speech. Shaking her head, she said, "You might be the sauciest person I've ever met. Besides me of course." Yolande broke into a wide grin and Linden started to laugh. The knot between her shoulder blades loosened, and she laughed harder than she'd laughed in months.

Linden smoothed out the skirt of her summer evening gown, a salmon-colored silk with a scoop neckline and cap sleeves. Yolande talked her into pulling some of her hair into a small top bun, allowing her longer layers hair to graze her shoulders and back. Checking her reflection in the tall looking glass in her bedroom, she fingered the crystal beads at her neck and decided Yolande knew what she was doing, although she'd never admit as much to her.

Linden took her time getting to the rose garden, where Nari and Alban were entertaining their guests with drinks, appetizers, and a soloist performing arias. A light summer breeze coursed through the garden, filling the air with the fragrant scents of rose and hyacinth. Although most visitors thought Delavan Manor itself was the main attraction, Linden loved losing herself in Delavan's extensive gardens, orchards, and woods.

Before Linden turned into the rose garden, Jayna stepped across her path, carrying a mug of sweet tea in one hand and calling out behind her, "Be right back. Let me see if I can find her for you."

"Jayna!" Linden hurried forward. "Why didn't you tell me you were coming?"

"I thought you knew. My mom was invited, so Nari said I

could tag along and keep you company." The leaders of the various Guilds, including Jayna's mother who now headed up the Royal Healers Guild, also sat on the Queen's Council of Advisors. Linden realized they must be the "important guests" Alban had mentioned that morning.

Jayna leaned over to whisper. "I've just met the most adorable guy, who told me you broke his heart when you were twelve."

"Toz Valti is here?" Linden's pulse stuttered, not because she still had a crush on Toz after all these years, but because she hadn't seen him since she'd broken up with him—by sending him a perfume-scented letter full of flowery prose. She'd totally embarrassed herself, and now she had to face her past.

"Here she is, Linden the heartbreaker!" Toz stepped onto the pebbled path, his arms opened wide. Linden laughed and stepped into his bear hug. He had the same blue eyes and dimples she remembered, only now he was a foot taller and his arms were solid muscle.

"Do you hate me for breaking up with your twelve-year-old self?"

"I'd never use 'hate' and 'Linden' in the same sentence."

"So, I have my second surprise of the evening. I had no idea you'd be here tonight!"

"Well I could say that I wrangled an invitation to see you again, but that would be only half true." Toz enjoyed taking his time when telling a story. Since his father owned all of the major newspapers in Valerra and led the News Guild, Linden supposed Toz came by it naturally.

"So, what's the other half truth?"

"My father was invited, and Nari suggested that I come as well, since she knew we used to be friends. *Close friends.*"

"I hope you haven't explained exactly how close we were?" Even though many boys and girls unofficially dated when they were fourteen or fifteen, Valerran girls weren't supposed to officially date until they turned sixteen. And they certainly weren't supposed to be kissing boys at twelve.

Toz bent over in a low, scraping bow. "Fear not, milady, your reputation is safe with me."

"Enough with the drama. Are you still at Morrell?" Linden had attended Morrell before moving to Quorne. According to the pamphlet Nari had picked up for her, *Morrell School for the Magically Gifted is Bellaryss's premier school for the study of Serving magic, where successive generations of mage apprentices are groomed to serve queen, country, and pure magic's high calling. Students are taught by renowned masters in literature, history, science, mathematics, fine arts, magic handling, and defensive arts.*

Toz nodded. "Barely, but I'm hanging in there."

"Now at least I'll know two people at school," Jayna said. "Linden and I are going to Morrell in the fall. Of course, for Linden, it'll be more of a reunion."

"So, who's still at Morrell that I might know?" Toz gave Linden and Jayna a rundown—and true to his newspaper heritage—shared a lot of gossip too. Linden's pulse smoothed out, returning to normal. She could honestly say she enjoyed seeing Toz again, but now only as a friend. They wandered through the rose garden, the maze garden, and a replica of the queen's topiary garden as they caught up on the past four years.

Reds and pinks streaked the sky when Goshen announced dinner would be served in the main dining room. As the guests started heading inside, Linden heard someone galloping up the gravel drive. The rider must have handed his horse to one of the servants, because he walked briskly around the side of the house and then paused to get his bearings. The summer twilight cast him entirely in shadow, almost as if he were a phantom conjured from the mists that descended on Delavan along with the dusk. Linden shivered slightly and rubbed her bare arms.

The man strode forward and greeted Nari warmly. She called Linden over to meet Ian Lewyn, the nephew of Harlan Lewyn, head of the Merchants Guild. Harlan sidled over to make the introductions. Harlan Lewyn's sandy-colored hair was streaked with white, and his square jawline was fringed on either side with bushy sideburns. He reminded Linden of a chubby chipmunk. His nephew, on the other hand, was powerfully built, with jade green eyes and a clean-shaven jaw. Ian bowed and then lingered over Linden's hand before kissing it. A pink blush spread across her face and neck. She considered fanning herself but didn't want anyone to notice she'd grown warm at Ian's touch.

"I'm sorry to be so late—one of my horses took a sudden turn and needed immediate attention."

"How's he feeling?" Linden asked.

"*She*'s feeling much better, having delivered a new foal!"

"Well then, congratulations!" Linden added with a smile, "To you *and* the proud mother."

Ian extended his arm to Linden and escorted her to dinner. Toz and Jayna sat across from them. They discussed horse breeding—Ian was a partner with his uncle—and the impact of locomobiles on their business. Ian was confident that locomobiles had a limited market outside the major cities. Toz wasn't so sure, since locomobiles represented progress.

There was a pause in the conversation, and Linden heard Nari ask, "But who's this Glenbarran 'master' I've been hearing about?" Nari's status as the highest-ranking master mage in Valerra meant she chaired the Mages Guild and held a position on the Queen's Council. Linden's heart sped up at the mention of a 'master'—an echo of her conversation with Oonie.

General Wylles answered, "I don't know anything about a Glenbarran master. Are you perhaps referring to the Glenbarran's new commanding general?"

"They have a new general?" Jayna's mother asked. "Since when?"

"Since the border raids have increased in ferocity, the one on Quorne being the first."

"What do we know about him?"

"Our scouts tell us he hails from up north, a Faymon who left his clan behind in Faynwood and joined the Glenbarrans." said General Wylles.

"Why would a Faymon leave his clan to lead the Glenbarran army? They're still fighting their own civil war in Faynwood," said Harlan Lewyn.

"I can never figure them out. Their fay blood makes them unpredictable. Great mages, though." The general returned to her braised salmon.

Alban glanced at Nari, who compressed her lips into a thin line. It was common knowledge that Nari and her late husband, Orion Arlyss, were Faymon immigrants who'd fled Faynwood as young people to escape the war. While it was true that Faymons shared a common fay ancestry, they were like everyone else—except for their blue-tinged hair and stronger magical gifts—both of which they inherited from their fay ancestors. Old prejudices, on the other hand, died hard.

"I'd like to hear more about these increasingly dangerous border raids, General," Toz's father said. "In fact, I'd like to embed some of my reporters in with your marine border units."

The general scowled at him, clearly more interested in finishing her meal than in discussing border raids. She looked around the table at the expectant faces. Realizing she had an audience, she shrugged and put down her knife and fork.

"There isn't much to tell, really. We're seeing both an uptick in the number of raids and more violence. We've lost eight marines in recent weeks." There was an intake of breath around the table.

"Why is this the first we're hearing about it?" Nari asked

sharply. Linden knew she was thinking of Quorne—where Linden's parents still lived—and of course Matteo, who'd be spending his summer with one of those marine border units, theoretically to 'observe' only. Marines had certainly been serving, and unfortunately dying, along the western perimeter for as long as Valerra had been a nation, but there hadn't been any casualties for at least a decade.

The general looked at Alban, who nodded. "This is strictly off the record." She waited for Toz's father to grunt his agreement.

"We've been intentionally keeping a low profile about developments along the border." She hastened to add, "I've been keeping the PM and the queen informed of developments, of course, but no one else."

"We're in direct negotiations with old King Barre's government. Unfortunately, the king is in poor health, and he can't come to the negotiating table himself. He's always been reasonable in the past," said Alban. "The king's son, Prince Roi, well, he's a different story."

"We've offered land swaps and even expanded the water rights along the Windrun River, but so far, nothing's appeased the Glenbarran prince," said Ellis Steehl, the queen's personal envoy, who attended all meetings of the Queen's Council and seemed to be a thorn in her uncle's feet, often questioning his decisions. Linden thought his pencil thin mustache and precise way of speaking made him better suited to serving as a headmaster than as the queen's special representative. There were rumors the queen's father had been excessively fond of their maidservants and Steehl was his son.

"So, we don't know what the Glenbarrans really want then, do we?" Harlan Lewyn asked.

General Wylles shook her head.

"All the more reason for me to embed some reporters,

General. The public has a right to know what's going on," said Toz's father.

"He's right, Gayle," said Alban. "We can't keep this quiet any longer."

The general crinkled her forehead, "Fine, Mr. Valti. You can embed two reporters—and don't ask for any more or I'll regret my leniency. Have them contact Colonel Revas at base camp headquarters for their assignments."

The servants brought in a flaming dessert, but no one seemed much in the mood for sweets at that point. Alban and Nari led the members of the Council to a large drawing room for after-dinner drinks and probably more political discussions.

Toz looked at Linden expectantly. "How about a game of billiards? I've been practicing for four years for a rematch!" Leave it to Toz to mention billiards in front of Ian Lewyn—not that Linden was trying to impress the handsome horse breeder —but she'd rather not parade all of her flaws in front of him the first night they'd met. Other than kissing boys at the age of twelve, playing billiards since the age of eight would rank up there as a serious violation of polite Valerran norms for any well-bred young woman.

"You play billiards?" Ian asked Linden. "And you've waited four years for a rematch?" He turned to Toz for an explanation.

"It's a long story," Linden said hastily. She turned to Toz, "You're on." She led them to the billiards table, located in a dark paneled room that smelled of pipe smoke. Linden selected her cue stick, chalked it, and began racking the balls.

Ian's eyebrows rose in a peak. "So, you really do know what you're doing?"

Linden frowned at him and decided to come clean about billiards. "Of course. How else do you think I was the unofficial, undefeated billiards champion at Morrell when I was twelve years old?"

Ian looked skeptical but Toz said, "It's true. In fact, I'm not sure whether I fell in love with Linden herself back then or her amazing game of billiards."

"Alright, let's see what you've got," said Linden, hoping to redirect Toz before he revealed anything truly embarrassing.

"Best two out of three?" Toz asked.

"That depends on our guests—it's not fair to bore them senseless with our re-match."

"Oh, by all means, I wouldn't miss this for the world," Jayna laughed. She knew Linden played billiards with her father back home in Quorne all the time. What Jayna didn't know was the reason Linden's father had taught her to play billiards: to improve her fencing skills through better hand-eye coordination. Linden smiled when she recalled her mother's reaction the first time she saw Linden playing billiards with one of Matteo's friends. She'd been furious—not at Linden but at her father—who'd calmly told her that Linden had the makings of a true billiards champion.

"I agree with Miss Buri, let the rematch begin," Ian said, his green eyes sparkling.

Linden might have failed at magic handling, lost her last three fencing matches, and been struggling academically in every subject, but she could play billiards in her sleep. She'd even started beating her father.

Linden gave Toz the first shot, which he missed. And then she proceeded to call out and put away every ball in the precise pocket where she said it would go. Although Toz did slightly better in the second round, Linden won that game just as handily.

Ian and Jayna announced her the undefeated champion and applauded, while Toz made his second mock bow of the evening. Linden offered the cue sticks to Ian and Jayna, but they both shook their heads.

"No thanks. I'll stick to horses, if you don't mind," Ian said as he stepped into the hallway, holding the door open for

Linden and the others. Linden exited the room last, after first re-racking the balls for a future game. Ian lingered, waiting for her.

"Ah, Miss Arlyss—" Ian began, but Linden interrupted him, "Please, call me Linden." Linden had grown accustomed to the more casual means of address in Quorne, and she preferred it to the formal and flowery mannerisms of the capital.

"Linden, I enjoyed myself very much this evening. To be honest, I hadn't really wanted to come, but my uncle insisted I accept your grandmother's kind invitation."

Linden glanced up at him, not sure where this was going. "I'm glad you enjoyed yourself."

"Yes, well, I'll be traveling for the rest of the summer for my uncle. However, I'd like to—"

"Oh, there you are, Ian. It's past time for us to leave," Harlan called down the hall.

"Yes of course Uncle." Ian looked at Linden as if he wanted to say more but nodded and then followed his uncle out of the house.

After everyone had left for the evening, and Nari and Alban had gone upstairs, Linden wearily changed out of her evening dress without rousing Yolande and slipped into a simple white nightgown. She spent a ridiculous amount of time adjusting her covers and then climbed into bed, hoping to fall asleep quickly. After tossing and turning for more than an hour, she crept downstairs and went to the kitchen to fix a cup of chocolate milk the way her father used to, which made her feel homesick for her parents and her casual, carefree life in Quorne, before the Glenbarrans had to ruin it all.

As she sipped her warm milk, she replayed the general's words in her mind. *"We're seeing both an uptick in the number of raids and more violence. We've lost eight marines in recent weeks."* Eight marines already dead, and her brother would be heading to his summer border posting soon. And so would his awkward, always-running-late roommate. Although Linden worried about Matteo, she considered him a model marine cadet. Her father had trained Matteo to be a proper soldier since he'd been a young boy.

Somehow, she didn't think Stryker was nearly as well prepared. The image of Stryker handfeeding the pigeon, his long eyelashes fringing his cheek as he looked down at the bird, didn't fill her with confidence. Linden didn't want to admit that she found herself worrying about the boy who could speak to birds, but when she thought of him posting to a border guard unit for the entire summer, she couldn't help herself. Her heart lurched in protest.

CHAPTER 6

Twelfth Week after Spring Solstice
Western Province
Border Guard Unit #9

Hey Linden,

You probably heard from Matteo that we posted to our assigned border units last week. And believe it or not, I've already had to draw both my weapons. Technically I shouldn't have bothered trying to use my pistol, but I was so nervous I forgot my training about the presence of magic disabling mechanicals.

    But that came much later, after I'd spent hours patrolling the old mud-brick ruins in Valerra's western province with Sgt. Desi. Did you know those ruins were once an ancient fay settlement, long before they withdrew further north into Faynwood? The only thing living in those ruins today are oversized country rats.

    We'd been waiting for one of Sgt. Desi's scouts, Zalu, to deliver intelligence on Glenbarran movements in the area. It was close to midnight when we heard the signal—two short hoots and one longer trill—and Sgt. Desi responded. I doused a chunk of wood with some of the maize oil they gave us at base camp and lit it up. We jogged around piles of old mud bricks, using the light from the torch to guide us as we closed in on the location of our scout. I remembered to carry the torch in my left hand, since the sergeant told me to always keep my right hand free to handle my weapon.

That's when we heard the sound of swords clanging nearby, and I shined my torch in the direction of the fighting. Desi pointed out two figures sparring and ordered them to stop, step back six paces, and drop their weapons. But one of the men lunged, thrusting his sword into the other man's side. The second man cried out and slumped over. The attacker then threw a dagger at me, knocking the torch from my hand.

I tried firing several shots at the Glenbarran assassin—I found out later that's what he was—but nothing happened when I pulled the trigger. So, I drew my sword and chased after him instead, while Desi ran over to Zalu. I caught up with the assassin, who turned around and charged me, aiming his sword right at my chest. Even though I was afraid (can I admit that to you?), my training kicked in, and I blocked a series of blows. I could see sparks flying all around us as we fought.

I noticed the assassin favored his left leg, so I pivoted to the man's left side and swept my sword upward. It was too dark to tell for sure, but I must have sliced his rib cage. The man screamed something—maybe an incantation—and threw back his head. Then he flailed his arms and fell to the ground, where his body burst into flames! It was the craziest thing I'd ever seen. By the time Sgt. Desi ran back over to check on me—poor Zalu had died by then—there was nothing left of the assassin but black, sooty ashes. Desi says it was the darkest magic he's ever seen along the border, and he's seen a lot of strange stuff over the years.

Well, I hear the sergeant yelling my name, so I'd better go. I hope you write soon. Have you started your magic lessons again?

Take care,

Stryker

Royal Marine Cadet 2nd Class

~

First Week after Summer Solstice
Delavan Manor
NE Bellaryss, Valerra

Hi Stryker,

I can't believe you've been in a sword fight already—aren't you supposed to be observing?—and I'm thankful your training kicked in when it did. I also can't believe you led with your pistol instead of your sword. You know the Glenbarrans always employ magic in a fight—what were you thinking? You're lucky you weren't killed before you could unsheathe your sword.

I think it's better to admit when you're scared. My father says true courage is fighting despite your fears. When I thought the grihm had discovered Delle and me during the raid, my heart almost flew out of my chest. And when I think about it even now—which I try not to—my pulse races and I break into a sweat. I have nightmares about it sometimes and wake up screaming. Fortunately, the bedrooms are so far apart here that I don't wake up anyone else. If I were back in Quorne, I'd have the whole household up with my screams—my mother and father and Kal, who'd click his beak in agitation—and Mille and Yogi, our servants. And then my mother would send me to yet another healer, who'd give me yet another set of bitter herbs to mix into my tea. It's just as well I'm here at Delavan.

To answer your question about my magic lessons—I started them last week, and you'll never guess who's tutoring me—my grandmother! We've had quite a week together. I accidentally started another fire, this time in her office, by mixing together two potions that should never be combined, but Nari reversed my spell so quickly that it did hardly any damage. One of her lab tables has a scorch mark across the top of it now. At least

Nari knows what she's signed up for, since she used a truth-saying spell to get me to tell her what really happened at Quorne. Consider yourself honored—you're the only other person who knows the whole story.

The good news is that Nari assures me I'm not crazy and won't become another Gloomy Oonie (she's my great-aunt who lives in a sanatorium). Nari says I'm a revelator, someone who's both a mage and a seer in equal measure, which I guess is pretty rare. I'm relieved to know that I'm "normal" for a teenaged revelator who's just learning how to manage her abilities, although Nari says I'll have to train twice as hard as I did before.

Well, that's my news for now. Stay out of trouble and remember to lead with your sword.

Be safe,
Linden

~

Third Week after Summer Solstice
Western Province
Border Guard Unit #9

Hey Linden,

Thanks for your letter—it's good to know your grandmother has taken over your magic lessons. I've learned a few things about revelators since you last wrote, and I feel much better knowing that a master mage like Nari Arlyss is looking out for you. Apparently, revelators are extremely rare, and if they're not properly grounded in Serving magic, they can go off the rails. I don't mean becoming unbalanced like you were worried about but abandoning Serving magic for Fallow magic. I'm not telling you this to scare you, but so you know the truth about why it's important to train hard. I'm done lecturing (you can stop scowling now).

Colonel Revas rode out to our camp this week and led one of our operations. He's normally stationed at base camp headquarters, but I think he wanted to inspect some of the border guard units himself. Our mission itself was a secret. All I can say is that we marched beyond the perimeter walls, patrolling as far as the Windrun River, and then returned to camp.

I can also say this: I'm glad you're living in Bellaryss, as far away from the western border as possible. I know you still have family in Quorne, and your parents must know a lot more than I do about the situation. If and when the time comes, I'm sure Colonel Arlyss will have plans for protecting the rest of your family.

Colonel Revas, by the way, is quite an accomplished master mage, and he's the one who told me about revelators. He and my father were best friends, and he's looked after me ever since my father died. The colonel helped me apply for a scholarship to the Royal Marine Academy, and he's helped me in other ways too. Last year I almost got kicked out of the academy, but the colonel stepped in and insisted I was innocent of the charges. (It's a complicated story that I'll tell you about sometime if you're interested.)

Please write soon and tell me how you're doing,
Stryker
Royal Marine Cadet 2nd Class

≈

Fifth Week after Summer Solstice
Delavan Manor
NE Bellaryss, Valerra

Hi Stryker,

Thanks for the information about revelators. I asked Nari about it, and she seemed surprised I knew so much (especially the part about being more susceptible to Fallow magic, which she ignored but I could tell bothered her). My whole family is over-protective and still treats me like I'm twelve. I'm going to be seventeen in less than two months!

We're going to pick a weekend around the Autumn Solstice when Matteo and my parents can come to Delavan Manor for my Teenth. As you've probably figured out by now, my family doesn't do anything halfway, so it's going to be the biggest Teenth celebration of the year. I think Nari is even going to invite the queen, who probably won't attend but you never know. I hope you can come too. Then you can meet all of the characters I've been telling you about, and you'll know I haven't been exaggerating at all. You'll also be able to meet Kal, which I'm really looking forward to—just think, the two of you can have a chat, and you can translate for me.

I've been thinking about what you weren't able to say in your last letter, I mean about the border. My uncle keeps telling me not to worry about my family in Quorne, but I can't help it. My parents have already canceled two trips this summer to visit me, and I'm sure it's because my mother can't leave the province with all of her duties. I've offered to visit them, but Nari says "things are not stable enough right now" for me to go back home for a visit. Hmm...I don't like the sound of that.

I'm glad you have someone like Colonel Revas who helps you when you need it. Can he help get you out of so much kitchen duty? It seems unfair you're stuck with it as often as you are. And I do want to hear about whatever happened to you last year (when you were almost kicked out of school).

Please be careful,
Linden

~

Seventh Week after Summer Solstice
Western Province
Border Guard Unit #9

Hey Linden,

Things have been heating up around here—we've had to repel two border raids in the past week. We suffered some injuries but fortunately no casualties. I heard some of the units further south had it worse (don't worry, Matteo's unit had a quiet week).

I saw grihms for the first time, and I'm not surprised you get nightmares. There was a pack of them running along the opposite bank of the Windrun River. They were on Valerran land, but they used the water as a natural boundary, almost like they were taunting us. Then some Glenbarran soldier blew a whistle and the whole pack bounded away.

I've seen a lot more action than I expected this summer, and Sgt. Desi told me the border guard units haven't been this busy for at least a decade. He even admitted he was surprised the cadets were left in place after things escalated—he thought we'd be pulled out and sent back to the academy early. He thinks central command is worried because we don't have enough marines to handle a full-scale Glenbarran invasion, so they're training us cadets just in case.

True or not, I'm ready to go back to school and hit the books. I'll appreciate the peace and quiet for a change, and I won't even complain about kitchen duty. I'm also looking forward to your Teenth and wouldn't miss it for anything. Say, how many dances can you save for me? Two? Four? Ten? I'll take as many as you'll give me, and I'll make Matteo practice the dance steps with me when we're back in school. I promise not to step on your dress!

This will be my last letter from the border camp. We're leaving the day after tomorrow, so please write back to me at the academy.

Your friend,
Stryker

Tenth Week after Summer Solstice
Delavan Manor
NE Bellaryss, Valerra
Hi Stryker,

I'm glad you and Matteo are back at the academy. Maybe by the time you graduate next year, the Glenbarran situation will be back under control. At least I hope so. I know Uncle Alban is doing everything he can to find a peaceful solution to the crisis.

I'm starting school tomorrow. I'll admit to being a little nervous, but I've met a couple of my old friends who still attend Morrell, plus I'll have Jayna with me, so it should be fine. And I have some good news—my cousin, Heidl, who was my old fencing master in Quorne, has moved to Bellaryss— she's been privately coaching me for the past few weeks and will be our new fencing instructor at Morrell. Nari made me tell her about the glowing green sword incidents and being a revelator-in-training, and Heidl said it made sense to her, whatever that means.

Anyway, Heidl's been training me hard, helping me to focus and ignore any sights or sounds beyond the immediate fighting circle. It's been working. I've had some good practice matches, and I've been able to disregard the occasional visions or sounds that are from a different time or place or might even be shadows of things that won't ever happen (at least that's how Nari explains them). Once I was sure I heard Matteo groaning like he'd been hurt. Another time I heard my grandmother crying, which she never does. Both times my hand shook, but I was able to keep my focus on my sword.

You should have received an invitation to my Teenth by now. You know I have to dance with everyone who asks me, just to be polite. But I'll save you at least two dances—just so long as you arrive on time. So, don't be late.

And definitely practice your dance moves with Matteo.

Your friend,

Linden

CHAPTER 7

Linden looked out the window of her uncle's locomobile, toying with the silver buttons on her green wool jacket. Boys at Morrell wore emerald green jackets, gray pants, and short black leather boots. Girls swapped out pants for calf-length gray skirts and taller boots. It took Linden a few weeks to get used to wearing a school uniform again. Just one more change she'd had to deal with after spending the past four years in Quorne.

As they pulled up in front of a stylish townhouse in central Bellaryss, the front door opened and Jayna popped her head out. "We're coming. Remy's spilled something on himself, so he's washing up." Jayna rolled her eyes. A couple of minutes later Jayna slid into the locomobile next to Linden, and Remy Zel climbed into the opposite seat.

Remy and Linden had played together in preschool, fought constantly in grammar school, and became friends about the time she moved to Quorne. Remy reminded Linden of a friendly bear, with his burly frame, wavy brown hair, and hazel eyes. He had an odd magical gift: he could start a fire at the snap of his fingers. Poor Remy had struggled to manage his pyromancy when he was younger and used to spend a lot of time in the headmaster's office.

"Sorry about that," Remy said, "I'll avoid Mrs. Buri's chopped cherry jam in the future."

"I thought you already had breakfast," Jayna said pointedly.

Remy shrugged. "Yours looked better than mine."

"I think we'll make it in time," Linden said. This was the first week of ride-sharing instituted by the government, and the Delavan driver would now be stopping to pick up Jayna and Remy, who lived next door to Jayna, on the way to school.

The ride-sharing program began as a practical response to the government's plea for all Valerrans to donate metal, rubber, and even "spare" locomobiles to the Royal Marines. Apparently, the marines were retrofitting locomobiles with extra armor to use in the border towns. Alban donated two locomobiles to the cause. Now ride sharing, especially in the capital, had become another way to demonstrate Valerrans' patriotism and support of the marines.

The Delavan locomobile groaned, a cloud of steam hissing from the engine, and drew up in front of the architectural smorgasbord that housed Morrell School for the Magically Gifted. The school looked as if seven architects had designed the school's seven wings, drawing their inspiration from different time periods and using different building materials, which, in fact, was true. Despite its helter-skelter appearance, Morrell was a highly selective school.

Linden, Jayna, and Remy climbed up the worn stone staircase to the huge oak doors that swung open when their feet landed on the top step. Even with her eyes closed, Linden would know they'd arrived at Morrell by the minty scent in the hallways—apparently the headmaster brewed peppermint tea throughout the day.

The three of them headed straight to history class, where students were giving oral reports on current events. Most teachers assumed Linden would be a naturally gifted orator, since politics ran in the family, but she hated public speaking and dreaded delivering her paper. She swallowed hard when her teacher called on her in class.

Linden's assigned topic was to present her recommendation on whether Valerra should declare war on Glenbarra. She knew the pros and cons better than anyone in class—she'd been hearing the arguments around her uncle's dining room table all summer. Most of the Queen's Council of Advisors wanted to declare war; Alban and General Wylles believed further diplomacy was possible, and desirable. Some called the prime minister a coward for not wanting to avenge the deaths of brave marines, but Linden knew his goal was to preserve their nation, with as little bloodshed as possible, from the increasing threat from the west.

Her voice trembled as she shuffled her notes and wrapped up her argument for pursuing further diplomacy. "...It's worthwhile remembering that Glenbarra is a vast nation with a standing army outnumbering Valerra's four to one. Declaring war on Glenbarra, before we've pursued every possible diplomatic solution, sets us on a dangerous path—one that has the potential for heavy loss of life across Valerra. It's a decision that must be made carefully, and only after every other option has been exhausted." Linden returned to her seat and wiped her clammy hands on her gray skirt.

When the teacher called on Mara Pensk to present her oral argument, the eyes of every boy in class followed her as she stepped up to the lectern. Mara, who filled out her school uniform in all the right places, had been Linden's nemesis from kinder-class until Linden moved to Quorne. She'd poked fun at Linden's petite stature, calling her a pixie. She'd ruined one of Linden's art projects, claiming it was an accident. She'd even started flirting with Toz after she found out he liked Linden.

Linden's approach had been—and still was—to completely ignore her.

Tucking her wheat-colored hair behind her ears, Mara launched into an impassioned plea for the queen to declare war on Glenbarra. Linden rolled her eyes and doodled on her notepaper. Her wandering attention snapped back at Mara's conclusion. "The recent attacks all along our border demonstrate Glenbarrans are done negotiating. In fact, the repeated forays into our territory amount to an act of war. Now it's time for our prime minister to drop his opposition and join with the Queen's Council in a formal declaration of war. Anything less dishonors the memory of our fallen marines. Anything less amounts to outright cowardice!"

Linden's temper flared at the careless words and obvious insult to Alban. While Linden was accustomed to hearing criticisms of her mother and uncle, in their official roles within the government, Mara had gone too far. Linden pushed back her chair and stood up. "You're uninformed...and overcompensating!"

Mara's skin flushed scarlet and she put her hands on her hips. "Overcompensating for what?"

For your father's cowardice. The words were nearly out of her mouth when Linden bit them back. Saying them out loud would just be spiteful, since everyone in class knew Mara's father had run from enemy fire as a young officer. He'd been punished for dereliction of duty and stripped of his command. It was also well known that another young officer, Ric Arlyss, had stepped into command that day and led his marines to a decisive victory.

"Ladies, ladies, that's quite enough. Take your seats please." Their history teacher fluttered her hands at both of them. Mara glared at Linden and stomped back to her desk.

After lunch Linden went to magic handling lab, where Jayna was seated at the lab desk they shared. She was trying to change an apple into an orange. Even though Linden hadn't started any more fires during her magic-handling lessons with Nari, she'd avoided shape-shifting spells all summer. And she definitely didn't want to be responsible for any more disasters at school. Last week, she was supposed to have changed a glass of water into a crystal dish. Instead, Linden had created a swirling fountain of water that spouted eight feet in the air and sprayed the entire class, not her best moment.

"Well, are you just going to sit there, or are you going to help?" Jayna asked, a little line forming between her brows.

"You know shape shifting isn't my thing. Besides, you look like you're doing well without me."

Jayna put aside her lab book. "It's funny you should say that. I was just telling my mom how lucky I've been, with the move and all. I was really nervous about moving to Bellaryss and starting at a new school, but having my best friend already here has made it so much easier. Thanks for introducing me to all your old friends, and for everything you've done to help me feel at home."

"Of course! You're my bestie, too, and I'm so glad you're here. You make school almost tolerable for me," grinned Linden.

Jayna smiled. "Now that we've established how glad we are to have each other, come help me with this spell. It doesn't involve fire. Or water, so you should be fine."

"Don't blame me if something bad happens."

"Don't be so dramatic."

Linden and Jayna carefully incanted the spell from their lab book. "Shift taste and texture, one fruit for another. From red, round apple to something oranger." The apple wobbled around their lab desk. *So far so good*, Linden thought. The apple slowly began to unpeel itself, spinning as the skin pulled away, picking up speed as it stripped itself from top to bottom. When it slowed down again, the girls could see the dappled orange skin re-forming around it. At least it was starting to *look* like an orange. Linden mentally relaxed a bit, enjoying being in the midst of the spell, seeing the magic unfurl before her eyes. Maybe she could handle shape shifting after all.

An image popped in Linden's head of a large crowd of people in a heavily forested area. Violets and bluebells carpeted the ground beneath the trees. She stood some distance from the crowd and spoke to them. Linden felt an overwhelming sense of belonging, almost as if she'd come home, although nothing about the place looked familiar. The crowd waved colorful banners and raised their voices, cheering for her. Linden reached out an arm to wave back, but Jayna was shaking her arm, and the voices were her classmates and Master Mage Rudlyn, their magic-handling instructor, ordering her to stop.

Apples and oranges and even a few stray leaves and flowers pelted the room, conjured by some unseen force. Several oranges smacked into Mara's backside. One bonked Rudlyn on the head. Other apples and oranges pinged off the walls and rained down on the classroom. The students had taken cover under their desks as the fruit piled up all around them.

"Linden snap out of it," Jayna was shouting and still shaking her.

Linden felt something give way inside her, and she was herself again. She looked around her, and the apples and oranges, leaves and flowers all tumbled to the floor. Rudlyn rubbed her head and said to Linden, "Miss Arlyss, a word in the hall, if you please." She looked around the classroom and pointed to Toz and Remy, "Go to the headmaster's office and request bags, boxes, whatever they've got, and lots of them. Class, you're going to be bagging and boxing up this fruit for the rest of the period. There's enough here for every student and teacher in the school to bring some home." Rudlyn looked around at the stunned class. "Any questions? If not, step to it!"

The two boys sprinted out of the classroom, and the rest of the students started picking the fruit off the floor.

Linden stared miserably at the tiled floor as she waited in the hallway. Rudlyn closed the door to the classroom and said, "What, in the name of all that is magical, happened in there? It seemed you were in some kind of a trance."

Linden debated whether to explain about her being a revelator-in-training, but Nari had emphasized the importance of maintaining a low profile. Rudlyn's bird-like eyes bored into hers, searching for answers. However, Rudlyn did more than simply stare, she used a probing spell to look for clues inside Linden's head. Probing spells were considered a breach of magical etiquette and not something that one mage ever used with another. Since Linden had just dumped fruit all over the classroom, maybe Rudlyn thought she had the right to probe around inside her head, but Linden didn't think so. Linden took a step back, wordlessly incanting a protection charm she'd learned from her father. It worked; the prickling sensation inside her head disappeared. Rudlyn arched her eyebrows as she waited for an explanation, obviously aware that Linden had just blocked her spell. They'd reached a teacher-student impasse.

Linden decided to use the classic medical excuse to divert Rudlyn's attention. She did have a headache, which happened after a particularly strong vision. Rubbing her temples and groaning, she said, "I'm sorry, ma'am, but my headache's been bothering me all period. I forgot the words to the spell."

Rudlyn pursed her lips. "Very well. In the future, please inform me of any headaches at the beginning of our labs. These little incidents are terribly disruptive to the rest of the class." Linden could tell Rudlyn didn't believe her, but she sent Linden to the healer's office anyway.

∾

Linden dropped her book bag in the front hall closet and went outside to look for Kal. The school's healer had force-fed her a disgusting brew, but it did the trick—her headache finally lifted —a minor miracle considering she'd listened to Jayna and Remy bicker the entire way back from Morrell. Remy, clearly smitten with Jayna, thought teasing her was the best way of demonstrating his affections. Poor Remy, his competition was Matteo. It was no contest. Linden decided she'd put her foot down tomorrow if Jayna didn't say something first. Otherwise, volunteering for early morning safety patrol shifts at school might be a preferable alternative to sharing rides with a love-sick Remy.

Linden heard her uncle's voice coming from the bluestone patio and walked over to say hello, pausing just beyond the hedge when she realized he had guests. She turned around to search for Kal in the gardens instead, but something in Alban's tone arrested her.

"Then we believe it's only a matter of time?" asked Alban, sounding resigned.

"I'm afraid so," said General Wylles. "With Prince Roi ascending to the Glenbarran throne, our chances for peace are bleak."

"Do you agree?" Alban addressed someone else sitting on the patio with him.

Ellis Steehl said, "We've known for some time that Prince— now King—Roi is unstable. General Mordahn is his closest confidant, and the general seems bent on attacking us."

"But why is Mordahn so set against us?"

"Who knows what drives a Faymon's heart?" Steehl realized his error immediately and coughed. "Present company excluded, of course."

"Of course," Alban replied curtly. Linden interpreted this as, *Actually, it's really not acceptable that you've just insulted my heritage*.

"Mordahn has been shifting troops to our western border." The general's voice dropped a decibel. "Last night, five of our scouts were dumped outside Loomyn's Gate with their heads tucked beneath their sword arms." Loomyn's Gate was one of the most heavily guarded gates along the perimeter wall.

"Despite the size of the Glenbarran army, their equipment is lower tech. Doesn't that provide us any advantage?" asked Steehl.

The general agreed the Glenbarran army lacked many of Valerra's technological advances, such as airships and weaponized locomobiles. However, the right dosage of magic could swiftly disable all our mechanicals, and Mordahn employed the darkest forms of magic.

"According to our best military mages, Mordahn is a master mage alright—but of Fallow magic. And that's what has me up nights. How are we going to counter that?" asked the general. *She sounds like we've lost already.* Linden's stomach knotted as she listened to confident General Wylles speak so dismally about the future.

"It seems the Glenbarrans won't be satisfied until they drive their army all the way to the Pale Sea. And the only thing in their way is Valerra," Alban said grimly.

"I'm hoping our seers can predict where they'll strike first. We can't possibly patrol the entire western boundary. We'll have our hands full just fortifying all the gateways!"

"Prime Minister, General, thank you for this briefing," Steehl said crisply. "I'll inform the queen of these latest developments. Perhaps *she* will think of some way to avoid an all-out war."

Linden heard Steehl's footsteps heading her way and took a few paces back so that it didn't appear she'd been eavesdropping. Steehl looked her up and down, his thin mustache quivering in disdain, as if he knew exactly what she'd been doing on the other side of the hedge. Nodding curtly, he walked past her without a word. Even though Ellis Steehl had been a frequent visitor to Delavan Manor since she arrived, she'd never warmed up to the man. As the queen's personal envoy, he enjoyed throwing around his weight a bit too much. Although he never said as much, Linden suspected her uncle felt the same way. Steehl's footsteps faded as he walked toward the front driveway. The door to his chauffeured locomobile opened and closed, and his driver pulled away in a spray of gravel.

Alban sighed. "Gayle, I know you well enough to realize you have a plan."

"I have plans and contingency plans. But if we can't hold them at the border—and given their numbers, their aggression, and their reliance on Fallow sorcery, that may be impossible—they'll march all the way to Bellaryss."

"Then we'll have to do everything possible to prepare and protect our people."

Linden backed away from the hedge and ran to the orchards, trying to forget everything she just heard. She ran until the bitter brew she'd drunk earlier rose up in her throat, and then she retched until she had nothing left inside her, except for the knot in her stomach that wouldn't go away. But Linden recognized that knot. It was fear, the same fear she heard in Alban's voice, and the general's.

Linden looked up at the sound of wings beating overhead. Kal landed with a soft thud nearby. She knelt down to scratch behind his ears. Kal clicked and circled around her. "Yeah, I know. It's worse than I thought. But what can one girl and one griffin do?"

Kal raised his wings and flapped them, as if to say, "Carry on!"

"I suppose you're right."

Linden stood up, wiped herself off, and headed back toward the house. She'd work even harder on her training—no more magical disasters at school. Maybe being a revelator would come in handy somehow.

Linden thought of her father and said to Kal, trotting beside her, "But hope isn't a plan, and wishing isn't a mission."

Right now, though, she wished for a mission or a plan that offered hope—and not just for her—but also for her uncle and the general.

CHAPTER 8

Linden tossed off her covers and hopped out of bed as bright shafts of sunlight streamed into her room. She opened one of her windows and leaned out, breathing in the early autumn air. The gloom she'd been feeling since overhearing Alban's conversation with the general melted away. Linden was more than ready for a shift in her mood.

She and Nari had been planning her Teenth party for weeks, and the day had finally arrived. Not only would she be officially coming of age in the eyes of Valerran society, she'd also get to see her parents, who'd left Quorne earlier in the week to make the trip to Bellaryss.

In the meantime, Matteo and Stryker would be riding over from the Royal Marine Academy and arriving sometime after lunch. Although she'd corresponded with Stryker all summer, she hadn't seen him since their first meeting at the academy's final dance of the school year. Linden refused to admit how much she was looking forward to seeing Stryker again, even though her pulse raced whenever she thought about him. So, she forced herself think about everyone else who was coming instead. They'd received a polite decline from the queen, who was indisposed but sent her regrets. Linden figured that queens were often indisposed and hadn't really expected her to attend.

Humming an old dance tune while she buttered her toast, she glanced up to say something and noticed Nari's hand shaking, a telegram trembling between her fingers. Linden felt all the blood in her veins turn to ice.

"What is it? Has someone been hurt?"

Nari looked up, blinking away a tear. Nari never cried. "Oh no, nothing like that. But I'm afraid your parents are stuck in a small town about a hundred miles west of here—they're fortunate the mayor let them use his telegraph machine. The main road into Bellaryss has been temporarily closed to all civilians; it's for marine use only. No exceptions. They'll have to return to Quorne without a visit after all." Linden heard the wistfulness in her grandmother's voice and realized she hadn't been the only one looking forward to a visit from her parents.

"I can't believe this is happening. I mean, it's not like we're at war. Why would the road be blocked?"

"There's no point in speculating since there's nothing to be done about it. Let's not let this ruin your special day," Nari said as she patted Linden's arm.

Linden swallowed down a lump in her throat. She missed her parents more than she allowed anyone to know, and she hadn't seen them since leaving Quorne last spring. She'd been certain that no matter what, they'd be together for her seventeenth birthday celebration.

"But Father is supposed to lead me through my first dance." Linden sounded whiney even to her own ears.

"I know I'm a poor substitute for Ric, but I'd be honored, my dear, if you'll have me," Alban said as he entered the room.

Linden tried not to let her uncle see the disappointment on her face. She smiled. "Of course. And I'll see Mother and Father some other weekend. It'll be fine," she said with false cheerfulness.

After breakfast Nari told Linden she needed some help in the attic, where Nari's pigeons lived. Most mages kept homing pigeons to send and receive express messages, preferring them to telegraphs that failed during power outages and around too much magic. Linden enjoyed working with Nari's pigeons, although Kal stalked away in a huff whenever he noticed a pigeon feather clinging to her skirts.

Linden had just climbed the stairs when a gray pigeon flew in through the open window and landed on an empty perch. Linden spoke soothingly as she removed a small roll of paper from the pigeon's right leg, and then her left. She gave the bird a special treat.

"Two messages?" Nari asked.

Linden handed them to Nari, who scanned the first message, re-rolled it and handed both to Linden. "They're for you. From Kamden and Ric."

"From my parents?" Linden looked at the pigeon more carefully and smiled in recognition. "Hortense!" The bird cooed as Linden gently rubbed her breast.

"Your father's extra precautions came in handy," said Nari.

Linden nodded. "Father always insists on taking pigeons along when we travel." Hortense often carried messages between Quorne and Delavan—but her home base was Nari's attic—so even when on the road, Hortense would fly true and return to Delavan.

She looked at her grandmother. "You were expecting another message from them, weren't you?"

"Of course. It's your Teenth, after all. One of the biggest days in a young woman's life—your formal coming of age. I knew they'd want to send you an express."

As Linden unrolled the first note, a platinum-and-diamond earring fell into her hand. She felt it thrumming with protection charms and recognized her father's handiwork. He must have spent hours carefully spelling the earring and its mate, enfolded within the second note.

The sight of her mother's spidery handwriting made her feel homesick all over again. She even missed the long list of chores her mother would write out for her on the weekends.

Dearest Linden,

Nothing but a closed road would prevent us from being there with you today. I'm furious with the Royal Marines. Ric is trying to soothe me but I'm going to lodge a formal complaint with General Wylles.

Here's what I wanted to tell you face-to-face, but this will have to do—I'm so incredibly proud of the young woman you've become— proud of your strength, your compassion, and how hard you're training to become a master of your own remarkable gifts.

With much love,

Mother

P.S. Remember to keep studying your lessons, especially Timely Spells.

Linden quickly wiped away a tear and refolded the note. She felt a pang of guilt over the mention of *Timely Spells*, since she'd stopped peering through its pages months ago, when all she found were the same old spells she'd already memorized. She promised herself she'd do better.

Linden opened the second note.

Dear Lindy,

I'm as furious as your mother about the road closure, but it's best not to encourage her, if you get what I mean. The road will reopen soon enough, but not soon enough to see you, my special girl.

I'm sorry I've let you down—I wanted to be the one escorting you tonight and leading the first dance. I know Alban will do fine, but it's not the same.

Take care of yourself, Lindy. And wear these earrings, all the time.

Your loving father

Linden put the earrings on and felt her anxiety drop down a notch. These were powerful charms, spelled with protection and something else, something almost peaceful, but not exactly. Linden closed her eyes to get a better sense of the magic embedded in her earrings: the eye of the hurricane, the calm before the storm, a warning as well as protection, then.

She opened her eyes, hugged her grandmother, and left to find Kal. But first she went back to her room to pick up *Timely Spells* and drop it into her bag, along with a small blanket and some treats for Kal. She and Kal needed some quiet time together before the craziness of her Teenth Day took over.

Kal padded along beside her as they entered the woods on the southern edge of Delavan's grounds. He must have sensed her mood, since he didn't scamper off once although they heard creatures scurrying in the underbrush.

Linden loved the Delavan woods—or pretty much any woods for that matter—for reasons she couldn't quite put into words. She loved the woodsy smells, a rich, mossy kind of scent that was sweeter in the spring, and more pungent in the fall, as decaying leaves carpeted the ground. When Linden entered the woods, the air seemed to shimmer just a bit, and she felt calmer somehow, kind of how she felt when she'd put on the earrings.

Linden tossed her blanket on the ground in front of an overturned log and gave Kal a treat. He clicked his beak a few times before settling down at her feet. Withdrawing *Timely Spells* from her bag, she leafed through it, searching for spells that had translated themselves since she'd last checked. But instead of finding new spells, she found new twists on spells she'd already been using, almost as if she'd graduated to the next level.

Linden found several different shape-shifting spells that seemed to focus on sealing the magic at each stage of the shift to help reduce mishaps. She also came across a water-douser spell similar to the one she'd botched so badly at Quorne. Instead of forming a waterfall, this spell formed a thunderstorm that generated considerably more dousing power.

It was well past lunch when Linden gathered her things. She paused at the edge of the woods to breathe in the soft autumn breezes that rustled the oaks, willows, and maples. Although the trees were dotted with gold and auburn, Delavan's lawns and gardens were still a lush green.

She heard the sound of hooves coming up the gravel drive and waited until the rider drew near.

"Matteo! Over here!" Linden flagged down her brother.

"I got a telegram from Mother and Dad and came as soon as I could," he said, dismounting to walk beside her.

"You mean about them being stopped by a road closure?"

"So, you heard?" Matteo asked sympathetically.

"It's alright—I mean, there's nothing I can do about it." Linden bit her bottom lip and then looked down the long drive. "Where's your roommate? I thought you and Stryker were coming together."

Matteo hesitated. "About that. He got stuck with kitchen duty again."

Another wave of disappointment washed over Linden. Her stomach clenched up like a fist. She couldn't believe Stryker would blow her off like this. Unless he'd lost interest and was too embarrassed to say anything because of Matteo. "So, he's not coming."

"I didn't say that. He's definitely coming, but he'll be late."

"How late?"

"He can't leave until his senior cadet releases him."

One of the stable hands took the reins of Matteo's horse to lead him away, and another servant alerted Nari and Alban of Matteo's arrival. Linden used the welcoming commotion to quietly slip up to her room, where Yolande found her an hour later snacking on a handful of nuts and reading a book, although Linden hadn't turned the page for the past twenty minutes. She kept losing her place and staring out the window.

Yolande folded her arms over her sizeable bosom and arched one eyebrow. "Really, Miss Linden. This party is being held in your honor, and here you are, leaves stuck all over your clothes and your hair all mussed up. Traipsing around like a tomboy, no doubt."

"I was *not* traipsing around. I was busy studying my spells." Yolande shot Linden a look of total disbelief but said nothing.

"The truth is I'm worried about my parents, and everyone else in the borderlands."

Yolande's tone softened. "I'm sorry your parents can't be here. Pure silliness on the part of the marines, I'd say." Yolande rubbed her back and sniffed. "Let's get you into your bath. I have something special in mind for your hair tonight."

"No formal up-dos for me," Linden protested.

"All the women will be wearing their hair up. The Teenth is a formal affair, you know that, and you're the star. Besides, tonight's your chance to turn a gent's head, and his heart."

"Please stop! I'm not interested in turning heads tonight. I want to have fun with my friends and not get a headache from one of your crazy up-dos."

"Of course, you want to turn heads. And what's wrong with looking for a husband among the likes of Ian Lewyn? You know my brother Dewel, he's head stable boy for the uncle?" Yolande waited for Linden to look up and pay attention.

"And?" Linden sighed.

"And, Dewel says now that young Mr. Ian is in business with his uncle, he's looking for a wife. And not just any wife, but a wife from a Serving Family." Serving Families were considered more powerful than others, because they practiced Serving magic at the master level. It didn't hurt that they led the various Guilds and were well off financially, too.

Linden rolled her eyes. "I don't see what this has to do with me. I'm only seventeen and not looking to get married."

"Not now, Miss Linden," Yolande said calmly, ignoring the storm clouds forming in Linden's gray eyes. "Of course, you'll not be getting married now. But in a year or two, who knows? Personally, I wouldn't pass up young Mr. Ian myself."

"You're already married to Goshen, who's devoted to you!"

"Yes, yes, I'm just saying if I were young and pretty and from a Serving Family like you, I'd set my cap for Mr. Ian."

Linden threw her hands up in the air. "You're hopeless! I'm going to take a bath and forget we had this conversation."

Linden felt better after her bath and tried not to fidget while Yolande did her hair. They compromised on a loose chignon that captured her mass of blue-black hair at the nape of her neck. Yolande helped Linden step into her dress, a periwinkle blue ball gown with white lace overlay and fitted bodice. Tiny blue rosettes trimmed the hem of the gown and neckline. This was her first sleeveless gown, another small milestone, since Valerran girls did not fully bare their arms until they'd come of age.

When Linden was ready to go downstairs Yolande winked at her. "You'll be turning heads tonight whether you want to or not."

The next few hours were a whirlwind for the family and staff of Delavan Manor. Linden thought the estate had never looked more beautiful. The days were growing shorter and the setting sun cast gold and russet shadows across the front of the mansion, so that its gleaming quartz façade looked gilded. The long winding gravel driveway led guests past woods and gardens and expanses of crisply manicured lawn. The ladies and couples arrived by locomobiles, each more luxuriously appointed than the last, with paneled doors and velvety cushioned seats inside.

Most of the Royal Marines on the guest list rode horses who, decked with plumes and braided manes, pranced up the driveway and around to the stables as if they were leading a parade. Guests climbed the pink marble staircase leading to the main entrance of the manor, which was supported by eight three-story fluted columns. Scores of torches illuminated the front of the mansion and the circular drive that edged around it. Alban, Nari, Matteo, and Linden greeted each guest as they entered their home, directing them to the grand ballroom on the west side of the mansion.

The grand ballroom was built inside a rotunda, with French doors on all sides that led outside to the patios, gardens, and private walkways of the estate. As guests entered, their eyes were drawn upward to the circular ceiling that soared thirty feet above their heads. An enormous crystal chandelier dangled like a multi-faceted diamond from its highest point, while the circumference of the ceiling was decked with green foliage and flickering tiny white gaslights, rising in concentric circles up to the highest point. Musicians played stringed instruments softly in the background, as servants circled with appetizers and drinks to fortify the guests as they waited for the ball to begin.

Linden was beginning to doubt whether Stryker would show up, despite Matteo's reassurances. Most of the guests had arrived and soon she'd be joining Alban for her first dance in the ballroom. There was a small flurry at the front door, and then Goshen announced their next guests.

"Miss Mara Pensk, escorted by Cadet Stryker Soto."

CHAPTER 9

Linden's heart shuddered in her chest. *Stryker and Mara? How could he?* Nari had insisted she invite all of her classmates, even Mara Pensk. That didn't seem like such a brilliant idea at the moment.

Mara kept a firm grip on Stryker's arm, and Nari, Alban, and Matteo greeted them warmly, although Linden could sense Matteo glancing at her sideways, waiting for her to say something other than a stiff "Welcome to Delavan." Linden refused to look into Stryker's eyes when she greeted him. He was several inches taller than her uncle and brother, and he towered over her, so it was easy to stare at his chest instead. Like Matteo, he was wearing the blue dress uniform of the Royal Marines. But rather than the rumpled pants and scuffed boots he'd worn last time, his uniform was crisply pressed, his boots polished, and his gloves—he was wearing *both* of them— were snowy white. Stryker looked confident, like he'd gotten his act together. Linden, on the other hand, swallowed hard and tried to ignore her fluttering insides.

Stryker shook hands with Matteo and Alban, and then

escorted Mara into the ballroom. Linden could feel his eyes on her, but she faced forward, ready to greet the next arrivals.

Finally, nearly all of the guests had arrived, and everyone was looking expectantly at Linden as she entered the ballroom with her family. She took a deep breath to steady her nerves as several hundred guests inspected her hair, face, and gown. She spotted Jayna standing along one wall with some of their friends from school. Jayna grinned and nodded encouragingly.

The orchestra leader announced the start of the ball. "Prime Minister Alban Arlyss will be escorting his niece, Miss Linden Arlyss, to the dance floor. Let the Teenth begin!" As the orchestra struck up the first chords of a traditional Valerran melody, the gaslights in the wall sconces dimmed around the rotunda, and the ceiling above shimmered like a thousand twinkling stars.

"You look lovely tonight, my dear. Ric and Kamden would be so proud." Alban smiled down at her as they danced.

Never one to hold back, Linden blurted out, "But why couldn't you do something so they could be here? You could've called the general. You're the PM, after all."

Alban glanced up at the ceiling for a few moments and then looked directly at her. "You know better than most the answer to that question."

Now it was Linden's turn to look away. Her family, and in theory all Serving Families, practiced a strict code of honor. What was good enough for everyone else was good enough for them. No special favors, and no looking the other way, either. Although Linden knew more than a few schoolmates who received preferential treatment from the headmaster because of their parents and what they'd promised to bestow on the school or the headmaster himself.

"Still, the timing stinks."

"The timing surprised even me. I wasn't expecting it so soon." Alban added, "We're speaking of family business, now."

"Family business" was Alban's private code that anything he said must not be repeated, as it reflected on his official role as prime minister. Alban led her around the dance floor, ensuring they circled entirely around so that everyone could see Linden in her finery. Soon other couples joined them on the dance floor, and Linden exhaled, relieved she was longer the center of so much attention.

The music changed tempo and there was a tap on Alban's shoulder. Matteo nodded with a friendly grin to his uncle, and Alban handed Linden over. Matteo bowed formally from the waist, offered his sister a white-gloved hand, and guided her through the next dance. He became an over-protective big brother whenever he was home, even though he was only two years older.

"I can see I'll have to keep an even closer eye on you. There are too many officers and gentlemen here maneuvering for a chance to sweep you off your feet."

"Don't be silly. You sound just like Yolande. Besides, you know I can take care of myself."

Matteo said, "I know you managed to evade a Glenbarran grihm in Quorne. You never should have been left alone like that."

"I wasn't entirely alone—I had a five-year-old to take care of. And how did you hear about it?" Linden added with a scowl, "Your unreliable roommate blabbed about it, didn't he?"

Matteo said hastily, "It wasn't his fault. He had too much grog the first night back at the academy. We started talking about the summer, and about other stuff, such as girls, and he told me because he really likes you and worries about you."

Linden snorted. "You could've fooled me."

"Oh, you mean about him showing up with that other girl. Stryker told me that— "

Linden interrupted her brother. "I don't even want to know. He shouldn't rely on you to make up excuses for him."

Matteo started to object, but his eyes wandered to the other side of the room and he said, "What's *he* doing here?" Matteo inclined his head and spun her around.

"Oh, you mean Ian Lewyn?"

"You know him?

"A little."

Matteo's face closed down. "I had no idea he'd be here. I just hope Stryker doesn't—"

"Did I hear my name?" Stryker smoothly cut in. He bowed to Linden and held her lightly around the waist, as if she might object any minute.

"I don't believe this is your dance," said Linden, refusing to meet his eyes.

Stryker pulled her closer—of course the orchestra had to select a slow dance for their next song—and he must have been practicing his dance steps, because he seemed almost *graceful.* "True, but I swapped with one of my friends at the academy."

Goshen had set up a small table next to the entrance to the ballroom, where he'd placed Linden's dance card, so anyone could sign up for a dance. She thought it was a silly, old-fashioned practice, but Nari overruled her. Linden had scribbled in a fictitious name a couple of times, to hold some spots for Stryker if he ever showed up. She wasn't sure she was going to tell him, though.

"What did you swap him for?"

"I'm doing his laundry for the next month."

"Oh, for goodness sakes, what's wrong with you?" Linden looked him in the face and felt herself growing warm inside her ball gown. His brown eyes, a shade darker than she'd remembered, locked on hers.

"I'd like to explain about tonight."

"You don't owe me any explanations."

Stryker plunged ahead. "I pulled kitchen duty at the last

minute, so I left really late. And then my horse threw a shoe and I had to find a blacksmith—"

"And you wound up escorting Mara Pensk. Yes, I understand."

"Oh about that, well, she gave me a ride when she saw me walking and—"

"Really, there's no need to explain!"

Stryker rumpled his hair, dark spikes of it standing up all over his head. Most un-marine-like. Linden hid a smile.

"Look, I know I've messed things up, but there's only one girl I want to—"

The orchestra leader called out the next song, which was a country reel, effectively shutting down all conversation. Linden's next dance partner, a perspiring member of parliament with a shiny pate, stepped up for his turn. As Stryker let go of her, Mara sidled up next to him, waving her dance card.

"Oh there you are. Looks like you're paired with me for the next two dances." Mara's gold gown was a few shades darker than her hair, and her fitted bodice showed off her curves. A perfect gentleman—Linden would expect nothing less—Stryker bowed, and they were off. Meanwhile, the MP stepped on her toes so many times Linden thought one of them might be broken.

When the orchestra broke for dinner, she was carried along with the rest of the crowd to the cavernous formal dining room that Nari used only for state dinners. Nari had reserved a long table for Linden, Matteo, and their friends. That morning, Linden had carefully placed her name card between Matteo and Stryker and put Jayna on Matteo's other side. When she finally arrived at the table nearly everyone else was seated, and she noticed Stryker's name card had been replaced by Toz's. Glancing around, she saw Stryker sitting at the far end of the table with Mara, who must have switched the cards. Linden counted to ten, slowly, plunked herself down next to Toz, and snapped her napkin loudly before dropping it in her lap.

Linden picked at her five-course dinner, hardly tasting her food. Relieved when the dessert course arrived, she took small bites of the layered chocolate and raspberry confection. Glancing up, she noticed Stryker staring at her. Their eyes met briefly, and then he turned back to Mara. Linden heard them laughing at something, their heads together as if sharing a secret. A small bubble of pain burst inside Linden's chest. "Happy Birthday Linden," she muttered under her breath.

"Did you say something?" Toz asked. Linden shook her head.

"In that case, I hear the orchestra starting up again. Should we head back?" Despite his numerous academic misfires, Toz had been well trained to behave like a gentleman. He guided her back to the dance floor, and he even managed to have her laughing when he imitated Mage Rudlyn. When Ian Lewyn tapped Toz on the shoulder to claim the next dance, Toz winked at her and slipped away.

"Miss Arlyss—I mean Linden—you're looking beautiful this evening. Are you enjoying your Teenth?" Ian wore a tight-fitting evening coat that accentuated his broad shoulders and narrow waist. His eyes wandered to her décolletage, which Madame Zostra, the best dressmaker in Bellaryss, had insisted on cutting into a low V neckline, much lower than girls were wearing in Quorne.

Linden blushed and remembering Yolande's remark about Ian looking for a wife, stammered. "Yes, um, thank you, I'm enjoying myself. How about you?"

"That depends."

"Depends on what?"

"On how the evening goes," Ian grinned. Linden decided she had no reply to what Yolande would have called his "cheekiness."

They both noticed Nari dancing nearby with the mayor, her silver-and-blue hair pulled back in a bun, her figure still trim. "Tell me, what's it like, growing up under the shadow of Nari Arlyss, one of the greatest mages of our time?"

"What an unusual question." A small line creased Linden's brow. "I'm not sure how to answer it."

"I hope I haven't offended you."

"Oh, not at all. It's just I don't think of her that way. To me, she's just my grandmother."

"And yet her reputation extends beyond our borders, surely you must know that."

"Of course. Nari is incredibly gifted, and I'm lucky to be her granddaughter." She glanced at Ian. "I'm at a disadvantage, since I know so little about you and your family."

"Well, there's not much to tell. I lost both my parents when I was quite young and was raised by my uncle. After leaving the academy, I served with the Royal Marines. I recently joined my uncle as a partner in his business interests, which includes horse breeding, among other things."

"So, how's that new foal doing?"

"He's going to be a champion, at least I think so." Ian added, "Your uncle has several Lewyn horses in his stable. Perhaps we could arrange to ride together? I'd like to introduce you to Newton."

"Newton?"

"Yes. Although most people think of him as merely a beautiful stallion, he's much more. He has the best self-awareness of any creature I've ever known. Newton is a proper gentleman."

Ian looked at Linden expectantly, and she realized he was waiting for an answer. It dawned on her this would start happening now. Young men (at least she hoped they were young) would begin asking her out for horseback rides or dinners in the city or walks in the park. She wasn't sure she was ready to deal with all the attention that came with her Teenth.

And yet, Ian was probably the most attractive man in the room, except of course for Stryker. What was holding her back? She and Stryker weren't exactly dating. Linden brushed aside any reservations.

"I'd enjoy a ride, so long as Kal could come along. He's jealous when I go riding without him."

"Who's Kal?" Ian's eyebrows shot up, as if she'd revealed a secret affair.

"My miniature griffin."

"You have a pet griffin?" Ian shook his head, looking both surprised and relieved. "How unusual. And what do you do with a griffin?

"Kal's my friend, my confidant, almost like my personal escape hatch."

"Escape from what?"

"Oh, escape from all of this," she waved her hand around the room. "Please don't misunderstand, I love my family. But there are times it's all so confining."

"I understand, I think. All of those expectations and duties."

"No, not exactly. I'm not sure I can explain. It's more about escaping from one part of myself to become something new. That sounds odd when I say it out loud."

"It makes sense to me. You're at an age when you still have a lot to discover. In a way, I envy you."

"Envy me, why?"

Ian narrowed his eyes. "Choices. You have many, many choices." The music ended and as Ian handed her to her next dance partner, he murmured, "Thank you for an enlightening dance. I'll see you again soon, as I've reserved another one." Linden noticed a number of female heads turning to watch Ian Lewyn as he headed to the bar.

The dance floor became crowded with couples, and Linden's ears rang from all the noise. When the orchestra took another break, she slipped outside onto the bluestone patio, which Goshen had lined with hanging lanterns and cheerful floral arrangements for the party. She shivered in the cool night air and rubbed her arms.

"Linden, here, let me." Stryker had followed her outside and came up behind her to drape a throw from one of the patio chairs around her. His hands rested for a moment on her shoulders, and Linden felt the urge to reach up and take one of his large hands in hers. Instead, she moved away and turned around to face him, embarrassed by her own thoughts.

"Thanks. I was getting overheated and needed some fresh air."

"I've been trying to find you since dinner. What happened to those dances you promised me?"

"Mr. Nibs."

"What? Who is Mr. Nibs?"

"I penciled in a couple of dances for Mr. Nibs. That's you. Because of course you were late. And then otherwise occupied. But you seem to be enjoying yourself."

"Mara Pensk saw me leaving the blacksmith's on foot, assumed I was probably a guest at your party, and asked if I needed a ride, which was a good thing because I'd have been even later. But all you've been doing tonight is avoiding me. I didn't even get to sit near you at dinner. And when were you going to tell me about Mr. Nibs?"

Stryker's eyes flashed, turning almost black. Linden tossed the throw onto the nearest patio chair and shrugged. "I thought you came just to be polite, because Matteo is your friend."

Shaking his head, Stryker closed the gap between them. He picked up one of her hands and held it against his chest. "I came here to see you. To be with you."

Someone cleared his throat. "Excuse me, but the music is starting, and Miss Arlyss is partnered with me for the next dance." Ian Lewyn stepped out of the shadows.

Stryker's head whipped around, and he pushed Linden behind him protectively. "Lewyn."

"Soto."

"Miss Arlyss is otherwise occupied. I suggest you sit this one out," Stryker growled. Linden couldn't see anything beyond his towering back and stepped out from behind him. Stryker's arm shot out and latched onto her waist, drawing her into his side. *What's happening here? Why is Stryker so protective? He's worse than Matteo.* Then Linden recalled her brother's reaction to seeing Ian earlier that evening. What had he said, something about Stryker and Ian?

"Why don't we let Linden make her own decisions?"

A muscle ticked in Stryker's jaw. "She doesn't know you like I do."

"I didn't realize the PM employed you as her guard dog."

Linden's eyes widened at Ian's rudeness. Still, Stryker had started it, whatever "it" was all about. She said, "Stryker, I don't know what you're thinking, but it's time for you to stop this. It's only one dance." She could sense things escalating out of control. Ian's hands were curling and uncurling into fists, and Stryker's body was as taut and tense as a newly strung bow.

"Listen to the young lady, Soto. She's as smart as she is lovely."

"You sixth son of a crossbreed!" Stryker dropped his arm from around Linden's waist and stepped toward Ian.

Ian charged Stryker, ramming his head into Stryker's stomach. Linden hastily backed away as the two men tumbled to the patio, punching each other as they rolled around. They knocked over several of the hanging lanterns, causing the grass along the edge of the patio to begin smoldering. Stryker leapt to his feet first and waited until Ian stood up before throwing a punch. Soon the two men peppered the air with grunts and yells as their flying kicks, punches, and hand chops connected. They looked pretty evenly matched to Linden, although Stryker was faster on his feet.

Linden didn't know what to do. She ran toward the French doors facing the patio, hoping to get some help, but she noticed quite a crowd gathering to watch. *Perfect! This is just how I wanted my Teenth to end.* She turned around and stalked over toward the two men, fuming.

Stryker had a puffy eye and his bottom lip had split open. Ian's nose was bleeding heavily, dripping down his chin and onto his jacket. She wanted to wave her arms and run into the melee, but she couldn't physically separate them. They were big, strong men with plenty of fight left in them. Before Linden could decide how to stop them from killing each other, the grass where the lanterns had toppled over burst into flames, and the fire spread quickly around the patio.

Not another fire! What is it with me, and fires? Linden remembered the new version of the water-douser spell she'd read earlier in the day. She raised her arms high and shouted the incantation, "Thunderclap and stormy cloud, drench this fire until it's out," repeating the spell over and over as a dark storm cloud swirled above them. Lightning bolts danced inside the cloud, and a clap of thunder rumbled above them. The cloud burst, drenching the fire, the patio, and the two men. Linden stood in the center of the storm, the water dripping down her face, plastering damp tendrils to her forehead, and soaking her bodice and once-flouncy skirt, which had gone limp and clung to her legs. She shifted her feet, her silk dancing slippers sopping and ruined.

Alban ran outside and pulled Stryker and Ian apart. He raised one bushy eyebrow at Linden, who'd dropped her hands once the fire was out.

"What in Queen's Crown is going on here? If you're going to kill each other, take your fight elsewhere."

Panting heavily, each man tried to blame the other for causing the fight. "Enough!" Turning to Linden, he asked, "Can you explain this?"

Linden's bottom lip trembled. More faces were crowding the French doors, and Matteo pushed his way outside to stand next to Alban. Her first instinct was to flee, to run and hide from the faces and the gossip. But this was her seventeenth birthday, her coming of age party. Time to stop running away.

Linden shook her head, brushed aside a wet strand of hair, and replied shakily, "I have absolutely no idea. But" and she looked first at Ian and then at Stryker, "I never want to see either of you again. Ever."

CHAPTER 10

L inden shuddered so violently her teeth made small clacking sounds. Her temples pounded as she shivered, from a combination of the chilly night air and the energy loss that came after casting a powerful spell. She remembered she'd eaten little and thought she might be hungry. Nari and Jayna appeared on either side of her, wrapped her in a long silver cape and pulled the hood up over her dripping hair.

Dull aches seized Linden's limbs and extended inward, settling around her heart. She leaned heavily on Jayna and Nari, who whisked her away from the prying eyes and whispered comments. They half-carried Linden around to the servant's entrance and up the back stairs to her bedroom. Jayna hugged her gently and left.

Yolande and Nari helped Linden out of her wet gown and into a hot bath. Although the pains in her arms and legs gradually lessened, she felt hurt and exposed from the inside out. She pulled on a fluffy robe and joined her grandmother, already seated on one of the comfy stuffed chairs in Linden's bedroom. Nari handed her hot tea mixed with something else, honeyed wine perhaps.

Linden sipped her drink and told Nari about Stryker and Ian and their fight. She left nothing out, because she had nothing to hide and couldn't understand how everything could've gone so wrong so fast. Sometime long past midnight Matteo joined them, and eventually Alban came in and pulled up a chair.

Alban said to Matteo, "I think you'd better tell them what you told me." Turning to Linden he said, "Apparently the relationship between Ian Lewyn and Stryker Soto is complicated. This doesn't excuse their actions, but it sheds some light on their behavior."

Matteo cleared his throat. Linden could tell he didn't want to share the details with her and Nari. "Ian Lewyn hurt someone that Stryker cared about. Her name was Madlyn Revas, and she was Colonel Revas's daughter. The colonel's been almost like a second father to Stryker, who thought of Madlyn as a sister, someone he should try to protect. Madlyn was beautiful and headstrong, and nearly every cadet fell for her during our first summer at base camp headquarters."

"But Madlyn only had eyes for Ian Lewyn, who'd graduated from the academy and was stationed at base camp. Ian and Madlyn saw quite a bit of each other over the course of the summer, and when Ian's uncle would visit while on business, he'd often bring gifts for Madlyn. At the end of the summer, we returned to school and forgot about Madlyn and Ian. Well everyone except Stryker, who continued to write to her. But she stopped writing back, and Stryker assumed she was busy with Ian."

"About two months later, Stryker received an express letter from the colonel. Madlyn was dead—and by her own hand. The man who'd seduced her, impregnated her, and then refused to marry or assist her in any way, was Ian Lewyn. Madlyn had felt so bereft and friendless that she took her own life."

There was a loud gasp from Linden. Stryker had tried to protect her, and she'd been furious with him. She thought of his black eye and split lip, and remorse ripped through her. How could she begin to apologize?

Nari compressed her lips and said, "I knew Ian's parents very well. They were good, decent people. I find it hard to believe Ian has fallen so low as to seduce and then abandon a young girl like this. Did she leave a note or tell anyone Ian was the father?"

Matteo shook his head. "No, but there's more. Apparently, Ian Lewyn left heartache wherever he went. Not only did he seduce Madlyn, but he'd done the same thing to the daughters of several merchants and farmers in the towns and villages that he passed through. And wherever Ian traveled, so did his uncle, probably to bail him out of trouble."

"When Stryker received the colonel's letter, he traveled to base camp headquarters to attend Madlyn's funeral. After the service, he tracked down Ian Lewyn, who happened to be having a drink at a local pub. Stryker publicly called him out. The two fought in the pub, in the street, and all the way to the guard post, where a senior officer finally broke up their fight."

"Didn't Stryker get in trouble for starting a fight like that?" asked Linden.

"If the colonel hadn't intervened, Stryker would have been kicked out of the academy. Unfortunately, Ian still has friends at the academy, and those are the same cadets that have been giving Stryker such a hard time by assigning him extra kitchen duty and chores."

"Where's Stryker now?" Linden asked.

"Healer Gracyn has him heavily sedated. He'll have to rest here at least through tomorrow." Matteo added, "He'll be fine,

Linden. I'm just sorry the two of them had to meet up at your Teenth. It was rotten luck."

Alban frowned. "Luck had nothing to do with it. Those two young men need to learn how to behave in polite company without trying to kill each other. And now Harlan Lewyn is threatening to sue us because he says Ian broke his nose on our property."

"Oh pish-posh, Harlan is all talk. I'll handle him myself if it comes to that." Nari waved her hand, and then noticing Linden stifling a yawn, she added, "I think it's time for all of us to turn in. It's been quite an evening, but then I'd expect nothing less from my granddaughter's Teenth."

Linden slept a few hours and woke up to twisted sheets and a pounding heart. She'd dreamt of the fight between Ian and Stryker, but in her dream, Ian had beaten Stryker until he dropped to the ground, lifeless. She threw a silk wrap around her shoulders and walked down to the guest wing.

Healer Gracyn had left the door to Stryker's room slightly ajar, probably because she was tending to more than one patient. Linden knocked quietly and the healer invited her inside.

"How's he doing?"

"Better. Finally sleeping. He's been restless all night, so I've had to keep him sedated to prevent him from compounding his injuries. He's stitched and bruised and pretty sore all over. I don't think he broke anything, but I've been watching him for signs of internal bleeding. I think he's out of danger."

Linden paled when Healer Gracyn mentioned stiches and internal bleeding. "Is he in pain at the moment?"

"Not now, he seems comfortable to me. Would you mind sitting with him for a short while? I have to check on another patient in the servants' wing."

"Of course, please go and take your time. I'll stay with him."

Linden sat in the chair next to his bed. She found a book on military history that Matteo must have left for Stryker in case he woke up. She tried to read it but kept looking at the same sentence over and over, so she set the book aside. She moved her chair closer to the bed and looked at Stryker's visible injuries. A bandage covered his right eye but couldn't hide the angry purple bruise on the side of his face. His swollen hands were covered with scrapes and cuts, and the healer had sewn neat stitches into his lip to repair the split.

Guilt knocked the wind out of her. She choked back tears, remembering how her pulse raced earlier in the evening when he'd walked through the front door. Of course, he'd arrived with Mara, but still, he'd looked handsome in his pressed uniform. Fit and healthy. Definitely uninjured. "I'm so sorry," she whispered.

"Don't cry. You make me think I'm dying," Stryker rasped crossly.

"You're awake! Healer Gracyn didn't think you'd be stirring for a while. Do you want me to find her? Is there anything I can get you? How about some water?" Linden started to stand up, but Stryker reached for her hand.

"Why were you crying?" Stryker tried to sit up and groaned out loud.

"What are you trying to do? Start some internal bleeding?" Linden stood and piled several pillows behind his back for support, which helped to boost him into more of a seated position. As she turned away to pour him a glass of water, he reached out and grabbed her wrist. Tugging gently, he pulled her down onto the bed facing him.

"Why were you crying?" he repeated.

Linden looked down at the coverlet, her heart beating a staccato rhythm in her chest. She'd never been this close to a half-naked man before, and this wasn't just any man.

He brushed away a stray lock of her hair and waited. She

touched his swollen hand. "Because of this," she said, and then gently traced the bruise on his face, "And this." She paused, "And because I didn't understand about Ian Lewyn, and now you have cuts and stitches and maybe internal bleeding." She closed her eyes to stem the tears, but they slipped out and trickled down her face.

Stryker used his thumb to wipe them away. "This is definitely *not* your fault. I picked the fight, and I'd do it again. I couldn't bear the sight of Ian Lewyn anywhere near you—I know what he's capable of."

Linden took a ragged breath. "Please don't pick any more fights. I'm rather good at taking care of myself."

"I'll grant you that. But I'd feel better—and you'd be less likely to get hurt—if you avoided him entirely. I know your brother feels the same way."

"I don't want to go anywhere near him, not after what Matteo told me."

"So, he told you about Madlyn Revas? I'm glad he did. Poor Madlyn." Stryker looked tired and rubbed his uninjured eye sleepily. "Maybe I'll take that water now."

Linden went over to a side table and poured out a glass of water from the pitcher. Stryker drained the glass quickly and leaned back against the pillows.

"It's time for you to rest," she said, placing his empty glass next to the pitcher. "I'm going to find Healer Gracyn."

Stryker nodded drowsily. "Just one thing more."

"Name it."

"Did you mean what you said, about not wanting to see me again?"

Linden bit her lip. Of course, he had every right to throw her words back at her. "At the time I meant it, but that was before I learned the truth."

"So, does that mean you *do* want to see me again?"

He's really going to drag this out of me, isn't he?

"It'd be nice if we could have a do-over, you know? Things got pretty messed up tonight."

"Like if I hadn't run late, showed up with another girl, and picked a fight that ruined your party?" Stryker winced when he tried to grin.

"Yeah, something like that," she smiled. "Now get some rest."

Linden slept until almost noon. She missed Matteo's departure—he left for the academy and made arrangements for Stryker's horse to be returned—and Healer Gracyn's pronouncement that Stryker needed complete rest for at least another day.

She dressed in a short-sleeved chambray dress, determined that Stryker was still asleep, and went to find Kal, who clicked his beak and flapped his wings when he saw her. Realizing she deserved Kal's scolding for not visiting him last night or this morning, Linden brought an offering of apple slices, one of Kal's favorite treats. They practiced his commands, such as retrieving and hunting without killing. Although Kal caught his own meals, Linden had taught him a modified form of falconry. When she headed back toward the house, Kal became unusually clingy and wouldn't leave her side. She snuck him through the servant's entrance and upstairs to the guest wing, where she saw one of the maids leaving Stryker's room with a tray. The maid's eyes bulged when she spotted Kal, but she curtsied quickly and left.

Linden knocked and heard Stryker's muffled response. "Come in."

She opened the door a crack but Kal pushed his way past her. "Kal! You weren't invited."

"So, this is the famous Kal," Stryker said, his face looking even puffier, his bruises darker.

Linden followed Kal and closed the door behind her. "He's

a bit moody today, so we won't stay long. Besides, he's not supposed to be inside the house."

Kal walked over to the bed and leaned against the coverlet so that Stryker could stroke behind his ears. Kal purred and clicked, and then he shifted around to face Stryker and offered him first one paw, then the other. Stryker whispered something and Kal's ears pricked forward. Kal clicked his beak rapidly and paced around Stryker's bed before lying down. Stryker looked surprised and leaned back against the pillows, lost in thought.

"Well?" Linden asked.

"Well what?"

"What did he say?"

"How do you know Kal said anything?"

"Hello! I'm right here. I could tell the two of you were communicating."

"You're not going to like it."

Linden frowned. "What could he possibly say that I wouldn't like?"

Stryker started to shrug but grimaced and said, "Kal told me that you need protecting."

Linden snorted. "He sounds like my father."

Stryker ignored her interruption. "And he's decided that my mission—which he says I can't or won't refuse—is to assist him in keeping your safe."

"Oh, come on. Do you really expect me to believe this?"

Stryker's unbandaged eye sought hers. "He's serious, Linden. And you're hurting his feelings right now by doubting his sincerity. And mine."

Linden knelt down next to Kal and put her arms around his neck. "Sorry, buddy." She pulled up a chair and said, "Did he explain how you're supposed to keep me safe?"

Stryker seemed embarrassed and looked away. "Not exactly."

"Which means you're not saying."

He yawned. "Thanks for introducing me to Kal. I hate to be rude, but I've got to get some shut-eye."

"Of course." She got up to leave and Kal padded behind her. When she got to the door, she turned to say something but heard Stryker's steady breathing.

Stryker slept through dinner and Linden didn't have another chance to speak with him. She scurried to get ready for school the next morning, dreading what Mara and some of the others would be saying about her Teenth. But Nari told her to go in and face it down. Staying home from school an extra day wouldn't stop the gossipers.

Jayna and Remy didn't bicker once on the way to school. Linden knew it was for her benefit and certainly wouldn't last past the morning. As they came through the doors, Linden saw Mara chatting with several junior girls. The girls had a good laugh until they noticed Linden standing nearby and scattered. Mara nodded at Linden, without any obvious sneering or smirking, so it felt almost polite. Linden stared after Mara, confused. Maybe Mara was coming down with something.

Toz stopped them in the hallway. "There's no point going to class, since the headmaster's just called an assembly." They turned around and followed Toz. Soon the hallway became jammed with students chattering about their weekend. She heard "Teenth" and "Linden" mentioned a few times, but she didn't try to figure out who was talking or what they were saying.

They found seats near the front of the auditorium, a huge high-ceilinged room with a raised dais and portable chairs and tables used for special events such as graduations, formal dinner dances, and school assemblies. Today it was configured for their assembly, with rows of chairs lining the room and facing the dais in the front.

The headmaster banged an ornamental staff on the floor of the dais three times. The students responded by stomping their feet on the polished wooden floor. Everyone took a seat and gradually the stomping quieted down. The headmaster banged his staff once more, and silence descended on the auditorium. He made a short speech, welcoming their guest and imploring the students to give him their undivided attention.

Ellis Steehl walked onto the dais, arrayed in the red and gold uniform of the Queen's Guard, an elite unit of trained soldiers sworn to protect the queen at all costs. Linden couldn't imagine Steehl sacrificing himself for the queen, even if the rumors were true and she was his half-sister. He seemed more the type to look the other way and grab the throne for himself.

Steehl stepped up to the podium. The headmaster gave him a deep bow before taking his seat at the end of the dais, next to Mage Rudlyn. A small buzz of chatter bubbled up but quieted down immediately when Steehl began to speak.

"Valerra is at a heightened state of alert due to several sightings of Glenbarran troops amassing along our western perimeter. Local militia in every city and town are conducting regular drills to ensure our preparedness. In addition, a number of Royal Marine units have been deployed to the borderlands to defend our queen and country, should the Glenbarrans attempt to invade our nation." *So that's why the general closed the main road into and out of Bellaryss this weekend,* thought Linden, *the marines were deploying troops and equipment to the borderlands.*

"I've come with a message from Queen Ayn. Your queen implores every student at Morrell to study harder than ever before. We need you, as never before. We need your hearts for service, your minds for leadership, your gifts for magic and healing and soothsaying—we need you to continue to serve our country well and truly in the years to come, after this current threat is behind us." Steehl then reminisced about his days as a student at Morrell, expressing his gratitude for the fine education he'd received, and claiming they were some of the happiest years of his life.

Toz snorted out loud, and Linden jabbed him in the ribs with her elbow. "Hush," she whispered, "Mage Rudlyn is staring right at us."

"This is pure propaganda," grumbled Toz.

"Agreed," she hissed. "But let's not get kicked out of the assembly."

"Fine."

Steehl continued his speech, glancing down at his notes on the podium. "These are grave times, and much will be required of every Serving Family. We may call on you to serve your queen and country while you are yet students. Your magic and your courage must never fail us." He went on to thank the students and faculty for their time that morning, and then turned to thank the headmaster. Steehl stepped away from the podium, the silent assembly of students clapping without much enthusiasm.

The headmaster and Rudlyn rose to shake Steehl's hand, and then Rudlyn escorted Steehl off the dais. "I'm going to follow them," said Linden.

"I'm coming with you," said Toz.

"Where are you two going?" asked Jayna, who'd been reading a healer's book on herbal remedies during the entire assembly, not listening to a word of Steehl's speech.

"Just checking something out. I'll see you in next period," said Linden, keeping an eye on Rudlyn's bobbing head and Steehl's straight back. "Come on, before we lose them."

Toz followed Linden behind the dais, bumping into her and nearly blowing their cover. Linden brought a finger to her lips, worried they'd been overheard. But Rudlyn was too busy talking to Steehl to notice a pair of students in their midst. As Steehl and Rudlyn made their way to the nearest exit, Linden heard Rudlyn say something about the Glenbarrans seeming unstoppable.

Steehl said, "I'll confess that I'm surprised—and impressed. Their Fallow spells are befuddling our mages and warriors on the battlefield. If this keeps up, we'll be serving King Roi before long." Rudlyn made a comment about Queen Ayn that made Steehl chuckle. They stepped outside, the door cutting off the remainder of their conversation.

"Did you hear any of that?" asked Linden.

Toz shook his head. "I can't believe Steehl is 'impressed' with the Glenbarrans' Fallow ways."

Crossing her arms, Linden said, "I wish I could have heard what Rudlyn was saying about the queen. I have a feeling it wasn't complimentary." The bell rang for their next period. They had five minutes to make it to the other side of the school for their mathematics class. "Let's get going before we're both late. I don't think you can afford any more demerits."

Toz gave her a mischievous grin. "I suppose if I get expelled, I can always join the marines. It sounds like the queen will be looking for students before long."

Linden rolled her eyes, jogging alongside Toz to their next class. She pondered Ellis Steehl's visit to their school and his comments afterwards to Rudlyn, curious at how well they seemed to know each other. Shrugging, she decided she had more immediate concerns. She'd neglected to do her mathematics homework in the excitement of her Teenth and would be earning a few demerits herself.

CHAPTER 11

The locomobile carrying Linden home from school pulled into the gravel driveway just as another Delavan locomobile passed them by. Linden stared after it, frowning. Nari might be going to a guild meeting, but those were usually held in the evenings. Alban had left after breakfast for parliament and said he'd be gone all day. Could it have been Stryker, heading back to the academy? Linden hefted her book bag onto her shoulder and ran up the front steps. Nari heard her opening the front door and walked out of the library, carrying an envelope.

"Who was that leaving in the locomobile?"

"Stryker Soto, who insisted on returning to the academy despite Healer Gracyn's protests. Apparently, he's on a full scholarship and can't afford to fall behind in his studies."

"Oh, I didn't realize." Linden tried to hide her disappointment. She had hoped he'd be around a few more days at least.

"He's quite a young man," Nari added, almost as an afterthought.

"So, then you approve of him?"

"Do you need my approval?"

Linden thought this sounded like another one of Nari's little tests. Lately her grandmother had been really pushing her to practice and study—everything from magic and fencing to history and math. Linden was learning to focus much better; even her grades were improving. She still struggled in her magic classes, but her water-douser spell the other night proved she could successfully wield magic. Well, some magic, some of the time. And she had Nari to thank for it.

On the other hand, Linden was seventeen and could make her own choices. "Although I don't need your *approval*, I do value your *opinion*."

Linden must have said the right thing, because Nari smiled. "While I believe Cadet Soto is somewhat hot-headed, he's young and will learn there are better ways to fight than with his fists. His instincts are right and true—he wanted to keep you safe—although I don't think Ian Lewyn is a threat." Nari started toward the library but stopped. "Oh, I almost forgot. He left this for you." She held out the envelope.

"Thank you." Linden added, "For everything." She took the envelope outside to one of the wrought-iron benches scattered throughout the gardens.

Hey Linden,

I'm sorry to leave without saying good-bye, but I've got to get back to the academy. I have homework to make up and—you guessed it— more kitchen duty. I didn't exactly show up empty-handed for your birthday, though. I had made you a pencil sketch from memory that Matteo said was a good likeness of you. But then it got all wet the other night, so instead, here's a sketch of Kal. I hope you like it.

Your friend (we're still friends, right?),
Stryker

Linden pulled out the second sheet of paper and gasped at the accuracy of Kal's portrait. Not only did Stryker have a good eye, but his pencil drawing of Kal's sharp eagle's face surrounded by a shaggy mane of fur managed to capture Kal's quirky personality too.

Linden found a frame for the sketch after dinner and put it on her dresser. She sat down to write Stryker a quick note of thanks, but it took her five drafts to get the words right.

Hi Stryker,

Thank you for your gift. I really like your sketch of Kal. It looks just like him—have you been formally trained?

I'm sorry I wound up ruining your original gift with all that water. I would have liked to have seen how you see me, if that makes any sense.

Don't push yourself too hard. You're still injured and need to heal.

Your friend (yes, still friends),

Linden

The next week passed quietly, and Linden's eventful Teenth was soon forgotten amid more serious concerns about the Glenbarrans and crazy King Roi. As seniors at Morrell, Linden and Jayna found themselves inundated with all kinds of extra assignments, projects, and additional service requirements after school. They visited the children's hospital, volunteered at the ladies auxiliary for displaced families, and collected donations for the city orphanage. While all Serving Families required their children to be actively engaged in hands-on service projects, the niece of Prime Minister Alban Arlyss needed to be more visibly involved than most students, and Jayna always accompanied her.

Linden was feeling overwhelmed by her schoolwork and

volunteer commitments, as well as news of more Glenbarran troop movements and pending battles in the borderlands. Her favorite part of each day was after lunch, when she could look forward to rigorous rounds of swordplay, followed by magic-handling lab. The exercise and intense concentration helped calm her worries about her parents, at least for a few hours. Although Nari begged them to leave Quorne, her mother refused to abandon her duties as governor, and her father agreed. Besides, someone had to look after all of Mother's relatives, who wouldn't leave their houses and farms and shops.

Linden detected a difference as soon as she entered magic-handling lab. Mage Rudlyn always ran the class with an iron fist, but today she seemed excited, as if she had a surprise. Her back ramrod straight, her dark brows knit together in concentration, Rudlyn addressed the class. "Ladies and gentlemen, I have it on competent authority that every magic handler in Bellaryss, from apprentice to master mage, will be called upon to serve the queen in the near future."

Here she paused as the class buzzed with chatter. When it quieted down again, Rudlyn continued. "It is not a surprise to any of us that our country—our way of life—is in peril. With most of our Royal Marines deployed in the borderlands to protect against an invasion, our city is left with a dwindling number of defenders. We will need to rely on the local militia, our citizens, and our magic."

"We'll be focusing all of our attention on learning magical defenses to help protect ourselves and our families. There are many different kinds of magical defenses that we'll be studying in the coming weeks. Please be prepared to work hard and practice even harder."

The class erupted in a dozen different conversations. Student apprentices were never permitted to learn magical defenses, beyond basic protection spells such as veils of drabness. Only mages were considered skillful enough to safely invoke this type of magic. Jayna's eyes widened in surprise, and Linden could hardly sit still.

Rudlyn raised her hands and the room fell silent. "To aid us in our lessons on magical defenses, I've invited a consultant who is this nation's foremost expert in defensive magic." She went to open the door.

"Class, please welcome Master Mage Nari Arlyss." When Nari entered the room, the class rose, applauded, and remained standing. As Rudlyn introduced each class member by name, the boy or girl bowed in formal greeting. When Nari paused before Linden and Jayna, Rudlyn did not skip a beat as she presented the girls. Nari inclined her head and winked, then moved on to the next set of desks. When she completed her inspection of the students, Nari returned to the front of the classroom. After asking the students to take their seats, Rudlyn once again addressed the class.

"What you'll be studying in the weeks to come will be among the most important lessons you'll ever have in this school. As with all magic lessons, these are to be practiced carefully, mastered competently, and shared with no one who is not a mage. This is especially important for the defensive spells you'll be learning from Mage Arlyss. Under no circumstances may these be discussed with anyone other than a mage."

Mara raised her hand. "Yes, Miss Pensk."

"If we learn these spells and employ them to help defend our city, wouldn't that make us mages?"

"Class, what do you think?"

Jayna raised her hand. "I believe we'd remain apprentices until we've completed all magic handling training assigned by our mage tutors."

"That is correct. As you know, upon graduation from Morrell, you're considered mage apprentices. Many of you will cease your magic lessons at that point, having determined to pursue other studies. Only a select few will continue their studies under the tutelage of a mage."

"That being said," Nari addressed the room. "Mage Rudlyn assures me this is the finest group of magic handlers she's seen assembled in one classroom. We expect most, if not all of you to continue your magic handling studies after graduation."

"I've been invited here to see just how talented you are—and to help prepare you to join mages and master mages in defense of our city and our queen." Another excited murmur rippled through the classroom. "Let's get started."

Nari instructed the students to move the lab desks against one wall and group the chairs in a circle, except for one that was placed in the center. She motioned to Linden to sit in the lone chair in the circle's center and instructed the students to stand outside the ring of chairs. Nari and Rudlyn stood off to one side. They slowly raised their hands in unison and chanted an incantation, murmuring so quickly that Linden couldn't make out the words to the spell. Suddenly the air shimmered around Linden and a wall of gentle breezes surrounded her. She could see everything around her, but her classmates were all talking at once, "What's happening?" "Where'd she go?" "What does it feel like in there?"

Rudlyn called out, "Linden, say something to your classmates."

"There's a soft breeze swirling around me...what're you seeing?"

"The air seems milky around you, almost as if you're standing inside a wispy cloud," said Jayna.

"It's like we can only see your shadow—we can't really see the details of your face or clothes," added Toz.

Rudlyn and Nari snapped their fingers, and a ring of fire surrounded Linden, the flames reaching to the ceiling. Several students panicked and Toz ran to get the mechanical flame douser from behind Rudlyn' desk. Just as suddenly, the flames subsided.

"That was amazing!" Linden shouted.

A whistling sound erupted in the class, as a series of tiny cannonballs began raining down around Linden. She looked up, grinning, as the cannonballs dropped harmlessly to the ground when they pelted the foggy shield. Next, a bombardment of little arrows came flying at Linden, followed by small swords, without owners, swishing through the air in an attempt to break through the shield surrounding her. As the din of mini cannonballs, flying arrows, and swishing swords died down, Linden began to clap. Soon the whole class was clapping and cheering. Nari and Rudlyn shushed the class and brought the room to order.

"Alright, the demonstration is over—now the real work begins!" Rudlyn said sternly.

Each school day thereafter, Nari and Rudlyn instructed the class on a variety of defensive spells. They learned how to cast a shield of impenetrable fog around a pencil, then a book, and then a desk. They learned how to deflect an opponent's fist, then dagger, then sword and arrow. It was incredibly hard work, and even the sassiest students stopped grumbling and concentrated hard. All went home exhausted each evening.

Still, none could imagine how their small triumphs in class would translate into a protective defense for their city—even with the assistance of every mage in Bellaryss. They could only hope they would have time enough to improve and perhaps become skillful enough to shield their own homes or deflect arrows from their loved ones. But to surround a city in a shield of fog? That seemed beyond the ability of any group of magic handlers, no matter how gifted.

~

Now that Nari joined Rudlyn in the classroom each afternoon, Linden's magic handling labs buzzed with excitement. And yet Linden found herself increasingly frustrated. While Jayna and her classmates made progress with the defensive spells, Linden fell further behind. Each of her spells wound up exploding or imploding or randomly malfunctioning. She studied, practiced at home with her grandmother, and studied some more. Rudlyn would repeat Boreus' old saying, "Focus your magic, funnel your energy, and find the spell's flow. Just remember to Focus, Funnel, Find, Flow." *What was it with magic handling instructors? Did they all learn how to be especially annoying as part of their job?*

Nari and Rudlyn were conducting the final exams for defensive spells, and Linden anxiously awaited her turn. She tapped her feet without even realizing it, until Rudlyn came by and asked her to be quiet so others could concentrate.

Rudlyn and Nari tested the class in groups of three. Linden, Jayna, and Remy were in the last group to be tested. Each trio needed to protect one white mouse from a playful kitten, as well as from bombardment by tiny paper airships and a small windstorm. If anything went wrong, Nari and Rudlyn were there to step in and preserve the mouse and kitten from harm. The other trios passed the exam—although the kitten was bored and seemed more interested in chasing her tail than the mouse.

When it came to their turn, Linden, Jayna, and Remy raised their hands, chanting the defensive spell over the mouse. "Raise impenetrable fog with this charm, protect those within from outside harm." The shield of fog formed around the unsuspecting mouse. The kitten sensed the mouse through the fog and pranced over, tail pointed, and amber eyes focused on the mouse. She jumped and was easily repelled by the shield. Next, Rudlyn sent paper airships into the air, which pinged against the shield and fell to the ground harmlessly.

Somewhere around the fifth time she repeated the

incantation, Linden realized she might have mixed in some words from a different defensive spell. She focused all the harder, her head starting to pound, as she repeated the incantation. "Raise fog and maelstrom with this charm, protect with strength from outside harm."

When Nari conjured a small windstorm to test their shield, something strange happened. Rather than blowing itself out as it had done with the other students, this wind started blowing harder. It blew so hard that it picked up the fallen airships and started flinging them around the classroom. As the wind whipped up, it lifted the students' hair, dislodged spectacles, and started tossing papers from desks. Growing in strength and velocity, the kitten was tossed into the maelstrom but Toz quickly grabbed her before she could be injured. Girls screamed and dove for cover as the wind tunnel tore books from shelves and spun chalk into the air. Nari and Rudlyn raised their hands and shouted the spell for unwinding active magic. Chalk, airships, books, and papers gently floated to the floor. The white mouse was nonplussed and seemed to be dozing. Nari looked thoughtful, her hands on her hips as she surveyed the resulting mess.

"Well," Rudlyn sniffed. "That was quite enough excitement for one afternoon. Let's sort out the papers and books and clean up this room."

"What happened?" whispered Jayna. "Everything seemed to be going so well and then all of a sudden—poof—we had a tornado in our classroom."

"You know what happened," Linden hissed. "I got nervous. You know what happens when I get nervous."

"It wasn't so bad...it was pretty exciting actually."

"Ladies," said Rudlyn pointedly at Jayna and Linden. "Please pick up papers in that corner of the room."

After school, Linden walked slowly up the steps of the manor. Nari was waiting as she entered the foyer. "Linden, please join me in my sitting room upstairs. I've made us some tea."

The next half hour passed pleasantly enough, with no discussion of magic or school, until Linden couldn't wait any longer.

"Are you angry with me? I'm sorry about what happened today. I was just so nervous."

"Of course I'm not angry with you. Quite the contrary— I'm proud and perhaps just a bit awed by the power of your magic."

"Proud? Awed by *my* magic?"

"Do you realize what happened today?" asked Nari.

"Sure. I created chaos and nearly caused Remy and Jayna to fail the exam." Linden stood up and walked to the window overlooking the formal gardens, stripped bare of any remaining blooms in the recent autumn windstorms.

"It's true you created magical chaos, but I never would have failed you, or any apprentice who demonstrated such promise."

"But I did everything wrong. I nearly hurt the poor kitten and flung stuff all around the classroom. It seemed to me that I failed pretty spectacularly."

"The kitten was safe with Toz. Mage Rudlyn and I were there to protect against any serious mishaps." Glancing toward her granddaughter, Nari gently asked, "What was the assignment, Linden?"

"To magically establish a protective shield around the mouse and ensure it came to no harm."

Nari nodded. "Precisely. And did you accomplish that?"

Linden shrugged. "Yes, but I flung the kitten in the air, tossed airships and papers and books all around. I created a mini-tornado in there. What would have happened if you and Rudlyn hadn't stopped everything?"

Now it was Nari's turn to shrug. "What do you think would have happened?"

Linden thought about it and slowly exhaled. "Well, I suppose the mini-tornado would have blown itself out, eventually."

"Yes, that's correct. Of course, now that I've seen a small demonstration of your power, we'll be focusing even more on techniques to help control your magic."

"But wait—are you saying it's actually a *good* thing I can create such a mess?"

"What if, instead of a small white mouse it had been Delavan Manor, and instead of paper airships it had been Glenbarran invaders, intent on destroying us? Would you feel as if you'd failed if you had created a windstorm to disorient them, perhaps even disarm them?"

Linden ran to her grandmother and hugged her. "Wow, who knew that creating chaos could be a useful thing!"

"Quite useful, and quite dangerous in the wrong hands," Nari took Linden's hand and guided her down onto the sofa next to her. "I've long believed you have a strong gift—the water-douser spell you deployed at your Teenth confirmed that for me. Revelators have the potential to become extremely powerful mages. All of your small disasters and frustrations indicate a greatness of power, which must be properly harnessed within the boundaries of Serving magic. However, you must understand you can never demonstrate such a powerful gift in school again."

"But why?"

Nari was silent and rubbed her forehead. "I'm weary, my dear. Let's leave this discussion for now. Please believe me when I say that it's vital you don't reveal the extent of your abilities again. It could put all of us—and especially you—in great danger."

CHAPTER 12

Twice a month Linden volunteered after school at the Valerran Museum, which boasted the largest collection of sculpture, art, books, maps, and scrolls anywhere in the world. The museum covered three city blocks and was constructed from the same pink and gold marble as most of Bellaryss' downtown buildings. Huge stone columns soared into the air on all sides of the imposing building, which was capped on top with a large gold-tiled dome. The burnished walnut doors in the main entrance were covered in ancient fay hieroglyphs, and the same hieroglyphs were etched at the tops of each of the columns. Unfortunately, the knowledge of fay ways and language had been all but lost, and even a master mage such as Nari could only divine the meaning of some of the symbols.

Although there were a number of entrances into the complex, Linden loved walking through the oversized walnut doors. It felt as if she were entering another time, another world. As she stepped into the cavernous space that formed the original structure of the museum, which now served as its library wing, she paused to look up at the domed ceiling. It was richly tiled in various shades of greens and browns that were designed to look like a forested canopy of leaves, vines, and tree branches above her head. The walls were covered in intricately detailed mosaics that recounted much of the old tales from Linden's history of magic classes. When she was younger, her mother had told her that standing directly beneath the forested dome on a new moon night would be like standing in the oldest part of Faynwood, where the Faymon Liege ruled all the clans. Even the fay people and creatures of the woodland recognized her authority. Her mother had told and re-told the old tales, which she'd explained were a combination of history, prophecy, and allegory. In other words, no one knew which stories were actually true. Linden had heard the tales so many times she'd memorized them by the time she was seven.

Linden's footsteps echoed on the polished stone floors as she headed to the Scroll Collection. It was her favorite room and almost seemed to hum with its own internal vibration. She'd once asked a young guard if he'd noticed it, but he'd looked at her so strangely she didn't ask again. But she felt it each time she stepped into the room—the vibration of old knowledge and an even older kind of magic.

The scrolls were carefully preserved inside glass cases, and only individuals with special credentials were permitted access to them. Linden's job was to dust the glass cases and to fetch the elderly librarian in charge of the scrolls if anyone requested access. There were seldom any visitors, so after Linden was finished dusting, she walked about the room, trying to find the source of the vibration. She'd gently place her palms on the walls, the cases, anywhere she could think of, but she hadn't found the source yet.

That afternoon was quieter than most, and the library was practically deserted. She decided to focus on the case containing the oldest scrolls in the collection and gently placed her palms on the smooth glass surface of the case. This time she uttered an incantation for opening secret places, for revelation. "Open what your magic has sealed; secrets, stories, and sights reveal!"

She felt a vibration like a shuddering breath beneath her fingers. The case vibrated harder, the glass panes rattling in their tracks, and one of the scrolls rolled open. Linden quickly removed her palms, and the vibrations ceased. She used her dust cloth to wipe away the smudges her palms had left on the glass, and as she was polishing the case, she glanced at the scroll that had been dislodged.

The scroll had beautiful illustrations all around the border and in the center. Although faint with age, Linden could tell this was a recounting of one of the fay tales. There was something familiar about it. As she looked more closely at the illustrations, she realized the leaves and vines were similar to those in the domed ceiling, and the illustration in the center was of the Faymon Liege herself; a nearly identical image adorned one of the mosaics in the main room of the library. Excited with her discovery, Linden tried to follow the story through the illustrations around the border.

Woven in and out of the leaves and vines were woodland animals, Faymon men and women, and the fays, easily identified by their vivid blue hair. The blue highlighted hair of the Faymons could be traced back to the much brighter blue hair of their fay ancestors.

Faynwood was clearly a happy, peaceful place until some danger forced the Faymon Liege to take up her sword. She died in battle and darkness settled in—woods and meadows and Faymon settlements were covered with a low-hanging black cloud. The darkness reigned for a time, with sword-wielding clans fighting each other.

Finally, another Faymon Liege—she was shorter and her

blue-black hair was longer—returned in a triumph of Serving magic, represented by lightening flashing all around her, and she pushed back the edges of the darkness until it was furled up like a small dark rug—still present, but contained. The larger illustration in the center of the scroll showed the new Faymon Liege surrounded by the people of Faynwood as she was crowned. Her crown seemed to have been woven from the leaves, vines, and berries of the woods, and it was placed on her head by a tall man in battledress, his sword hanging at the ready by his side. While Linden was familiar with all of the well-known fay tales, the crowning of this Faymon Liege by a warrior was new. She couldn't imagine why she hadn't heard the story before.

Someone coughed behind her, and Linden spun around. Toz's father had entered the room and was standing next to Linden. Linden often saw Mr. Valti at the library, studying the ancient scrolls and mumbling to himself. He looked curiously at the scroll that Linden had accidentally unrolled. Mr. Valti excitedly withdrew a pair of spectacles from his pocket and examined the illustrations more closely. Then he set down his satchel on the floor and withdrew a handheld photographic machine and small, folding tripod.

"Where is the librarian on duty?" he asked as he set up the tripod, mounting the photographic machine on top.

"He's in another wing, but I can fetch him for you."

"Who's been in this room during the past two hours?"

"No one but me, sir."

Mr. Valti looked at her over the top of his spectacles. "No one?"

Linden shook her head. "No sir, Mr. Valti. No one."

He repositioned his tripod a few times before pointing the photographic device at the newest illustration in the scroll. At the click of a button, the machine whirred to life, capturing the image. Mr. Valti counted aloud to one hundred and then withdrew a silver-plated copper square from inside the photographic machine.

"What exactly happened in here, young lady?" he asked, staring at the image of the Faymon Liege he held in his hands. "I want to hear every detail from the time you entered this room until I arrived a few minutes ago."

Linden briefly recounted what happened, leaving out the part about trying to find the source of the vibration. "So, when I leaned on the glass case, that one scroll became dislodged and rolled open."

"And you're certain that's the entire story?" Mr. Valti asked skeptically.

"Yes sir, it is."

Mr. Valti carefully wrapped a piece of linen around the square containing the image, slipping it into his satchel. He removed the photographic machine from the tripod, refolded the legs of the tripod, and placed both tripod and machine inside his bag, next to the image. Straightening, he removed his spectacles and returned them to his jacket pocket. "Curious. Very curious indeed. You see, I was in this room not more than two hours ago and examined that particular scroll. It's related to the research I'm doing on the old fay prophecies," he paused to scratch his chin thoughtfully. "And I can assure you, that center illustration is new."

"Perhaps you just missed it?"

"Of course I didn't just miss it. I tell you, it's new. It wasn't there two hours ago."

"But that's impossible."

"I agree it's highly improbable, but when it comes to fay magic, nothing is impossible. I'd say that somehow, by dislodging the scroll, you released some long dormant fay magic." Here he paused again and muttered under his breath, "Just as I thought."

"Excuse me?"

"Never mind. I've had my suspicions all along, of course."

"Oh—I hope I'm not in any trouble?"

"Quite the contrary, quite the contrary," replied Mr. Valti almost cheerfully, as he tipped his hat in her direction and strolled out of the room.

What an odd man, Linden thought, shaking her head as she tried to reconcile the dimpled, mischievous Toz with his crusty, contrary father. She was convinced Mr. Valti was confused and must have examined a different scroll, perhaps from a different case entirely. She packed up her book bag and went outside to meet the Delavan locomobile for the ride home.

As she headed toward the stairs and her bedroom to change, she overheard voices in her uncle's study down the hall. The door swung open and a harried messenger bowed to her on his way to the front door. Linden walked into her uncle's study and was struck by how much older Alban looked. His black hair, once salted with blue highlights and a touch of gray, had turned mostly silver during the past few months. "Glenbarrans," she muttered.

But Alban heard her. "Yes, I'm afraid so. The reports are worse than expected. There are more Glenbarran troops amassing in the western borderlands every day, and there is at least one unconfirmed report of them having broken through the northwestern perimeter."

"That can't be!" Linden felt as if a chill wind had chased all of the warmth from her uncle's office. "Have we heard from Mother and Father yet?"

Alban picked up a telegram from his desk and handed it to her. "DESPITE REPORTS OF ENEMY TROOPS STOP ALL IS QUIET HERE STOP EXECUTING OPERATION REFUGE STOP."

Linden saw the telegram had been sent that morning and blew out a puff of air. At least her parents had been safe when they'd sent the message. "What's Operation Refuge?"

Her uncle put his arm around her. "One of the reasons Ric and Kamden refuse to leave is they are working on getting as many of the city's residents as possible to safety, among them Kamden's extended family. Some have already left Quorne. Others are packing up now, realizing the threat is real. And then there are some, like your Aunt Oonie and several of her sisters, who are elderly and need special care. Your parents won't leave them behind. You should be enormously proud of them."

"I am proud of them—and now I wish I'd never left Quorne. I want to be with them, especially if the Glenbarrans attack again."

Alban raised one eyebrow and said, "Why do you think your parents sent you away when they did? They'd never have let you stay in Quorne this long. It's not safe, not for them and certainly not for you."

Linden swallowed hard and nodded. "And what happens if the Glenbarrans really have broken through the perimeter? Couldn't they make it all the way here?"

"Remember, even if it's true they've broken through, Bellaryss has never been taken by an enemy. We'll stop the Glenbarrans, even if they come right up to our city gates."

"But the marines are scattered across in the borderlands. Who will defend us here? And what about the queen and royal family? Have they been notified?"

Alban smiled through his weariness. "I would be a poor prime minister if I didn't keep the royal family informed. We're putting plans in place to ensure their safety. Have no fear on that score. And as far as defending our city, we've already called up our reserves and the local militia."

"What can I do to help?"

Alban looked out the window as a stiff westerly wind shredded the remaining leaves from the trees. The rain, which had held off all afternoon, began to fall in earnest. "Until you hear otherwise from me, live your life, Linden. Live it fully, completely, with no regrets. Live fearlessly. If we allow the Glenbarrans to get inside here," he tapped the side of her head. "Then they've already won. Do you understand what I'm trying to say?"

"I think so."

"Good. Well, I have to prepare for several parliamentary votes this coming week." Alban turned back to his desk. "And remember House Rule Number One."

"Always!" House Rule Number One was simple: Absolutely nothing heard at Delavan Manor regarding the government or individuals in the government could be repeated. Period. Servants had been sacked for sharing what they thought was innocent gossip. That was no excuse in Alban Arlyss's household. National security and personal integrity were paramount.

Linden bit her bottom lip as she changed out of her school uniform. Tossing her green jacket on her bed, she slipped off her white blouse and stepped out of her gray skirt. Yolande hadn't been feeling well that morning, so Linden told her to take the day off and rest. Linden had managed to dress herself just fine when she lived in Quorne, and although she needed Yolande's help getting into her new dresses and gowns, she could manage just fine otherwise. She pulled one of her old dresses from Quorne out of her wardrobe, a scoop-neck gray jersey that fell to her mid-calf, far from fashionable but comfy and easy to wear.

She fretted over her parents and relatives still living in Quorne. While she always carried with her a nagging worry for her family, it had just erupted into full-blown anxiety. Linden tried to calm her mind with a few deep breathing exercises. She knew she shouldn't attempt to practice any of her magic lessons while in such an agitated state. She gave up and went to find Nari.

Linden told Nari what she'd heard from Alban. As usual, Nari was impassive. Linden wouldn't have been surprised to learn Nari knew of the latest developments even before her son. Nari looked deeply into Linden's eyes and asked her what was really on her mind.

"It's Mother and Father, of course. I want to know they're safe and will remain safe, no matter what," she answered with a scowl.

"So, you want to see the future? Or do you want to control it?"

"Well, um." Linden faltered, then added softly, "Neither. I just don't want to lose anyone I love."

"Neither do I. None of us wants to face loss and pain, and with rumors of war swirling about that's understandable and reasonable." Nari paused for emphasis. "Now, tell me whether you'll be able to concentrate on your magic handling lessons today."

Linden snapped back to the present, surprised at how well her grandmother knew her. She realized what had just happened. Nari had forced her to verbalize her fears, and in doing so, she'd been able to clear her mind enough to focus on her lessons. She nodded.

"Good. Do you have any questions or anything else on your mind before we get started?"

Linden thought back to when Nari had first told her she was a revelator. "Remember when you explained about me being a revelator? What did you mean when you said I had two competing gifts, and even you don't know what I'll be capable of doing?"

Nari put a bookmark in her reference book and motioned for Linden to join her at one of the lab tables in her office, which adjoined her bedroom suite. Nari picked up several test tubes and holding up one with gold-colored liquid, she said,

"Take this elixir and sprinkle two drops on those dried rosebuds."

Linden took the tube from her grandmother. As the liquid hit the buds, each brown petal uncurled itself and became a soft velvety yellow, glistening with dew. Linden gently touched one of the petals.

"Alright, take this elixir and sprinkle two drops on them." Linden grasped a second tube, this one with purple-colored liquid, and carefully sprinkled the drops. Her eyes widened as the roses changed into a deep shade of gray.

"Now, put on this lab coat and wear these goggles," Nari said, as she donned a pair of goggles. "I want you to combine two drops from each tube and sprinkle the mixture on the roses. Step back before the drops hit the petals."

Linden barely had time to step back before the roses exploded, showering them both with brown, smoky petals. The front of Linden's lab coat was sprayed with a brownish, sticky substance. "Yuck. What just happened?"

"Two magical substances, which work quite well on their own, were combined without any thought given to how well they would work together. The result, as you can see, was the destruction of the roses themselves. Now consider what might happen if two magical gifts, each imperfectly understood by their owner, were haphazardly thrown together. The results could be disastrous—to the magic handler and anyone else in her path."

"Which is why you keep telling me to study and practice, study and practice!"

"Precisely!" agreed Nari. She smiled and patted Linden's hand. "You're a smart young woman and prodigiously gifted. You'll learn what you need to know when you need to know it."

The speaking tube in Nari's office sputtered to life; she had a caller downstairs. Nari grumbled about the interruption, removed her mage's lab coat, and left Linden to continue working on her magic lessons. After a while, Linden wandered over to her grandmother's bookshelf and ran her fingers along the titles: *Seventy Spells for Seven Seasons, Handbook of Herbal Healing Arts, Magic Handler's Primer, History of Serving Magic, Advanced Magic Handling, Seers and Prophets of Valerra, Collected Tales of the Fay Nation*. Linden's fingers stopped at the last title. She was familiar with all of the other volumes and was working her way through *Advanced Magic Handling* under Nari's exacting instruction. But Linden had never seen the *Collected Tales of the Fay Nation* in her grandmother's library before. She pulled the heavy volume down and almost dropped it when she saw the front cover. It was the exact same illustration she'd seen in the library—the crowning of the new Faymon Liege by a tall man in battledress. She opened the front cover and had another surprise. All of thick vellum pages were blank, which meant the book itself was ensorcelled.

Linden carried the heavy volume over to an uncluttered spot on the scarred lab table. She started with some basic reading spells. Nothing. She tapped her fingers on the table, thinking. She moved on to spells for storytelling and unwinding. Still nothing. Frustrated, she glanced around Nari's office and stopped. She walked over to the crystal globe and placed the book, open in the middle, on the floor beneath it.

It fit snugly between the three carved legs of the globe's tripod. She carefully placed her hands on the crystal globe and focused on the spell for opening secret places, which she'd just used in the Scroll Collection room at the library. "Open what your magic has sealed; secrets, stories, and sights reveal!"

The glass beneath her hands grew warm and something inside the depths of the crystal began swirling. Linden's pulse raced, anxious to learn what the spell might unveil. Illustrations accompanied by hieroglyphs began to form inside the crystal's depths. She couldn't make any sense of the hieroglyphs and uttered a translation spell. "Translate for me what's on the page, into my language from ancient fay."

The globe shook beneath her hands. The hieroglyphs began reforming themselves, squiggles and curlicues tumbled into each other and then paused in mid-glass, becoming recognizable words. The illustrated pages flipped past quickly, providing a snapshot of fay history and their complicated relationship with the Faymons of Faynwood. But it all went by so fast Linden couldn't understand what she was seeing. And then the lesson stopped halfway down a page, where new hieroglyphs slowly formed and translated, one word at a time. *They*. Linden held her breath as the next word formed. *Are*. They are...what? She wondered aloud. The final word formed: *Coming!*

The glass darkened and started shaking again, so violently that Linden was afraid it would tumble from its stand. But she felt frozen in place, unable to free herself from the spelled globe. Nari's reflection appeared in the globe and then her grandmother's arms were around her, pulling her hands away. Linden was panting hard, beads of sweat forming on her forehead and trickling down her face.

"I thought I told you never to use the globe by yourself. You're not ready!" Nari seemed more frightened than angry.

"I'm sorry, I was just so curious about your book on the fays," Linden gestured to the floor beneath the globe, but the book wasn't there.

"You mean this book?" Nari pointed behind her, to the same illustrated book of children's fay tales that her mother used to read to her. Linden shook her head and knelt down, touching the wooden floorboards under the crystal globe. The floor was warm and vibrated slightly at her touch, but there was no sign of the book. Linden stood up and said, "*Collected Tales of the Fay Nation*. It was in your collection, over here." She walked over to the wall of books.

"I've heard of it, but I've never owned it. Actually, no one 'owns' that book. It chooses its owner." Nari pressed her lips together firmly and said, "I think you'd better begin at the beginning. Why this newfound interest in the fays?"

Linden followed Nari out of her office and into her sitting room, plopping down on her grandmother's comfortable sofa. Nari had some tea sent up from the kitchen, and then she sat next to her and waited. Linden told her grandmother everything she could think of, beginning with the vibrations she always felt in the Scroll Collection room at the library, and the ancient fay scroll that had rolled open when she touched the glass. She explained about Mr. Valti's visit, what he said about the "new" illustration of the Faymon Liege, and how the same illustration had appeared on the cover of the *Collected Tales of the Fay Nation*.

"Well, that explains what my caller, Cy Valti, was going on about." Nari paused and seemed uncertain how to proceed. "Linden, do you recall our conversation about taking care not to reveal too much of your magical powers?"

"Of course. I've been careful to stay focused in school and not let myself get carried away."

Nari patted her knee. "I know you've been careful. But unfortunately, Cy Valti, who's like a dog after a bone, believes—rightfully so, I'd say—it was your magic that caused the new illustration of the Faymon Liege to be drawn upon the ancient scroll. He believes you did that intentionally, to draw attention to yourself."

Linden sputtered, "Why that's ridiculous. He's such an old busybody."

"Busybody or not, he now possesses knowledge—potentially dangerous knowledge—about your gifts that I'd prefer remained private."

"Why do you keep using the word 'dangerous' when referring to my magical gifts?"

"Because you're not yet in full possession or control of your magical gifts, and until you are, those gifts pose a danger to you and those who care about you. Your magical misfires actually reveal the extent of your talent, which is enormous, and if your talent falls into the wrong hands, it could be misdirected and harm yourself and many others."

"How could it fall into the wrong hands?"

Nari looked sternly at Linden. "How do you think the Glenbarrans' Commander, General Mordahn, became so powerful? As a young man, he was a mage of average abilities. But he's learned to exploit the magic of others. Mordahn is a good example of what absolute power mixed with Fallow sorcery can lead to—a warped but mighty master mage and vicious military tyrant." Nari shook her head sadly. "The point is that you should treat your magic as if it's a rare treasure and only share a few trinkets with anyone outside the family."

Something about Nari's story prompted Linden to ask, "How do you know so much about Mordahn?"

"We were once betrothed."

"What?" Linden's mouth opened and closed several times. She couldn't imagine Nari as a young woman, let alone engaged to General Mordahn, who by all accounts was a vicious, nasty man. "You were going to marry General Mordahn? How could you?"

Nari frowned at Linden. "We were promised to each other when I was not quite sixteen."

"Did you love him?"

"I thought so at the time."

"What happened? Did grandfather fight with him?"

"No, nothing like that. We were from different clans and met in happier times before the civil war. But his clan had always been the most difficult to manage. During a dispute between the clans, Mordahn's father killed my parents."

"That's horrible!"

"Chaos spread like wildfire in Faynwood, with all of the clans taking sides. I barely had time to bury my parents before fleeing, but not before sending word to Mordahn, breaking off our betrothal."

"What did he do?"

"Mordahn pursued me across Faynwood. He nearly captured me more than once. He was hurt and angry and possessive. Without the help of my clan and my tutor, a deeply spiritual mage, I'd never have escaped."

"Do you think that's what drove him to Fallow magic?"

"No, I don't. People are hurt and disappointed all the time and they don't turn away from Serving magic as he has."

"Does anyone else know about this?"

Nari shook her head. "Once I arrived in Valerra, I put all of it behind me. I told one other person about Mordahn, and that was your grandfather. And I'd like to keep it that way. These are painful memories for me."

"Of course." Linden put her arms around Nari and wondered how many other family secrets were still waiting for her to uncover.

CHAPTER 13

The next morning, Yolande helped Linden into one of her new riding outfits, a smart-looking fleece-lined burgundy jacket with gold buttons, perfect for the chilly autumn days. She belted her jacket over a pair of chocolate-colored slacks. Yolande pulled Linden's hair into a long ponytail and started to pin a burgundy top hat onto her head, but Linden pushed her hand away. "I'm not wearing that silly thing."

"But it's the fashion, Miss Linden. It's quite the rage in town."

"I like to ride with my head uncovered. Besides, I'm only riding on the estate. Who's going to see me?"

Yolande scowled but set aside the hat. "Fine, but don't blame me if you look under-dressed."

Rolling her eyes, Linden pulled on a pair of brown leather boots and grabbed her matching leather gloves. She headed downstairs for an early breakfast before she went riding, which she only got to do on the weekends because of her busy school and volunteer schedule. She took one look at Alban and Nari huddled over their morning tea, and her heart dropped to her stomach. She knew bad news when she saw it, and Nari and Alban looked like their world had just ended. But then again, if hordes of troops and grihms really were about to invade the borderlands, maybe it was the end of the world as they knew it.

"What's wrong?"

Nari's lips formed a thin line. "General Wylles confirmed the Glenbarrans have broken through the perimeter. Royal Marines are engaged in heavy fighting less than twenty miles from Quorne. Your uncle will be making a formal declaration of war at noon today."

Linden not only lost her appetite, but her stomach turned over. She ran from the room before she retched all over the breakfast table and closeted herself in the powder room down the hall. After she was done, she washed her face and rinsed her mouth. She walked back to the dining room on wooden legs.

Alban looked at her and nodded toward a chair. "You'll hear this soon enough, so let me give you the rest of the bad news."

"Mother and Father?"

"As far as we know, they're still working to get the rest of the family out of Quorne, although now it's going to be much more difficult for them." Alban paused and said, "Your brother has been called up."

"What do you mean, called up?" Linden frowned in confusion. Matteo was a student. Sure, he was at the Royal Marine Academy, but he was still in school. Along with Stryker. Was he being called up to? Her uncle kept talking but Linden had to ask him to repeat himself.

"The general has decided to call up all of the marine cadets, as well as the instructors. They're closing the academy for the time being."

"But that's not fair, they're not really soldiers, they're students!" Linden shouted.

Alban raised his eyebrows. "They're marine cadets, and their country needs them."

Linden took a deep breath and asked the critical question. "When?"

"They've been given one day to move out of the dorms, visit family, and get ready for their deployment. Matteo is coming here later this morning, and he's bringing Stryker with him," Nari said. "They'll need our support, and our love."

Linden closed her eyes and nodded. She felt dizzy, like the world was spinning faster than normal. She wanted things to slow down and go back to the way they were, before the Glenbarrans raided her school in Quorne, before she'd ever laid eyes on a grihm or heard the name of Mordahn, back to when the world felt settled and safe and ordinary.

Linden saddled up her favorite horse from Alban's stable, a headstrong palomino. She rode for two hours, crisscrossing the entire estate, her mind a blur of thoughts and images as she struggled to comprehend how much her world was shifting.

When she returned to the house, her hair a tangled mess, a subdued Yolande helped her bathe and dress. Neither one of them had the heart for chitchat. Linden selected an amber flannel dress that gathered neatly at the waist and flared around the legs. Yolande brushed out her hair so that it fell in loose layers around her shoulders. Linden pulled on her brown leather boots and went downstairs as soon as she heard male voices drifting up from the front hall.

She gave Matteo a big hug and glanced at Stryker, who was talking to Nari. Relief washed over Linden when saw his face had completely healed. Then she remembered what the attendant had said about Stryker at the military ball, five months earlier, when the woman had repaired Linden's torn dress. She'd said he was gorgeous to look at, and it was true. When he locked eyes with her and smiled, her insides melted, completely. This time she wasn't going to mess it up with misunderstandings and hurt feelings.

She walked over and hugged him—a quick, sisterly hug since her grandmother was standing right there. But he didn't seem to care. Stryker hugged her tightly and kept his arm around her waist afterwards.

After lunch Matteo left to visit Jayna, while Stryker borrowed one of Alban's locomobiles and took Linden for a drive. They wound up going to the beach, because Stryker hadn't seen the Pale Sea all summer and wanted to see it before heading to the border. Linden brought a brown woolen cape with her, and Stryker wore his long black trench coat from the academy.

An hour later, Linden and Stryker descended a ridge of sand dunes and stood in the powdery sand, watching as pale turquoise waves pounded the coast. The ocean floor was covered with polished white stones that reflected back the sunlight and gave the Pale Sea its name.

"There's something I've been wanting to tell you."

Linden's pulse sped up, not sure where this was going, hoping he had feelings similar to hers. "What is it?"

"Do you remember when I was last here, and Kal and I 'communicated' as you called it?"

"Of course."

"And I told you Kal said my mission was to keep you safe? And you asked me how I was supposed to do that?"

"I tried to ask you about it, but you'd fallen asleep."

"Well, I can't exactly explain how, but Kal gave me a glimpse of the future. More like your future."

The wind whipped Linden's hair around her head. She pushed some hair out of her eyes. "So, what'd you see?"

"A series of lightning-fast images that all jumbled together.

You wielded a sword several times, fighting Glenbarrans or grihms, I wasn't sure. And I saw you with a group of weary-looking mages, chanting an incantation. But the last image I remember clearly, maybe because that's when I came into the picture. You stood in a clearing, surrounded by huge trees. And I was beside you, wearing a uniform I've never seen—not a marine's uniform—and I seemed to belong there, somehow." Stryker ran a hand through his dark hair. "I'm not explaining this well."

Linden frowned. "So then what happened?"

"That was it—a series of images. And I was in one of them, in your future."

"Is this why you wanted some private time with me, to tell me this?" Linden asked, angry with herself for thinking Stryker might have had other reasons to be spending time alone with her, like maybe he had feelings for her. No, instead, he'd wanted to tell her about some vision that probably came from all the herbs Healer Gracyn had made him drink and had nothing to do with Kal.

"Yes. I mean, I thought you should know. After all, Kal is your griffin."

"Thank you," Linden said coolly. "If that's all, then perhaps we should get back to the locomobile. It's getting chilly." Linden turned and started to walk back up the sandy ridge.

Stryker reached out, grasped her arm, and spun her around to face him. "Now wait just a minute. I think there's something bothering you, and we're out of second chances. I'm leaving tomorrow. There won't be time for any do-overs. Tell me what's going on, please."

Linden hesitated, remembering her vow a few hours earlier about avoiding misunderstandings. But that's all they ever seemed to have. "Nothing's going on. I appreciate your concern for me, and for Kal. I'm glad we've had this talk. And now it's time to head back."

She tried to pull away from him, but he had a firm grip on both her arms.

"You're driving me crazy," he rasped hoarsely, his brown eyes flashing darkly. "I don't know if I'm coming or going with you."

Linden stopped fuming long enough to listen. "Why am I driving you crazy?"

"Isn't it obvious?"

"Not at all."

Stryker pulled her toward him, tilted her head back, and brushed his lips against hers. She ran her hands around his waist and drew him closer, inhaling a trace of wood smoke and pine needles. He sucked in his breath, pressing his mouth against hers. Everything slipped into slow motion for Linden. She heard the sound of each wave as it crashed into the beach, the cooing call of every seagull flying above her head, the whistling of the wind as it passed through each blade of sea grass on the dunes. Her heart pounded so hard in her chest she was certain Stryker could hear it.

He reluctantly pulled away and heaved a sigh. Running his fingers through her hair and sending shivers up her spine, he whispered, "Do you have any idea how I've longed to do this?"

Linden shook her head and asked shakily, "What took you so long?"

Stryker laughed. "I'd planned to say something profound and then kiss you at your Teenth, but we both know what happened that night."

"Let's not talk about my Teenth. Not my best moment."

"And definitely not mine. Although I think any girl who can call down a thunderstorm to put out a fire and stop a fight—all at the same time—is pretty special. Pretty amazing, actually."

Linden thought he might be teasing her, but his eyes were almost black, which she was beginning to realize meant he was serious. "You really mean that?"

Stryker didn't say a word. He took her face in his hands and kissed her again, more gently this time, starting with a petal-soft kiss on each eyelid, and then on the tip of her nose, and finishing with a firm yet sweet kiss on her lips.

He wrapped his arms around her in a giant bear hug and rested his chin on top of her head. "I could stay here like this with you all day, but you're shivering. Let's get you inside the locomobile."

Linden nodded, not trusting herself to speak. She felt shaky all over, from the inside out. With Stryker's arm draped around her waist, the two of them scaled the dunes and climbed into the locomobile. Despite the steering wheel and knobs and dials that got in their way, they managed a few more kisses before Linden decided they really did have to head back to Delavan.

Nari planned a quiet, elegant dinner that evening. Linden selected a V-necked plum-colored silk gown with an empire waist and asked Yolande to leave her hair loose. Yolande accepted the challenge and wove pink and plum ribbons through her dark waves. Matteo invited Jayna, who looked lovely in a green satin dress. But Linden knew her friend well and saw the worry in Jayna's eyes, the same worry Linden shared—for Matteo and Stryker and her parents.

No one said anything, of course, but anxiety and fear bubbled up inside her. Linden looked at Matteo and Stryker, both so full of life, her brother with a smile playing at his lips because Stryker had just told them a funny story, and she started to cry. Startled, both of them looked at her with concern, and Stryker started to rise out of his chair. Nari came over to Linden, and putting her arms around her, guided her firmly from the dining room and into the library.

"I can't help it, Nari, when I look at them sitting there, all I see are those same chairs empty tomorrow night. Matteo and Stryker will be deployed to who-knows-where, and they could be injured or worse, and I still can't believe this is happening. Why here, why now, why us?"

Nari smiled wistfully. "You're asking the same question that all good and decent people ask, when they come face-to-face with injustice and war. We will lose good men and women in this fight, I'm afraid. But you must be brave and not discourage Matteo and Stryker with your tears."

Linden dabbed at her eyes and straightened her back, ashamed of her emotional outburst. "Yes, of course."

They returned to the dining room, but Stryker kept glancing at Linden as if waiting for another bout of tears. Instead, she pushed against the ache in her throat and chest and smiled at their stories of school days, of mischievous antics and happier times. *They're girding themselves for battle, they're taking with them the best of their hopes and dreams and memories.* She joined in the storytelling then, telling one or two of her own, all the while committing to memory the sight of Matteo and Stryker, their heads thrown back in laughter, surrendering to the moment.

Linden and Stryker decided to go for a walk in the bright moonlight. They knew this was their only chance for a private moment together for some time, since Matteo said they needed to leave for base camp headquarters right after breakfast. The evening was chilly, and Stryker insisted Linden return to her room for a warmer jacket before they left the house. They walked, hand in hand, around the various garden paths, strewn with curled, brown leaves that crunched underfoot, each struggling to deal with their first separation, so soon after admitting they cared for each other.

Stryker ran his hand through his hair and turned around to face Linden. He clasped both her hands in his and drew her closer. "I don't know where I'll be headed after tomorrow—only that it'll be some time before any of us will be able to communicate back home."

Linden swallowed down a gigantic lump in her throat. "I know."

"'Home' is such a small word, but it packs such power, especially when you're being deployed. When I think of my childhood home, I naturally think of my mother and father." Stryker paused, "And when I think of my future home—that is the home I want someday, when the Glenbarran threat is behind us—I think of you."

Linden's heart skipped a beat and she gripped his hands more tightly.

"We've finally gotten a shot at our do-over and now I'm leaving again," Stryker sputtered in frustration. "I've never met a girl like you, and even when we're not together, you're never far from my thoughts. What I'm trying to say is this—I've fallen for you."

She felt like she'd been tossed onto a child's carousel during the past day, her life a dizzy whirlwind. Linden wanted to tell Stryker she loved him, but she was afraid he'd be embarrassed and feel like he had to say the "L" word too, and she didn't want that. So, she settled. "I feel the same about you."

Stryker brought his face down to hers and kissed her slowly and deeply, lingering over her neck and lips. He forced himself to pull away and look into her eyes.

"I hope, when I return, we can pick up where we've left off. No more missed opportunities," he said. "For now, this will have to do."

Stryker dug into his pocket and pulled out a gold chain with a heart locket attached. The locket was encrusted with small diamonds, opals, and pearls that encircled a dark-red garnet in the heart's center. "Go ahead, open it." Linden popped the locket open and looked up, a question on her lips. There was a tiny strand of dark hair inside.

"I wanted to give you something of mine, to remember me while I'm away.

"It's beautiful." Glancing at the key fob on his belt, she said, "Can I have your pocketknife?"

Stryker arched an eyebrow, wordlessly handing over his knife. Linden cut a small strand of her own hair and placing it in Stryker's hand, pointed at his key fob. Recognition dawned, and unclipping his key fob from his belt, Stryker took the strand of Linden's blue-black hair and gently placed it inside his fob, snapping the case closed.

"Now you can carry something of mine with you, wherever you go."

"Thank you," he said, his voice sounding a bit shaky. "You don't know how much this means to me." He cleared his throat. "Here, let me help you with this locket."

Linden unbuttoned her jacket, and Stryker slipped the chain around her neck. He nodded appreciatively when he saw the locket resting just above the soft curve of her breast.

"It's perfect, Stryker. I promise to keep it safe until you return." She rested her hands on the lapels of his coat. "Promise you'll return to me?"

Stryker cupped her face and kissed her thoroughly. He sealed his lips over hers and ran his hands through her hair and down her back before drawing her against his chest and holding her there, as if to imprint the memory. "Promise you'll wait for me?"

"Promise," she said.

Linden had barely closed her eyes, and Yolande was shaking her awake. Although it was still dark outside, Linden could see a streak of light in the east. Yolande helped her slip into a square-necked navy wool dress. Linden hardly took notice of her appearance, her thoughts swirling around inside her head, a mish-mash of worry about Matteo and Stryker deploying for the border, and her parents still trying to figure out how to leave Quorne.

Stryker and Matteo were already at breakfast, their plates piled with eggs, ham, and toast, their last meal at home for a while. Linden's heart was heavy, her stomach twisted in knots. She poured herself some tea and nibbled on a piece of toast. Stryker finished first and smiled at Linden. "Let's go for a quick walk outside."

Matteo looked up. "Very quick, we're leaving in a quarter hour. They're saddling the horses now." Stryker nodded and took Linden's hand. She grabbed a long navy cloak from the closet on her way out.

They didn't even have time to walk in the gardens. Instead, Stryker guided Linden around the back of the house and onto the bluestone patio. Glancing around to ensure they had privacy, he drew her into his arms and kissed her, his mouth urgent as his hands wound through her hair. He drew a ragged breath. The air was so chilly their breath formed misty puffs. "What I wouldn't give for even one more day with you."

"Don't die. Please." Linden whispered.

Stryker wrapped his arms around her and held her tightly. "I don't intend to. Whatever happens, wherever we wind up— I'll find you." They heard Matteo's voice calling them, and hand in hand, they rounded the side of the house and headed to the stables. Stryker gave Linden's hand a squeeze and walked quickly to his horse. Linden ran over to her brother and gave him a hug. Nari and Alban were there as well, Nari kissing both young men and Alban shaking their hands. They were on their horses then and heading down the gravel drive. Linden watched until she couldn't see them anymore.

One of the servants assigned to feed the pigeons ran down the four flights of stairs from the attic, sailed onto the gravel driveway, and breathlessly handed an express message to Nari. Nari thanked her and unrolled the message. "It's from Ric!

Here, Linden, please read it. I don't have my spectacles with me."

Mother, Alban, Matteo, and Lindy,

We've managed to leave Quorne, having paid handsomely for a spot in a traveling merchant caravan—the only "safe" route out of Quorne is south, away from the fighting to the north and east and west. The caravan leader is a man I've known for years. He's trustworthy enough, and brave enough. We'll travel through the Barrens and settle in the Colonies, until we can return home. The three aunts are with us, as are Yogi and Mille, and Boreus and his family.

Love and prayers all around,

Ric

Nari swayed and Alban reached out a steadying hand. "Oh Alban, when will we see them again? My son south of the Barrens and my grandson heading to war."

Linden put her arms around Nari, and the two of them struggled to hold back their tears. She missed her mother and father more with each week that passed. She longed to show her parents how much she'd progressed with her magic handling and to tell them about Stryker. When would they be together again? Linden couldn't possibly travel to the Colonies through the Barrens herself. And they were out of range for telegrams and carrier pigeons. She wiped her eyes and forced herself to be thankful they'd escaped from Quorne.

Alban patted both of their backs and kept repeating, "This will all work out. Nothing's as bad as it seems at the moment." Linden wished she could believe him, but she thought it might be a long time before things worked out. She knew as well as anyone the hidden meaning in her father's message: if the fighting had moved east of Quorne this quickly, then the marines were already struggling to contain the invasion.

CHAPTER 14

Linden wrestled with the normalcy of daily life in Bellaryss, whether at the shops or markets or school. It felt strange to her, as if people were pretending there wasn't a war happening, since the fighting was so far away. Sure, many of the residents had relatives they were worried about, either because they lived near the western border or because they'd been deployed. But people carried on as if nothing had changed or would ever change in Bellaryss.

Linden decided to avoid one of Morrell's honored traditions, the Senior Dinner Party organized each year by Mage Rudlyn. As a respected teacher with palace connections, Mage Rudlyn never failed to convince a prominent Serving Family to host the event. All of Linden's friends, even Jayna, eagerly anticipated this quirky rite of passage. This year, the dinner party was being hosted by Harlan and Ian Lewyn, which gave Linden the perfect excuse to decline. When she received the engraved invitation, she promptly pitched it, but Nari found out and insisted Linden attend.

"I'm no fan of Harlan Lewyn, but that's no reason to bow out of this party. It's a special occasion, and you told me last month you were looking forward to it. Why the reluctance now?" Nari's curiosity sometimes bordered on nosiness.

"Two reasons. First, we're at war, and the whole tradition seems frivolous to me. Second, Matteo and Stryker have specifically asked me to avoid Ian Lewyn, and you know the reasons."

Nari held up her index finger. "Then let me address your reasons, one at a time. I'll begin by asking you a question. Do you think your parents or Matteo or Stryker, for that matter, would want you moping around, putting your life on hold for months or longer, until this war with Glenbarra is over?"

Linden sighed. "No, of course not, but you know how Stryker feels about Ian Lewyn."

Nari held up a second finger. "And that brings me to the second reason. I've been thinking about what Matteo said about that young woman and Ian. It's a troubling story."

"It's very troubling, a truly horrible story. Poor Madlyn Revas!"

"That's not what I mean. Of course, I feel sorry for that poor young woman. No, something else has been troubling me. There's something to this story that doesn't add up."

"But Matteo and Stryker wouldn't make up a story like that."

"I'm not suggesting that at all. No, it seems publicly at least, the facts are what they are. But I believe there's a story within a story here, and that Ian may still be guilty, but perhaps of a lesser charge."

"What do you mean?"

"I'm going to make a few discreet inquiries of my own. In the meantime, please tread cautiously around Ian Lewyn, as Matteo and Stryker have asked, but let's not assume we know the whole truth, either."

The evening of the party arrived, and since Jayna's mother was attending to a patient with a severe lung inflammation,

Nari escorted both girls. Jayna chatted eagerly while Yolande helped them both dress. Jayna wore a dark gold gown and matching peplum jacket. Madame Zostra had made Linden a blue-and-ivory striped gown, with a blue spencer jacket and a little blue derby hat to complete the outfit. Linden started to refuse the hat, but Yolande put her hands on her full hips and Linden didn't feel up to an argument.

Nari and the girls were running late when they arrived at Harlan Lewyn's elegant three-story brownstone in Bellaryss' poshest downtown location, one of several residences for the Lewyn family. As they ascended the steps, the front door was thrown open by a towering, lanky butler, whose booming voice announced them.

They entered an over-crowded drawing room. A discussion of the latest fashions occupied one side of the room; a small quartet played on the other side of the room, with couples or singles lining up to wait their turn to sing, Mara among them; and several card games occupied the area in front of the large arched windows. Linden spotted Remy with a large pile of chips in front of him, grinning broadly. On the side of the room closest to the entrance raged a vigorous debate of current events.

This was nothing like the "formal dinner party" Linden had expected. The noise in the drawing room was deafening. It seemed as if these well-to-do Valerrans—students and adults alike—were determined to cram as much enjoyment as they possibly could into one room, in one night. She looked at Nari and could almost feel her stiffening beside her. Her grandmother appreciated the finer arts and intellectual conversations with a few friends and acquaintances over intimate dinners. This was a discordant clash of sounds—cards being shuffled, instruments being tuned, someone now running through her scales, and voices, many of them raised to be heard above the din.

Ian Lewyn strode forward to welcome them. He greeted Linden last and lingering a bit over her hand, said softly, "I'd like a private moment with you before dinner. Would you grant me that?"

Linden would have preferred to avoid him altogether but opted for politeness. "Certainly," she replied.

They followed him back to the current events conversation, where the topic was the Glenbarran threat and the government's plans. Toz Valti sat next to his father on a sofa, looking bored. Linden acknowledged Toz's smile with a small one of her own. Jayna gave Linden a quick squeeze on the arm and scampered over to the musical entertainment across the room. All eyes turned to the new arrivals: the prime minister's niece and mother, who also happened to be the head of the Mages Guild.

Linden and Nari sat on a pair of wing-backed chairs. Inclining her head, Nari said, "Please, do continue. Don't let us stop your speculations."

"Speculations, Mage Arlyss? Whatever can you mean?" asked the oily voice of Harlan Lewyn.

"Why, only that every one of us—myself included—has imperfect knowledge of the Glenbarran threat, and our country's response to that threat. So, we speculate."

Several men guffawed. "You use the term as if it were a dirty word," responded Harlan Lewyn.

"I merely suggest that some of us enjoy speculation and debate, while others actually have to bear the burden of governing and defending our freedoms, including our freedom to speculate." Nari smiled serenely. Linden tried not to smirk as she saw Harlan Lewyn's complexion darken. Ian remained silent, observing the exchange with interest.

"Spoken like the leading matriarch of Valerra's Serving Families. We would do well to follow her example," said Mage Rudlyn diplomatically. "You must forgive our host," she nodded in Harlan Lewyn's direction. "He can become quite passionate —but I do prefer passion to apathy, myself."

"Here, here!" said Harlan Lewyn with a smile.

"We each do our part to help queen and country," said Mr. Zel, who'd wandered into the conversation from one of the card games. "Many of us belong to a consortium of private businesses who are doing everything we can to support our marines." Remy had entered behind his father and sat down by Toz.

"And growing your profits as a result!" exclaimed Toz. Toz's father frowned at his son's outburst but said nothing.

Harlan Lewyn laughed appreciatively. "Well said, Toz. Tell me, what of your family's businesses?"

"If you're asking whether our businesses generate a profit, then the answer is 'of course.' However, I believe it's our duty to run our businesses with an eye toward caring for the employees and not just the owners," replied Toz.

"Have a care, there, Cy. I believe you've raised a radical thinker." Mr. Zel joked.

"His mother did that for me. However, one could do worse than have an independent thinker for a son," said Mr. Valti.

Linden looked at Toz, whose eyes glittered defiantly, and she raised her glass. "A toast to independent thinkers everywhere!" She and Remy clinked their glasses with Toz's. He flashed his high wattage smile and mouthed "Thank you."

"Speaking of independent thinkers, Valti, why aren't we reading more about the war situation in your papers? I'd think your reporters would be all over it," said Harlan.

"Because our reporters haven't been allowed anywhere near the perimeter walls for the past few weeks. There's been a news black-out, and you heard it here first." There was a general murmur of surprise.

"So, you don't have anything newsworthy to report?"

"I didn't say that," Mr. Valti replied. "However, I can report only what the government and our military commanders allow, out of concern for Valerra's security."

"Reading between the lines, it seems as if we have something to fear," said Mage Rudlyn. The lively, chatting group grew quiet.

"We'd do well to fear the Glenbarran threat." Linden spoke into the silence. "After what happened at Quorne and in other villages along the border, we should never be complacent."

"Well said, Miss Arlyss," Ian stood up, smiling. "Perhaps you'd welcome an opportunity for a quick walk before dinner? All this talk of war is beginning to spoil my appetite."

"Why yes, thank you," Linden nodded, wishing she hadn't agreed to a private moment with Ian. She excused herself and followed Ian out of the drawing room. They stopped to pick up her jacket and walked to the rear of the townhouse, stepping outside into a small courtyard garden, dotted with a dozen or so varieties of roses, many finished for the season but some stubborn few still in bloom. A flagstone path wound around the garden and stopped beside a fountain, which was sending gurgling spouts of water into the air, although it would soon have to be silenced for the winter.

Ian paused before the fountain and turned to face Linden, his green eyes clouded. Linden couldn't trust him, but she also couldn't treat him like the criminal her brother and Stryker believed him to be. She agreed with her grandmother—something didn't quite add up.

"I want to apologize for my part in the fight with Cadet Soto. I regret striking him and embarrassing you and your family. I should have simply walked away."

"Thank you for apologizing," Linden replied, not knowing what else to say. Out of loyalty to Stryker, she wasn't about to point out that Stryker had started it all by insulting the man.

"Although if I'm going to be totally honest, I'd have

thought your family would want your suitor to be more financially secure and less temperamental than Cadet Soto."

Linden glared at Ian, fuming. Stryker was her boyfriend, not her suitor, although strictly speaking, she supposed he might be considered a suitor. In any case, Ian was out of line. "This might be the most unapologetic apology I've ever heard. How dare you insult Stryker, particularly in light of your character flaws." Linden spun on her heels and headed toward the house, but Ian reached out and grasped her arm to stop her. "Unhand me this instant, Mr. Lewyn," she said, her anger vibrating in her voice.

He raised both hands, palms up, and took a step back. "I'm sorry. But just for the record, I'd like to know what character flaws you're referring to."

"My brother told me how you treated poor Madlyn Revas, and apparently other women as well. It seems your uncle has gotten you out of trouble on more than one occasion."

Ian's jaw locked and his eyes were steely. "I see. So that's my reputation around here? These are grave flaws indeed. Untrue, of course, but serious charges."

"You deny what happened to Madlyn?"

"I deny that my actions had anything to do with her taking her life. She was an emotionally disturbed young woman."

"But what about her pregnancy? And your refusal to help her in any way?" Linden blurted out.

Ian sputtered, "Pregnancy? If she was pregnant, it wasn't by me." Ian lowered his voice, "If the truth be told, she was more interested in my uncle than me."

"Ah, there you two are. Enjoying my garden, I see." Harlan came up behind them, clapping Ian on the shoulder and squeezing until Ian winced. Linden pretended not to notice, quickly changing the subject. "Your roses are amazing. What's your secret?"

"Why it's magic, of course." Harlan laughed heartily at his

own joke. "Actually, my mother had quite the green thumb, and I seem to have inherited her gift. Here," Harlan walked over to the last yellow rose still in bloom and using a small pocketknife, cut the stem.

He stripped away a few thorns from the bottom of the stem, so it could be handled, and he presented it to Linden with a slight bow. "A beautiful rose for a beautiful young woman. Watch those thorns, though. They'll draw blood if you don't take care." He stared at Linden through hooded eyes. Shivering slightly, she murmured her thanks and headed inside to the large, formal dining room.

There were no seat cards at the two long tables set up in the dining room, so students naturally gathered at one table, with parents and teachers seated nearby. Linden sat down next to Jayna with a sigh of relief.

"Where've you been? I looked all over."

"Looking at the courtyard with Ian and his uncle." Linden held up her yellow rose.

"With Ian?" Jayna whispered, "I thought you couldn't stand him.

"I'm not a fan, that's for sure. But it's complicated." Linden looked at her best friend. "Nari asked me to be nice."

Jayna nodded. She trusted Nari as much as she trusted Linden. "She has her reasons, I'm sure."

"But his uncle is another matter."

Mage Rudlyn stood up to thank Harlan and Ian for hosting the dinner party. Servers arrived with the courses and conversation around the table shifted to school and other, safer topics. The Glenbarran threat wasn't mentioned once during the four-course meal. While the food was delicious—the Lewyns had spared no expense on the Senior Dinner Party—Linden still couldn't wait until dessert was served. She knew Nari would wait a polite interval and then they could take their leave.

Linden leaned back against the plush seat of the Delavan locomobile and kicked off her heels. She listened to Jayna talk about the party and speculate whether Mara was going to continue pursuing Ian Lewyn, who so far had ignored all of her attentions. Nari directed the driver to pull up at Jayna's townhome. Waving goodnight, Jayna said, "Thank you for letting me tag along with you. I really enjoyed myself tonight." Linden blew Jayna a kiss as the driver pulled away. Dropping back against the seat, she stifled a yawn.

"Are you going to tell me about your stroll in the garden?" Nari asked as she pointed to the drooping rose, wrapped in a damp handkerchief to help preserve it, compliments of the Lewyn's cheerful butler.

Linden sat up straighter to gather her thoughts. She recounted her conversation with Ian, and her observations of Ian's uncle, including how he treated Ian and his odd comment about the rose. "He was creepy and made me feel uncomfortable."

"Imagine how Ian must have felt, losing his parents and going to live with that uncle."

"But that doesn't excuse Ian's behavior, well that is, if he did what Matteo and Stryker say that he did."

"No, it excuses nothing. But as you shared tonight, Ian vehemently denies wrongdoing."

"But is it even remotely possible that Madlyn actually liked Harlan Lewyn?" Linden wrinkled her nose in disgust.

"I've learned never to speculate where matters of the human heart are concerned."

Their driver pulled the locomobile up to Delavan's main entrance to let them out. The front door opened, and Alban stepped out. He shuffled down the steps to meet them, his shoulders hunched forward. "What's the matter, Alban?" Nari asked, climbing out of the vehicle with a speed that belied her age. Linden followed her out, holding the limp rose in her hand.

Alban looked at them through bloodshot eyes. "It's Matteo, he's been injured. His unit suffered heavy casualties."

"Not my grandson!" Nari cried out. "Where is he?"

"He's been taken by a medevac airship to the headquarters hospital." Alban put his arms around Nari. "They have some of the best healers anywhere in Valerra."

Linden stood numbly on the gravel drive, too overwhelmed to do anything but squeeze her eyes shut. She recalled the happy images of Matteo she'd tucked away and refused to believe the worst. He would survive. Matteo simply had to come home. And so, did Stryker, out there somewhere as well, in the line of fire.

CHAPTER 15

Fifth Week after Autumn Solstice
Western Province
Border Guard Unit #9

Dear Linden,

We deployed so rapidly from base camp headquarters that I had no time to send you a note. When we arrived, they handed us uniforms and equipment, and loaded us onto airships that dropped us at the forward camp. From there, Matteo and I split up—he went to Ravyn's Gate up north with his unit, while I was sent to Sergeant Desi's unit at Loomyn's Gate.

Our mission is to hold the perimeter gates against the Glenbarrans. They've already broken through at Suthavyn's Gate, near Quorne. I'm sure your parents have left by now, so please don't worry about them. Your father knows when a battle's been lost and it's time to retreat. And the thing is, no one can figure out how the Glenbarrans broke through, because we were winning on the ground despite their larger numbers—we have better equipment, better-trained marines, and better mages, for that matter. But the marines guarding Suthavyn were outflanked and taken out from behind.

Sergeant Desi says the Glenbarrans are using Fallow magic to disguise their movements and evade detection by our mages. He thinks they must have tunneled under or climbed over the perimeter walls somewhere and then doubled-back to attack. We've been casting extra defensive spells, just in case. I don't have to tell you that none of us is sleeping well these days—a few hours, tops. And then there's a trumpet blast to warn us of a pending attack, and the arrows start flying overhead to give us some cover. That's when we charge through the gate and line up along the outer perimeter wall like human armor, our shields up and swords ready.

I hate it, Linden, the sound of men and women screaming when an arrow or sword strikes them down. The grihms make more of a howling noise when they're struck. And when it rains, we slip and fall in mud that's turned reddish brown from the gore all around us. There are days when I wonder whether I'll be able to keep my promise to you. But then the trumpet blasts and we retreat behind the wall for another few hours. I close my eyes and pretend I'm holding you again, and I know I can fight for at least one more day.

The sergeant is collecting our letters to send home now, and so I'll say the one thing I didn't get to say before I left.

I love you,

Stryker

Royal Marine Corporal 1ˢᵗ Class

P.S. The sergeant just told me we're retreating from Loomyn's Gate. I guess the Glenbarrans have broken through to the north. There's no point in writing back since I don't know where we're heading next.

By the time Stryker's letter got to Linden, Mr. Valti's newspaper reported the Glenbarrans had broken through the perimeter at multiple checkpoints. The newspaper also started publishing weekly lists of the wounded —Matteo's name was there alongside hundreds of others—of the dead, and of the missing. Linden scoured the lists for

Stryker's name as soon as the newspaper arrived, her stomach churning as she went first to the list of deaths. She breathed slightly easier when she got past that list. Then she checked the lists of the wounded and the missing.

She felt like she could breathe normally again when she got past the names of the missing, but then she started worrying about the next week. When Linden spotted other names she recognized, some of the older brothers and sisters of her classmates, she felt awful, but not as awful as if it had been Stryker's name, which made her feel guilty.

Linden re-read Stryker's letter so many times she kept it inside a book to prevent the edges from tattering. Her eyes blurred with tears at the hard parts and then she smiled at the last part, when he wrote "I love you."

Linden worried about her uncle. Alban rarely seemed to rest these days, constantly receiving and sending messages, holding emergency sessions of parliament, or consulting with the queen and Ellis Steehl. Having lost the perimeter, the marines were falling back to defend Valerra's interior, especially the main roads leading to Bellaryss. They also sent marines to fortify Wellan Pass, the primary passageway through the ring of hills that surrounded the city. If Mordahn's troops breached those hills, then they would literally be storming the walls of the capital next.

Meanwhile, the queen and Alban jointly issued an evacuation order for anyone in the presumed path of Glenbarran destruction, from the western perimeter all the way to the gates of Bellaryss. At the same time, General Wylles mobilized retired veterans of previous battles who resided in the capital. They joined the city's local militia to reinforce the walls and gates of the city, working in partnership with mages to ensure both military and magical defenses were at the ready.

Nari was just as busy, leading meetings of the Mages Guild, which Linden, Jayna, and the other students from Mage

Rudlyn's classes were permitted to attend. There, the mages discussed various magical strategies for defending the city, including curtains of impenetrable fog, defensive shields, protection charms, and other techniques. They debated and negotiated with one another and couldn't seem to reach a consensus. After one particularly troublesome session, Nari flung herself into the locomobile and blurted out, "Fools! Those men know that defensive shields have limited life expectancy; after a few hours they'll simply disintegrate. I'm at my wit's end with the lot of them!"

"I don't know how you put up with them. I have no stomach for politics—either the politics of government or the politics of magic." Jayna shook her head.

"Maybe you could compromise and agree to a staggered strategy, like curtains of impenetrable fog for the first phase, defensive shields for the second phase, and so forth. What do you think?" Linden asked.

Nari looked at her granddaughter and chuckled. "A sound negotiating strategy. I'll take your suggestion under advisement."

Despite all of the preparations for war within the city's walls, many things went on as before, more or less. Farmers and merchants continued to trade, although supplies of certain items were beginning to run low. Healers and apothecaries were seeing more patients, largely for balms and tinctures to calm nerves and settle stomachs. Students were going to classes and doing their homework, but attention spans were shorter.

Linden worked hard to maintain her same focus at school, and yet she wondered, deep down inside, where she and her classmates would be next year. Would they be able to graduate? Would Bellaryss be under siege? She'd noticed that Nari and Cook had started hoarding food and supplies. Goshen had put up extra shelves in the root cellar to store the overflow.

Linden, Jayna, and Nari were at the market near the main

city gate when a new influx of displaced families, weary from their journey, arrived by foot, wagon, and horseback. Children cried, women sagged under the weight of carrying infants in their arms, and the men stared hollow-eyed with worry and fear. There was a loud scuffle at the gate as a constable tussled with a middle-aged farmer. Nari set her mouth in a firm line and marched over to intervene.

"What seems to be problem, Constable?" Nari asked in her commanding voice, causing both men to stop in their tracks.

"This man's papers are not in order, ma'am." The young constable, who looked to be no more than nineteen, tipped his hat at Nari, Linden, and Jayna.

"Please explain."

The constable looked surprised at the intrusive elder, so Linden quickly said, "This is Mage Nari Arlyss, Constable."

Recognition dawned on the constable's face and he bowed. "Pleased to make your acquaintance, Mage Arlyss." Hooking his thumb at the man he was questioning, the constable continued, "He has identification papers for himself, his daughter, and his missus, but the babe was born on the way. The babe hasn't had his naming ceremony yet, so there are no papers."

"And do you propose to leave that man and his family without protection, beyond the city gates, just sitting ducks for the Glenbarrans?"

"I'm following orders, Mage Arlyss. Everyone must have proper identification to enter our city."

"Constable, on my authority, let this family and those traveling with them through the gates."

"If you please, mum," said the farmer, who'd been silently watching the exchange. "What of our animals? We canna leave 'em outside the gates for those crazy Glenbarrans to destroy."

Linden spoke up. "What if every Serving Family or landowner with sufficient property took some of the animals?

We could keep many of them safe right here within Bellaryss. He's right, if we do nothing, they'll all be slaughtered."

Nari thought for a moment and made her decision. "How many people and animals are traveling with you?"

The farmer scratched his chin as he thought about it. "Eight in my extended family, plus three horses, two dairy cows, three sheep dogs and twenty sheep, who are scattered on the hillside below." The man pointed behind the city gate. "But mum, another family, an older woman and her granddaughter, joined us on the way. We've been traveling together for the better part of two weeks now."

"What's your name, sir?" Nari asked.

"BeBe Jermyn, at your service, mum." The man bowed low, sweeping his wide-brimmed hat off his head in one smooth movement.

"Well Mr. Jermyn, we can accommodate your family and your animals at Delavan Manor. I'm sure some other arrangements can be made in town for the other family traveling with you. However," Nari looked at the farmer and said kindly but firmly, "This is not charity. You'll work for your meals and will care for your own animals. Is that clear?"

The man's Adam's apple bobbed up and down as he said, "Oh yes, mum, absolutely mum." Linden noticed he quickly wiped a tear from his eye.

"And the Buri family will be able to accommodate the other family traveling with you." Jayna said firmly, "Under the same conditions as Mage Arlyss, of course. They'll work for my mother."

"Are you certain your mother will approve?" Nari asked.

Jayna nodded. "Mother will want to help, and we have the room."

Nari looked at the constable. "Well then, Constable, please process these families and allow them and their animals into the city. We accept responsibility for their care."

"Yes ma'am," the constable replied, anxious to please the mother of the prime minister.

"And Constable…"

"Yes, ma'am?"

"Common sense, young man. Exercise common sense as you exercise your authority. If I learn of any more silliness about babies without identification papers, I'll be back for another chat. Is that clear?"

"Aye, Mage Arlyss, of course." The constable bowed, eager to get on with his work and away from Nari. Linden and Jayna glanced at each other and suppressed smiles.

When the Jermyn family arrived at Delavan Manor, Linden and Nari brought them to the back parlor of their home, which was used as a small clinic by Healer Gracyn. The healer saw to all of the injuries—at least the physical ones—among the refugee family. BeBe's daughter, Jorri, a slim girl of about eleven with large hazel eyes, had injured her arm fleeing from their home. Linden tried to engage Jorri in conversation as they waited to see the healer, but her mother said Jorri hadn't spoken since she'd taken one last look at her home from the back of their wagon and saw a Glenbarran trooper grab a stray dog and snap its neck. When it was finally Jorri's turn to be seen by the healer, Linden watched as Healer Gracyn cleansed Jorri's wound and applied a hot poultice of salt water and herbs. Then she let the wound air dry and applied a clean dressing.

"Her wound's badly infected. She'll need to come see me every day for the time being," the healer explained to Jorri's mother. Linden's heart went out to the child and she volunteered to cleanse Jorri's arm and change the dressing each day after school, hoping the young girl would eventually open up to her.

Each day that Jorri walked into the back parlor to have her dressing changed, Linden was hopeful Jorri would say even one word. Jorri's face lit up when she saw Linden, but she still didn't speak.

About ten days after arriving at Delavan, Jorri took her usual spot on the raised wooden bench that served as the examining table. She stared at her arm as Linden removed her soiled dressing.

"They're bad men, killing just to kill," Jorri whispered as Linden was bent over her arm, cleansing the wound.

Linden looked up and thought about how to answer her. "They killed the dog and others," she replied carefully.

Jorri nodded. "Nub is safe." Linden knew that Nub was Jorri's kitten, which she'd carried in her school bag as her family fled their home. Nub was one more rescued animal now safely tucked away at Delavan.

"You were brave to save Nub."

Jorri nodded solemnly. "You were brave too."

Linden was curious. "When was I brave?"

"Back in Quorne, when you protected that little girl from the grihm."

Linden dropped the fresh dressing she was about to apply. Her hands shook as she picked it off the floor and threw it away. "You're a psychic, aren't you?" she asked. Psychics required physical touch to activate their ability—this was clearly the case with Jorri.

Jorri nodded. "Brave Linden," she put her arms around Linden, her hands patting her back. Linden swallowed a lump in her throat and hugged the little girl. "Thanks."

"They are coming," Jorri whispered. Linden felt a chill down her spine—the same three words she'd seen in the *Collected Tales of the Fay Nation* in her grandmother's lab.

"We'll be safe here, Jorri," Linden said with more conviction than she felt.

Jorri shook her head. "No one is safe."

During the days following Jorri's arrival, a constant influx of refugees entered through the city's gates. The word spread rapidly about the arrival of refugees and the need to provide shelter for them and their animals. Linden and Jayna started a project at Morrell to raise funds to help educate refugee children, while Nari and Alban appealed to the Serving Families and landowners to provide accommodations. Nearly everyone stepped up to the challenge, as more displaced families arrived each day. Even the Lewyns took in a family, and they accommodated a large number of horses at their breeding farm.

The refugee flow gradually tapered off, with small bands of people and their livestock continuing to trickle through. And then the city's gates were quiet. The constables and palace guards scanned the valley below for any sign of life. No people, no animals, nothing stirred but the wind in the grasses.

This could mean only one thing: the Glenbarrans were coming.

CHAPTER 16

The Valerran Tribune
Weekend Edition
Ninth Week after Autumn Solstice

Wellan Pass Falls After Six-Day Battle

By Embedded Reporter Marcus Hobe

The city of Bellaryss—and our nation—owes a debt of gratitude we can never repay to the brave men and women who died defending Wellan Pass. For six days, a thousand of our marines repelled at least ten times that number of Glenbarrans.

Wellan Pass Commanding Officer Colonel Revas constantly rotated marines to defend the pass against the onslaught. Valerrans on the frontline rode through the narrow pass on their horses, moved partially downhill, and fought by sword or spear against the Glenbarrans advancing up the hill towards them. Meanwhile, Valerran archers took up positions in trees at the top of the hill and fired down on the enemy.

As Valerrans fell, their fellow marines dragged them back through the pass and others took their place. By the sixth day, about half our marines and a large number of horses were dead or injured, and many more Glenbarrans lay in the plains below Wellan Pass. Undeterred by their heavy losses, the Glenbarran's Commander, General Mordahn, sent fresh horses, troops, and grihms into the battle, while our number of uninjured marines dwindled.

Even worse, none of our mages' defensive incantations seemed to work against whatever Fallow magic General Mordahn employed. Our marines were unable to use firearms or mortars since all of the magic flowing about rendered them useless. Colonel Revas called in airship assaults on the Glenbarrans spread across the plain below them. But as the airships attempted to fire on the enemy, they exploded in mid-air.

During a brief lull in the fighting, Colonel Revas gathered the senior officers who were still standing in a cluster. He asked them for an honest assessment.

"I think it's time we pull back behind the city walls," said Captain Uhl, of Border Guard Unit #4. "We still need men and women to defend Bellaryss. At this rate, we'll have no one left to fight for our queen." The other officers agreed.

Colonel Revas ordered them to prepare to retreat to Bellaryss. "The challenge now is to figure out how to evacuate as many of our wounded as possible before the Glenbarrans make it all the way through the pass."

A young corporal and his sergeant suggested creating a diversion. Their proposal was initially met with skepticism, but in the end, saved the lives of countless marines who would not have survived the retreat otherwise.

While the wounded were loaded onto litters and carried or dragged to Bellaryss, two dozen officers and enlisted men, all of them mages, volunteered to take up the rear of the retreat, assisted by a dozen archers who provided them cover. The plan was simple: use Serving magic to redirect the river that flowed down the eastside of the range, toward Bellaryss and the Pale Sea, and send the water through the pass to disrupt the attack.

In the midst of the chaos of the retreat—horses neighing, men shouting, injured groaning, and chaplains praying—the mages formed a line near the bend in the river and began the incantations.

A thin stream of water gurgled and spun in the air, then jumping its bank, veered toward the pass. As the mages repeated the incantations, more streams of water joined the original stream, until the entire river was pulsing and running past their feet toward the pass and the plain below.

In the trees, the archers were firing as quickly as possible down on the Glenbarrans charging the pass. However, the Glenbarrans were coming even more quickly, and a few came streaming through the pass, swinging swords at the mages nearest them. Several officers were struck down and fell into the now surging river.

Glenbarrans shouted as they were knocked off their feet and washed down through the pass, but our mages continued the incantations. After the river stabilized in its diverted course, the colonel nodded to a pair of mages. They lowered their hands and stepped away, and the line of mages moved in to close the gap.

Despite losing two mages, the river held its new course. Saluting their fellow officers, the pair joined the retreat toward Bellaryss. Gradually, about every quarter hour, another pair of mages stepped away and retreated. This reporter left while there were still half a dozen mages diverting the river.

A group of exhausted mages employed Serving magic to divert the flow of the river that day, and they maintained the spell long enough to ensure the wounded could make it safely to the gates of Bellaryss. The young corporal and his sergeant volunteered to remain behind to bind the spell for as long as possible. While these men may be lost to us, their display of Valerran bravery and Serving magic will go down as among our finest moments of this war.

L inden's hands trembled, rattling the paper as she read to the end of the front-page news article. The plan to divert the water flow sounded like the kind of insanely brave idea Stryker would cook up with his sergeant. She quickly turned to the back of the paper and scanned the long list of names under Missing In Action: Sergeant Rao Desi. Corporal Stryker Soto.

Linden screamed, "No, no! He promised me!" and crumpled up the paper into a ball. She'd been having tea with Nari in the library when Goshen brought in the newspaper. Goshen knew Linden checked the names every week for "her young man."

Linden's heart exploded into a knot of pain in her chest, making it hard to breathe. She threw the balled-up paper onto the floor and dropped to her knees, sobbing. Nari bent down to unroll the paper and read it.

Linden wept until she hiccupped and had to catch her breath. Her throat hurt and her eyes felt scratchy and sore. Nari handed her a handkerchief and patted Linden's tangled hair. "I so sorry about Stryker. These lists break my heart every week. Matteo, Stryker, and so many others."

"Why did Stryker have to go and be brave? Couldn't he just have focused on surviving the war?"

"You're assuming he's the unnamed corporal in the article?"

Linden nodded. "It sounds just like him."

Nari didn't try arguing with her. "You could be right. And

you're likely one of the reasons he would have volunteered to remain behind until the end."

"Me? He knew I promised to wait for him! I want him back home, with me, not out there somewhere, missing or—" Linden choked back the rest of her sentence.

"All of those marines, Stryker included, were fighting to protect you and me and every other resident in Bellaryss, including the queen. Wellan Pass was their last hope of turning back the Glenbarrans. He knew exactly what the stakes were, and you mustn't blame him for making the best decision he could under horrible circumstances, a decision that saved the lives of many others."

Linden shifted her position on the floor and cried more softly now, her hands clasped around her knees. Nari helped her get up and sit next to her, rubbing her back like she used to do when Linden was five or six, back when it was easy for grandmothers to make everything better.

Later that evening Linden found Nari with her ear pressed against the door to Alban's study. When she tapped her grandmother's shoulder, Nari jumped and then put her finger to her lips. She made room for Linden, who raised one eyebrow at her grandmother, but nestled in right beside her to eavesdrop.

"We're in full retreat." General Wylles spoke over a three-way patched radio transmission with Alban and Ellis Steehl. "While we expect trouble throughout the countryside, we know the main target is Bellaryss and Queen Ayn."

"Can you send additional troops to defend the city?" Alban asked.

"Only the men who survived the Battle of Wellan Pass and made it safely back to Bellaryss," General Wylles replied grimly.

"Many of whom are wounded." Alban was thinking out loud. "What about an airship drop with troops?"

"Most of our airships have been destroyed. The few remaining airships are needed for medevac and supply runs."

"We're on our own, then."

"You still have the Queen's Navy." General Wylles reminded him. The Queen's Navy was comprised of a small fleet of ships that patrolled the Pale Sea along the shoreline. Valerra had never been attacked by sea, so the Navy's work was geared toward rescuing stranded fisherman and conducting routine coastal patrols.

"With enough ships to evacuate the royal family, and perhaps ten percent of the population," Alban calculated out loud. "We'll need to invoke Article 99."

"Agreed," said Steehl.

"I never thought I'd see this day," said Alban.

"We just didn't believe it could happen to us," General Wylles admitted. "Valerra has more advanced technology, a better trained military, and more mages skilled in Serving magic than Glenbarra. But we never factored in a ruthless commander like Mordahn, who'd use crossbreeds, terror tactics, and Fallow sorcery to defeat us."

"I'll inform the queen and ensure her safe departure," said Steehl crisply.

"And I'll call an emergency session of parliament." Alban sighed as they disconnected. Nari knocked on the door and walked into her son's office, while Linden lingered in the doorway.

"It's worse than we could've imagined," he said.

"What about Matteo? Can we find a way to bring him home?"

Alban's shoulders sagged. "I spoke with Gayle. She said Matteo is safer at the headquarters hospital than he'd be in Bellaryss. General Mordahn is avoiding the heavily defended targets such as base camp headquarters. Instead, he's attacking softer targets, terrorizing villagers and farmers, all the while plowing his way to our city gates."

Nari noticed Linden lingering in the doorway and sent her for some tea. Linden walked on rubbery legs toward the kitchen, her anxiety for Matteo and Stryker twisting her stomach. She saw Yolande rubbing her lower abdomen and speaking quietly with Healer Gracyn. They both stopped speaking when they saw Linden. Healer Gracyn excused herself and left.

Yolande told Linden that some families, after reading about the marines' defeat at Wellan Pass, decided to try to leave town before the Glenbarrans reached the city's gates. They feared the food shortages that would accompany any siege, and they feared General Mordahn even more. Their options, however, were severely limited. Now that Wellan Pass had fallen, there would be no safe passage anywhere to the west. These families had two choices: pay one of the traveling merchants to take them out of the city and through the Barrens to the Colonies or find passage on an outgoing ship in the Bellaryss Harbor.

Neither of these choices was especially attractive, since they both involved the exchange of large amounts of cash, required blind trust in strangers who may turn on you if there were profit in it, and involved destinations that were unknown, dangerous, and potentially deadly. And the families had to decide soon, as ship berths and spots in traveling caravans were going quickly, and rumors were flying that General Mordahn and his grihms would be descending upon them and laying waste to their city at any time.

Linden asked Yolande if she'd ever heard of Article 99.

"I've heard of it, Miss Linden, but I don't know much about it. It's an ancient law."

Linden noticed Yolande seemed a little breathless and peered at her more closely, "Are you feeling alright? Do you need for me to call Healer Gracyn back?"

Yolande's eyes crinkled at the corners. "No thank you, miss. I'm with child, about four months along."

It took Linden a moment to respond. "You're with child? How wonderful! Are you sure you don't want to see the healer?"

Yolande shook her head. "It's not me I'm worried about, Miss Linden. It's my wee one. How will I raise a child in all of this?"

The morning after he'd received the general's devastating news, Alban accessed the Bellaryss Radio Transmitting Frequency, used only for emergency broadcasts, to address the people. Nari and Linden were in the office with Alban, behind a roped off area, to give him moral support. The office had been transformed into a radio communications center, with several technicians wearing headsets sitting in front of large transmitting equipment, twirling dials, and making notations on their pads. The head technician finally turned to Alban and nodded. Alban took a deep breath and began the most difficult speech of his career.

"Friends and residents of Bellaryss: There are many stories —truths, half-truths and rumors—flying around our beautiful city right now, and Queen Ayn has asked me to set the record straight."

"Here is what we know: Our countryside is overrun with Glenbarran troopers and their trained crossbreeds, known as grihms. There are pockets where our brave marines are holding their own, but our commanders tell us the main prize these invaders are seeking is our beloved queen and her city. This cannot happen. We must fight this threat down to our last man and woman. Whether you are a mage, a blacksmith, or a grocer, we need you to stand firm.

"Please listen carefully to the following important instructions.

"All city schools will be closed until further notice. We must ensure that students, teachers, and staff are with their families at this difficult time and do not become separated when the assault on our city begins, which we expect will happen within the next day or two.

"We are asking all mages to report to Morrell School Auditorium at sunset this evening. Apprentice mages must also attend this important meeting.

"For everyone else, please cooperate with the local militia leaders in your wards. Every able-bodied individual will be called upon to defend our gates and walls. Drills will begin in each ward at dusk tonight.

"This is the most perilous time in our nation's history. Our queen, our people, and our way of life are under attack, and the outcome is uncertain. For this reason, the queen is invoking an old law that was passed when Bellaryss was a young city. The law was designed to ensure our people would survive no matter what the peril. I'm speaking of Article 99." Here Alban paused for a sip of water and took a deep breath.

"Article 99 is quite simple: Each family of Bellaryss may select one person, between the ages of fifteen and fifty, who will evacuate with the queen. A family is defined as three generations: grandparents, parents, and children, and it includes any children who are under the family's guardianship, even if they are not blood relations. A family may decide to forfeit their spot with the Queen's Navy and give it to another family. A list of all Bellaryss families is maintained at the Registry and will be used to ensure only eligible individuals or their designates may evacuate with the queen. Newly arrived refugee families have already been entered into the Registry and may also select one family member for evacuation.

"We will have an orderly evacuation. Evacuees from each

city district will gather at the Royal Marina at their appointed time, which I will provide at the end of this broadcast. Those selected will be processed through security and will set sail with the Queen's Navy once everyone has boarded the ships.

"Each person selected may pack one bag only. There will be no exceptions to the age restrictions or the amount of luggage. Anyone attempting to gainsay these rules will be arrested and their family disqualified.

"No other family members may congregate at the marina. Please say goodbye to your loved ones in private, and send your sons or daughters, husbands, or wives on their way as soon as possible. The Queen's Navy waits for no one and must sail this evening. If you are late, you will forfeit your spot.

"The Navy will be sailing to the Colonies, where the governor and residents are preparing to accommodate our evacuees. There the queen will rule *in absentia* until peace returns to Valerra, as one day it surely shall.

"I realize that each of us has a gut-wrenching decision to make within the next few hours. My own heart is breaking as I speak. Please know we will do everything possible to ensure Valerra's survival and look forward to our reunion one day. In the meantime, let us pray for our queen and our country in the coming battle for Bellaryss."

Alban paused and then read the timetable for evacuees from each district to report to the Royal Marina. Since Delavan was located in the farthest district from the marina, it was assigned the last spot; evacuees had to report to the marina an hour before dusk. When he was finished reading the timetable, Alban looked at the technicians who had set up his office for the transmission and waited until they gave him a thumbs up. Alban disconnected and dropped his head in his hands. After the technicians had packed up the equipment and left, Nari went over to her son and put her hands on his shoulders. "You did what had to be done. Your father would have been proud of you."

"Proud that we've lost control of the border, that our country is under attack, that we can only save ten percent of our capital's citizens? I think not," replied Alban bitterly.

"You know this war's been coming, and you've done everything in your power to help our country prepare for it. You're not responsible for the destruction wrought by evil men. Don't lose heart, Alban—that's one of the things that truly differentiates us from our enemy."

"It's going to take a lot of soldiers and weapons to survive this invasion. They are coming, for all Valerrans, and especially for the Serving Families." Alban groaned at the telegraph receiver on his desk, pinging in the background with a batch of new messages.

Nari paused and said softly, "First, we have family business to take care of. You know it as well as I do."

Alban nodded and lifted his head to look at Linden, who'd been watching them closely. "Linden, please go pack. You'll take our family's spot with the Queen's Navy."

CHAPTER 17

L inden couldn't imagine leaving her home again, leaving her family, and leaving Stryker. And who would look after Kal if she left? Linden was sure the queen wouldn't want a pet griffin on board one of her ships. She felt blurry around the edges, like someone was using a giant eraser to remove bits and pieces of her. Although it was done with the best of intentions, pretty soon there'd be nothing much left of her.

She shook her head. "I'm sorry, but I'm not leaving."

"Linden, please understand we only want to keep you safe," Alban said.

"Of course, I know that" Linden said. "But this is my decision. No one else can make it for me. I'm not leaving."

"But do you really know what you're saying? What will happen here when Bellaryss is attacked?" asked her uncle.

"I'm old enough to understand the risks. I know it won't be easy, and I might even regret it, but this is my home. My life is here with you, and with Stryker when he comes home." Linden held up Stryker's locket. "I know things may get much, much worse. But I also know we have to stop General Mordahn and the Glenbarrans—and it's up to all of us to stop them. Whatever it takes, I belong here, alongside both of you."

Nari walked over and embraced Linden. "We can't lose you too," she whispered. Linden hugged her grandmother. "You won't. I promise."

Nari pulled away to look into Linden's eyes. "You must promise me this: whatever is happening at the time, wherever you are when our defenses fail, when you're told to run, *you will run*. Do you understand?"

"You believe the city will fall, don't you?"

"Yes," Nari said simply. "I do."

Linden thought Nari and Alban would put up more of a fight, but she was happy to comply. "Yes, when I'm told to run, I'll run. But how will I know where to run to?"

"You'll know when the time comes," said Nari with a firm nod.

"Then it's settled," Linden said with more confidence than she felt. Sometimes Nari could be so confounding.

"What about your spot with the Queen's Navy? Have you given any thought to who should be going in your place?" Alban asked.

"I want Yolande to take my spot. She just told me she's with child."

"Goshen is the only son in his family. I wouldn't be surprised if his family wants him to go as well," said Alban. "Alright, go speak with Yolande. I'm certain several others from our staff also will be leaving with the Queen's Navy. We'll assemble on the drive in three hours to see them off." He turned back to his desk, his shoulders more slumped than before. Linden went over and kissed his cheek. He smiled wistfully and went back to the thankless job of running a country at war—a war it was losing badly.

∼

After a lot of cajoling from both Linden and Goshen, Yolande reluctantly agreed to take Linden's spot. Linden helped Yolande close her bulging bag, a curious role reversal that wasn't lost on either of them. Linden threw her arms around the often cranky, but always trustworthy, Yolande. "I'm going to miss you!" Linden whispered.

Yolande was openly weeping. "Who's going to look after you? And make sure you're dressed proper? I'd best not be going." She put her bag down on the floor.

"Oh no you don't. You and Goshen deserve a chance at a new life, to raise that baby of yours far away from this war. You're going." Linden marched Yolande down the stairs from the servants' quarters.

As they neared the landing, a maid was scurrying up towards them to let Linden know she had a caller. Linden walked into the front parlor to see her cousin Heidl standing by the fireplace. "Heidl, please sit down!" Linden said.

Heidl shook her head. "I can't. I've been offered a place with the Queen's Navy and have stopped by only to say good-by."

Stung by the departure of another family member—Linden recalled how hard she'd worked to avoid her numerous relatives not so long ago—she forced a smile. "I'm happy for you, although I'm going to miss you."

Yolande was standing at the entrance to the parlor. "Beg your pardon but I overheard. Miss Heidl, I'd be honored to assist you during the journey, if you should need my services."

"You'll be leaving as well?" Heidl was surprised. Yolande nodded shyly. "Well, I'm glad to hear that," she smiled at Yolande. "At least I won't be going to the Colonies completely friendless."

Heidl turned to Linden. "I'd better go. My driver is waiting outside." She started to walk away but turned back around. "Be brave, little cousin, because trouble is heading your way. And remember to focus!" She hugged Linden, gripped Yolande's hand, and left through the front door.

The house, by this time, was in an uproar. Several of the younger staff also prepared to leave with the Queen's Navy, as well as one of the Jermyn cousins. Those who remained behind —most of Delavan's household—lined up outside, on both sides of the drive, to say goodbye to their friends and family. Most of the women and more than a few of the men cried openly. Alban, Nari, and Linden stood next to the locomobiles that would be taking the departing staff to the Royal Marina.

Alban thanked the staff for their many years of service to the family, and after one more exchange of handshakes and hugs, the various members of the departing staff got into the waiting vehicles. Yolande gave Linden one more hug and pressed something into her hand as she left. Linden was too distracted to pay much attention to it until the locomobiles had pulled out of the driveway and were on their way. She glanced down at the small drawstring bag in her hand, which Yolande had embroidered with tiny leaves.

"What's that?" Nari asked.

"A parting gift from Yolande," Linden said, fingering the drawstring.

Linden opened the bag and gasped as she drew out a miniature painting of the Faymon Liege being crowned by a warrior in battledress.

"I don't understand this at all. How could this particular image find its way to me three different times, in three different ways? And why would Yolande give this to me?"

By now most of the staff had made their way indoors or to their various duties around the estate, and Alban had gone back inside. Nari took the miniature to examine it and shivered as a chilly wind swirled around them. She rubbed her fingers across the miniature, and the wind picked up dried leaves from the driveway and sent them swirling around their feet. Nari handed the miniature back to Linden and the wind ceased, the dried leaves tumbling to the ground. Linden shook her head in confusion.

Warmed by the fire in her grandmother's study and curled up in an armchair sipping strong black tea with a hint of bergamot, Linden was feeling better. Less emotional and more focused. "What do you make of this?"

"It's clear the fays are sending you a message."

"You mean the fays still communicate with humans?"

"Of course they communicate with us!" Nari answered with all the authority of a master mage. "What are they teaching young people today in our schools?"

"But I thought those were just bedtime stories my parents used to tell me."

Nari smiled fondly, her thoughts far away, back to when her children were young. "Ric used to love those fay tales. He'd remind me he was descended from a long line of Faymon warriors, which meant he—all of us—have ancient fay blood running through our veins."

"Do you know how much fay blood we have?"

"You're not asking the right question."

Linden thought about what she really needed to know and asked, "Why are the fays communicating with me now?"

"Much better." Nari hesitated, as if she wanted to say something more but stopped herself. "They've contacted you three times, which means they've finished that circuit. I'm sure you'll hear from them again, but it won't be the same message. They like to message in threes."

"Why in threes?"

"It's the fays—they have their reasons, and they'd be completely different from mine. I might say because it's a prime number, or it represents completeness, or some such thing. They might say because the woodland sloth has three toes."

"It makes no sense."

"It makes fay sense, which means you need to take it on faith they have their reasons."

Nari walked over to the window and noted the slanting rays of the sun. "We'd better be leaving soon for our meeting at Morrell. I suspect this is going to be a long night." Nari paused. "In fact, this may be the last time we'll be alone together."

"For some time. Alone together for some time, right?"

Nari turned around and gave Linden a wistful smile. "I want you to know that no one could be prouder of her granddaughter than I am. You're kind, compassionate, and smart—and you've been working so hard to master your magic. You'll be an amazing Serving mage, Linden, absolutely amazing."

Linden walked over to Nari and hugged her. "You're an amazing grandmother."

∽

Linden found Kal moping near the kitchen garden and his gazebo. "What's wrong with you?" Kal's wings drooped as he slowly padded over to her.

Kal clicked his beak half-heartedly and bumped into her leg. She knelt down to rub behind his ears. "Nari thinks we'll be gone for a while, helping the mages with the defensive spells. You'll be safer here at Delavan than with me."

Kal flapped his wings as if to say, *I'm coming too!*

"Kal, please promise me you'll stay with Uncle Alban. He needs looking after, too." Kal circled around her feet once and then lifted his right paw. "Thank you." She ran her fingers through his mane, patted his smooth back, and swallowed down a huge lump in her throat. As the time drew closer for her to leave Delavan with Nari, her apprehension grew stronger. She decided it was old-fashioned fear, and she shook herself.

"Love you," Linden whispered into Kal's mane.

Linden changed out of her dress and into her warmest woolen skirt, a black and blue plaid. She buttoned up a long-sleeved white blouse, layered a black sweater on top, and pulled on her most broken-in leather boots. She decided to avoid long capes and coats, especially if she would be conjuring fog and shields for long periods of time. She'd need to be able to move her arms about freely. Instead, she selected a fleece-lined black leather jacket with a hood and grabbed a pair of gloves.

On the way out of the house, Nari and Linden stopped to say goodbye to Alban, who was on a patched radio transmission again with General Wylles. There was more static and noise than last time, and Linden was certain she heard shouts in the background. Looking even more harried than usual, Alban waved briefly in their direction and returned his attention to the general.

As their locomobile wound down the drive, Linden turned around to catch one more glimpse of Delavan Manor. The setting sun cast its pillars and roofline in a golden glow. The trees had lost their leaves and stood like silent sentries along the drive. In the distance, the Jermyn's sheep were grazing on a hill, each like a puffy white cloud fallen from sky to earth. Jorri came running out of the cottage where her family lived and waved to them. Linden asked the driver to stop and got out of the vehicle. Jorri threw her arms around Linden.

"Jorri, what is it?"

"I want to say good-bye."

"Why good-bye? I'll see you again."

Jorri looked at Linden with something like pity. "Not for a long time."

Linden squinted at Jorri. "Another vision?"

"When they tell you to run, you have to run." With that,

Jorri gave her a peck on the cheek and ran back to her family's cottage near the edge of the Delavan estate.

Linden climbed back in the locomobile, a quizzical expression on her face.

"Jorri is going to be quite a psychic one day," Nari said thoughtfully.

"And quite a handful, too." Linden shook her head. "It's strange to think of the ships leaving the Royal Marina right now and crossing the Pale Sea for a new land."

"Any regrets at not leaving with them?"

"None at all. This is where I need to be."

"I know." Nari patted Linden's arm.

Linden looked at her grandmother in surprise. "Then why did you try to get me to leave?"

"Because I wanted you to be safe. Because I'd hoped I was wrong."

"Wrong about what?"

"About how much we're all going to need you."

Nari and Mayor Noomis called the meeting to order. As the two highest-ranking master mages in Valerra, they shared joint responsibility for certifying mages and for facilitating meetings, although they'd never had to prepare mages and apprentices to defend against the Fallow magic and physical danger of a pending Glenbarran attack. It was well known in the mage community that Nari and the mayor disagreed on just about everything. Yet despite their many differences, they respected each other's leadership and magic handling skills.

After the crowd in the auditorium settled down, Mayor Noomis said, "We've just been informed the Glenbarrans have advanced through Wellan Pass. We can expect to see them assembled outside our city walls by dawn or thereabouts.

General Mordahn is leading the column of Glenbarran troops and grihms heading our way." There was a collective intake of breath, and the room erupted into shouts and cries of "No!" or "Queen's Crown!"

"In peace and quietude, we lead and serve!" Nari's voice boomed across the auditorium. She'd assumed the commanding voice of a master mage. Although a small woman, Nari seemed to grow larger as she spoke. "As you know, Mayor Noomis and I occasionally disagree on the best magical approaches to a situation." She acknowledged her colleague with a small bow, as a few of the older mages chuckled. "However, we stand here tonight united in our purpose: to defend Bellaryss against all attacks of Fallow magic."

"Mage Nari is correct," Mayor Noomis continued more loudly, as he also assumed his commanding voice. "There is no greater calling for any mage or apprentice than to defend our people against the coming darkness. We've all heard the stories of the Glenbarrans' Fallow magic and dark spells."

"What we require of you will tax every ounce of strength you have." Nari picked up the thread. "We ask that you draw upon all of the magic within you—that you hold nothing back in the defense of our city." Now the room was completely silent.

"That's asking much," said Harlan Lewyn evenly. Others whispered among themselves. Linden took a deep breath, waiting to see the reaction in the room, fully expecting some mages to walk out of the building and not look back. Her grandmother knew this wouldn't be easy. If mages used all of the magic at their disposal, they would weaken to the point they'd be unable to use even a simple spell in their own self-defense. It could take weeks for them to gather their strength —and to collect the sparks of magic they'd dispersed. Some mages might never regain their full magical strength again.

"Anything less and we'll be defeated," Mayor Noomis

shouted across the room. "We know what we're asking. You must give of yourselves freely. Anyone unwilling to do so should leave now." Mayor Noomis paused, sipped from a glass of water, and waited half a minute. No one left the auditorium.

"Thank you," Nari said. "And now we come to our plan. We'll stage multiple lines of magical defense. First, Mayor Noomis will ask for your assistance to conjure and maintain curtains of impenetrable fog. This will form the initial defense along our city's walls and gates. For the second line of defense, Mage Rudlyn and I will take the apprentices to the Fortress Tower and help them cast a defensive shield over the palace." Linden's eyebrows shot up, excited to be going to the Fortress Tower, the oldest and highest part of the city's outer walls. The palace, which was built centuries later, connected to the Fortress Tower.

"The shield is a precaution we hope we'll not need," said Mayor Noomis.

"What if it all fails?" asked Harlan Lewyn.

"Then we fight with sword and spear and arrow. We save as many innocent lives as we can by non-magical means. We help guide the way to shelters, assist healers with our herbs, instruct the young in how to be brave." Nari paused and her eyes bored into Harlan Lewyn's. "Did that answer your question, or do you have something you wish to add?"

He shrugged. "Well said, Mage Arlyss."

"I do have a question," said Cy Valti, Toz's father, as he stood up. "I've read in the ancient scrolls there will be a union of Faymon and Valerran magic, under a powerful mage who will help defeat our enemy in our time of direst need."

"We can't rely on ancient scrolls—we must prepare to defend ourselves tonight," Nari replied bluntly.

"Even if what the scrolls reveal are true and the answer to our prayers may be in our midst?" asked Mr. Zel. Remy's father was standing next to Cy Valti.

"Even so," Nari said.

There were murmurs in the background as mages and apprentices began whispering to one another.

"Enough!" Mayor Noomis boomed. "We have work to do!"

Nari shouted the final instructions above the din. "Mages, please meet with Mayor Noomis in front of the dais. Mage apprentices, please meet with Mage Rudlyn in the back of the auditorium." Linden was seated near the dais and watched as Mayor Noomis organized the mages into teams, each under the direction of a senior mage. He provided the teams with the incantation they'd use to conjure the curtains of fog before departing for the city walls and gates.

She turned and headed to the back of the auditorium where the apprentices were gathering. Linden and the other students from Morrell—those who remained after the Article 99 evacuation—waited in one of the aisles for their instructions from Mage Rudlyn and Nari. Linden looked around. Of the original seventeen mage apprentices from her magic handling lab, they were down to five. The rest had evacuated with the Queen's Navy, or they'd left Bellaryss with their families by boat or caravan. Remy, Toz, Jayna, and Mara remained.

"I assumed your younger sister would be leaving." Linden said quietly to Jayna.

Jayna nodded. "Mother and I wanted Annah to have a chance at a new life. I'm still worried it was the right call, though. Sailing to the Colonies at fifteen won't be easy, either."

"I'm convinced sending as many away as possible was the best decision. At least your sister and the others will have a future free of grihms and Fallow magic."

"I would've thought your uncle and grandmother would insist you leave with the queen."

"They did."

"But you stayed any way. I didn't really think you'd leave without saying goodbye, but part of me wanted to show up tonight and not see you here." Jayna paused and asked, "Any news about Matteo?" Jayna had wept when Linden told her about his injuries, and she asked about his condition every chance she got.

Linden filled her in on the conversation Alban had with the general. "So, Matteo is better off at the headquarters hospital than back here in Bellaryss. At least for the time being."

Jayna's eyes widened. "Well I'm glad the general thinks he's safer where he is. But I don't like what that means for the rest of us. Aren't you scared?"

"Crazy not to be."

Nari nodded at the small group of students and said, "Let's be off. We have a great deal of work to do."

Rudlyn led the apprentices and Nari outside through one of the school's side exits. "I'm sure you realize the gravity of your responsibilities. The palace is the symbolic seat of Valerra, and we must ensure it is defended should the impenetrable fog curtains fail," Rudlyn explained as she walked briskly through the deserted streets.

Bellaryss was normally bustling well into the late evening hours, with ladies and gentlemen attending opera or theatre or joining friends for dinner parties. The only sound now was a lone hoot from a moon owl.

The subdued group of apprentices followed Rudlyn and Nari through the twisting cobblestone streets. Remy stumbled and fell to his knees. Linden and Jayna bent over to check on him, with Toz right behind them. Remy rose shakily to his feet, gripping Linden's hand as he stood up. "I'm fine, just tripped on a loose stone and twisted my ankle."

Nari paused, glancing behind her. Remy said, "I'm coming, Mage Arlyss. I just need to take it a bit slowly." She nodded and continued walking toward the tower. Remy, still holding on to Linden, walked with a limp. "I'm sorry I'm holding you back," he said.

"Nonsense, we can catch up." Turning to her friends, Linden said, "Go ahead without us. We'll be there soon enough." Jayna and Toz shrugged and jogged to catch up with Rudlyn, Nari, and Mara.

Remy continued to limp along at a snail's pace. Soon, everyone was out of sight, and it was just Remy and Linden slowly ascending the twisting road that led up to the Fortress Tower.

"I'm sorry, Linden, really I am," Remy said as he stumbled again, gripping her waist to regain his balance.

"What on earth for? You can't help—" the remainder of Linden's words were smothered inside a damp cloth that Remy had clamped over her mouth and nose.

CHAPTER 18

While she struggled to breathe, Remy wrapped his powerful left arm around her shoulders and gripped her tightly against his chest. *How could Remy betray me like this? And why?*

Linden turned her head to the left and right, trying to escape from the sickly-sweet odor. *Chloroform*, she thought drowsily. She was familiar with its sleep-inducing properties from Healer Gracyn. Linden knew she was no match for Remy's sheer strength, so she did the only thing she could think of: she started kicking his shins.

She landed a particularly vicious kick and he yelped, loosening his grip. Linden turned her head slightly and bit his arm. Remy howled as Linden wriggled free. Spinning around, she landed an upward thrusting kick in Remy's groin. He groaned and doubled over.

"What'd you do that for?" Remy screeched, trying hard not to cry from the burning pain between his thighs.

Linden fumed. "What's wrong with you, Remy? You just grabbed me and stuffed my mouth with chloroform. You're either crazy or working with the Glenbarrans!"

"Queen's Crown, you got it all wrong. I'm not trying to hurt you, I'm trying to protect you!" Remy said through gritted teeth.

"Protect me? From what?"

"From our crazy fathers," said Toz, coming up behind them. Remy nodded in agreement and Toz gave him a hand up.

Toz looked him over carefully. "She kicked you in the cabbages, didn't she?"

Remy moaned. "She shredded my cabbages, more like."

"Told you she could be a handful."

Linden's breathing was almost back to normal, but she coughed from the aftereffects of the chloroform. "What are you talking about? Your fathers are odd—especially yours, Toz —but why do you need to protect me from them?"

"Because my father believes you're a mage of historic power who can save us from General Mordahn," replied Toz, looking embarrassed. "So, he and his bizarre secret society want to kidnap you—for your own safety—and help you harness your magical gifts."

"And my father completely agrees with him," grumbled Remy.

"That's crazy. I struggle with my magic all the time and often fail pretty spectacularly."

"We know," they replied simultaneously.

Before Linden could reply, they all heard the moon owl again, followed by an answering hoot. Toz looked at Remy. "We've got to move before they get here." Turning to Linden, he said, "Look, this was the best plan we could come up with on short notice. In retrospect, it was really dumb. But if you don't follow us now, we're all going to get caught."

Linden examined the two of them. Remy met her eyes, and she could *see* he was full of remorse. Toz's eyes were full of fire and defiance—she *felt* his anger toward his father. "Fine. But no more stupid plans involving trying to save me. I can take care of myself." Both boys nodded solemnly. Remy started to jog, Linden and Toz following him.

"Where're we going?" Linden asked, as Toz pulled open a door that blended seamlessly into the ancient stone walls rising on both sides of them.

"We're meeting your grandmother and the others at the eastern entrance to the Fortress Tower."

Toz pulled the door shut and hastily cast a spell to seal it, at least temporarily.

"You mean my grandmother knew about this ridiculous plot of yours to 'protect me?'" Linden sputtered.

"'Course not. She knew something was up, so she and Rudlyn bound me with a truth spell. I spilled my guts, and your grandmother actually boxed my ears." Toz rubbed his right ear as though it still hurt.

"Serves you right for such a bone-headed plan," Nari said as she came up behind them, glaring at the two boys.

"Someone's coming," hissed Rudlyn. "To the guard station, quickly, it's just around the corner."

They ran towards the guard station inside the base of the Fortress Tower. The station looked like a large closet that someone had bolted onto the tower's underbelly. Linden hesitated. She'd never been a fan of tight, confined spaces. Ever since she'd hidden from the grihm in the healer's closet in Quorne, she avoided them all the more. Nari held out her right hand and beckoned Linden with her eyes.

Linden took a deep breath and grabbed Nari's hand. A powerful surge of energy jolted through Linden's hand, up her arm, and into her chest. She glanced at her hand; her grandmother's eyes were closed, and she was whispering an incantation as she gripped Linden's hand.

Linden squeezed Nari's hand, sensing something amiss. Rudlyn bolted the door to the guard station and directed Remy and Toz to move the large supply shelves in front of the door.

Linden dropped to the floor and put her head between her knees, her heart hammering in her chest. She was beyond caring who knew of her claustrophobia at this point.

"Where are Mara and Jayna?" asked Remy.

"Visiting the Royal Armory next door. They've been gathering supplies and weapons from the palace guards, in case the Glenbarrans penetrate our magical defenses." Rudlyn explained.

"Shh!" Toz whispered. "They're close by!"

They heard shouting, swords clashing, and a lot of grunting, followed by more shouting and swearing. Linden couldn't tell how many men were fighting outside the door. Finally, the yells quieted down. They waited at least five minutes in complete silence, and when all was still quiet, Toz and Remy cautiously moved the supply shelves away from the door.

Linden was the first one through the door, anxious to get out of the tiny guard station. She pulled open the door and ran smack into Ellis Steehl's chest.

"Why Mr. Steehl, what a surprise. We thought you'd left with the Queen's Navy." Mage Rudlyn said loudly.

Steehl grunted at her and pointed to two men he'd gagged and hog-tied, squirming nervously on the ground. "It looked like there were a couple more following you, but they got away." Spotting Remy and Toz standing behind Linden, he withdrew his sword, pointing it at the boys. "And there are two suspicious ones, right behind you!"

"No, it's alright." Linden put her hand out and pushed his sword away. "They told me their fathers wanted me for some ridiculous reason, but they're with us."

"It's true, these are foolish boys, but not evil ones." Nari joined Linden in the doorway, her mouth compressed in a thin line.

"Where are you heading?" Steehl asked.

"First the armory, then the top of the tower," said Rudlyn.

"What about them?" Linden asked.

"I'll have the guards toss these men in the dungeon for now. I can deal with them later." Linden saw Remy and Toz glance at each other and shrug. The men probably belonged to their fathers' secret society.

While Steehl left with several guards to secure the two men in the dungeon, Linden, Remy, and Toz joined Jayna and Mara, who were busy equipping themselves with swords, knives, and short bows from the armory. First, they hauled weapons up the narrow, winding stone steps leading to the top of the tower, and then they hauled food, water, and other supplies.

As Linden stepped out of the stairway, she looked up and could see stars surrounding her above the walls of the tower, which were two feet thick and four feet high. At thirty feet across, the six-sided Fortress Tower could comfortably accommodate an entire unit of guards. Overhead curved the graceful arches of a wooden nave, designed to shelter the Bellaryss Bell and its handlers from the worst of Valerra's elements. A narrow, walled passageway connected the Fortress Tower to the palace's six smaller towers. When royal guards patrolled the perimeter, they walked around each of the seven towers and the passageway that connected them, taking about a half hour to complete the circuit.

Rudlyn began issuing instructions to everyone, even the palace guards, who seemed somewhat dazed to find themselves without their queen and under the command of a bossy schoolteacher. Linden stood, rooted on the spot, as wave after wave of something—some premonition she couldn't quite identify—washed over her. She shook herself and spotted Nari staring out across the gently sloping valley floor to the west. Somewhere below, General Mordahn was amassing his troops and grihms for battle. Linden walked over to her and asked her softly, "What was that crazy business with Toz and Remy's fathers?"

"Pay them no attention," said Nari. "They believe, based on rumors about your magical gifts, that you are some mythical mage with the ability to repel the Glenbarrans. You are not. No single mage has the power to overcome the Fallow sorcery of Mordahn. The Glenbarrans have become too powerful." Linden's brow creased in confusion. The idea of being some mythical mage was almost laughable if it also weren't frightening.

Nari put her arm around Linden and then squinted, looking out beyond the city's walls. She pointed to tiny pinpricks of light on the valley floor, likely torches the Glenbarrans were carrying as they advanced, since the lights seemed to be moving. "Look," said Nari. "We have the best view anywhere in the city. They're coming. We must raise the alarm."

Nari turned and shouted, "Remy and Toz—come quickly. We'll need you to take turns ringing the bell." She instructed the boys and before long the sonorous sounds of the Bellaryss Bell were pealing across the tower and city wall. "Keep it up. We need others to pick up the ringing, so everyone knows the Glenbarrans are on their way." Soon they could hear other bells ringing across the city, from chapels, government buildings, and even some private residences. The constables rang their claxons, while guards and volunteers, working under the glare of large steam-powered searchlights, unrolled concertina wire outside the city walls to create an additional barrier the Glenbarrans would have to cross before entering Bellaryss.

Nari surveyed the valley below, watching as the tiny pinpricks of light continued to advance. "And so Valerra falls," she said sadly. Linden's scalp crawled at the finality of Nari's words and she closed her eyes, refusing to acknowledge the advancing army below. *No, there must be some way to fight back.*

Since bells were now ringing throughout the city, Nari told the boys they could stop ringing the bell and join the rest of the apprentices. "It's time to begin the work that you've been training for. We'll start by casting a defensive shield around the Royal Marina. I want us to practice on the marina first, to flex our muscles a bit," Nari said.

Toz glanced around. "Where's Mage Rudlyn?"

Nari glanced out to the western horizon once more and hesitated before answering. "She had a question for Mr. Steehl."

Linden placed her hand on her grandmother's arm and asked, "What's wrong?" With the Glenbarrans nearly at the city gates, Linden realized that was probably a silly question, but she sensed a deep sorrow in Nari that went beyond anything the Glenbarrans would be doing in the next few hours. Something very personal was troubling her grandmother.

Nari gave her a sad smile. Gently patting the side of Linden's face, she said, "Everything and nothing, my dear child. Whatever comes next, I know you will do the right thing." Turning to the rest of the group, Nari called out, "Let's focus, apprentices, on the task at hand. Follow me."

The apprentices gathered on the eastern wall of the tower, which looked out over the Pale Sea. They held hands to boost the strength of their spell, Nari linked to Linden, who held her hand out to Jayna, who was next to Mara, then Remy and finally Toz. "Conjure a shield around this spot, defend with strength against onslaught!" they intoned in unison. Linden concentrated on the Royal Marina directly below them.

Slowly, the apprentices, with Nari's help, began to raise the defensive shield. First, Linden spotted a few small eddies in the harbor below, then a shimmering misty wall began to rise from the edge of the sea and arch over the marina. Linden saw stars through the shimmery wall, but it seemed as if they were faded smudges, barely twinkling behind a wavy glass. The sea lapped at the base of the shield but didn't penetrate it.

"Excellent!" said Nari. "Now, let's extend the shield to the palace itself. Slowly now, that's it." Nari unlinked her hand from Linden and walked over to each student, encouraging them to maintain their focus and allowing one apprentice at a time to step away and take a short break. When she wasn't supervising the shield, Nari spent a good deal of time looking out of the western side of the tower, overlooking the valley and the tiny points of light below.

A half-moon had risen in the clear night sky. The students took turns taking small breaks. With just five of them, only one student could step out at a time and rest. The four other students worked extra hard to maintain the shield, with Nari supervising and occasionally stepping in to help strengthen the incantation.

A few hours after midnight, Rudlyn returned to the tower with Steehl and several guardsmen behind her. Rudlyn clapped her hands and said, "Well done, mage apprentices. All's quiet around the city walls, and the impenetrable fog curtain is in place. You may stand down for now, until the defensive shield is required."

Linden and the others looked to Nari for additional instructions, but Nari was impassive. She looked steadily at Rudlyn and Steehl and then nodded once to the apprentices, who readily broke their focus. As soon as they relaxed, the shield receded. In truth, Linden doubted whether just five apprentices could have maintained the shield for much longer without fresh magical energy from Nari or another mage. Linden felt drained and needed to rest. She couldn't imagine casting even a simple child's spell at the moment. All she wanted was a warm bed.

Turning toward Rudlyn, Linden was about to ask a question, but the look on Rudlyn's face froze the words on her lips. The chatter among the others also died down, when it became clear that Steehl and the palace guards—if they even were palace guards—had their swords drawn.

Mage Rudlyn shouted, "Freeze all magic swirling about, stop our spells till the hour runs out," temporarily blocking the flow of their magic. No one could cast spells for the next hour, even Rudlyn.

"Drop your knives, swords, and any other weapons that you may have hidden on your persons," Steehl boomed to the stunned group.

"What's the meaning of this?" Linden asked sharply.

Nari moved next to Linden and gripped her shoulder tightly, as if willing Linden to silence.

"The meaning of this? It's not obvious? I'm in charge here, and you'll be coming with us now." Speechless with shock, Linden and the other students quietly obeyed, dropping their swords and knives onto the stone floor of the tower.

"Search them carefully. They're a tricksome group," Rudlyn commanded the guards. Linden glanced at Nari in dismay but quickly realized her grandmother didn't seem surprised. A short, muscular man with five gold hoops in his left ear began to frisk each student. He found a set of brass knuckles on Remy and punched him in the stomach. As Remy doubled over, Steehl said, "That was just a warning. Empty your pockets, now."

The rest of them pulled out small knives, an awl, a jagged arrowhead, and even a piece of broken glass. Linden reluctantly dropped a pocketknife Matteo had given her on her tenth birthday. After they were thoroughly searched, the guards herded them down the stairs.

Linden stumbled on the steep tower stairs, but Toz grabbed the hood of her jacket from behind and pulled her back up. *How could Mage Rudlyn have fooled me for so long? And why are Rudlyn and Ellis Steehl working against Nari and the rest of us?*

They reached the ground floor of the palace, where more guards joined Steehl, and were hustled into a single line. "Take them to the dungeon," grunted Steehl. A jolt of fear coursed through Linden at the mention of the palace dungeon. It conjured up images of dark, dank, rat-infested cells with no light and little air. She felt chilled to the bone, as if already inside one of the cells, and shivered.

As they were led away, Toz grabbed at one of the guard's swords. Linden shouted, "Look out!" as a second guard rushed in, his sword raised above his head. Linden tried to pull Toz aside, but Nari stepped in front of them both, and the guard's long sword came down on her neck instead. Nari's head dipped to one side, and she slid to the floor.

CHAPTER 19

"No! No!" Linden shrieked, dropping to her knees, and screaming Nari's name, knowing deep down that her grandmother was already dead.

Linden swayed on the floor, sobbing and gulping for air. She clutched her stomach as if she'd been stabbed in a hundred places, each wound raw and exposed. Linden heard muffled crying from Jayna and Mara, maybe even from Toz. Taking a ragged breath, Linden reached over to close her grandmother's eyes. She pulled off her jacket to cover Nari's face, her hands shaking with emotion.

Placing her hands over Nari's still form, Linden indwelled some of Nari's passing sparks of magic, as a way of memorializing her grandmother. Images of Nari in happier times, chuckling over a funny story or raising her eyebrows when Linden botched a spell, came flooding in, as fresh waves of grief washed over her. Linden rose slowly to her feet and turned toward the guard who'd killed her grandmother. In a blind fury, Linden charged him, but Toz grabbed her and held her tightly against him. The guard put the tip of his sword against Linden's throat, nicking the skin so that a small trail of blood trickled down her neck and onto her white blouse.

Jayna was crying. "Please, no more killing. Please stop."

Rudlyn said, "Then behave yourselves." Linden was still sobbing when Rudlyn walked over and slapped her hard across the face, leaving a handprint on Linden's cheek. Jayna and Mara came along either side of Linden and tried calming her down.

Jayna smoothed Linden's hair out of her eyes and whispered, "Focus, Linden. We need to stay calm and focused. Look at me." Linden glanced over, her eyes glassy. "Good, now let's listen to our instructions. *To serve, we must survive.*" Jayna whispered one of Nari's favorite sayings. Linden nodded silently, tears coursing down her face. Linden knew Nari died saving her and Toz, and she was going to make sure her grandmother's death meant something. No one else was going to die—at least not tonight.

The guards dragged them away and tossed them into the palace dungeon. They bound their hands in twisted steel manacles. The twisted steel counteracted magic and couldn't be conjured open. They shoved the girls into one cell and the boys in the cell next to them, the two cells separated by a thick stone wall. The two men that Steehl had tossed in the dungeon earlier must have been in another section, since there was no one else around. Their captors first padlocked their cell doors, and then they shut and locked the heavy iron door that separated the dungeon from the remainder of the palace's lower level. Suddenly, all was silent in the underground chamber, except for Linden's occasional hiccups and sniffles, and skittering noises along the walls made by the dungeon's permanent residents.

The boys waited in respectful silence for as long as they could, which was probably about twenty minutes, and then Remy said through the bars, "I'm really hungry. I wonder when they'll be feeding us?"

Mara rolled her eyes and stalked over to the cell door. "Is that all you can think about, Remy? Your stomach? Linden's grandmother was just murdered. We're in no mood to talk about food."

There was a long pause, and then Toz said, "I'm really sorry, Linden, I didn't mean for your grandmother to get killed. I guess I went a little crazy when I heard they were putting us in the dungeon. I came with my father here once when he interviewed a prisoner for his paper." Toz gulped and whispered, "I vowed I'd never do anything to wind up in this place."

"Well, we're stuck here now. There's no way we'll be breaking out of these manacles." Mara banged hers against the cell bars for emphasis.

"I think we should try to get a few hours of sleep," Jayna said, her healer's instincts kicking in. "We could all use the rest." Linden curled up on one of the mats on the floor, while Jayna pulled one of the scratchy wool blankets over her. All Linden wanted to do was to blot out every memory of the last few hours. Drifting into a restless sleep, she woke up some hours later to see Mara and Jayna hovering near her. Mara handed Linden a cup of water, a piece of bread, and a boiled egg.

"One of the guards came by with this an hour ago. It's not much but try to eat something."

As Linden numbly ate the prison food, memories of the previous night came flooding back. The image of the sword coming down on Nari kept replaying over and over in her head, bringing on fresh tears.

A few hours later, the heavy outer door opened and Mage Rudlyn trooped in with two palace guards. Pointing her finger at Linden through the cell bars, she said, "That's the girl he wants to see." The muscular guard with the five ear hoops unlocked the cell door, hauled Linden to her feet and marched her out of the cell, shutting and locking the door behind them. They entered a dimly lit passageway formed from scarred blocks of stone. Linden made a mental note of their route; she figured if they ever escaped, she'd make sure they headed in the opposite direction.

Despite her grief and exhaustion, it dawned on her that someone thought she needed two palace guards and a mage escort, even though she was half a foot shorter than any of them and manacled in twisted steel. As she pondered why, some of her grief-stricken fogginess was replaced by wariness. They wanted something from her, and they wouldn't take rejection too kindly.

They climbed several flights of stone stairs and paused on the fourth landing. Rudlyn led the way through an arched doorway, where the stone flooring gave way to thick, patterned carpets in reds, blues, and golds. Rudlyn paused in front of a large burnished walnut door, trimmed in gold leaf, and emblazoned with a coat of arms Linden didn't recognize. The guard with the earrings grabbed Linden's arm roughly and pushed her into the room. Crossing to the other side of the long chamber, its walls covered with murals, he forced Linden to her knees. He placed a beefy hand on her neck and shoved her head to the floor.

"That's enough, Brunky," Steehl said.

Brunky released his grip on Linden's head, and she pushed herself back up to a kneeling position. Steehl leaned back against a gilded throne. Rudlyn took her seat next to him, in a smaller, simpler chair that no one could mistake for a throne. Both the throne and chair were raised off the floor and sat on a carpeted platform.

Steehl beckoned at Linden to stand up. He flicked his wrist at Brunky, who moved to Linden's side in a flash. Grinning, the guard grabbed Linden's hair and twisted her head back, exposing her throat to the six-inch blade held in his other hand.

"Now, now, Brunky, let's not spoil our fun too quickly. You know how I enjoy taking things slowly."

"Of course, your Grace." The knifepoint withdrew a fraction from Linden's throat. *What have I done to deserve this? My grandmother killed, my friends in a dungeon, and a knife at my throat.* Numb with exhaustion and grief, she clenched her teeth, unable to comprehend why Steehl and Rudlyn were pretending to be royals.

"Do you know why you're here?"

"Not a clue." Linden's voice dripped with sarcasm.

Steehl leapt down from the throne and slapped her hard across the mouth, splitting her lip. "There, see what you made me do? I do hate a scene." Steehl waved Brunky back.

"But I see I'll have to teach you some manners, young lady, something your overindulgent uncle neglected to do." Steehl backhanded Linden so hard she nearly lost her balance. He smacked her again, and with her hands manacled in front of her, she couldn't stop her fall and pitched face-forward onto the floor. He kicked her hard in the stomach, knocking the air out of her.

She curled up defensively on the floor, clutching her stomach, and he said, "Much better." He bent down to grab Linden by the hair. "Would you like to know why you're here?"

Linden whispered, "Yes."

Steehl pulled her hair until she winced. "Yes what?"

"Yes, your Grace."

"That's better." He brought his hand to her throat and squeezed until she started seeing stars. *What a stupid way to die*, she thought, gagging and feeling herself go limp. *Strangled by the queen's personal envoy.*

Rudlyn coughed loudly, which seemed to snap Steehl's concentration. He released Linden and jumped onto the dais, returning to his throne. Turning to Rudlyn, he said, "Would you care to do the honors?"

Rudlyn examined Linden, who'd managed to push herself to a seated position on the floor, blood from her lip and nose dripping onto her lap. "If you weren't so stubborn, none of this would be necessary. You always were such a prickly girl."

Linden glared at Rudlyn, her anger bubbling up inside. "My grandmother would be alive if you hadn't betrayed us. How could you?"

"You little fool—you know nothing of betrayal! Ellis and I are the ones who've been betrayed, by our own sister."

"Your *sister?*"

"Ayn refused to acknowledge us publicly as members of the royal family. Ellis served at her every whim, and I was a mere schoolteacher. Me, the daughter of a king!"

Their odd partnership—Ellis Steehl and Mage Rudlyn—made a bit more sense, two illegitimate children of the king banding together. However, Linden couldn't imagine how they'd get away with this level of betrayal for long. The Serving Families were still in charge of Bellaryss for the moment, and the Valerran militia and reserves still patrolled the streets. "So now what? Even if you're in charge, the Glenbarrans are at the gates."

"True," Steehl said, "Clearly, Mordahn has power on his side. He's mastered Fallow magic in ways previously unimagined. The Glenbarrans will win. The question is: how much blood needs to be shed before Valerrans lay down their weapons? And that's where you come in. You're going to help convince your poor befuddled uncle that it is in Bellaryss's best interests to surrender."

"How could surrendering be in our best interests? We've all seen their brutality."

"Aye, the Glenbarrans can be quite fanatical in pursuit of their goals. But I can assure you, Mordahn would rather have

Bellaryss—the jewel of Valerra and the entire continent—relatively unscathed. So much easier than rebuilding and far less mess. He can be quite civilized when he wants to be."

"What's in this for you?" Linden asked, curious to understand what motivated their twisted thinking, beyond their desire for power. She didn't think the Glenbarrans would be willing to power-share in any case.

"My sister wants to be treated as a true member of the royal family, which is her birthright. No more teaching magic tricks to stupid girls like you. And I want to rule Valerra as the potentate, under Mordahn's authority, of course. Really, all we want is peace." He spread his hands out, palms up. *They're both delusional*, thought Linden.

"My uncle will never cooperate."

"Oh, we think he will, when he learns his mother is dead, and that you're next—you and your friends. He'll cave in, and when he does, the rest of the mages will follow suit."

Linden determined in that instant that whatever it took, whatever the sacrifice, she would find a way to fight and defeat them. She calmed the rage stirring inside and stared defiantly at Steehl.

"Perhaps we ought to give her some time to think this over? Perhaps until tomorrow morning?" Rudlyn said. "She's smart enough to realize that with or without her help, Bellaryss will fall. She needs to ponder how much blood will be spilled in the process."

Steehl agreed. "Till tomorrow, then. If your answer is no, your body and that of your friends will be delivered to Alban Arlyss as a warning of what's to come, if he and the other Serving Families don't cooperate. Think it over carefully." He flicked his wrist and the guards hauled her to her feet and half-dragged, half-carried her back to her cell.

CHAPTER 20

When the guards opened the cell door and tossed Linden inside, one glance at Jayna and Mara told her how awful she must look. Jayna started to cry, her healer's instincts taking second place to her emotions. It was Mara who gently cleansed Linden's face and helped her onto the mat. Linden grabbed Mara's hand and said, "Thank you. And I'm sorry."

"Sorry for what?" Mara looked confused.

"For all of our stupid spats. All this time, we could've been friends."

Mara arched one perfect eyebrow. "Don't get ahead of yourself," but she smiled. "I'm sorry too. I guess it was jealousy on my part."

"And stubbornness on mine."

"When you're finished mooning over each other, could you tell us what's going on?" Toz called out from his cell.

"It's not good." Linden spoke quietly. Her throat felt raw and she hurt all over from the beating, not to mention her heart ached over Nari's death. She felt inside her blouse for

Stryker's locket, remarkably still there and in one piece. That was a small consolation.

"We can't hear a thing!" Remy whined. So Jayna and Mara helped Linden to move her mat nearer to their cell door, so she could tell her story to everyone at the same time. She spoke haltingly and held nothing back. When Linden finished speaking, Mara looked at her and said, "We're not surrendering. We can't! We've got to fight back with every ounce of magic we have."

One by one, everyone one of them agreed: death over surrender. Linden was so moved that she paused, thinking perhaps they were right. But her survivor's instincts kicked in. "I don't want to surrender either. And yet, I want to live to fight another day. I keep thinking there must be a third option."

"Like what?" Toz asked glumly through the iron bars of his cell door.

Remy said, "Perhaps Linden is right. After all, *she's* the one our fathers think has all the answers."

Linden rolled her eyes and paused. Squinting, she raised her manacled hands and pointed at the dungeon wall with her index fingers. "Do you see that?" Jayna and Mara shrugged. "Look more closely. See that moss, there? It's not the same color as the rest of the moss in this dungeon. And it seems to be, well, *wiggling*."

"Very odd," Jayna agreed.

"No, not odd." Linden lowered her voice. "It's a magical signal of some kind. We need to decipher it. Quick, find something we can use to write with."

Mara, somehow, still managed to have her reticule with her, which she pulled out of her jacket pocket. She withdrew a tube of rouge. "Will this do?"

Linden nodded gratefully and took the tube from Mara. "Here, help me up." The girls helped Linden shuffle over to the area directly underneath the discolored moss. As the moss wiggled, the letter S formed. Linden scrawled it on the rough wall. The next letter was I. There was a pause...and then N formed. The moss continued to form and re-form, ceasing after eight letters: SINGFREE. The girls tried various options until Linden said thoughtfully, "It's two words. Sing. Free. Do you think we need to sing for our freedom?"

"But how could singing help to free us?" Mara wondered aloud.

The girls looked at each other and then went over to the cell door to confer with Toz and Remy.

"What could it possibly mean?" said Jayna.

"How could a song get us out of here?" mumbled Remy.

"Are you sure it said to sing?" asked Toz.

As they continued to debate, Linden hobbled back over to the moss. It stopped wiggling and the letters faded away; message delivered.

Something tickled at the back of her mind, some clue she was missing. "Wait a minute. They do feed us periodically, right?" Linden asked.

"I should hope so!" said Remy from the next cell over. "Whatever passes for breakfast in a dungeon wasn't enough for me. I'm starving."

"You're always starving," grumbled Toz.

"That's it then!" Linden exclaimed.

"What's it?"

"Even though we can't cast spells with these twisted steel manacles on our wrists, we can still sing."

"How will singing get us out of here?" Toz asked.

"Ah," grinned Mara. "I can hear it now. A lovely lullaby, perhaps?"

"It will need to be one of the old fay lullabies," said Linden, nodding.

"I don't know any," Jayna sighed.

"Me neither," echoed Toz and Remy.

"How could you come from magical families and not know even one fay lullaby?" Mara wondered. She looked at Linden and started ticking off lullabies. Linden shook her head at each one—either the melody was too difficult or the verses too complicated.

Mara snapped her fingers. "What about 'Come Now Softly.'"

Linden nodded. "Perfect! Alright everyone, gather by the cell doors and listen to Mara and me. We'll have one chance to get this right."

"Won't the song put us to sleep, too?" Jayna asked.

Linden held up her manacles. "Not as long as we're wearing twisted steel. *We* won't fall asleep, but *they* will!"

They practiced the lullaby for hours, but still no food. In fact, Remy began to worry they'd been forgotten and would be left to starve. Finally, Jayna said, "Shush! They're coming."

Everyone lounged carelessly against the rough walls of their cells. The outer door clanked open and four surly guards shuffled into view—two with weapons drawn and two bearing trays of food. The guards opened the boys' cell door first and slid the tray into the small space. They locked the door and moved to the girls' cell.

The door clanked open and as the tray of food was pushed into the cell, Mara began to sing in a strong contralto the haunting first notes of the lullaby. Everyone else joined in:

> *"Come now softly, lead me nigh*
> *Where dreams come true, and hopes runs high*
> *Sprinkle your fay dust, stay by my side*
> *Keep me from harm all through the night."*

The guards stopped moving and listened, entranced. First one guard yawned, and then another, and Linden eased herself closer to the tray of food, still sitting in the open doorway of their cell. She smiled at the sleepy-eyed guards and continued to sing. The nearest guard wobbled slightly and then slid down to the ground. He rubbed his eyes and curled himself into a tight ball, fast asleep. One by one, the other guards slid to the ground and were asleep.

Everyone continued to sing as Jayna stepped over the food tray and searched each of the guards for the key ring. Mara and Linden followed her out of the cell, pausing only to grab whatever food they could carry with them. After searching the first three guards thoroughly, they realized the last guard, the biggest and surliest of them, must have the key ring. Everyone continued to sing as Jayna studied the man's breathing to ensure he was really asleep. Satisfied, she leaned over to snap the key ring off his belt fob. One hairy hand reached up and grabbed her hair, while the other hand held a blade to her throat. "Stop singing, ye troublemakers, or she won't see tomorrah."

"Ear plugs!" Jayna screeched as the blade nicked her neck.

"Stop now, or she won't be stayin' for breakfast!" he shouted.

Mara stopped singing, as did the rest of them. The guard rolled onto his knees, still holding Jayna by the hair. The other guards began to stir. As the guard tried to stand, his blade hand wobbled, pulling away momentarily from Jayna's neck. She stomped on his right foot and pivoted slightly toward him, ramming her right elbow into his abdomen. He dropped the knife in surprise and Linden rushed him, jumping on his back, her muscles groaning from the exertion. Mara and the boys started singing again, and the remaining guards settled back to sleep.

Linden rode the guard like a recalcitrant horse. Grimacing, she reached into the guard's right ear and pulled out an earplug —likely made of dried mud and spittle—and then did the same with the guard's left ear. As the first chords of the lullaby surged around him, the guard unclenched Jayna's hair and his shoulders slumped. After swaying slightly to the haunting melody, he pitched forward. Jayna had barely enough time to hop out of the way as he collapsed face first on the ground. Linden waited until she was certain he was under the lullaby's spell, and then she and Jayna rolled him over.

Linden grabbed the key ring and ran over to open the boys' cell door. Toz and Remy ran out, each stuffing some bread and cheese into their pockets. They continued singing while Linden went through each key on the ring for the right one to open their manacles. She was on the twelfth key when she heard it click, and Jayna's manacles slid from her wrists. Linden quickly unlocked everyone else's, and Toz unlocked hers. The boys dragged the guards into the cells and locked the doors behind them. With Remy, Mara, and Jayna singing the lullaby in front of the cell doors, Linden and Toz crept to the large dungeon door and creaked it open a crack.

They stepped into the corridor, more of an intersection of three passageways. Linden signaled to Toz to avoid the one straight ahead—that one led upstairs to the throne room. Instead, Linden took the left passage and Toz the right. They each went about thirty paces, until they could see around the next bend. They crept back to the dungeon door. "Well?" Linden whispered. Toz held up his fingers. Five guards to the right. Linden held up her fist. No guards to the left. Toz nodded and opened the dungeon door, signaling to the others. Once everyone had stepped into the corridor, they locked the outer door behind them. Linden and Toz led them down the passageway to the left.

They sprinted in short bursts, then paused to listen for any sounds of guards behind or ahead of them, and they sprinted again. They ran several hundred feet when they heard the sounds of men shouting and boots stomping nearby. They froze in place, searching frantically for a door they could hide behind. Remy spotted an old grate that covered a hole in the stone floor of the tunnel. He and Toz pried it away, and they motioned to the girls to jump down. Linden took the lead and jumped into the stinking pit, which reeked of raw sewage and rotten food. Jayna followed behind, holding her nose. There was scuffling above, and Mara was pushed into the hole. She put her hand up to her mouth, gagging at the stench. The girls grabbed her and pulled her back so that first Remy and then Toz could jump down.

They heard the sound of boots pounding nearby and Toz shoved the grate back in place as quietly as possible. A pair of boots stopped directly above them. Toz and Remy pulled back against the slimy wall as light from a lantern passed over the grate.

Cast a veil of drabness! Linden hadn't studied the spell in months, but it came to her unbidden. She hissed, "Drape us in a veil of gauze, hide us from inquiring eyes," and the drabness descended over them.

The guard's light wavered and then moved away from the grate. He called out, "There's no sign of them here." The light dimmed and the sound of boots faded as the guards continued down the passageway.

"Let's get out of here and let the mages know what's really going on at the palace," said Linden.

"Which way?" Toz asked. Linden pointed in the direction they'd been headed. Now that they were in the cramped sewer that ran beneath the palace tunnels, they had to run hunched over, as the stone roof above them, which had been excavated from the caves in this part of the palace's underground system, was about four feet from the ground. There were iron grates like the one they'd slipped into every so often, and occasional shafts of light from the gas lamps in the tunnels above pierced the darkness below.

Although Linden would have preferred to pick her way carefully through the raw sewage, and her stomach revolted every time she stepped on something squishy, she led the way at a good pace. The sooner they reached some sort of an exit, the better. She had to stop once, when Mara whispered, "Hold on," and then leaned over to vomit on the nearest wall. She wiped her mouth with a lace handkerchief she pulled from her pocket and then said, "Ready." Linden had to admire Mara's ability to maintain proper decorum, even in the bowels—quite literally—of the palace. If she hadn't been so frightened and exhausted, the idea of it would have made her laugh out loud.

"Hush!" Jayna said. They stopped moving and caught their breath. "Hear that?" Jayna asked. Everyone shook their heads. "The sound of rushing water, almost like a waterfall."

"I don't hear a thing," Remy said. No one else could, either.

"Jayna, why don't you take the lead, since you'll be able to hear what's up ahead before the rest of us," Linden said. Jayna sidled around Linden in the cramped space and took the lead, the five of them crabbing along through the palace's sewer. They'd gone another fifty paces when Jayna stopped. Everyone heard it now: rushing water straight ahead.

"What's that?" Toz grunted.

"Sounds like a waterfall," said Jayna.

"We better figure something out quickly, because this disgusting garbage we're walking in seems to be rising. Eek— it's above my boots!" Mara was gagging again.

Linden looked down and saw the dark, stinking sewage was rising quickly now and beginning to swell around them. "I think it's flushing itself," Remy shouted.

"What?" asked Linden.

"My father's company installed a new system in the palace about five years ago—apparently the stench from this ditch was wafting up even during the queen's balls. Now it flushes twice a day." They heard a swooshing noise behind them and saw a wall of raw sewage heading their way.

"Run!" Linden said. They took off, running as quickly as their cramped legs could take them. Jayna slipped and Linden caught her from behind. "Faster—it's gaining on us."

"What about the—" Jayna never finished her sentence. Instead, she disappeared right in front of them. Linden looked around her, and then she was swept away as well, carried on a swelling mass of sewage that arched over the edge of the palace wall and dumped her in the Wye River, which headed out to the Pale Sea. The frigid water jolted her system and she came up, gulping for air. She heard more splashes behind her as Mara, Toz, and Remy followed her into the river. Linden scanned the water for Jayna but didn't see her surface.

"Jayna!" she screamed, searching frantically for her friend.

"Over here," Jayna shouted. She'd grabbed onto the branch of a large tree that had fallen into the river. Relieved, Linden searched for something she could hang onto. The current had swept her past the fallen tree. She glanced back to see the others clinging to the fallen tree, safe for the moment.

The river's current picked up, the water churning white around Linden. Instead of fighting the current, she relaxed into it, forcing herself to remain calm. Straight ahead was the open sea—if she didn't drown in the surge of river water coursing into the sea itself, she'd be dashed against the rocks that lined the sea wall. To her right she saw a small sand bar with a twisted tree stump, weather beaten from a hundred storms, still clinging to the loose soil. She knew she had one chance— she had to get to the sandbar before she swept past it.

CHAPTER 21

Linden held her breath and dove beneath the surface of the water, and then kicked and stroked in the direction of the sandbar. The current swirled around the small protrusion of earth, and Linden swam with the current. She came up for air and reached her arms up out of the water, grasping at the tree stump. She nearly fumbled, but a sudden surge of water swelled beneath her, and she was able to hug the tree as she levered herself out of the water, half crawling and half pulling herself up the tree stump and onto the sandbar.

She laid down, panting, the sound of the surf crashing around her. She stayed like that, every muscle of hers screaming, until she'd caught her breath. Rolling over, Linden sat up to get her bearings, her teeth chattering. Behind her was Bellaryss, cast in a pinkish glow by the setting sun. Ahead was the Pale Sea. Yolande and Goshen and Heidl were somewhere out there, sailing with the queen to what she hoped was a better, safer place than this one. Linden stood up and shivered in the chilly autumn air, her waterlogged clothes sticking to her skin.

She picked her way carefully along the sand bar and onto the rocky beach—she knew her friends would be looking for her—but quietly, so as not to risk capture. She began the long climb up the forested bluff that lined the Pale Sea, clamoring over fallen branches, slipping on the rocks that studded the face of the bluff. She was about two thirds of the way up the bluff when she heard a twig snapping nearby. She froze and found a fallen tree to duck behind.

"Shush! You're so loud you'll wake the dead in Glenbarra," Mara said, scolding the boys. Linden stood up from behind the tree and whispered loudly.

"Over here." She jumped up and down, trying to stay warm.

Jayna reached her first and threw her arms around Linden. "We didn't know whether we'd find you." Jayna tried to inspect Linden for any apparent injuries, but Linden was in no mood to be coddled.

"I'm fine, really, just some more cuts and bruises to add to what Steehl already gave me. And I'm wet and cold." She noticed they were dry—filthy, with matted down hair and smelly, with bits of raw sewage stuck to their clothing—but they weren't dripping wet like she was. "How'd you dry off so fast?"

Jayna said, "Remy used his fire-maker."

Linden said through blue lips, "Remy, fire-maker, please." She'd forgotten about Remy's pyro gift, which he rarely used because of his multiple school suspensions whenever he did. He used to think it was amusing to yank a few hairs out of some poor girl's head, and then snap his fingers to create a little flame that burnt the hair up in a flash. He didn't need to shape-shift something to create the fire or cast a spell to call up fire. He just snapped his fingers. An odd magical gift, but one that Linden gratefully accepted. Remy snapped his fingers and held a warming ball of fire between his palms. He walked around

Linden, raising and lowering the fireball so she'd dry off quickly.

"Thank you, Remy. Much better." She was still cold, but at least she wasn't wet.

"Where to?" Mara asked Linden. It was the first time she acknowledged Linden as their leader, of sorts.

"Well, I think we should go to Mayor Noomis to tell him about Steehl and Rudlyn and ask him to get a message to my uncle. And then we could help the mages defend the city walls. But this needs to be a decision that each of us makes individually. The closer we are to the city walls, the closer we are to where the Glenbarrans will attack."

"I'm in," said Remy.

"Me too," Toz agreed. Jayna and Mara nodded as well.

"Alright. Let's figure out the safest route to the city walls and Mayor Noomis and stay as far away from the palace as possible."

"Do you think we can go back to Morrell for a quick shower and change of clothes first?" Mara asked. Everyone kept an extra uniform in their school lockers; you never knew when a magical experiment would go wrong and coat you in slime or douse you in oil or soak you with water.

"Good idea. Maybe we can raid the cafeteria, too," said Remy.

"And grab some blankets from the healer's office. Our coats are ruined," said Jayna.

They found Mayor Noomis a few hours later, taking a short break in the guard station at the main entrance to the city gate, which had become the de facto headquarters of the mages as well as the militia. He looked surprised to see five Morrell apprentices, all wearing green-and-gray Morell blankets over their school uniforms. Toz had the brilliant idea to cut holes in the blankets so they could wear them poncho-style.

Mayor Noomis pulled a limp handkerchief out of his coat

pocket to mop his brow. Linden could see the strain of maintaining the curtains of impenetrable fog already taking its toll on the mage. She wondered how long he and the other mages could sustain it, even with their help. She also knew only one thing could be sapping the master mage's energy like this—Fallow magic. And yet she didn't feel anything pulling at her near the city walls. Nothing deadening or seeping or draining. Linden and her friends told Mayor Noomis about the double betrayal of Steehl and Rudlyn, Nari's death, and the need to get a message to her uncle. Mayor Noomis' shoulders drooped even more, and his enormous mustache seemed to sag around his full mouth.

"To think we've been betrayed from within, and Nari Arlyss is gone." He shook his head, and then realizing he was speaking with students who'd already suffered much more than he had, the mayor roused himself. He dispatched a messenger to Alban at Delavan Manor, and he sent for the chief constable, who questioned them closely about what happened at the palace. When the constable had gathered enough facts, she sent a highly trained force to surround the palace.

The sun was up by the time Mayor Noomis returned to the guard station to give them an update. "Did they find Steehl and Rudlyn?" Toz asked eagerly.

"Afraid not, son. By the time they stormed it, Steehl and Rudlyn were gone." Mayor Noomis shook his head, as if putting the betrayal behind him. "Well, apprentices, there's fog to be spun, and we could use your help." He led them to the heavily fortified western wall, just outside the main guard station, and went to find the mage in charge. Linden tried to hide her surprise when Mayor Noomis returned with Ian Lewyn, who was all business and quickly put the apprentices to work maintaining the fog curtain. The apprentices' primary duties were to relieve exhausted mages along the western wall, so the mages could rest briefly from the magical strain. At first,

Linden felt fine and couldn't understand why the mages, who were better trained and had years more of experience, were wearying so quickly. Then she felt it: a slithering, throbbing sort of ache that started in her feet, crept up her legs, circled her waist, clenched her heart, strained her arms, and squeezed her head. After less than an hour of maintaining the fog, she was panting. She looked down the wall at her friends, and they were struggling as well. Linden cast about in her mind for some remedy, something that could counterbalance the Fallow sorcery. She felt certain there must be a way to push back, but the more she tried to think of a remedy, the more her head hurt, and she couldn't concentrate on anything but holding the fog in place.

Before anyone came to relieve them, first Mara and then Jayna collapsed. They were quickly taken to the infirmary, where they were revived by one of the healers, who told them they could not return to the wall. Instead, she put them both to work in the infirmary, preparing healing potions and putting together first aid kits for those along the wall. Everyone was preparing for an assault, and they knew the wall would be the front line of the battle for Bellaryss.

Eventually the mages returned to relieve Linden, Toz, and Remy, who collapsed in the arms of the nearest mage. Toz stumbled to his knees and needed help walking to the infirmary. Linden had a pounding headache, which began to lift as soon as she stopped chanting the incantation that sustained the fog. She was sent to the infirmary along with her friends, to be examined by one of the healers. After they were feeling better, Toz and Remy were sent to work in the mess hall near the guard station, preparing meals for the mages and militia who manned the city's walls. Linden, however, was told to remain in the infirmary for a consultation with the master healer.

"But I'm fine, really—I'm ready to return to wall duty," said

Linden, trying not to let her frustration show. She was bursting with the need to do something, anything, to fight back.

"Yes, I'm well aware of that," replied the master healer. "What I want to understand is how you can be absorbing so much Fallow magic at such a tender age, and yet be ready to return for more. It was too much for your friends."

"Perhaps I have more pent up anger?"

The master healer shook her head. "No, anger may boost your adrenaline, but it will not shield you from the dark energy of Fallow magic. I can find no reason to hold you here, however, I won't permit you to work the same schedule as a mage. You're still an apprentice and must rest more frequently from wall duty."

Linden went back to work with the mages along the wall, and although they tried to give her more breaks for rest, it was obvious the mages were struggling with the same headaches and exhaustion as she was, so she returned to duty as quickly as possible.

On Linden's second day of wall duty, Kal found Linden during one of her breaks. She threw her arms around him and then scolded him for leaving Delavan.

"Nothing could keep him at Delavan, so he came with me," said her uncle.

Linden and Alban hugged in silence for several moments, remembering Nari and realizing the loss was too fresh, too deep to articulate even to each other. He cupped her face in his hands and said, "At least you're still safe. To think I couldn't protect my own mother." Pausing, Alban added, "The constable and her crew transported your grandmother home to Delavan yesterday. We held the funeral rites for her this morning."

Linden heaved a shuddering breath and said, "I'm glad she's home now." Alban nodded mutely, wiping a tear from his cheek. He looked old, older even than Nari, his hair now entirely silver streaked with dull blue, and his skin sagging around his eyes.

"Why did you leave Delavan? Will General Wylles be able to contact you here?" Linden worried her uncle might be so distraught that he abandoned his duties.

"I lost contact with the general two days ago. No telegraphic messages, no patched transmissions. Nothing but static. After I buried your grandmother in our family plot, I decided it was time come here, to the wall, to help defend Bellaryss with the other mages. At least there's something that I can still do. But before I left, I activated Mother's last spell."

"What spell?"

"Your grandmother cast a shielding spell the evening before you left Delavan, and she entrusted me with the final incantation—sort of a key—which would activate everything. But first, I had to explain to all the servants and our refugee family what was about to happen. I gave them a quarter hour to decide if they were staying or leaving. Everyone decided to stay, which is best, because they'll be far safer. So, I left Delavan by horseback, stopping only when I reached the boundary of our estate. That's where I unlocked the final key to the spell, and it all disappeared."

Linden was having difficulty following the threads of Alban's story, "What disappeared?"

"Why Delavan, of course. Gone. Mother's spell completely vanished it." Seeing the shocked look on Linden's face, Alban quickly added, "Oh, don't worry. It's still there, but it's completely shielded and invisible. Now for those at Delavan, life continues as before, but they can't venture beyond the boundaries. However, they have all they need to survive and even thrive—crops, fruit trees, livestock, and plenty of fresh water."

"That's amazing. I can't imagine how hard Nari must have

worked on that spell. But if it's shielded, how do we get back inside?"

"I'm sorry, I thought you understood about shielding spells. For us—for anyone not sealed inside the spell—well, we can't go back home."

"I can never go home again?"

"Now I didn't say that, exactly. But you'll have to wait five years, which is the length of the spell. Mother wanted to be certain Delavan would still be there for you and your brother. She trusted General Mordahn and King Roi would be defeated by then, and you could safely return home."

"Five years! Nari thought the war could last that long?" Linden shuddered at the idea of battling Glenbarrans for five years. Who would be left standing? "What if the war is over sooner?"

"Mother told me you'd find your other home."

"My other home? What was she talking about?"

"She said when you needed your second home, you'd find it." Alban squinted into the sun. "Delavan is the past, Linden, and both of us have to move forward. Now could you show me how I can help the other mages here at the wall?"

For eight days and nights, Valerra's best mages—and one mage apprentice—battled against Fallow magic. The headaches and exhaustion worsened, until finally only Linden, Alban, Mayor Noomis, Ian, and a handful of others remained. The fog curtain had been thinning for several days, and they could hear the guttural grunts and shouts of grihms and troopers on the other side of the wall. Constables, militia, and the marines who'd retreated to Bellaryss from Wellan Pass were positioned all along the parapet, arrows, spears, and swords at the ready, waiting until the curtain of fog fell and the Glenbarrans charged the concertina wire and the wall.

Linden heard a gurgling scream from one of the mages. She glanced over and almost fainted at the horror before her: blood poured from the man's eye sockets, nose, and mouth. He raised his hands to his face and then pulled away bloody palms, the sight of which increased his keening. Two healers ran over to the screaming mage, insensate from pain and blood loss. He fell into their arms and was led away, whimpering like a sick puppy. A short while later the master healer came to the wall and after briefly conferring with Mayor Noomis, pulled Linden into her arms. "Enough."

"I'm younger and stronger than that poor man. I'm staying," said Linden, swaying with weariness.

"You don't understand. We must move away from the wall and let the soldiers take over. You've done more than enough— you and the mages bought countless Valerrans time to escape these eight days past. Now come, lass, away from the wall."

"She's right. The time for Serving magic has passed. Now we must give way to swords and arrows and carnage," Alban said grimly, massaging his temples and sagging against another healer for support.

Linden looked over at Mayor Noomis, who was helped away from the wall by one of the soldiers. The mayor looked so much older than he had a week ago. He paused on his way to the infirmary and locked eyes with Linden. Nodding once, he moved on. One by one, the last few mages, including Ian Lewyn, were helped to the infirmary.

White wisps of fog swirled around them as they left the wall, the fog disintegrating rapidly behind them. Linden leaned heavily on the master healer for support. As they headed toward the infirmary, she heard shouts from the soldiers and a whizzing whir as the first arrows started flying in the battle for Bellaryss.

CHAPTER 22

L inden dreamt she was walking among tall trees along a narrow, uneven path. She almost lost her footing twice, and the man walking with her had taken her hand. Although she couldn't see his face, she felt safe with him. The man started jogging and Linden, her legs heavy, tried to keep up. He kept urging her to hurry as the pungent smell of smoke filled her nostrils. "Fire," he yelled, "Come on, Linden, we've got to move!"

She woke up to Ian Lewyn shaking her shoulder. Smoke was filling the infirmary room, and he handed her a damp cloth to put over her face. He helped her out of the cot, and they went through the room, checking each bed to be sure everyone was out. As the smoke thickened, they dropped to their knees and crawled towards the door.

"My uncle and my friends? Are they safe?" Linden choked out. She wondered why no one used a water douser spell, but then realized the mages were still weakened by their wall duty to take on such a large fire.

"They're outside. Your uncle panicked when he couldn't

find you. He tried to run back in, but I beat him to it." The smoke was stinging her eyes and filling her lungs.

"Thank you," she rasped. Ian grunted, "Don't thank me yet."

He pushed her in front of him, lower to the floor to get whatever oxygen remained. Flames were licking at the bed curtains and roaring up the walls. Linden couldn't see the door, but Ian kept pushing her along. A beam came crashing down behind them. Ian moved next to her. "Almost there," he gasped. They belly-crawled a few more feet, and a pair of hands grabbed her under the arms and dragged her out of the doorway. Someone else grabbed Ian and pulled him away from the building. Alban and Toz pulled her farther away from the flames. They heard a loud swoosh behind them as part of the roof caved in. Other buildings smoldered nearby, with men and women lined up along the path of destruction, trying to douse the flames with buckets of water.

"What's causing all these fires?"

"The Glenbarrans have a new weapon, a catapult that fires an egg-shaped projectile that explodes on impact. The catapult operates on a completely manual pulley system, so it's able to deliver its deadly packages despite all of the magic swirling about," explained Toz.

"But we can still cast smaller shields to protect some of our buildings, can't we?"

Alban said, "Aye, but the mages who are still healthy enough are busy protecting the palace, the cathedral, and the museum. When we heard the infirmary had been hit, we ran over to help with the evacuation."

"You must've woken up before me, then, if you were out with the other mages."

"You've been asleep since yesterday," said Jayna, her eyes clouded with worry. "Your magic was nearly spent."

Linden still felt exhausted, but she hadn't been drained down to her last spark. At least not yet. "What's the plan?"

"The Glenbarrans are building scaffolding, and despite our militia's best efforts, they'll soon be scaling the walls. For every Glenbarran who's killed in battle, it seems that two more rise in his place. We need to drop back to the museum and prepare for the ground assault," Alban answered grimly.

"Why the museum?"

"The mages took a vote and agreed to conserve our remaining magic for the museum. It contains our most precious artifacts, books, and scrolls. We must preserve our cultural heritage."

"And" said Ian, who was still hoarse from the smoke inhalation, "It has the added benefit of housing an enormous collection of weapons."

"But those are just a bunch of old swords and knives. What use would they be to us?" asked Toz.

Alban shook his head. "What do they teach in the history of magic classes these days?"

Everyone looked at Alban, who sheepishly answered his own question. "Ah well, it's clear that Mage Rudlyn's mind was on other things."

Turning to Toz, he added, "It's said that some of those 'old' swords, knives, and bows you're so quick to dispense with were actually spelled by the fays themselves and carry special protection."

"Ensorcelled swords? Maybe I can beat Linden yet," Remy said.

"I think we'd better concentrate on beating the Glenbarrans."

"I brought you a fresh change of clothes—another school uniform, but at least it's clean," Mara had a neat package under her arm that she handed to Linden. Wrinkling her nose, she added, "Though you might want to wash the soot and dirt off first."

"Definitely, and thanks."

The mages and apprentices set up their own version of a base camp inside the Valerran Museum, cast a tightly bound defensive shield and established foot patrols in the main section where the library wing was located. Ian took everyone to the Weapons Room. At first, they tried to select their own weapons from the display cases but quickly discovered that didn't work. Remy picked up a scimitar with an onyx handle, but every time he tried to practice with it, he dropped it. Toz picked it up and tried to hand it back to Remy, but as soon as he touched the handle, it pulsed with a golden glow. Remy put his hands up and said, "Take it—it's yours!"

When something similar happened to Ian, he suggested that the mages and apprentices place the various weapons in a long row and slowly walk past them in a single file, picking up each one and looking for any reaction. One by one, each of them found weapons that fit their personalities and talents.

A lightweight sword covered in green hieroglyphs and a jeweled handle found its way to Linden, along with a matching short dagger. She realized she'd 'seen' this sword before, when she'd been fencing with her old practice sword and her blade seemed to shimmer with green hieroglyphs. Both sword and dagger were sheathed in burgundy leather scabbards, which Linden strapped to her waist. The pair seemed tailor-made for someone with her smaller frame. The same was true for the others. Jayna's sword had an intricately carved mahogany handle and a polished steel blade. After everyone was armed, Ian organized the apprentices and mages who were not on patrol duty and forced them to do drills several times each day, so they could practice fencing with their new weapons.

Linden, Mara, and Jayna discovered an assortment of women's clothing in a storage room in the basement. Linden asked one of the senior mages, who also happened to be a docent at the museum, about the intriguing styles—leggings, slacks, and split skirts, along with formal gowns—and the material, which seemed woven of various iridescent fabrics, in golds, silvers, and copper shades, as well as blues, greens, reds, and purples. The docent explained they were historical replicas of the clothing worn by Faymon women prior to the civil war. She glanced down sympathetically at Linden and her friends, still wearing their tired-looking school uniforms, and told them they could help themselves to whatever they fancied. The three girls spent a gleeful afternoon sorting through the outfits. Linden chose a tunic and matching leggings in a silver-blue fabric to wear, and she selected a second set in a shimmering purple. She layered a vest made from a lightweight silvery mesh over her tunic for extra warmth and protection. Mara selected a pair of slacks and jacket in dark green, while Jayna went with a deep copper shade.

In the meantime, Mayor Noomis and Alban sorted the most portable artifacts at the museum according to their cultural significance, and they assigned to each apprentice a set of artifacts to carry with them inside lightweight backpacks designed by the mayor for that purpose. The packs were spelled closed to preserve the valuable contents. Linden dropped the shimmery purple tunic and leggings into her pack before Mayor Noomis sealed it, pointing out the clothes were of some cultural value. Mayor Noomis arched an eyebrow but didn't argue.

Remy carried the oldest Valerran book in the library, laying out the constitution and early laws, while Toz carried miniature portraits of the Valerran kings and queens and a brief history of each reign. Mara carried a golden belt decorated with fire opals that seers claimed had been forged by the fays. Both Jayna and Linden carried sets of scrolls. Jayna's contained all of the known herbal and medicinal remedies for various ailments, and the best methods for cultivating herbs, flowers, and plants. There was also a scroll that charted the stars and planets, and another containing maps of the continents and seas. Linden's was a collection of ancient fay scrolls, covered in hieroglyphs, including the scroll with the story of the Faymon Liege being crowned by the tall warrior. Alban added *Timely Spells*, which he'd brought with him from Delavan, to the other artifacts Linden was carrying.

Although no one spoke of it, Linden knew the mages had pledged their lives to protect the apprentices, and the few artifacts they carried with them, when General Mordahn and the Glenbarrans attacked the museum. And she knew they would attack—like bloodhounds on a scent, they would sense the presence of Serving magic in the building. The periodic updates from the mages on guard duty added to the general level of anxiety inside the museum. Each day, the Glenbarrans got closer to overwhelming Valerran defenders along the wall. It was a matter of days before the Glenbarrans would be fighting Valerrans in the streets.

Ian mapped out several escape routes and ensured the apprentices knew how to find each option. One was an old tunnel that was part of the underground system leading to the Pale Sea; another was a series of safe rooms that connected with each other and opened into a small shop on a side street. The shop was camouflaged and heavily spelled—even the Glenbarrans wouldn't be able to track them there—or so they hoped. The last option was a hidden staircase inside the library that led up to the rooftop, where a flying aero-cycle, discovered by Toz and Remy in the Cycling Collection, had been set up for a quick get-away. However, none of the options were foolproof.

If they reached the Pale Sea, would they find any sea-worthy boats? If they made it to the shop, would they be able to evade the Glenbarrans long enough to get out of the city?

And how would they be able to get to a safe zone from the rooftop, assuming they could figure out how to get the aerocycle in the air? Linden kept her doubts to herself and focused on the fencing drills.

The more Linden observed Ian, the more convinced she became he was a different man from his uncle and that Nari probably had been right about him. She'd learned from the mayor that Harlan left wall duty after the first day. He returned to his horse farm and prepared to defend his own property. Apparently, his civic duty didn't extend to the rest of Bellaryss.

She was polishing her blades after a particularly demanding drill, and Ian was standing nearby. Linden turned to him. "When did your uncle start asking you to cover for him?"

Ian dropped the knife he was sharpening. "What do you mean?

"It's become clear to me that you're nothing like your uncle."

Ian didn't say anything. He picked up the knife and placed in on the worktable beside the sharpening stone.

"You weren't involved with Madlyn or the other women, were you?" Ian shook his head. "Why did you take the fall for your uncle?

Ian looked away. "My uncle took me in after my parents died and raised me as his own son. I felt it was my duty to protect him. If that meant covering for him, I figured it was a small price to pay. Besides, Madlyn and the other women seemed to like him—he can be quite charming when he wants to be. I hadn't realized—until you told me—that Madlyn was pregnant."

"Are you sure it was just his charming nature that attracted those young women?"

"What are you saying?"

"Your uncle is a powerful mage, after all, and I wouldn't put it past him to do something unscrupulous."

"You mean like a seduction spell?"

"That's exactly what I mean."

"I don't know—and I don't want to find out."

"Nari was convinced all along that you were innocent."

Ian glanced at Linden with something like admiration. "Your grandmother was quite a woman, and you're just like her."

"I'm nothing like her," said Linden, shaking her head. "Nari possessed more magic in her pinky finger than I'll ever be able to muster."

"You're wrong. I've seen what you can do when you're wielding magic—remember your Teenth?"

"I'd rather not." Linden smiled.

"Well, it was an impressive display for any mage, especially an apprentice. Believe me, you've inherited her gift."

There was a loud crash, and the entire building shuddered as the defensive shield collapsed with a whoosh. The air was rent with shouts and grunts as a claxon blared from somewhere inside the building. Ian and Linden picked up their swords and sprinted toward the commotion.

He stopped and grabbed her by the shoulders. "Where do you think you're going?"

"I'm going to fight the Glenbarrans."

"Oh no you're not—you're going to lead the other apprentices out of here."

"I'm not leaving my uncle or you behind."

"Can't you see this isn't about you or your uncle or any of us? It's about the survival of Serving magic. You have to preserve it, even if it means leaving everything and everyone behind. It's your duty."

Linden knew he was right, but she wasn't ready to give in. "Look, I promise that if it looks like we're losing badly, I'll escape with the other apprentices. I hate the thought of running, but I will."

Ian looked at the determined set of her jaw and shrugged. "Fine, just remember you promised to run—and as your commanding mage, I'll tell you when it's time."

Linden nodded and jogged toward the sounds of swords clashing and men shouting. Ian stepped in front of her as they rounded the corner and bounded into the Great Hall. Linden gasped at the sight of so many grihms—their wolfish snouts snapping and snarling—swinging swords and axes with a ferocity that left no doubt about their bloodlust. With their magic nearly spent trying to maintain the shield, the mages were fighting for their lives. The grihms were fighting because they enjoyed it.

Linden glanced around. She didn't see Alban, but Remy and Toz, their backs to each other in a tight circle, were fending off several grihms, sparks flying as their blades clashed. She tapped Ian's shoulder and pointed. He nodded, leaned in, and quickly kissed Linden on the lips.

CHAPTER 23

I an charged into the fight followed closely by Linden, who didn't have time to process what just happened. The nearest grihms heard them and spun around. An especially gruesome one charged Ian, who blocked the grihm's upward thrust and threw his dagger with his left hand, hitting the crossbreed in his neck. The grihm screamed in agony, and two more ran into the fight.

Linden took on the smaller of the two, who still towered above her. He bared his canines and brought his ax down toward her head. She spun out of the way, nicking his side with her sword. He screamed in fury and swiped at her with his ax. Linden sidestepped and using two hands, swung her sword upward, knocking his ax to the floor. He quickly withdrew his dagger, but before he could throw it, Ian ran him through from behind. The grihm screeched loudly and slumped onto the ground. The grihms who'd been fighting Remy and Toz turned and charged Ian and Linden. More of them came running into the Great Hall. Ian pushed Linden behind him and yelled. "Run! Run far away—and that's an order!"

Remy and Toz, who was bleeding from a cut above his eye,

came alongside Linden and dragged her away from the fight. "We've got to run. Don't look back!" She couldn't stop herself from looking and saw Ian surrounded by four grihms. She tried to run back to help, but Toz and Remy had a firm grip on her, and half lifted her as they ran. When she turned her head one last time, she didn't see Ian standing any more. Several of the grihms realized they were escaping and took up the chase.

They were running so hard they collided right into Jayna and Mara, who'd been anxiously waiting for them next to the hidden staircase, which was the closest escape route. Kal dashed by them on the stairs and scampered ahead to the roof. Jayna grabbed Linden and pulled her into the small space beneath the staircase, as Remy and Toz crammed in behind them. They slid closed the wooden panel that camouflaged the staircase and bound it with a hastily whispered spell. They heard the grihms run past, growling and snuffling, searching for them.

As quietly as possible, the five began their ascent to the roof. Linden's legs were shaking, whether from fear, muscle strain, or rage, she wasn't sure. Probably all three. She was sure Ian was dead, and the other mages would be soon enough, including Alban. No one could survive against those odds for long. As she climbed, she actually *felt* each mage's passing, as sparks of Serving magic were dispelled into the atmosphere. She was too exhausted to grieve properly for them. She whispered a simple prayer of peace for them and kept climbing.

They were about two-thirds of the way up the staircase when they heard something crash into the sliding panel below. Grunts and yowls told them the grihms were on their trail. They dispensed with silently creeping up the stairs and sprinted to the roof. Jayna and Mara reached it first and ran over to the aero-cycle, which had five pairs of flappable wings attached to a five-seat tandem cycle. Toz had scrounged around and found an assortment of goggles, which he'd stacked in a neat pile on the roof.

The tandem cycle's frame and canvas-wrapped wings were constructed from lightweight titanium. The wings were mounted on a pair of metal poles directly above basket-shaped seats. Each seat sat above a spoke-and-hub wheel with rubber tires, connected to a pair of pedals. Aero-pilots guided the tandem cycle using wooden handlebars mounted on the same metal poles that held the wings in place. The aero-cycle required vigorous pedaling by each pilot in order to gain enough speed for flight; the pedals connected to a pulley system that turned the five wheels and flapped the five pairs of wings overhead.

While the museum's rooftop extended three city blocks, no one knew whether the aero-cycle could become airborne quickly enough for an escape. Ian had wanted to test it, but the mages decided it might reveal their location prematurely. The cycle rested on kickstands mounted to the frame beneath each seat. When aero-pilots were ready for flight, they kicked back the stands with their left legs and started to pedal with their right, swinging their left feet onto the pedals to maintain the momentum. Ian and the boys had propped the cycle upright, facing north, although it leaned somewhat precariously to the left since the only thing holding it upright were the kickstands.

Jayna and Mara were climbing into their seats when Remy, Toz, and Linden ran onto roof. Remy and Toz turned to help Linden close the heavy rooftop door. The boys dashed over to the aero-cycle, jumped into the seats, and buckled themselves in, but Linden hesitated.

"Hurry up, Linden," Jayna called, but Linden was still focused on the door, calming her mind. There was a commotion on the other side, and a pair of grihms stormed through, ripping the door off its hinges. As the grihms loped onto the roof, Linden indwelled all of the disparate sparks of

Serving magic she had felt at the passing of the mages. Their latent magic coursed through and around her. She tingled with fresh magical energy, like a jolt of electricity flowing from the roots of her hair to the tips of her fingers and toes, her muscles pulsing with power. Everything around her slowed, and she heard only the beating of her own heart. The grihms charged, thinking she was defenseless, her magic long since drained. She pointed her sword, and the hieroglyphs all along the blade glowed like fiery green opals. Linden shouted an ancient fay war cry, "Evakunouz!" which Matteo had told her basically meant "Retreat or die!" She charged, brandishing her sword in front of her with both hands.

The grihms took one look at the glowing blade coming their way and dropped theirs on the roof. They turned and fled back down the stairs, whimpering. Linden uttered a quick defensive spell to shield the open doorway from any more intruders. She sheathed her sword, jogged to the aero-cycle, and hopped into the fourth seat, directly in front of Remy, who handed her a set of goggles. Her friends watched in stunned silence as she buckled her seat belt and gave them the thumbs up. Toz, in the front seat, signaled, and they all kicked out their stands and started pedaling rapidly. The mechanical wings slowly opened and flapped languorously, but they were nearing the end of the roof and the wings would have to flap much harder if they were going to fly.

"Faster, pedal faster!" Toz shouted. Linden's legs were burning with the strain. The aero-cycle reached the end of the rooftop and took a nosedive, heading straight toward a cluster of Glenbarrans whose swords were drawn and pointing upward. Kal flew alongside them, clicking his beak sharply at Linden.

While Toz and Remy were yelling, "Faster!" and Jayna and Mara were screaming and pedaling in a strange symmetry, Linden reached deep inside herself and cried out an incantation. "Take flight and soar from trees and ground, wing and beak and feathers sky-bound!"

Her brother had used the spell to send mourning doves into flight on her sixteenth birthday—a spell he'd learned from Stryker. Matteo had taken her outside and told her to close her eyes. Then he shouted the incantation and two dozen speckled white, beige, and gray doves rose from the grass and soared into the sky, flying in large looping patterns. She'd hoped it would work on mechanical flying machines as well. The nose-diving aero-cycle shuddered in mid-flight, skimmed the treetops surrounding the museum, and dipped into another nosedive. The spell wasn't designed for large inanimate objects. Now everyone was screaming as they sped towards the ground, and Kal flew in frantic circles above them.

Linden desperately searched her memory for anything that could keep them airborne. She remembered an incantation from *Timely Spells* for teleportation, which was used rarely by mages, and then only to move an object from one surface to another. Nari used the spell to move books from her shelf to her lab table. Linden modified the first portion of the spell, which commanded an object to be airborne, shouting, "Propel this cycle into the air! Keep it aloft till I say where."

She couldn't incant the rest of the spell because it required precise directions on where to land the object. The aero-cycle shimmied, righted itself, and began climbing until they reached a safe cruising altitude of several hundred yards—well out of range of any Glenbarran arrows or catapults. Linden wondered what the tandem aero-cycle looked like from the ground: an odd flying contraption with five pairs of wings flapping and five students pedaling for dear life, trying to keep from falling out of their basket seats. Gliding alongside the aero-cycle was a miniature griffin, weaving figure eights above and below them.

Relief and grief coursed through Linden in equal measure. She was relieved the teleportation spell seemed to be working and grieving for everyone they'd just lost. More than anything, she wanted to curl up somewhere and mourn in private, but she had to keep the aero-cycle aloft by repeating the spell every so often, and she had to keep pedaling.

Remy tapped Linden's shoulder and shouted above the noise of the wind and wings, "That was incredible, what you did back there with the grihms. Remind me never to get on your bad side!"

"Where to?" Jayna called into in the wind. Linden remembered what Nari had said, when it was time to run, she would know where to go. Linden didn't have to think twice. "Head north," she shouted, "We're going to the Sanrellyss Sisterhood."

"I thought the sisterhood was hidden from all but the most powerful mages," Mara called out.

"It is, but it's the only place I can think of where we'll be safe," Linden hollered into the wind.

They pedaled for several hours. Once they reached the Pale Sea, they cycled into an air current that took them in a northeasterly direction. Nothing stretched around them for miles except the sea itself. Linden continually scanned the horizon. She couldn't describe what she was looking for, but she trusted she would know it when she saw it.

Eventually she found it: a tiny white speck in the sea. "There, can you see it? It's a small island in the Pale Sea." Linden pointed to the speck.

"Where?" asked Jayna and Mara.

"I can't see anything but water," shouted Remy.

"What island?" said Toz.

Linden was the only one who could see the island—so she had to be the navigator for her friends. She described what she was seeing, shouting various instructions so they would slow down and not miss the island entirely. Since Toz was in the front of the aero-cycle, he was struggling with how to bring them in for a landing when he couldn't see anything but open sea.

"Are you absolutely sure something's there?" Toz asked her for the third time.

"Yes, of course I'm sure," Linden answered crossly. She'd been arguing about the island for the past thirty minutes.

"This isn't wishful thinking?"

"I can even see the cloisters and people walking around. Over there I see rows of trees. Must be an orchard."

"What kind of orchard?" Remy wanted to know.

"Who cares?" Mara snapped. "We have more important things to worry about than your stomach."

"A man's got to eat to keep up his strength," Remy grumbled.

"Linden, I need you to be my eyes," Toz called out. "Where should I put this thing down?"

"Bank thirty degrees starboard. There's a nice pasture over there." Linden was pointing, but Toz couldn't see her. She stopped incanting the teleportation spell because she couldn't provide the exact coordinates for landing on the island. They had to set down the aero-cycle manually, without any magical support.

Linden noticed Kal flying in graceful spirals directly toward the island and realized he could see it too. She cupped her hand and shouted, "Kal, go to the front and guide Toz down." Kal flew next to Toz and then banked toward the pasture. Toz pointed the aero-cycle after him.

Linden continued to call out instructions. "Stop pedaling, everyone. Put on the brakes."

"Where are the brakes?" Toz yelled.

"We're coming in way too fast," Linden shouted even louder.

"Are we going to crash?" Mara screamed.

"I found them!" Toz shouted.

"Found what?" Linden yelled into the wind.

"The brakes!"

"Then use them now!" Linden and Jayna hollered in unison.

Toz stepped down hard on the brakes, which caused the entire aero-cycle to convulse. They landed with a loud crunch, toppled to their port side, and skidded for several hundred feet, until their cycle smashed into a stand of trees, ripping off half its wings.

Linden's belt snapped and she was thrown from her seat, landing in a patch of lichen headfirst. Her last conscious thought was of Stryker—she felt his presence in a physical way that she hadn't since he left Delavan—almost as if he were nearby, but she knew that wasn't possible. He was fighting the Glenbarrans somewhere, or had been captured, or worse. She couldn't bring herself to think about anything worse, so she stopped thinking and drifted into a blackness that felt like release or peace or possibly even death. She wasn't sure which, but it was where all memory ceased and she could rest, undisturbed by thoughts of troopers and traitors and grihms.

CHAPTER 24

L inden woke up in a simple, whitewashed room, resting on a narrow bed. It was the first clean set of sheets she'd slept on in weeks and although they were rough-spun cotton, they smelled of soap and sunshine. *I'm still dreaming,* she thought groggily. Then she remembered the betrayals and battles and so much fresh loss. Nari, Alban, and Ian, all gone.

Wiping her damp eyes on the sleeve of her nightgown, she sat up abruptly, trying to push her sadness and fears away. The room swirled and Linden quickly leaned back against her pillow and closed her eyes. She brought her hand to her head, fingering a bandage someone had carefully applied. Something warm and heavy dropped into her lap, and Linden's eyes snapped open.

Kal clicked his beak happily and paced in circles around her legs before settling down at the foot of her bed. "I'm happy to see you too," Linden smiled.

There was a knock on the door and a female servant brought in a tray.

"Where am I?" Linden asked. The woman shook her head,

setting the tray on top of the bed. She brought two fingers to her lips, to indicate she was mute, and pointed to a pendant around her neck. It was a small gold circle with a pair of wings in the center. Linden had seen the symbol of the Sanrellyss Sisterhood before, in Nari's library. She realized she was inside the cloisters that housed the secretive sisterhood of mages sworn to protect Serving magic and ensure it was never misdirected or misused.

The Sanrellyss servants took a vow of silence. Some said the serving men and women had become mute over time, and their children were born without the ability to speak. The honor of serving the sisterhood, however, far outweighed any physical limitations. The servant clapped her hands twice, and Kal jumped off Linden's bed and sat obediently in front of the woman, who slipped him a slice of apple. Linden's eyebrows rose. The servant had obviously figured out the way to Kal's heart. She silently backed out of the room, bowing gracefully as she closed the door.

Linden's stomach growled. She couldn't recall when she'd last eaten a real meal. Lifting the embroidered linen cloth from the tray, she handily devoured the fried pepper omelet, roasted red potatoes, and baguettes with fresh butter and currant jam. She was sipping her second cup of tea when the door to her room opened and the same female servant delivered an official-looking envelope addressed to "Sister Linden Arlyss," sealed with the Sanrellyss Sisterhood's symbol in dark blue wax.

"Wait, please." The woman stood still.

"There were others traveling with me—two girls and two boys. Are they safe?" The woman smiled broadly, nodded, and backed out of the room.

Relieved that everyone had arrived safely, Linden turned her attention to the envelope. She broke the wax seal and withdrew a piece of cream-colored parchment containing a short note:

Dear Sister Linden,

   Long ago I tutored your grandmother, and now I am pleased to welcome you and your companions to our community.
   Once you have rested, Magda will arrange a time for us to meet.
   Verily Yours In Service,
   Mage Mother Pawllah
   Sanrellyss Sisterhood

Linden ran her fingers over the signer's name: Mage Mother Pawllah. Nari had spoken reverently of an exceptional woman who'd tutored her and remained her spiritual and magical director throughout her life, but she never revealed her name.

Linden pushed aside the tray, swung her legs onto the floor and slowly stood up. She felt stronger after eating and no longer dizzy, but she still had a dull headache. She pulled the rope for the serving woman, anxious to meet the Mage Mother. After bathing and dressing—the only available garments were the long pale blue robes, white headscarves, and white ankle boots of the Sanrellyss Sisters—she opened her door. Linden trod softly, listening for sounds of life, and Kal dogged her steps. A small woman walked toward her, carrying a long garment draped across her arms. Her reddish wisps of hair, streaked with blue, peaked from beneath her headscarf.

"Please, could you tell me how to find Magda?"

Her face dimpled as she smiled at Linden. "I am Magda."

Linden stepped forward, excited to find someone who answered her. "Are you permitted to speak?"

Magda dimpled again and said, "As one of Mage Mother Pawllah's envoys, I speak as the need arises. If you would allow me." She indicated the garment she was carrying. Linden nodded, unsure what to expect. The woman unfurled a cerulean blue wool cloak, which she expertly draped around Linden. She pulled up the hood, careful not to displace the white headscarf. She didn't seem satisfied until Linden was covered head to toe in the thick woolen fabric. Magda wore an identical woolen cloak.

Handing Linden, a pair of matching blue wool gloves, Magda said, "Please follow me." Turning sharply on her heels, she led Linden and Kal down a series of labyrinthine stone corridors, some covered with threadbare rugs, their footsteps echoing as they walked.

"Where're we going?" Linden asked as they stepped outside onto a small cobbled patio surrounded by thick yew trees.

"You wish to see Mage Mother Pawllah, no?" Magda asked, her eyes squinting as the sun burst out from behind a cloud.

Linden nodded. Magda led her through a gap in the yews that Linden was sure hadn't been there a moment before. She looked over her shoulder and the gap was gone. *There's extraordinarily strong magic in this place,* she thought. They began to ascend a steep hill, following a snow-covered path that wound its way around to the top. As they climbed, snowflakes swirled around them, and the wind grew colder and fiercer the higher they ascended. Grateful for the cloak, Linden fastened the top button around her neck to help stay warm.

"How far is it?" Linden asked, but her words were carried away by the wind. Linden's breath came in short huffs as she struggled to scale the hill, leaning into the wind that seemed to want to push them off the rocky incline into the valley below.

When they reached the top, they were back among the stone walkways and whitewashed walls of the cloisters. "What kind of magic is this?" Linden breathed. Smiling, Magda gestured for Linden to follow her inside the cloisters. She pointed out a large coat hook near the entrance, where Linden hung up her woolen cloak, stowing her gloves inside its pockets. Magda hung up her cloak as well and then continued down the corridor, her boots clacking on the stone floors, stopping abruptly before an oversized door made of burled hickory. A serving woman opened the door and ushered them inside.

"Please, do come here by the light, sisters!" a reedy voice called out. Linden spotted a small, brown-skinned woman, shrouded in blue shawls, sitting in an armchair near the fireplace. Mage Mother Pawllah was ancient—much older than Nari or any other woman Linden had known—and yet, her hair was a vivid shade of blue, without a streak of silver or white. *Nari's beloved tutor was a fay? Why did she never mention her by name?*

Linden bowed low when she entered the room and Pawllah beckoned her to come closer. Linden walked over and knelt down before the ancient mage. Pawllah placed her gnarled right hand on Linden's head in a blessing. Her commanding voice, which was surprisingly strong for one so old, reverberated off the walls and echoed around them. She spoke in the buzzing language of the fays, her words sounding like a swarm of bees to Linden's untrained ears. Linden wondered whether Nari could speak fay and thought she probably had learned the basics of the language while growing up in Faynwood.

When she finished reciting her fay blessing, the old mage said, "Welcome, Protector of Serving magic." She nodded at a nearby chair where Linden sat down.

"Well met, Protector of Serving magic," said Linden. "And thank you." Linden had so many questions, but she held back, waiting for the right moment to ask them. It wasn't every day that an apprentice had an audience with an accomplished fay master of Serving magic, especially someone so old she'd tutored her grandmother.

Pawllah addressed Kal. "Welcome, Companion of Protectors." Kal laid down before the old woman, who patted his head. Kal clicked his beak so fast he almost sounded like he was sending a coded message.

Still petting Kal but addressing Linden, she said, "My dear child, I've long awaited your arrival."

Linden looked into the dark eyes, sparkling with curiosity. "And yet I never knew your name until today."

Pawllah nodded. "Your parents wanted to protect you as long as possible."

"Protect me from what?"

"From the burden that awaits you."

Linden drew her brows together. Why had her parents never bothered to tell her about the mysterious Mage Mother Pawllah? And her burden? "I don't mean to be disrespectful, but I'm already feeling burdened. My parents had to abandon our home and flee across the Barrens, and I don't know whether I'll ever see them again. My grandmother was killed protecting me from traitors, and my uncle and many other mages died to save my friends and me. And then there's Stryker, who's missing, and Matteo, lying injured in a hospital." Linden stopped and took a deep breath, her emotions rubbed raw and exposed. "Wouldn't you call those burdens enough?"

Pawllah spoke gently. "Aye, of course. You've experienced far too many losses and misfortunes in your young life. And yet, these misfortunes will equip you for what lies ahead."

Linden looked away from Pawllah's searching black eyes. Her voice shook as she said, "I don't want it, any of it." Linden knew Nari would scold her for being so selfish, but she was heartsick and tired. "Let someone else carry the load for a while."

"It's not just because of your loss and pain, Linden. But because of who you are—it's your privilege, your inheritance—and yes, your burden."

What inheritance—and burden—could this old woman be talking about? How does she know so much about me? Linden's natural curiosity won out. Tilting her head to one side, she asked, "What sort of burden?"

"The burden of profound knowledge, and with it comes a lifetime of unflagging duty and extreme service. How I wish I could take on the burden myself, but my time has come and gone. Do you know what I'm referring to?"

"I think it's what my grandmother was trying to prepare me for, when I went to live with her in Bellaryss. But as much as I've tried, I've struggled to be a good apprentice."

The old mage shrugged. "So, did I, in my youth. Powerful magic is not easily tamed. It takes years—a lifetime, really—to completely master it."

Linden hunched her shoulders, still unconvinced.

"Tell me, little sister, how did you and your friends escape, carrying valuable artifacts with you, and make your way safely here, hidden as we are from all but the most gifted mages?"

Linden recited—haltingly at times—the last battle at the museum and the deaths of her uncle, Ian, and the other mages. "And then we crashed into the pasture..."

"And is this something that a few months ago you would've been able to manage with your own magical gifts?"

Linden shook her head. "No, not at all. It would've been unthinkable." An awareness of what Pawllah was trying to tell her clouded Linden's features. "No," she choked, "It can't be."

Pawllah nodded. "Just before her death, Nari transferred the full force of her Serving magic to you." Linden swallowed the lump that rose in her throat whenever she thought of Nari's death. And then she remembered the jolt she felt when Nari took her hand while they were locked in the guardroom— and how Nari had looked at her, willing her to understand.

"A young revelator who possesses the full inheritance of a master mage must recognize that with a great gift comes a great burden, which serves as the counterbalance to so much power. What I'm trying to say, little sister, is that you must continue your studies."

Linden realized what Pawllah was really saying. "Are you offering to tutor me?"

"Of course. It's my duty and my privilege to instruct you in the proper use of your gifts."

"But how can I stay here, safely pursuing my studies, while Valerra is under attack? I want to fight against Fallow magic, not retreat from it."

"Valerra is no longer under attack."

"What do you mean?" A small ray of hope bubbled in Linden's chest.

"Valerra has fallen."

Linden leapt from her stool. "Impossible! The Glenbarrans can't have subdued the entire country in the past few days."

"You mean months. The past few months."

Linden's legs trembled and she flopped back down on the chair. "Months?"

"You've been in a coma for two months."

CHAPTER 25

"Two months." Linden's voice broke. "I don't know if Stryker's alive, captured, or—"

"Who is Stryker?"

Linden closed her eyes briefly, trying to bring his face into focus. "My...special friend."

"Ah, I see." Pawllah signaled to Magda, who helped the ancient woman stand up. "Come. Let's learn what we can about your Stryker." Magda led them to one end of the long room, pausing before a peacock blue door. She whispered an incantation and the door opened. They entered an enormous octagonal room that looked like part observatory, part laboratory, and part library. If Linden weren't so preoccupied, she could have happily holed up in this room for a long time.

Pawllah, leaning heavily on Magda's arm, led them to what appeared to be some type of land surveyor's scope. It was about ten feet long and had a lens that was three feet across. An old sister—almost as old as Pawllah—was fiddling with some dials on the side of the scope. When the sister saw Linden, her face softened. Pawllah introduced Linden to Sister Xavir.

"Is the young lass finally awake? Been asking after home? Well let's see if we can give her some insight."

"What exactly is this invention?" Linden had never seen anything quite like it.

"It's called an electromagnetic insight scoping device," said Xavir. "It will provide you with at least three views—or insights —anywhere you wish to point it."

"Why would I want three views, or insights, when I'm really trying to get at the truth of what's happening in Valerra? Wouldn't one view be enough?"

"We've found that if you have anywhere from 2.8 to 3.3 insights about any given point of view, you'll generally be able to garner the truth. That's why the electromagnetic insight scoping device will deliver at least three insights." She nodded, satisfied with her answer—which left Linden even more befuddled.

"Linden is particularly concerned about her young man." Pawllah had taken a seat nearby.

"And my brother—I'd like to see if we can find him, too."

"We'll scan Valerra for the past three months, so you can see what's unfolded. Then we'll attempt to focus in on your brother and your friend."

"How can we focus in on just one person?"

"When you wear these neurogoggles, I'll be able to isolate your psychic connection to your loved ones during that three-month window, and I'll thread it into the scoping device." Linden looked at Xavir and scratched her head.

"Its ancient magic paired with modern science," said Xavir.

"And a pinch of faith for good measure." Magda winked.

"Step up here, there's plenty of room, and please put on these neurogoggles." Xavir indicated a raised platform in front of the large scope. As Linden climbed the platform, Xavir handed her a pair of large brass goggles. "Prepare yourself, lass," she said softly.

Apprehensively, Linden took a deep breath, put on her goggles, and stood in front of the lens, which was dark at first and reflected back her pale face. Slowly the darkness swirled and shifted away. She saw village after village overrun by Glenbarran grihms and troopers, with Valerran children crying in the streets, dogs barking, and women running with toddlers in tow. The view shifted to battlefields littered with dead and dying marines. Then the city of Bellaryss came into focus. Linden saw fierce fighting all around the city walls, the city's defenses collapsing, and Mordahn's army pouring in, overwhelming the city's militia.

The neurogoggles vibrated, as if recalibrating, and she was at the palace just as Nari stepped in front of the guard's sword to protect her and Toz. Linden's heart splintered again at the sight, and then she was at the museum, when Ian and her uncle fell to the grihms in their final battle. Shifting again, she saw an underground tunnel where a small band of wounded marines seemed to be hiding from the Glenbarrans. Linden scanned their faces, many heavily bandaged, and thought one of them strongly resembled Matteo, but she couldn't be certain.

The focus shifted to a heavily wooded forest and she was following two men, one of whom looked familiar. He turned to speak with the other man, and her pulse raced when she saw it was Stryker—thinner than she'd ever seen him, with a thick beard and a deep cut on his face, but he was safe. Linden felt certain Stryker was somewhere in Faynwood—he and the other man, who seemed to be leaning on him, headed deeper into the woods. The lens went dark. Linden's bottom lip quivered, and she pinched the bridge of her nose, trying to stem the tide of grief threatening to overwhelm her.

"Your young man—did you find him?" Pawllah asked gently.

Linden nodded. "Yes, he's alive. But my brother, it's difficult to say. As for the rest," she indicated the scoping device and shook her head. "As you said, it's over. Valerra has fallen. In Bellaryss, the shops and markets are closed. Thugs roam the streets and food supplies are running low. It's awful." She stumbled off the platform and collapsed onto the floor.

Linden woke up on a sofa in a darkened room, her head hurting as much as her heart. She wanted to close her eyes and wipe away the images she'd seen. At least Stryker was alive. That was something to hold onto.

She heard skirts rustling and steps shuffling nearby. A gnarled hand gently reached over and felt her forehead. "You're slightly feverish. Please drink the tea on the table nearby—it'll bring down your temperature." Pawllah slowly lowered herself onto a tufted chair next to the sofa.

"How can you bear it?"

"What, my dear?"

"The burden of so much knowledge. What I saw—all of that death and destruction and loss—I want to forget all of it."

"So, you'd rather live in a fantasy world, blissfully unaware of what's happening outside your door?"

"Not exactly, no. I *do* care about what's happening to those poor families and our marines. I just don't want to see it when I close my eyes at night."

Pawllah nodded. "That's understandable. However, how else would you be able to fight evil if you don't see it? If you don't name it and recognize it?"

Linden picked up the cup and sipped the hot, sweet brew. "You sound just like my grandmother. Or my grandmother sounded just like you."

Pawllah smiled wistfully. "Nari was my best student and dearest friend. But you—well, you're going to be my *absolute best* student."

Linden looked at Pawllah. "Here? Now?"

"Of course. You must complete your studies to become a proper master mage."

"But it'll take me years to become a master mage—I'm still an apprentice!"

Pawllah laughed, a pleasing sound like the tinkling of small bells. "Only mages are able to make the trip to my residence here in the cloisters."

"Wait a minute." Linden put her cup down. "Then are you saying—I'm actually a mage?"

"You're not just any mage, but with a bit more effort, you'll become a master mage."

"And what about my friends? What'll they be doing while I'm studying with you? I'm sure they're anxious to be going."

"Quite the contrary. They seem to be enjoying themselves here. The young men are studying with the brothers in the monastery on the other side of the island. Sister Jayna and Sister Mara are living in the cloisters, honing their magic skills along with several other promising young apprentices." Pawllah added, "Your friends have been concerned about you. You've chosen your companions wisely."

"I don't think I've chosen any of them, except perhaps for Jayna. It seems to me we've all wound up together by default instead of choice."

"Your magic did the choosing," Pawllah replied simply.

Linden thought about Mara, Toz, and Remy. "Interesting choices."

"Perhaps, but each companion was chosen for a reason."

Linden arched her eyebrows skeptically. A smile flitted across Pawllah's face. "You remind me of Nari as a young woman. So skeptical and wary."

"And yet she walked right into the trap set by Rudlyn and Steehl."

Pawllah furrowed her already wrinkled brow. "Nari expected to be betrayed that night, which why she transferred her magic to you. Ever since the raid at Quorne, your safety has been her chief concern."

"But why? My parents got me out of Quorne within a couple of days."

"Your parents insisted you leave Quorne because they shared your grandmother's concerns."

"About living in the borderlands?"

Pawllah sipped from a glass of water. "What did your grandmother tell you about that Fallow sorcerer, Mordahn?" Linden repeated everything Nari had told her, including that Nari had once been betrothed to Mordahn, and that his father had killed Nari's parents.

"I'm not surprised Nari didn't tell you the rest of Mordahn's story," Pawllah said. "After Nari fled from him, and most Faymons reviled him for what his father had done, Mordahn isolated himself and his clan. He blamed his father for drawing first blood, which ultimately led to civil war. He took no sides, content to be left alone. More than a decade passed, and he eventually married one of the women from his clan, a cheerful woman who bore him a daughter. That little girl captivated Mordahn's heart. And so, for a time, he was happy."

"Then what turned him?"

"As the fighting among the clans escalated, the Faymons became more and more bloodthirsty. The low point came when your grandmother's clan attacked Mordahn's clan, burning everything in their path. Mordahn had been hunting with a small party and when he returned, his wife and daughter were dead. He wrapped himself in his pain and bitterness and grief, and his magic became darker. The darker it became, the more Mordahn lost himself inside it. He became bent on vengeance against Nari's clan.

"Mordahn never forgave her clan for killing his wife and daughter. He channeled his hatred, turning himself into a powerful warrior and master of Fallow magic. Over time, Mordahn sought to destroy not just the clan who destroyed his happiness, but he set his sights on the Serving Families of

Valerra, as well. His goal became the destruction of Serving magic wherever it exists."

"I can't believe a civil war that started fifty years ago could lead to all this."

"Not so hard to believe, when you mix pain, bitterness, and vengeance together. It's a recipe for despair. And why it's critical for you to become a master mage as soon as possible. You must be fully prepared for your mission."

"What do you mean, my mission?"

"You tell me. What do you want to do?"

"Find Stryker. Find a way to defeat Mordahn. Find my brother if he's still alive and bring him home." Then Linden remembered that Delavan was shielded and inaccessible, so she added, "Or somewhere safe."

"To accomplish that you're going to need help. A lot of help."

"I know. And I'm guessing you have something in mind."

"It's simple: complete your studies with me and then ask your companions—who'll become mages soon themselves—for their help."

"Mage Mother, please don't misunderstand me. I appreciate all that you've done for me—and for my friends. But I can't stay here for a long time, studying, while so many are suffering."

"It won't take long. Nari schooled you well. Give me sixty days of hard work, and you'll be a master mage."

"When will I get to see my friends?"

"In order to access my residence, your friends first will need to become mages themselves. I'd estimate it'll take them another six weeks or so. Probably a bit longer for the two young men. I recommend waiting to see your friends until everyone has completed their training. Fewer distractions all the way around."

Linden thought about the opportunity—perhaps the only

one she would have to become a master mage like her grandmother—and she nodded. "I'd be honored to complete my studies with you. And once I've completed them, I hope you understand that I'll have to leave."

Pawllah agreed. "Of course, you must leave. I'd expect nothing less from you." Calling to Magda, Pawllah said, "Please show our newest student to her quarters."

Linden bowed to Pawllah and waited for Kal to rouse himself from his nap. "Kal, are you coming?" she asked. Kal clicked his beak and buried his head inside one of his wings. Linden frowned, worried that Kal was sick. Pawllah chuckled and said, "Your griffin prefers to sleep in my quarters, it seems. Don't worry, you'll see him every day." Linden arched an eyebrow but followed Magda out of the room. Magda had already donned her cloak and paused while Linden pulled her long blue cloak off the coat hook and buttoned it up. Linden noticed Magda pulling on her gloves, so she did the same, wondering how far they'd have to walk to her new quarters.

When Linden stepped outside, the wind nearly knocked her over. Her hood blew back, and she pulled it more snuggly around her headscarf. She turned to ask Magda a question, but the other woman was already trudging uphill. Linden leaned into the wind, her face stung by small specks of ice swirling in the air, like tiny needles pricking her skin. Her legs ached with the effort, and she tried calling out once to Magda, to ask her to slow down, but her voice was carried away by the wind. Linden's heart sank when she came upon a sheer rock face and watched as Magda began scaling the wall. Linden drew closer and saw handholds and footholds in the surface of the rock. She put her right foot in the first hold, lifted her arms to grasp the handholds, and hauled herself up, grimacing with the effort. Linden thought perhaps they could have found more reasonable accommodations for someone who'd just woken from a coma. She was physically weak and emotionally drained, not in the best of shape to be mountain climbing. Linden grit her teeth and continued the climb, her legs and arms shaking with the effort. When she neared the top, her left leg gave way, and Linden yelped. Magda reached down and grasping her arms, pulled her up and over the precipice. Linden fell to her knees, panting, waiting for her pulse to return to normal. "How much farther?" she asked.

"We're almost there," said Magda cheerfully. She helped Linden to stand up and turned back to the path, which wound around the ice-covered mountain slope. Linden stayed as close as she could to the solid mountain on her left, because there was nothing but thin air on her right. As they continued to ascend, Linden slipped on the icy path and slid partly over the edge, her legs dangling.

Linden cried out, "I'm going over!" Magda came beside her in an instant, giving her a firm hand up. Linden's legs trembled as she stood on solid ground again. Too weary to thank Magda, she nodded, wondering why she'd agreed to study with Pawllah. If this was how the sisterhood treated its students, she wasn't sure she was interested in staying. As if reading her thoughts, Magda said, "The way gets easier, with time and practice."

Linden trudged along behind Magda, gingerly putting one white boot in front of the other, until they rounded the icy slope. Linden blew out a puff of air, grateful to step onto a level surface just below the mountain's peak. A tidy bright blue yurt sat tucked against the peak, well protected from the fierce gusts of wind buffeting them. *What was it with the color blue and Mage Mother Pawllah?*

Pointing, Magda said, "Here are your quarters. You'll find a pillow and plenty of blankets. Your magic will not work here, so use the blankets to keep warm. There's a sack inside containing crackers, jerky, and dried fruit, as well as a jug of water. You'll take your midday meal with Mage Mother Pawllah."

Magda turned to leave, but Linden put out her hand to stop her. "Wait, please. Will you return in the morning to help me get back to the Mage Mother's residence?"

Magda shook her head and said gently, "You're now training to become a master mage. You must find your own way to Mage Mother Pawllah each day. Be ready at daybreak and be sure to keep your sword close by." She handed Linden her sword and scabbard from the Valerran Museum, which Magda had been carrying inside her heavy cloak. Magda started to leave, but pausing, added, "Oh, I almost forgot. The way is always uphill." Then Magda turned and trudged quickly up the icy path, her footing steady and true.

The way is always uphill? Linden didn't know whether Magda meant that as a metaphor or as actual directions to Pawllah's residence. *How could the way always be uphill? It makes no sense.* Her teeth chattering, Linden scurried over to the yurt and stepped inside, grateful to be out of the wind. She secured the flap with ties and surveyed her new quarters. They were about as basic as any she'd seen, and just as Magda had described, a food sack, a jug of water, a large pillow, and a stack of blankets. Linden laid her sword down on top of the blankets and opened the food sack. After satisfying her hunger with dried berries and a piece of jerky, Linden sipped from the water jug. Pulling off her boots, she piled the blankets on top of herself and fell asleep to the sound of the wind whipping around the peak.

CHAPTER 26

"Sister Linden, it's time for your morning lesson."

Linden rolled over onto her back, yawning and rubbing her eyes. The voice calling to her from outside the yurt apparently thought she was taking too long to wake up. "Come now, lass, you need to rouse yourself. Mage Mother is very particular about keeping to the schedule."

Linden adjusted her headscarf. Untying the yurt's flap so she could poke her head through, she found an older man dressed in a long brown cloak, sitting on a rock that he'd dusted free of snow. The man's silver beard reached halfway to his waist, and a long silver braid, streaked through with blue, hung down his back. "I'm sorry, but I didn't know anyone would be arriving at, um," Linden saw the first few streaks of pink in the sky. "At sunrise. And I wasn't aware of the schedule. I'll be right out."

Linden strapped her sword around her waist, pulled on her boots and cloak, and stepped outside. Bowing, she waited for the man to introduce himself and explain the reason for his early morning visit. He hopped off the rock and bowed from the waist, his long braid swishing forward onto his shoulder. "I'm Brother Hume, here for your sword fighting lesson."

"Sword fighting?" said Linden. "But I'm supposed to be studying magic handling with Mage Mother Pawllah."

"Aye, you'll have plenty of time for your magic lessons. But we begin each day on Sanrellyss Island with physical activity. In your case, Mage Mother wants you to be practicing with your sword. May I see it?" The older man reached out his hand with a slight bow.

Linden tilted her head, not willing to hand over her sword to someone she'd just met, even if he were a monk. "Some other time, Brother Hume. Tell me, have you met any Valerrans on the island these past few weeks?"

Ignoring her question, Brother Hume frowned. "Why can't I see your sword?"

Linden reached inside her cloak to withdraw her sword, pulling it from its leather sheath. The sword glowed green, the hieroglyphs along the blade lighting up. "My sword only responds to my touch, and I'll not hand it over until Mage Mother vouches for you herself."

The old man chortled. "Mage Mother said you were no fool, and she's right about that." Drawing his bushy eyebrows together, he said, "You're right to never hand your sword over to anyone, regardless of how innocent the request may be, until you know beyond doubt they can be trusted. My brother, believing he was handing his sword over to a smithy for sharpening, died at the end of his own weapon."

"That's awful. I'm sorry to hear it."

Brother Hume nodded and withdrawing his sword, asked, "Are you ready?"

Linden looked at his sword, comprehension dawning. "You mean here, on top of a mountain? Isn't that a bit dangerous for practice?"

The monk smiled and pointed behind Linden's right shoulder. "There's a nice, flat field right over there."

Squinting at the old man, Linden shook her head. "I know what you're trying to do. I'm not going to lower my guard by turning around when I know very well there's nothing but my yurt and the mountain peak over there."

The monk grinned. "Well done. I can usually catch the newer mages with either the first trick or the second. All right, I'll lead the way over to the practice area. But first, would you mind getting me a drink of water from the jug inside your yurt?"

Linden still didn't know who Brother Hume was, or even whether Pawllah had sent him. Besides, he'd never answered her question about seeing any Valerrans on the island. If he lived in the monastery with the other monks, then he would have met Toz and Remy at some point during the past two months. She knit her brows together and shook her head. "Perhaps later, but for now, please lead the way."

Chuckling, Brother Hume said, "I'm impressed. You passed all three tests. You've demonstrated you have your wits about you. Now, let's see what you can do with that green sword of yours. Follow me."

Linden expected another tricky question from the monk, but instead he walked past her and kept on walking, right past Linden's yurt and onto a snow-covered field. Linden blinked, feeling slightly disoriented. Instead of standing near the mountaintop, she found herself at the base of the mountain, her yurt tucked snuggly against the rock wall she'd climbed the day before. Tipping her head back, Linden spotted the cloisters about two-thirds of the way up the mountain. Remembering Magda's words, she shook her head. *The way is always uphill.* Linden followed Hume onto the practice field and watched as he walked twenty paces away from her. Turning around, he flexed his legs and brought up his sword. "Sword up, Sister Linden. Let's begin."

"But we have no protective gear."

"Are you afraid you might get hurt?"

The old monk was beginning to wear on Linden's nerves. "No, I'm not afraid. Just surprised." She flexed her legs and gripped her sword, waiting to see what Hume would do. She didn't have long to wait. For an old man, he sprinted toward her with remarkable speed. Hume held his sword across his chest in a protective posture until he was nearly upon her, and then he swung his sword in a powerful arc, knocking Linden's sword out of her hand. His movements were so smooth and fast that Linden hardly registered she'd lost her sword. Hume used the tip of his sword to flip hers into the air and catch it in his left hand. Handing her sword back to her, he said, "Let's try that again. Now this time, I want you to charge me."

Linden trudged away, debating not for the first time what she was doing on Sanrellyss Island, and why she'd agreed to be tutored by Pawllah. She turned and faced Hume, who'd taken up the same posture and was waiting for her to charge. Linden preferred to bide her time in a fight, wait until the other party grew weary before she poured on a burst of energy. On the other hand, she was badly out of shape after two months in bed and needed as much physical exercise as Hume and Pawllah demanded.

Linden held her sword at her side and charged toward Hume. As she neared him, she slipped her sword under his, trying to knock it from his grip. However, the monk pirouetted around her and batted her sword away. Linden's sword landed in the snow. Hume once again used the tip of his sword to flip hers into his hand. Bowing, he returned her sword and said, "Again, only this time, stop holding back because I'm an old man. I may be old, but you're going to have to come through me if you want to start your magic lessons with Mage Mother.

Now charge me as if I were one of those grihms I keep hearing about."

Linden stalked away, frustrated she couldn't hold onto her sword for even five seconds against Hume. She charged again and again, Hume knocking her sword to the ground each time. On her ninth try, panting heavily, Linden looked at the silver-and-blue haired monk and thought: *I want my breakfast, and to ask Pawllah more questions, and to sit down near the fire. I want to become a master mage like my grandmother, and I want to surprise this crazy old monk by knocking that sword out of his hand. I'm going to have to do something different.*

Hume had a slightly quizzical expression on his face, as if he were wondering how much longer this first lesson was going to take. Linden's sword had turned a dull green, almost tarnished looking. She brought her sword up to her chest and recalled that moment on the roof of the museum, when the two grihms charged her. She remembered her grief and fury and magic, all flowing through her—from her hand to her sword—and she knew this time, she was going to drop Hume's sword. Shouting "Evakunouz!" she ran toward Hume, the hieroglyphs pulsing along her blade. As she neared the cagey old fighter, she pivoted to her left, because she'd noticed he favored his right leg slightly. She momentarily dipped below his line of vision, and in one fluid motion she popped up on his right side, thrusting her sword under his arm and punching his weapon out of his hand. Hume's sword landed in the snow. Linden used the tip of her sword to flip his sword into her left hand. Bowing, she handed it back to the old master.

Hume threw back his head, laughing heartily. "I can see I'm going to enjoy fencing with you, Sister Linden. Now off you go, to your lesson with Mage Mother. I'll see you tomorrow, same time." He added, as an afterthought, "I never did answer your initial question, because I knew you were trying to establish my bona fides. Brother Toz and Brother

Remy are somewhat undisciplined lads, but they're coming along nicely. Brother Carmine has them minding the goats every day. It's been good for them." Nodding, he turned around and headed across the snowy field toward his monastery. Linden tried to imagine Toz and Remy as goatherds and quickly gave up. Sighing, she started up the steep path to the cloisters. The wind howled around her, whipping her hood back from her head, and she slipped on the ice several times, but she kept climbing, the thought of a hot cup of tea spurring her forward.

Magda greeted her at the entrance to the cloisters, her red-and-blue hair mostly tamed under her headscarf. "You're right on time, Sister Linden, come on inside and warm yourself by the fire in Mage Mother's room."

Linden hung up her cloak and entered Pawllah's room, bowing to her ancient tutor. Kal padded over to her, clicking his beak happily. Linden gave him a hug and rubbed his fur. Considering his warm spot near the fire, instead of the chilly yurt she'd slept in the previous night, she whispered, "You chose wisely."

A small breakfast table and two chairs had been set up in front of the fire. Pawllah indicated the chair opposite her and said, "I'm sure you must be chilled. Please take a seat and help yourself to breakfast." Linden eagerly heaped bacon, eggs, toast, jam, and roasted potatoes onto her plate. She poured herself a cup of tea, added cream and sugar, and leaned against the chair back, the piping hot teacup feeling good in her chilled hands. Taking a sip, she set the cup down and devoured her breakfast.

After Linden's plate was clean and she'd moved onto her second cup of tea, Pawllah said, "Brother Hume tells me you did very well today. He's quite pleased."

Linden put her cup down on the saucer and shook her head. "I don't think I did very well today, not at all. But how did Brother Hume manage to get up that steep path faster than me, and without being seen?"

Pawllah winked and said, "We older mages have our ways." Linden pondered that and concluded Hume must have used magic to move around so quickly. She wondered whether he'd eventually teach her the spell. In the meantime, she'd have to get used to being outrun and outperformed. Nodding at Linden, Pawllah said, "Let's begin with your shape-shifting spells and any related counter spells. Please run through them, in any order you'd like."

Linden glanced around Pawllah's sitting room. Except for the burled hickory door leading to the hallway, and the peacock blue door leading to Sister Xavir's laboratory, bookcases and cabinets lined three of the walls. The fourth wall contained the fireplace and two windows. A pair of sofas and several armchairs occupied the center of the room. Without a lab table or other area for magic demonstrations, Linden hesitated. "Where would you like to me to conjure?"

Pawllah spread her hands and said, "Right here."

"But some of the spells are messy. And if I make a mistake, well, I could ruin something."

Pawllah shook her head. "I'm not worried."

Linden took a deep breath, knowing she could do this and feeling apprehensive all the same. Raising her hands, palms outward, she spoke the most basic shape-shifting incantation. She shifted the forks, knives, and spoons on the table into wafer-thin silver bookmarks, each retaining the delicate scrollwork that had decorated the tableware. Pawllah picked up one of the bookmarks and said, "This is quite lovely. A fine specimen." She saw Linden raising her hands to incant the counter spell. "Change the others, but I'd like to keep this one as a bookmark."

Linden nodded and adjusted her spell to reverse five of the six shifted items. Pawllah had a fork and a knife again, but her spoon remained a bookmark. Linden took a sip of tea, relieved her first spell worked as planned. She mentally ran through different shape-shifting spells, trying to determine which to exhibit next, when Pawllah said, "Please show me your fire-shifting spell, countered with a tightly controlled water-douser spell."

Linden compressed her lips, realizing she had to come clean, even though she'd ultimately gotten past the worst of her problems with Nari's help. However, Mage Mother Pawllah was now her tutor and had a right to know. Linden said, "Maybe I ought to forewarn you about my spells." As she recited a few of her challenges and downright disasters with fire shifting and water dousing, Pawllah chuckled merrily, thoroughly enjoying Linden's most embarrassing moments.

Pawllah's dark eyes crinkled at the corners. "Your stories bring back fond memories of my own disasters. I once set all my mother's freshly laundered clothes on fire, and by the time I used the counter spell, her clothes were charred and ruined. I'd waited too long to douse them before changing them back. My mother was furious. She wouldn't let me play with fire for a year after that."

Linden hadn't shared the part about setting her classroom on fire, but seeing how Pawllah understood about accidents, she told her. Pawllah actually giggled at Linden's story and wiped her eyes on her napkin. She asked, "What happened? Were you suspended from school?"

Linden shook her head and told Pawllah the entire story about the raid at Quorne, including seeing a grihm face-to-face and using the veil of drabness spell. Pawllah sobered quickly, and reaching across the table, she grasped Linden's hand. "Your magic, however unruly at the time, saved that little girl and you that day. I can assure you the average apprentice would not have been able to accomplish half so much." Pawllah added, a gleam in her eyes, "Now, let's see that fire-shifting spell of yours. How about shifting my door over there?"

Linden frowned at the hickory door, which she knew would flare up quickly if she didn't douse it immediately with water. Rising from the table and raising her arms, she carefully incanted the fire-shifting spell. "Shift from hickory door to flames so bright. Stop when burning true and right." The beautiful door burst into a fireball, its flames licking the white doorframe and stone flooring. Linden heard screams and shouts coming from the hallway.

She focused on the water-douser spell, wanting to get it exactly right, a perfect blend of dousing power with precision. She threw her arms in the direction of the flames, incanting the spell. "Water flowing through these hands, soak burning wood and fiery flames." Jets of water spouted from her fingertips and arcing over the sofas and chairs in the middle of the room, sprayed the door in a continuous stream until the fire was extinguished. Linden wrapped up with a cleansing incantation to remove the soot from the door, doorframe, and floor. She noticed some scorch marks etched into the hickory, but they seemed to add extra character rather than detract from the door's appearance, or at least she hoped that was how Pawllah and others would see it. Linden lowered her arms and sat down in her chair, her brow damp with perspiration.

The door burst open and Magda, her normally cheerful countenance scrunched with worry, ran into the room. "That fire gave me a scare. I didn't know whether to douse it myself or wait for Sister Linden to take care of it." Turning to Linden, she added, "A group of novitiates were walking past when the door burst into flame, causing a minor panic."

Pawllah smiled. "Yes, I'm to blame for that—I suggested the door. But Sister Linden had it well in hand."

Magda spotted the scorch marks but didn't comment on

them. "Hmm, well, I'll leave you to your lessons then." Bowing, she closed the door firmly behind her.

Turning to Linden, Pawllah clapped her hands and said, "Delightful! I'd almost forgotten how much fun it is to tutor a young mage. Don't worry about those scorch marks, I rather like them. Let's move on to protection spells, beginning with that veil of drabness you cast in Quorne."

By the time Linden climbed up to her yurt that night—it had shifted position back to the mountain's peak—she barely had enough energy to remove her boots and crawl under the blankets. She couldn't imagine another fifty-nine days of fencing lessons with Hume and magic lessons with Pawllah. She thought of a thousand ways she could fail and never become a master mage. As Linden dropped off to sleep, an image of her grandmother came to her. She could hear Nari telling her, in her no-nonsense way, to focus on the immediate obstacles and leave the future to take care of itself. Linden blew her a kiss before the image faded away.

Linden hadn't seen Jayna, Mara, Toz, or Remy since they'd crash-landed on the island four months earlier, although she received periodic updates from Magda. Everyone had finally achieved mage status—Remy had just been qualified the day before—and they were all arriving the next day for a "graduation" ceremony planned by Magda and the other sisters. The snows had receded from the foothills and meadows, which were dotted with white and yellow crocuses and daffodils.

Pawllah and Linden were enjoying a leisurely breakfast. Linden had completed her master-level training and moved back to the cloisters the day before, relieved to be sleeping in a bed again, if only for a short while. Pawllah asked, "Are you still planning to leave the island after the graduation ceremony?"

Linden nodded. "Yes. I'd like to wait until I've spoken with my friends and give them some time to think over whether they want to join me or stay here. In either case, I plan on leaving in a few days."

"Have you decided where you'll go?"

"To Faynwood, to search for Stryker. I realize he may not be there. I've tried finding him again using Sister Xavir's scope, but I haven't had any luck. Yet it's the only potential lead I have, and I feel drawn there."

Pawllah's black eyes took on a dreamy quality. Linden wondered whether the old woman was having a vision. "Faynwood is the right destination, but you don't have to worry about finding Stryker—he'll find you."

"How?"

"He'll find your family, and you'll be right there among them."

Linden shook her head. "But I don't have family in Faynwood."

"Oh, but you do, my dear Linden. You have countless family members living there," said Pawllah.

"I have that many relatives? Who are they?"

"Why the Faymons, of course."

"I understand my grandparents were from Faynwood, but do I have that many relatives?"

"Naturally. The Faymon Liege is considered the head of the family for all the people in Faynwood."

Linden went still. "What're you saying?"

"You are the Liege of Faynwood, and the clans are preparing for your arrival."

CHAPTER 27

L inden put down her fork and sputtered. "But, but... that's ridiculous! I'm not a ruler or a royal. I'm as unqualified as anyone I know." Linden peered more closely at Pawllah, who enjoyed a glass or two of blackberry wine with dinner each evening.

As if reading her thoughts, Pawllah said grumpily, "Don't look at me with that imperious stare of yours—I never have wine in the morning." And then more gently she added, "Why do you say you're unqualified?"

Linden ticked off the list on her fingers. "I hate giving speeches, cuddling little babies, christening buildings and boats, sending soldiers off to war, and generally ruling over anyone other than myself. And I have enough difficulty ruling over myself most of the time."

Pawllah laughed in her tinkling way and patted Linden's hand. "You've listed the duties of a typical Valerran royal. Let me tell you about the last Faymon Liege, who led her people until she perished in battle fifty years ago. She was stubborn, unruly, and opinionated, as well as beautiful, kind, and loyal. And her magic, well it was so volatile when she was a young girl that she set part of Faynwood on fire. Her mother despaired of her ever learning to control her magic, and her father despaired of finding anyone brave enough to court her." Pawllah paused.

"Go on."

"Well, she grew up and became a talented leader of her people and wed a man as stubborn and opinionated and kind as herself, a Faymon warrior from a neighboring clan. And together they had one child, a brilliant young woman, who managed to escape with her fay tutor during a deadly battle. That battle led to the civil war in Faynwood, which still rages on today."

"What happened to the young woman who escaped?" Linden asked casually, trying to appear disinterested in how the story ended.

"She fled to Valerra, where she became a powerful master mage in her own right and eventually married another refugee from the civil war. She had two sons who grew to become skilled mages and leaders. The younger son became a highly decorated colonel in the Valerran military and married a gifted woman from one of Valerra's Serving Families. Together they had two children, a boy and a girl."

"The boy followed in his father's footsteps, but he was injured during the war with Glenbarra. The girl, however, now that's an interesting tale. She's stubborn, unruly, and opinionated, and yet also beautiful, kind, and loyal. And she's fast becoming the most powerful master mage in generations, as powerful as her great-grandmother, Faymon Liege Ayala." Pawllah paused to nibble on a piece of scone.

"Nari was the young woman who escaped from Faynwood?" Linden half-asked and half-stated the question. Pawllah nodded and continued to look at Linden expectantly.

"And you were her tutor, weren't you?" Pawllah smiled shyly, acknowledging her part in the incredible story of Faymon survival.

"But why didn't Nari return to become the next Faymon Liege? Why wait for a new Liege until I came of age?"

"Liege Ayala heard rumors Fallow magic was taking root within Faynwood, in Arrowood, the westernmost province that shares a long border with Glenbarra. She and her husband rode to Arrowood to confront the clan chief, Mordahn's father, who killed them. After Ayala's death, which sparked the civil war, seers predicted we must wait until the third generation to crown a new Faymon Liege." Pawllah spread her hands, palms outward, "And here you are."

"How sad the Faymons have been fighting each other all these years," said Linden. Wondering out loud, she asked, "Who's been ruling the Faymon people since my great-grandmother's death?"

Pawllah smiled. "That's an excellent question for a future ruler to ask. Since the Faymons are ruled only by female Lieges, and no females of the ruling clan's line were available, tradition dictates that a male relative governs until the new Liege is crowned. The current Faymon Elder—that's his title—is one of your cousins, Reynier Arlyss."

Linden stood up and started pacing the room as a floodgate of memories opened: her mother taking her to the museum, where they would stand before the mosaics and her mother would tell her stories about the fays and Faymons who inhabited Faynwood; Nari teaching and drilling her, and telling her she had a destiny to fulfill; and her father, who'd tuck her into bed at night when she was young and whisper in her ear, 'Good night, my little Liege.'

Linden spun around and faced Pawllah. "Our home was ransacked—and my portrait stolen—during the raid on Quorne. Those Glenbarran troopers, who were under Mordahn's authority, were looking for me, to kill me, weren't they?"

Pawllah nodded. "Aye, they were, and it's a good thing they

didn't find you in the school at Quorne or at the museum during the siege, or you never would have escaped. You've been under the protection of many Faymons and Valerrans since the moment of your birth, and your own family has suffered greatly protecting your secret. Now it's my duty—and my privilege—to see you're safely delivered back to the Faymon clans."

Pawllah squinted her eyes, as if staring into the distance. "There's one more thing you must know before you leave here. It's about being a revelator." Linden waited for Pawllah to continue. "I've only known two other revelators, as they're extremely rare. One was your great-grandmother, Faymon Liege Ayala."

"And the other?" Linden wasn't sure she wanted to know the answer, but she wasn't surprised when Pawllah said, "And the other is Mordahn."

"Is that part of the reason why he's so powerful?"

"Aye, and also why he's been so good at tracking your whereabouts at Quorne and in Bellaryss. And he'll be tracking you again once you leave here. The only reason he hasn't attacked here is that Sanrellyss is completely shielded from anyone who practices Fallow magic."

Linden shivered at the thought of being tracked by Mordahn. She folded her arms and nodded. "Can his Fallow magic be defeated? My grandmother told me I wasn't strong enough yet."

"That was before you'd completed your studies. Of course you can defeat him, and you won't have to face him alone. Fallow magic responds to the whims of a single mage; Serving magic serves the needs of all. Fallow magic doesn't last."

Then Pawllah did an astonishing thing. She slowly levered herself out of her chair, and bowing deeply before Linden, she said, "I pledge my life, my home, and my mage's honor to my Faymon Liege, Linden Arlyss."

Linden was speechless. She helped Pawllah to stand upright

and kissed both her cheeks. She said softly, "I owe you so much —my family owes you so much—and I'm honored to call you my tutor and my friend." She must have said the right words, because Pawllah's face broke into a wide grin.

"As we've reached the end of our lessons together, and you'll be busy with your friends when they arrive, I'd like to give you my formal blessing now." Pawllah beckoned to Linden to sit back down and placed her hand on top of Linden's head.

Linden felt a tingling surge of energy course through her body. Pawllah closed her eyes, swayed gently, and then said in her commanding voice, "Linden Arlyss, you have many gifts, gifts of leadership, courage, friendship, charity, and pure magic. Of them all, your greatest gift is loyalty—to your family, your friends, and your people. You must discern and unite with all those who pledge themselves to defend Serving magic. Some will sow the seeds of insurgency against King Roi's reign, while others will reap the peace that follows. You, my Liege, will do both." Pawllah paused and then concluded with the mage's farewell blessing, "May your magic serve in peace and lead through service. This is the true path." Linden kissed and thanked the old mage who'd saved her grandmother all those years before and walked slowly back to her own room. She needed time to think before her friends arrived the following day.

Mara and Jayna threw their arms around Linden when they saw her. She had barely enough time to greet and hug her friends before everyone was whisked away by Magda, who was all business as she helped the graduates dress in full mage's regalia. They each wore long flowing robin's-egg blue robes with pointed sleeves and white rounded collars that dipped to a point in the back. Linden also wore a gold velvet beret perched at a saucy angle to indicate she had attained master mage status.

Pawllah, Magda, and all of the mages of Sanrellyss Island—both brothers and sisters—assembled on the front lawn of Pawllah's residence, which sat two-thirds of the way up the highest mountain on the island. Linden was touched by how much effort the mages had put into the graduation ceremony; they wanted to create a semblance of normalcy for her and her friends, who were refugees from their homeland, their pasts haunted by painful memories, their futures uncertain.

After speeches and a few stories about each of the graduating mages, including more than one funny mishap about Remy and Toz tending to the brothers' goats, everyone gathered within the inner courtyard of the cloisters, where a blue and white tent had been erected for the occasion. Scattered about were wooden tables laden with jugs of iced tea and blackberry wine, finger sandwiches, flaky pastries, cheese wheels, and dried fruits.

Pawllah stood up to say a few words. "I want to add my congratulations to those of the sisters and brothers. Each of you has accomplished much in the short time you've been here —we've been fortunate to have five such gifted and brave young people in our midst. Your actions during the siege of Bellaryss and your escape demonstrated remarkable courage, and the artifacts you saved were precious to the Valerran and Faymon cultures. It's been our pleasure to instruct you in the ways of Serving magic. Well done!"

After all of the guests made the rounds, congratulated the young mages, and said their goodbyes to Pawllah, Linden and her friends had some private time together. They went for a walk along the rocky hillside on which Pawllah's residence perched so precariously. When everyone had a chance to talk about their experiences over the past several months, and they had a few more laughs over Toz's imitation of Remy chasing down one of the errant goats, silence descended on the group.

"What're we going to do now?" Jayna asked.

"We know we can't go back home," said Remy.

"Each of us needs to decide for ourselves. Basically we have two choices: stay on Sanrellyss Island and serve with the mage community here, or head to Faynwood and align ourselves with the Faymon clans there to defeat Mordahn," said Linden.

There was a sharp intake of breath at the mention of the Faynwood. "Why do you think we'd be able to align with the Faymons? We know their reputation," Toz asked reasonably.

"Pawllah told me that since my grandparents were from Faynwood, my Faymon relatives would welcome us. And I have another reason to go—I'm fairly sure Stryker wound up there."

"So you plan to enter Faynwood, an unwelcoming place for outsiders, form an alliance with the Faymons, find Stryker if he's even there, and then go after Mordahn? Sounds crazy to me," said Mara.

"It *is* crazy, but it also seems right. Of course, it's up to you if you want to join me."

Mara looked intently at Linden and took a deep breath. "Crazy or not, I'm in."

"Me too. We've got to stop Mordahn, and we're going to need help from the Faymons to do it," said Toz.

"Is that what you really want?" Linden looked at Toz, who nodded. Then she looked at each of her friends.

"Look, I'm a lover not a warrior," said Remy. Everyone groaned. "It's true. But if I stay here, Brother Carmine is going to make me herd goats forever. The only reason I studied as hard as I did was to get off this island. If I have to kick Mordahn's butt while I'm at it, that's fine by me." Linden shook her head and laughed.

"I want to be able to go back home someday," said Jayna. "I miss everything about home."

"So many Valerrans lost their lives—I dream of them sometimes," whispered Mara, and then she added in a stronger voice. "I want to fight back."

"Then I think we've got a plan: go to Faynwood, locate my Faymon relatives—and Stryker if he's there—and enlist their help in standing up to Mordahn."

"There sure are a lot of 'ifs' in this plan," said Remy with a sigh.

"How'll we get to Faynwood?" Toz asked.

"I'll ask Mage Mother Pawllah for her help."

"When're we leaving?"

"How about the day after tomorrow?" Linden waited and everyone nodded.

The full moon shone brightly through Linden's window blinds, casting stripes of light across her bed. She tossed and turned, trying to sleep, but finally threw off her covers, slipped into a dressing gown, and went outside. Kal opened one eye and rolled onto his other side.

Perched on one of the rock formations that dotted the hillside, Linden stared up at the night sky and studied the constellations Nari taught her when she was a child. She wanted to put her sadness behind her. If she'd learned anything under Pawllah's guidance, it was to cherish the memories of her loved ones while at the same time focusing ahead. Yet when she thought about the future, she couldn't think about it with any clarity.

Linden begged Pawllah not to tell anyone—especially her friends—that she was the Faymon Liege-in-Waiting. She still found it nearly impossible to believe herself. And the last thing Linden wanted was to be teased by her friends about being a ruler, and being a Faymon ruler made it all the more laughable, given that many Valerrans believed the Faymons to be vain, tricksome people with little regard for anyone outside of Faynwood. The fact that they were gifted mages and seers also created resentment among some of their less gifted neighbors.

In less than two days, she and her friends would be leaving the safety of Sanrellyss Island and heading deep into Faymon territory. They'd spent several hours that afternoon discussing various preparations and divvied up their duties. Linden was responsible for transportation, for arranging it and ensuring they had safe passage through Faynwood. She planned to discuss it with Pawllah and Magda in the morning. In the meantime, she sought to quiet her mind, using the many techniques she'd learned as a master mage. She sighed, realizing she was trying too hard.

"Are ye 'aving trouble sleeping, mum?"

Linden started and turned toward the voice. "The full moon is making me restless." She peered around but saw no one.

"Ah, so it's the moon that you're blaming, mum?"

"I suppose I'm already restless, and the full moon isn't helping." Linden frowned at being called 'mum.' It was not a term generally applied to young women. "Who are you? And, where are you?"

A short, stout man in a peaked cap stepped out from behind another rock formation. The pungent smell of pipe smoke wafted on the breeze. Doffing his cap, the man's blue-streaked brown hair tumbled out. He bowed low and introduced himself. "M'apologies. Cap'n Raffindor, at yer service, mum. Though m'friends call me Raff."

"Good evening, Captain...Raff." Linden said. "Are you having trouble sleeping as well?"

Raff guffawed. "Still early for me, mum. I only need a few 'ours a sleep, so I'm having me evenin' walk an' smoke before turnin' in."

"I wish I could say the same. I need my sleep and find myself wide awake tonight. Too much on my mind, I suppose."

"Aye, m'Liege, 'tis no surprise."

"How do you—" Linden stared at the man.

"Come now, mum, all the fays and Faymons on this island know yer true nature."

"I see," said Linden, shifting around on her rock-seat. She didn't relish the thought that everyone on the island seemed to know her true identity, while she could hardly believe it herself. "I'd hoped to keep it a secret, at least for now."

"Of course. Keeps things simple, like." Raff nodded sagely. "When do yer want to depart?"

Linden was surprised again by Raff. "Day after tomorrow. Why?"

"Why I'm yer Cap'n, mum! I'll be sailing t'ship that takes us t'Faynwood. Lookin' forward to it, I might add. Haven't seen some a'me kinfolk for a spell." Raff removed the pipe from his mouth and tapped it against the side of a rock. He pocketed the pipe in one of the many pockets of his voluminous coat, and then indicating the rock opposite Linden, he asked, "May I?"

"Of course."

Raff settled himself and said, so gently that his words seemed to float in the breeze, "Fear not, young Liege."

"Why do you think I'm afraid?"

"'Cause ye jus' learned yer Liege o' the Faymons, and ye've left all else behind ye. Anyone'd be fearful, mum."

Without acknowledging her fears, she asked, "And what advice do you have for me?"

"Press on. No peace comes from lookin' behind ye, and no amount of scurryin' keeps the future at bay."

"My sentiments exactly," smiling, Linden inclined her head at Raff. "Captain Raff, I believe we'll get on well. Now, when I can get a glimpse of that ship of yours?"

Raff pulled out his pipe and began refilling it as he spoke. "She's in dock on t'other side o' the island, gittin' her final prep a'fore the trip. She'll be ready an' waitin' on ye mornin' after tomorrow."

Linden sincerely hoped it was a reliable sort of transportation but thought it rude to ask. She was getting sleepy and stifled a yawn. "Well, it's been a pleasure, Captain. I'm off to my room. I'll see you at sunrise day after the morrow."

"Aye mum," Raff bowed and faded into the shadows.

CHAPTER 28

The morning of their departure dawned clear and chilly. Linden rose well before sunrise, too excited to sleep, and slipped into a long-sleeved teal blue traveling dress that the sisters had made for her. She carried a teal shawl, also made by the sisters, which she'd need once she stepped outside. Pawllah, Magda, and Raff joined the travelers for a breakfast of omelets, brown spelt toast, rashers of bacon, pomegranate juice, and strong black tea.

After breakfast, Pawllah gave her blessings to the group and hugged each of them. When she reached Linden, she whispered softly in her ear, "Serving magic will lead you, my Liege. This is the true path." She slipped *Timely Spells* into Linden's hands. Linden kissed the old woman's wrinkled brown cheek and murmured, "This is the true path." Pawllah had nursed her, tutored her, and loved her when she most needed it. She'd miss her.

After that Raff took over, directing his crew to carry the supplies, trunks, and knapsacks supplied by the sisters down the hill to one of the waiting carts. One of the trunks contained the ensorcelled weapons the group had obtained in the Valerran Museum, since Pawllah pointed out they were now the rightful owners of the swords. Magda handed Raff a small leather trunk, which he carefully stowed with the other belongings. Raff led Linden and her friends down the sloping hillside to the last cart, lined with wooden benches on each side. They climbed in and tried to make themselves comfortable. Raff jumped onto the driver's seat, picked up the reins, and set a brisk pace as they followed the supply cart down to the harbor. Kal flew in figure eights overhead, dipping low over their cart and then soaring up into the sky. As they rounded the hillside, Raff shouted proudly, "Thar she is, ladies 'n gents, that's the Aurorialyss. Ain't she a beaut!"

There was a collective gasp from everyone in the cart. The ship was shaped like a giant swan, including a long, graceful neck that curved upwards into a perfectly rendered swan's head at its bow. The ship was painted to look like a swan too; white and gray paint had been applied in layers to create the appearance of feathers, including a pair of wings that seemed to fold into the sides of the ship. The head had two black eyes that overlooked a large beak at the tip. Each of the masts sported large, billowing sails that were sky blue with white puffy clouds scuttling across them.

Linden and the others murmured their appreciation, although she could tell some of their earlier enthusiasm was muted. She understood why: it was the strangest ship she'd ever encountered, and she wondered whether it was even seaworthy. She trusted Pawllah, though, so she smiled at Raff and told her how impressive it all was. Raff beamed, started to bow but catching Linden's eye, he nodded. Once they arrived at the dock, he ushered them onboard the ship and began shouting orders. Raff's crew intrigued Linden. Most were Faymons, easy to spot with their blue-streaked hair, but there were also a few Valerrans and one feline crossbreed named

Orlette. Before long, the Aurorialyss left the harbor behind and sailed into the light blue waters of the Pale Sea.

The water was calm and the sails full, so the ship made good time the first day. That evening, Linden and her friends dined with Raff and his first mate, Evaleah, a tall, ebony-skinned Valerran with a single braid of dark hair hanging down her back and a patch over her left eye.

Linden was surprised by the variety and flavor of the captain's fare—the ship's cook prepared lightly seasoned whitefish, roasted root vegetables, fresh herb salad, and crusty brown bread, served with mulled wine. Over dessert, a spice cake coupled with strong coffee, Linden thanked Raff for his hospitality, which he waved away with one callused hand. Then she asked the question on everyone's mind. "We've heard the currents are unpredictable this far north. What's your best guess for when we'll reach the coast of Faynwood?"

Raff pulled out his pipe, and noticing Mara's wrinkled nose, hastily pocketed it again. "Well, mum, 'tis a mite unpredictable like. Anywhere from two days to two weeks."

"Two weeks at sea!" Mara exclaimed, "But Sanrellyss Island isn't that far from the Faynwood coastline." She turned to Evaleah, who shrugged and said, "Captain's right. Depends on the currents. And of course, once we leave the protective shields cast by the sisterhood around the island, and as far out as their magic will carry, well then, it's anybody's guess."

"So you're saying it's a matter of natural and magical forces?" Jayna asked.

"Always is when you're traveling near Faynwood. I wouldn't worry too much. The only time we've run into any real trouble is when we've been ferrying folks with powerful enemies on their tails. Doesn't seem to be a concern here, though."

Everyone at the table, except for Raff and Evaleah, dropped their eyes, until Toz cleared his throat. "Well, that's not exactly accurate.

"What's not exactly accurate?" Evaleah raised her right eyebrow.

"We have powerful enemies," Toz replied.

"Although we lost them in the mists when we headed east over the Pale Sea, before we crash-landed on Sanrellyss Island some months ago." Remy hastened to add.

"I'm sorry Evaleah, I thought you knew we've been on the run since we left Valerra," Linden said quietly.

Raff intervened. "Evaleah knows Valerra is in th' grips 'a Mordahn's thugs. What she didn't know was th' part you 'n yer friends played in defendin' the capital fer so long." He glanced at Evaleah. "Yer's in the presence of heroes, matey. And heroes like these young folks sometimes make powerful enemies."

Evaleah stood up abruptly. At first Linden thought she had taken offense and was leaving the table. Instead, she bowed deeply and said, "Come what may, I'm honored to serve with any who survived the siege of Bellaryss and escaped to tell of it."

"All of us on the Aurorialyss are honored to serve with you." Raff added as he rose. The others stood as well. "Best be getting some shut eye while's we can. We'll have th' sisters' protection for a few hours yet. Let's use it t' bunk down a bit."

"I'll supervise first watch, Captain," Evaleah said, saluting before she turned to head above deck, her long braid swishing behind her as she walked.

Raff guided his guests to the lower deck, where the girls shared a large stateroom and the boys shared a separate cabin. Linden had trouble falling asleep and opened *Timely Spells*, curious to see what would translate. One new spell appeared: an incantation for unbinding magic. She turned the spell over in her mind until she dozed off, waking up a few hours later to a squawking foghorn that blared throughout the ship.

"What on earth can that be?" Mara asked grumpily. "It's the middle of the night."

289

"Remember what Raff said?" Jayna replied. "We have—or had—a few hours left under the sisters' protection."

"So what? Can't we just go back to sleep?"

The entire shipped lurched to one side as if it were rolling over. Another wave hit and the ship lurched to the other side. There was a loud knock on their stateroom door that Linden hopped out of bed to answer. A young deck hand, a boy no more than nine, stood before them, his wet blonde-and-blue hair plastered to his head and his slicker dripping on the floor.

Linden opened the door wider. "Please, come inside and dry off, Mister...what's your name?"

He shook his head, his eyes wide in alarm. "Me name's Fen, but no thank ye, mum. Raff's sent for ye—all of ye—to come help above deck."

"What can *we* do, young man?" Mara asked primly.

"'Tis Fallow magic, mum. We need Serving mages to help us fight back. Ship's takin' on water and Raff says the wind's too wild fer us to last long."

Linden whirled into action. She threw a rain slicker on over her nightgown and thrust her feet into boots. "Show us the way!" Jayna and Mara followed behind, hastily grabbing slickers as they clambered after Linden and Fen. As they neared the main deck, Jayna shouted above the roaring wind, "What about the boys?"

"They're already helping out, but their magic's not strong enough."

Before he opened the door to the main deck, Fen put out his hand to stop Linden. "Just a minute, mum. Each of ye must wear one." He looped a belt forged of heavy brass links around each girl's waist, and then left a long piece of the chain dangling down to their feet, with a latch on the end. "What's this?" asked Jayna. "Won't it slow us down?"

Fen strapped on his own chain belt. "This'll keep us from washing overboard, mum," he yelled over his shoulder as he struggled to open the door. Linden helped him and together they pulled it open and were lashed by the rain. Fen reached up and attached his belt to a pulley system that ran the length of the ship, and then latched each of the girls as well. Linden hadn't noticed the pulley system the evening before, so she thought it might have been rigged up after they turned in for the night.

Fen guided them down the center of the main deck to where Toz and Remy were attempting to start another round of incantations as a large wave rocked the ship, soaking all of them. The surge of water knocked Linden off her feet and sent her skidding across the deck. Thankful the chain around her waist held, she got to her feet and shouted above the wind, "Quick, grab each other's hands—we need to start a counter-wave reaction that's powerful enough to calm these seas." Mara and Jayna grabbed Linden's hands, and the boys joined them in a tight circle.

Fen stepped up and joined them as well. "I'm an apprentice, mum, an' know m'spells for sea-farin'." The Aurorialyss rocked and creaked beneath them, the waves continuing to pound the ship. "She can't take much more a' this!" Fen yelled as another wave sent the ship rolling once again.

Linden shouted in her commanding voice, "In peace and quietude do we work!" The waves continued, but their power seemed to abate somewhat. She spoke above the roaring water, but no longer had to shout. "We're going to cast a plowing spell."

Toz said, "You're the master mage, so have at it."

Linden nodded and started the incantation, which the others took up, repeating the words of the spell, "Curl watery waves into a trough, and let this ship plow all the way through!" They focused so hard their hands began to feel warm. Gradually, the action of the waves slowed and then, finally, the waves seemed to curl backwards, reversing their trajectory, and creating a watery path, almost like a river, for the Aurorialyss to plow its way through to the coast. Linden concluded with a binding incantation to hold the plowing spell in place, and everyone finally dropped their hands and stepped back. Fen unhooked each of them from the overhead pulley system and stowed the brass chain belts.

"Thank ye for savin' the Aurorialyss," said Raff as he joined them, having given command of the bridge over to Evaleah. He doffed his hat and bowed, and with a twinkle in his eye he added, "Always a pleasure t'have mages onboard."

"We were likely the cause of all this," Linden spread out her hands to indicate the shredded sails above them and the bits of wood and debris all over the deck, which was already being swept up by the crew.

Raff shook his head. "'Tis nothing that can't be mended. Besides, if these currents you spelled for us hold, we'll be making land in two more days."

"We'll make sure it holds," Mara said over her shoulder. Clutching her stomach, she dashed over to the side of the ship and retched. Jayna put an arm around her and helped her below deck.

"Mara's right," Linden said. "We'll need two mages on deck at all times to reinforce the plowing spell. I'm wide-awake and volunteer to take this watch."

"Me too," Fen piped up eagerly.

Remy and Toz mumbled their thanks and stumbled off to their cabin, clearly drained and a bit seasick themselves. One of the deckhands brought over two chairs so that Linden and Fen could sit next to each other. Linden periodically repeated the plowing spell and Fen echoed it. They continued this way for a while, until Fen began fidgeting in his chair and taking sneak peeks at Linden sitting next to him.

Sensing he had something on his mind, Linden said, "You can speak freely with me, Fen."

Fen nodded. "Thank ye." He took a deep breath, "Well, I suppose I'd best be out w'it." Fen paused and whispered, "I pledge allegiance to m'Liege and by t'way, we're cousins." Fen nodded solemnly.

Linden looked at him, her eyebrows drawn together. "Who told you?"

Fen shifted his gaze. "I overheard Cap'n telling Evaleah who ye really were—and why we had to keep ye safe."

"I see. And about being my cousin?"

"Now that's a bit more complicated. See, my great grandma was married to yer great grandpa's half-brother, and they had one child, my mum."

"Ah," said Linden with a smile, although she gave up trying to figure out whether Fen was a second or third or fourth cousin.

Fen smiled back happily, and they watched the sunrise, the sky and water turning pinkish gold along the horizon. A much refreshed-looking Remy and Toz relieved them later in the morning. As Linden turned to go below deck, she thanked Fen for his help and reminded him that she didn't want her identity widely known just yet. Fen nodded and looking wiser than his years, replied, "Of course, mum, yer friends won't really understand until we're amongst our own kind. Then all will be clear."

Surprised at his words but too tired to think more about them, Linden donned a fresh nightgown and tumbled into her cot, Kal clicking his beak on the floor nearby. Grateful to be safe for the moment, she refused to speculate about finding the Faymon clans of Faynwood, and what her friends would say when they finally learned the truth about her Faymon heritage.

CHAPTER 29

The next two days brought calm seas—so long as Linden and her friends took turns maintaining the plowing spell—and on the morning of the third day, Fen, who had climbed up to the crow's nest for a better look, shouted "Land ahoy!" A cheer went up from the deck and the crew began bustling about.

Evaleah scanned the heavily wooded coastline through her scope as the ship approached. Pausing to refocus, she brought the scope back up to her good eye and then hollered across the deck, "Troopers, I see Glenbarran troopers lining the shore! Turn her about, mates. Let's get some distance between us and the coast." Deckhands scrambled about, shouting orders, throwing ropes, and adjusting the massive sails.

"Incoming!" yelled Fen from his perch in the crow's nest, "They're firing on us!" Flaming arrows began flying at the Aurorialyss. Several landed on the deck, sparking into flame, as deckhands scrambled to douse the fires with buckets of water.

"Quick," Linden stopped one of the deckhands, "Summon the other mages." She and Toz stood on the main deck, maintaining the plowing spell while the others were still resting down below.

"We need to switch to a defensive spell," Linden shouted above the din around them.

Toz nodded. "But we won't be able to hold it long without the others."

"We can start by defending just the port side, which is facing the shore." Linden replied as she started the incantation. "Shield of water protect this boat, defend with strength against onslaught." Toz joined her, and the waters on the ship's port side began to rise in a kind of frothy wall—just in time, as they were pelted with a shower of fiery arrows that hit the shield of water rather than the ship itself and fell harmlessly into the sea.

"Brilliant," said Mara as she ran over with Jayna and Remy to multiply the power of Linden's spell.

"Let's raise the water-wall higher, to protect the masts and young Fen up there," Linden called out.

The five mages joined hands together, focusing on raising the wall of water all around the ship. The ship rocked, snug in its watery cocoon, and Linden thought they might be out of danger when a dense black cloud formed above their heads. The cloud reformed itself into a misty rope that lassoed the wall of foaming sea surrounding the ship, collapsing their safety net in an enormous wash of water over the deck. A loud crack rocked the ship. Looking over her shoulder, Linden's heart skittered. Grapple hooks lined the ship's starboard side, and grihms were loping across from a looming, creaking hulk of wood and iron and sooty gray sails that had broadsided the Aurorialyss.

"It must be Mordahn and his Fallow spells," yelled Fen, who shimmied down from his perch.

"Starboard! Swords drawn!" Raff bellowed to the crew.

Evaleah grabbed a rope from the bridge and swung down,

knocking two grihms overboard and running a third through with her sword. The deck swarmed with grihms and Glenbarran troopers, ship's crew and mages, their axes, swords, and daggers flashing in the sunlight. Screams, grunts, and cries competed with the clang of metal on metal and the hiss of blade on flesh.

Linden drew her sword as one of the grihms zeroed in on her. Wavering when he saw the blade pulsing with green hieroglyphs, he swiped at her with his ax. Linden leapt aside, her blade slicing the grihm's arm. Yelping, he transferred his ax to the other hand and swung again. As Linden's sword smacked into the grihm's ax, he was thrown backwards onto the deck. Picking himself up, the grihm attacked again.

Linden pivoted, lunging at the grihm and stabbing his other arm. Screeching, the grihm charged her on all fours, baring his canines and knocking her over, her sword falling to the deck. He snapped his powerful jaws, his breath hot on her face. She curled up defensively, covering her head with her arms, waiting for the jaws to clamp around her neck. But the grihm screamed, arched his back, and toppled over, as Fen reached down to help her up with one hand while holding the grihm's bloodied ax in his other. Linden grabbed her sword, her thanks on her lips, when a brawny trooper grabbed Fen from behind and tossed him overboard.

"Fen!" Linden cried, bringing her sword up in both hands. She noticed the grihms and other Glenbarrans continued fighting but managed to clear a space around the large man who'd tossed Fen. He pounced on Linden, his sword whooshing past her head. Linden ducked, sidestepped, and swept upwards with her sword, but the trooper flashed past her, swinging again and this time cutting her left arm. Linden hissed in pain and took a deep breath. She had to react like Brother Hume had taught her.

Screaming a war cry, she charged the other man, her blade

blazing green. He hesitated a fraction of a second, just long enough for Linden to pirouette to his left side and punch out with her sword, jabbing him in the thigh. The trooper cried out in anger and spun around to face her, favoring his left leg. *Good, now we're more evenly matched.*

He jogged toward her, more slowly this time, and lunged. She parried and danced out of his way. Screeching in frustration, he rotated around on his good leg and thrust his sword at her right flank. Linden hopped out of the way in the nick of time, the blade whipping past her abdomen.

The man charged her again, his sword movements quick and deadly, despite his injured leg. He stood over a foot taller and used his size to his advantage, jabbing the point of his blade at her face and neck to distract her. Linden found herself parrying blow after blow, just to keep herself from serious injury. He maneuvered her with his swordplay, backing her toward the side of the ship.

Narrowing her eyes, Linden looked for a distraction. One of the grihms dropped his ax nearby, and it clattered to the ground. The man's eyes flitted down momentarily, and Linden used that instant to scuttle away from the ship's side, out of the reach of his sword.

The trooper withdrew a dagger from his belt and flung it at Linden, hollering an incantation that crackled in the air. She cast a hasty protection charm, but the dagger flew true, punching its way through her right side and puncturing her lung. She screamed as she pulled out the knife, the pain searing hot. Her breathing became more labored, but she brought up her sword, ready for one more bout.

The man laughed, a mirthless sputtering noise that made Linden's insides turn cold. Taking in his powerful build and shoulder-length brown hair, lightly salted with blue, she frowned. He was a Faymon fighting as a Glenbarran, but this couldn't be Mordahn—the man looked to be thirtyish—and yet a part of her recognized him as the sworn enemy of every Serving mage.

He'd clearly grown tired of the swordplay and snapped his fingers, conjuring a powerful spell that bound her arms at her sides, her sword dangling uselessly from her right hand. As he squeezed the magical bonds tighter, Linden dropped to her knees, gasping for air.

Toz spotted her distress and yelled, "Linden! I'm coming!" but Mordahn spun up a privacy shield so that no one else could enter the fighting circle. With the hilt of his sword, Toz banged on the transparent grayish dome surrounding Linden and Mordahn, worry lines creasing his brow as he yelled Linden's name. A grihm zeroed in on Toz from behind, and he had to turn away to fend off his attacker.

As Linden struggled to breathe, Mordahn began to laugh. "What's wrong, little mage? Expecting someone else?"

She squinted and looked into his flat, expressionless eyes, and she saw the eyes of an old man, an old sorcerer who practiced Fallow magic. "You've won. You've defeated Valerra, destroyed the Serving Families. What more do you want?"

His mouth twisted as he spat out, "To finish what I started. Nari Arlyss's clan will never rise again."

Scenes of death and destruction wrought by this man flashed through her mind, as if she were peering through the electromagnetic insight scope again. "Despite your Fallow spells to reverse aging, you're still an old man. And old men die, just like everyone else," she rasped.

Mordahn sneered. "Same self-righteous streak as Nari. Enough chit chat."

All around her, Linden's friends and ship's crew battled the Glenbarrans, the two sides fairly evenly matched. She had no clear sense of who would come out the victor, and she could do nothing to help her friends. She had to focus on Mordahn, keep him talking as she tried to figure out how to break the invisible chains that held her.

"What are you afraid of? It must be something that really scares you, haunts your dreams even, otherwise you'd not hunt me down like this."

"Nothing scares me. Nothing can touch me anymore," grunted Mordahn.

Linden squinted at him, meeting his glower. She had a flash of insight, a vision of a brighter future, one free of Fallow magic. She knew, with the gift of foresight, that she had a role to play in that future. Like her, Mordahn was a revelator—a powerful mage and seer. She reasoned that he must have seen that same vision as well, perhaps many times before the raid at Quorne.

"You fear the future. You've seen me there, haven't you? You know that Serving magic will bind your dark magic in the end."

Mordahn's voice sizzled like heat lightening. "Brave words for a little mage, on her knees, breathing her last."

Linden squared her jaw and said through gritted teeth, "I'm on my knees but I'll be breathing long after you're in the ground." Linden drew on the indwelling power of ancient magic, of her Faymon clan and fay spirits long since gone, and uttered the incantation for unbinding from *Timely Spells*. "Serving magic run true and free, unbind this Fallow sorcery!"

Mordahn's Fallow magic withered. Like dead vines falling to the ground, the magical chains holding her were unbound. She climbed to her feet. Clutching her right side where the dagger had punched through, she pointed her sword at Mordahn, charging him with all the remaining energy she had left.

Their blades collided, their magic exploding into a mass of green and gray sparks that rained around them, melting Mordahn's privacy shield, and burning skin and fur and wood. The sound of blades clanging and sparking, grihms yelping, and men and women shouting, rang in Linden's ears. She recalled Stryker's letter to her, describing one of the battle scenes he'd witnessed in the borderlands, and the thought of him gave her a burst of adrenaline.

Linden met Mordahn's every lunge and pivot and thrust, her sword's hieroglyphs shimmering as she struck back with equal force. They met each other, blow for blow, and she could sense his energy beginning to flag. "Time to end this!" yelled Mordahn. He sprinted toward her, sword outstretched, aiming for her heart. She sidestepped left, and swept up, batting his sword away and sending it clattering to the deck. She was too weak to press her advantage and Mordahn snatched up his sword again.

Roaring in frustration, Mordahn leaped in the air, sweeping his sword from side to side, trying to cleave Linden in half. She dropped to her knees to avoid his killing blow and clasped her sword in front of her defensively, the blade pointed up toward the sky. As Mordahn's sword swept over her head, a projectile of fur and wing and beak hurtled toward Mordahn's knees. Mordahn tripped, falling on top of Linden's sword. She pushed him away as he fell, and he toppled onto his back, her sword stuck fast in his chest.

Wheezing heavily, her lung collapsing inside her, she rose to her feet shakily. His eyes clouded with pain, Linden watched as Mordahn's thick brown-and-blue hair thinned and grayed, and his face and body shrank in on itself, his muscles shriveling with age. As the skin on his face sagged and his eyes hollowed, he looked closer to seventy years old than thirty.

The grihms, sensing the demise of their master, jumped back across to their own ship, and the troopers who were still standing followed them. Linden noted there didn't seem to be much loyalty among the followers of Fallow magic.

Mordahn moved his lips. "This is not the end."

"Perhaps not, but you'll not be rising again."

Mordahn rasped with his last breath, "You have much to learn. There are others."

Raff reached Linden first. Pulling her sword out of Mordahn's chest, he wiped it off and handed it back to her. She numbly accepted it and shoved the sword back in her scabbard. Kal leaned against her legs protectively, as if Mordahn would try to harm her again. She reached down to pat Kal's back and whispered, "You just saved my life. How can I ever thank you?" Kal rubbed his head against her leg.

Raff's crew, led by Orlette, boarded Mordahn's wood and iron hulk and surrounded the grihms and troopers. The grihms seemed fascinated by Orlette, who hissed them into submission. She took command of Mordahn's ship, which they would use to transport the prisoners to Faynwood. The Glenbarrans who'd been firing on them from the coastline had fled—or perhaps they'd been captured. In any case, they were gone.

Linden looked around for her friends. Toz, bleeding from a cut on his neck, leaned heavily on Remy, who was streaked with blood. Jayna's clothes were scorched and her nose was bleeding, but she seemed fine otherwise.

"You're bleeding from your arm and your side," said Jayna. "Let's get you down to the healer right away."

Linden swayed slightly but shook her head. Scanning the deck, she asked, "Where's Mara?"

"She jumped overboard after Fen," said Remy.

Then Linden remembered that Fen had been tossed overboard and closed her eyes. She couldn't bear to lose Mara and Fen. Not now that Mordahn was finally dead. "Any sign of them?"

"We've been searchin' for 'em," said Raff.

"We've got to find them," said Linden, grimacing at the effort it took for her to take a simple breath.

"Aye, mum, but it's a large sea."

CHAPTER 30

L inden leaned over the ship's rail, searching the water for any sign of Fen and Mara. As the minutes passed with still no sighting, Raff walked over to her and shook his head.

"No, we're not leaving. We can't." She'd never have believed it six months earlier, if someone had told her that she and Mara would become friends, but she couldn't imagine continuing without her. She wasn't giving up on Mara, nor on young Fen, her third-or-fourth-or-whatever cousin and probably greatest fan.

"Aye, but they won't survive much longer in these chilled waters."

Linden didn't answer. Dizzy with blood loss and wincing with every breath, she'd lost the feeling in her hands and feet. She'd been drenched along with everyone else when the cold wall of water collapsed on the deck. The wind had picked up, whipping her hair around her head and raising goose bumps beneath her damp gown.

Evaleah squinted through her scope and let out a whoop. "I think I see them, Captain." Raff turned the ship toward two tiny specks bobbing in the waves. When they got closer, he let down a skiff with a couple of sturdy deckhands to pluck Mara and Fen out of the water. As the deckhands lifted Mara to a stretcher, Linden squeezed her friend's hand. Teeth chattering and in shock, Mara and Fen were ferried immediately to the healer's quarters below deck.

Relieved they were safe, Linden turned her attention to everyone else. "How'd your crew fare, Captain?"

"Four of me mates are gone, mum, and three sorely wounded. Pretty much everyone 'as cuts and scrapes, but we'll mend."

"We never should have boarded your ship." Linden spread out her uninjured arm to indicate the burned deck and singed masts, the bloodied crew, and the bodies—friends and foes falling where they died—scattered on the deck. She couldn't believe she'd been the cause of all this destruction.

Raff removed his cap and said softly, "'Tis war, m'Liege."

"I'm sorry, for all of it." Linden coughed, spitting up blood. Her legs gave out and she dropped to her knees, pitching forward onto the wooden boards of the deck. Kal squawked and flapped his wings.

Raff flagged down Evaleah. "Give me a hand, we need to carry this lass to th' healer right away! She's turning blue."

Linden closed her eyes, too weak to do more than draw a ragged breath. Raff and Evaleah lifted her from the deck and carried her down the steps. With so many injured, the ship's healer had run out of space to work and they laid Linden on her bunk inside the stateroom. Raff retrieved the healer, who took one look at Linden's blue lips and said, "Her lung's collapsed. Grab my kit." A few minutes later, Linden felt something sharp puncturing her side and screamed. As the healer suctioned out the air inside her rib cage, Linden passed out, waking several hours later to find Jayna staring down at her. Linden's right side felt on fire, and she grimaced as she took a breath.

"You're finally awake. Kean, the healer, said if you didn't come to soon, you might not. He's not the comforting sort of healer, not like my mother," said Jayna. "Can I get you anything?"

Linden shook her head. "I hope it gets easier to breath, that's all."

"Kean said you were struck by an ensorcelled dagger. He couldn't clear out all the dark magic in Mordahn's spell."

"What does that mean?"

"You'll always have a twinge of pain in your lung, and it'll likely worsen if you're in the presence of too much Fallow magic."

Linden sighed, and then wished she hadn't, because even that hurt. "Let's hope we can avoid Fallow magic, for a while at least. Where are we?"

"Captain is sailing toward a hidden inlet that he knows, way up north. He says we'll arrive tomorrow."

Linden drifted off to sleep, waking early the next morning to find Mara and Jayna sitting on Jayna's bunk, speaking in hushed tones. "What are you two whispering about?" she croaked.

Jayna and Mara looked at each other guiltily. Mara, who'd picked up a slight head cold after her dunking the day before, sniffed as she said, "I was telling Jayna about you being the Faymon Liege."

Linden pushed herself into a semi-sitting position, wincing as she shifted on her bunk. "When did you find out?"

Jayna's mouth opened and closed, but no sound came out. Mara said, "When young Fen thought we'd be 'sailing to the yonder shore' as he put it. Fen told me that you were the Liege of all Faynwood, including the clans that don't recognize your authority. Although to be honest, I'm not sure how well that would work out. He also mentioned, about half a dozen times while we were bobbing in the waves, that he's your cousin twice or thrice removed."

"So, it's true?" asked Jayna. "Why didn't you tell me?"

Linden felt badly about the hurt look in Jayna's eyes and hastily explained. "I only learned about it from Mage Mother Pawllah the day before our graduation. I was shocked—still am —and I wasn't ready to tell anyone. I'm not sure even now how I feel about it, but I don't think my feelings matter at this point."

Jayna nodded, looking somewhat mollified, and said, "Well of course your feelings matter. If you don't want to do it, you don't have to."

"It's pretty complicated." Linden explained about the Faymon prophecies, the blood feud between her clan and Mordahn's, and about the strange coincidences when she kept seeing the same image of the new Liege being crowned.

Mara said, "If I were you, I'd go through with the crowning ceremony and then see what happens. Even if it doesn't work out, the crown would be yours, and they're worth a fortune."

Linden smiled. "The Faymon Liege wears a crown woven from the leaves, vines, and berries of the forest."

"Huh?" said Mara.

Laughing, Jayna said, "I don't think Linden would be going through with it for the crown."

The three girls roused themselves enough to get dressed. Jayna helped Linden into her teal-blue traveling dress and white boots. They shared tea and toast in their stateroom, and then went above deck to scan for the coast. It seemed as if the entire ship had the same idea: everyone was on deck, looking out the port side for a glimpse of the towering trees of Faynwood. Fen brought a chair over for Linden, still too weak to stand for long. She glanced starboard and sure enough, Mordahn's ugly hulk was sailing along beside them.

One of the deck hands spotted the coastline, and everyone applauded. The inlet was well camouflaged by a thin spit of forested land jutting out into the sea. As the ship entered the inlet, Evaleah sounded the ship's foghorn three times. The crew clambered to their posts, pulling in the sails and letting down the anchor. Orlette piloted Mordahn's ship, dropping anchor behind them.

Frowning, Remy asked, "Why are they aiming arrows at us?" A small army of mounted warriors occupied the beachfront, their archers taking careful aim in their direction.

Raff spun around, swore an oath, and shouted at the two nearest deckhands, "Hoist 'ar colors up quick-like, 'afore we start anoth'r war!"

As the purple and gold flag was run up the pole, Raff explained, "We sail beneath th' colors a' th' Faymon Elder's clan and be under 'is protection."

"Have we landed among hostiles?" asked Mara, sneezing into her handkerchief.

"We're in Shorewood territory, a clan friendly to the Faymon Elder. So, we're safe. Those men just don't know it yet," said Evaleah, nodding at the Faymon warriors who'd taken up battle positions all along the shoreline. "On the other hand, we just arrived with a ship that reeks of Fallow magic. They're wary for good reason."

Raff rubbed his chin. "I'd best be headin' over in th' skiff, waving me white flag."

"I'll join you," Linden said.

"These boys can be quick to strike, so you'd best stay here."

Linden turned to Fen, "Would you please fetch my shawl?" Fen bowed and raced below, returning a few minutes later with the teal shawl made by the sisters.

Raff shrugged. "As ye wish, mum." Two of the crew readied the skiff and rowed them over to the sandy shore. Linden removed her boots, lifted her skirts, and Raff helped her out of the skiff so she could wade to shore. When they reached dry land, Raff stood at her right side so that she could lean on his arm for support while she slipped her feet back into her boots. Nodding at his ship, he said, "We're flyin' the Elder's colors! Is't any way to treat 'is honor's friends?"

There was a ripple of motion as a bearded man with military bearing and a scar bisecting one dark eyebrow dismounted, moved through the ranks of his warriors, and stepped in front of Raff and Linden. His frown turned into a wide grin, "Raffindor—how long's it been? Two, three years?"

Raff nodded and smiled broadly. "Aye, m'Elder, it's be'n goin' on four years since we las' met!"

The Faymon Elder clapped Raff on the back affectionately and then turned to Linden, shivering slightly on the windy beach. Bowing politely, he asked, "And who's our guest, Captain?"

Raff hastened to make the most important introduction of his life. Bowing, he said, "M'Elder, Reynier Arlyss, 'tis 'ar Faymon Liege, Linden Arlyss. An' quite the master mage too." Raff added helpfully.

Reynier smiled warmly at Linden and bowed deeply. "I pledge my life, my home, and my mage's honor to my Faymon Liege, Linden Arlyss."

Linden thanked him, feeling awkward and exposed on the little strip of beach. Reynier turned and shouted to his countrymen. "This is our Faymon Liege come home, Linden Arlyss! Show her your allegiance!" The entire company of leather-clad warriors, sitting atop their sturdy horses, lowered their weapons and bowed their heads. Their blue-streaked hair seemed almost to shimmer in the sunlight. In one voice, they shouted, "We pledge our lives, our homes, and our mages' honor to our Faymon Liege, Linden Arlyss."

Reynier turned to Linden and said, "Come with me. I can see you need to sit down somewhere more comfortable than a

TONI CABELL

skiff." He escorted Linden through a cluster of lushly scented trees to a simple warrior's tent, which probably belonged to him. Bowing again, he handed her over to a serving woman, but Linden put her hand on his arm.

"Those trees, what are they called? They smell so familiar, yet I've never seen them before."

"They grow only in Faynwood. That's the Linden tree."

"I was named for a *tree*?"

"Not just any tree, but one that perfumes the air a few weeks each spring, reminding us to hope."

The serving woman called in a healer to change Linden's bandages, and then she helped Linden into a flowing purple gown piped with gold thread and cinched at the waist with gold braid. Linden sat on a seat cushion before a small table large enough for two people. The woman placed a bowl of hot soup on the table. After Linden had eaten her fill, the serving woman announced the Faymon Elder. Reynier bowed upon entering the tent and sat across from Linden.

"You must have much on your mind, my Liege," Reynier said.

"I have much on my mind, and on my heart," Linden replied, gazing steadily at Reynier. He reminded her of someone—and then it came to her. Although he was older by several years, he reminded her of Matteo. Same straight nose and strong chin, same strength and kindness packed into a single word or gesture. His dark brown hair, the same shade as Matteo's, had identical bluish streaks along his hairline and temples.

Reynier nodded. "Of course, my Liege."

"Please, call me Linden. We're cousins after all, and it'll take a while for me to become used to the title."

"As you wish, Linden," Reynier smiled. "We've a great deal to do within the next eight days to prepare you for your crowning ceremony."

"Eight days! That soon?"

"We can't wait longer, as the Faymon clans who support us have been awaiting your arrival impatiently, and the clans who don't support us will use any means—including any delays—to divide us." Reynier went on to explain that Linden needed to prepare a short speech for her crowning ceremony.

"Couldn't I draft my speech and have someone else it read aloud to the clans?" The thought of giving a speech at a large public gathering of the Faymon clans made Linden's palms go clammy. She resisted the urge to wipe them on her gown in front of Reynier.

"Absolutely not! You have Liege Ayala's blood running in your veins." Reynier added, more gently, "The clans understand you are new to all this, but they expect to see their new Faymon Liege at the crowning ceremony, not a frightened Valerran transplant."

Linden thought of her uncle and her mother, whose firm grasp of politics she'd often witnessed. "I understand. Please forgive any lapses as I become adept in Faymon ways and duties."

"I have every confidence in you, my Liege." Reynier outlined how she'd be spending the next eight days. First, they'd travel to the spiritual center of Faynwood, a forested bluff spelled by the fays with protection charms, where every Faymon Liege before her had been crowned. That's where she'd be meeting the Faymon Council and clan chiefs who supported her, meeting her people, and preparing for the actual ceremony.

"And what about my friends, who've fought alongside me, traveled with me, and have no home in Valerra? What of them?"

"Every Liege has companions, an inner circle of trusted friends and advisors. They're as welcome here in Faynwood as you are."

"Yet they're not Faymon by birth."

"The Faymon clans we're aligned with understand we must engage more with those outside our land—we must work together to destroy Fallow magic. For too long we've isolated ourselves, fought amongst ourselves, and now the rest of the continent has fallen." Reynier paused. "Tell me about that Fallow ship and how you came upon it in the open sea."

Linden told Reynier about the battle with Mordahn, his death, and what he'd said about there being others. Reynier rubbed his beard. "Mordahn dead at last. That's something to celebrate. But he couldn't have come this far, done this much damage, all on his own. There are other Fallow mages out there, equally powerful."

"Agreed. And they must be stopped." Looking at Reynier, she added, "We have to be ready—by uniting all the Faymon clans. Anything less, and we'll surely fall the way of Valerra."

"Well said, my Liege. Faymons must stop killing Faymons."

CHAPTER 31

"**A**re you ready?" Jayna asked as she adjusted Linden's ankle-length watered silk gown, which flashed a kaleidoscope of purple, blue, red, and green every time she moved. The formal gown had an empire waist, cap sleeves, and square neckline, its bodice, sleeves, and hem embroidered with leaves, vines, and berries in gold thread.

At her waist she wore the circlet of fire opals Mara carried from the Valerran Museum. Pawllah had packed the circlet in the small leather trunk that accompanied them to the ship. Inside was a note from her, explaining the circlet had belonged to Liege Ayala and now was Linden's. Also packed inside the small trunk were the shimmery purple tunic and leggings that Linden had carried in her backpack. Pawllah's noted indicated the clothes must have some significance to Linden, and so she included them with the circlet of opals. Linden planned to commission a whole line of tunics and leggings for her to wear in Faynwood, along with split-skirt dresses and gowns.

Linden fingered Stryker's pendant at her neck absentmindedly. She checked her reflection in the tall looking glass that one of the servants had thoughtfully placed inside the cavernous Liege's tent. Her blue-black hair fell about her shoulders and down her back in long layers, and her father's earrings, which she'd never removed, still sparkled as brightly as they had on her Teenth. She twirled around to check that her dress moved freely—she knew many Faymons would be lining the pathways along the ridge and even climbing the trees for a glimpse of their new Liege.

Her mind went back to another evening, eight months earlier, when she was getting ready for her Teenth. *So little time, really, but so much loss, not just for me, but also for Valerra.* Kal clicked his beak and she bent down to rub his fur, which she'd brushed to a bright sheen despite his protests.

Mara ran into the tent, hung all about with tapestries, its floor covered with woven carpets. She bent over to catch her breath. "Linden, you won't believe who I saw!" she exclaimed.

"Who?" asked Linden.

"They wouldn't let me get too close, but I shouted his name, and he turned around. I could hardly believe my eyes, but he's here."

"Who's here?" Linden and Jayna demanded.

"Stryker—he's with a group of Faymons, but it's definitely him."

"Stryker—where?" Linden reached out a hand to steady herself against the looking glass. *Stryker's alive, and here!* She lifted her skirt, preparing to dash outside to search for him, when one of her maidservants announced the Faymon Elder. Linden didn't want to talk to her cousin at the moment. She'd spent more than enough time meeting with Reynier this past week as he prepared her for the crowning ceremony—that's all she'd been doing it seemed—meeting with the Faymon Elder and the Faymon Council, meeting with the chiefs and advisors from Shorewood and Ridgewood and her own clan, Tanglewood, meeting and listening and learning.

"Please let him know I can't see him—" but Reynier was

already walking through the silk panels that formed her doorway. She turned away in frustration until a familiar voice stopped her.

"Linden!" Stryker stepped around Reynier and ran to her, his arms outstretched. She spun around, ready to step into his arms, so filled with yearning she could only whisper his name. But her lips parted in surprise. *Could this really be Stryker?* The gentle doe-eyed boy was gone, replaced by a tall bearded man with a fresh scar on his cheek. His thick, dark hair curled over the collar of his black Faymon dress uniform, which strained across his muscled chest and clung to his torso like an oiled glove. Her heart thundered, pounding so hard the tips of her fingers and toes tingled. She reached out a hand, "Stryker?"

His arms were nearly around her waist when Reynier shouted an incantation, and a luminous wall surrounded Linden, trapping her inside. Stryker uttered an oath as he pounded on the wall, sending gold sparks flying whenever his fists made contact. The wall shimmered slightly, and Stryker spotted a doorknob where there'd been none a moment earlier. He grasped it, pulled the door open and stepped through, and then quickly slammed it shut in Reynier's shocked face.

One more step and they were in each other's arms, laughing and crying and laughing again. Stryker let Linden's hair spill through his fingers as he whispered, "I came back." Linden smiled, relief mingled with joy. She inhaled his familiar scent of wood smoke and pine needles. "Aye, you did—you kept your promise."

Stryker cupped her face in his hands and kissed her, slowly and searchingly, as if to satisfy himself that Linden was really standing in front of him. Linden grazed the scar on his cheek with her fingertips, recalling Pawllah's promise that Stryker would find her among her Faymon family. She sent up a silent prayer of thanks they'd both arrived safely in Faynwood, refugees from their homeland, but together once again.

"Your name appeared in the list of the missing after the battle at Wellan Pass, and I—" she stopped and closed her eyes, and then willed herself to continue. "I never gave up hope, but there were days when I thought I wouldn't see you again."

Stryker touched the scar on his cheek. "Aye, I earned this and a couple of broken ribs at Wellan Pass." He clasped her tightly against his chest. "There's something I've regretted not saying to you before I left Delavan. I wrote it in a letter, but it's not the same."

Linden drew back and looked up at him, waiting. Stryker tipped her head back and kissed her firmly on the lips. He ran his hands down her back and gripped her narrow waist, drawing her closer to him. Her stomach performed crazy somersaults, his kisses leaving her yearning for more.

"I love you," he said as he nuzzled her hair. "I'm crazy in love with you."

She wound her arms around his neck. "I love you, Stryker."

After several more long, satisfying kisses, Linden asked, "How on earth did you find me?"

Stryker gave a throaty chuckle. "It was your cousin who found us—me and Sergeant Desi, that is. We managed to escape from Wellan Pass before the Glenbarrans broke through, but we couldn't make it to Bellaryss in time. So, we rode north until we connected with a small unit of marines about ten miles outside of Faynwood. We made ourselves a nuisance, attacking the Glenbarrans at night, stealing their supplies, even their horses, until they finally came after us."

Stryker paused, his brown eyes glittering darkly. "Only the Sarge and I escaped with our lives, and Desi was wounded. We managed to cross into Faynwood and nearly died from exposure, when Reynier discovered us. In the midst of trying to determine why we were wandering around Faynwood, a wild boar charged Reynier from behind. I didn't even think. I pushed him out of the way and ran the boar through with my sword." Stryker grinned. "I guess that simple act has turned me into something of a folk hero, at least with your clan. And apparently, there's some sort of a prophecy about a tall warrior in battledress crowning the new Liege. So here I am."

Linden cradled her head in the center of his chest, knowing she owed Reynier a debt of gratitude she could never repay. Then she pulled back and looked at Stryker, who smiled down at her. He still had the bearing and confidence of a Royal Marine, but she noticed there was a humility about him that was new. He reminded Linden of her uncle in the final weeks before the fall of Valerra, burdened with the knowledge that whatever he did or said, innocent people would still die.

And it came to her, then, something her grandmother had tried to explain during one of their many lessons in the months before everything fell apart. Nari had told her there would be times in her life when it would seem that darkness had won. When her courage, her faith, and even her hope would falter. In those moments she would have to hold tight to one comfort, one truth: love never fails. She thought of those who'd sacrificed for love of one sort or another—whether love of country, family, friends, honor, or Serving magic—Nari and Uncle Alban, and Ian and so many other mages and marines, lost defending Bellaryss, that great fallen city. And Matteo, injured and missing as well.

Looking at Stryker she whispered, "Love never fails." He arched an eyebrow, "You sound just like Nari."

That's when they noticed the tent seemed to have filled with people gesturing and talking. The entire Faymon Council was inside Linden's tent, staring at the pair with stern expressions. But Linden's friends were smiling at them—Raff and Evaleah and Fen, as well as Remy, Toz, Jayna, and Mara. Stryker waved at a smiling man, also attired in black battledress, and she figured he must be Sergeant Desi. They heard Reynier muttering various incantations to open the door in the luminous wall that cocooned them. Sighing, Linden said, "I suppose we really ought to step out and face Reynier."

"*You* put that door in the wall, didn't you?" Stryker asked.

Linden bit her bottom lip. "I've learned a few tricks."

They both laughed and then he said, "Before we face Reynier, there's something you should know." Stryker explained that according to Faymon custom, they couldn't be together—ever. Reynier had told him she'd have to agree to an arranged marriage with a Faymon warrior from another clan. A Valerran by her side would never do.

Linden's anger flared and she drew her brows together. Compressing her lips like Nari used to do, she said, "We'll see about that." She clapped her hands twice and the walls dissolved around them.

Everything was much louder without the walls, especially with several dozen people speaking and shouting over one another to be heard. Reynier was growing more frustrated by the second and in a commanding voice he shouted, "Be still! The Liege needs some privacy before the ceremony begins. Please leave us now." With quick bows and curtsies, everyone filed out of the tent. Even Jayna and Mara left when they realized Reynier wanted to speak with Linden and Stryker alone.

Reynier put his hands behind his back and paced around the tent. He paused once or twice to speak, thought better of it, and then resumed his pacing. After his fifth turn around the large tent he stopped in front of Stryker, whose arm was draped around Linden's waist, and frowned.

"Reynier, we didn't mean to create such a spectacle," Linden said quietly. "It's been many months and—"

Reynier held up his hands, stopping her mid-sentence. "Say no more. That was quite clear to everyone who witnessed your reunion." He paced some more. "And yet, this cannot be."

"What cannot be?" Linden asked, her voice louder than she intended.

Reynier sputtered, "You, the Faymon Liege, and Stryker—a Valerran man. It won't do."

"You forget yourself, Cousin," Linden said stiffly. She didn't want to fight with Reynier, but no one was going to dictate her love life. *And an arranged marriage? Ew!*

"How do you mean?" Reynier seemed genuinely confused.

"Liege Ayala's daughter, Nari Arlyss, a woman with as much Faymon blood running in her veins as you, has deemed this man worthy. What right have you to overrule the Liege's daughter?"

Stryker cleared his throat. "Of course, we want to do everything we can to respect Faymon traditions. I'll gladly ride out with you and your clan—so long as it's understood. We are promised to each other. No one and nothing is going to change that."

Reynier's brow furrowed in thought. He paced slowly about the tent one more time, moved his shoulders ever so slightly and then nodded. "I suppose if Liege Ayala's daughter has deemed him worthy, then I cannot stand in the way. However, Stryker must follow our customs, learning our history and defending our clan." Reynier looked at them, waiting.

Stryker spoke first. Stepping forward, he bowed before Reynier and said, "It will be an honor to serve with you, my Elder." Linden walked over to Reynier, stood on her toes, and kissed his cheek. "You are a wise man."

Reynier sighed deeply and then said, sheepishly, "My Liege, I have a favor to ask." He waited until Linden nodded. "Would you show me how you inserted that impenetrable door?"

"Someday, perhaps." Linden smiled slyly.

Reynier's eyebrows shot up, and then his warm laugh embraced them all.

~

The Faymon high priest led the procession, carrying the simple crown woven of Faynwood itself, of its vines and berries and leaves and magic. Directly behind him walked the Faymon Council members and clan chiefs. The two clans still at war with the rest were not represented. Behind them were the Liege's companions, Mara and Remy, Jayna and Toz, and then Stryker and Sergeant Desi. Then came the musicians, pipers playing a haunting fay melody, and drummers tapping out a rhythmic marching beat. When the high priest at the head of the procession paused, the drummers picked up the tempo, hit a final thrump on their drums, and the woods fell silent. Everyone stopped moving; even the birds stopped twittering.

Reynier and Linden stepped out of her tent, with Kal walking between them, his tail held high, his mane framing his small eagle's face. Two clansmen carrying banners—one for the Liege and the other for the Elder—followed behind. A loud cheer went up throughout the woods. The women trilled in their high-pitched voices and the men stomped their feet, shouting a Faymon victory chant. The procession resumed as the raucous crowd, trilling and chanting, followed Linden and Reynier.

They took a circuitous path to the crowning ceremony, winding from Linden's tent past a colorful collection of tents surrounding a large open marketplace, overflowing with tables laden with food and drink for the celebration following the crowning. Leaving the marketplace behind, they followed a worn stone path through the woods, where a canopy of trees formed a natural arch overhead, and Linden knew a number of Faymon children would be perched in the branches for a good look at their new Liege. It was a beautiful spring morning for an outdoor ceremony, with violets and bluebells carpeting the ground, and mourning doves, cardinals, and red-winged blackbirds chattering in the trees.

The high priest led them up the path to a grassy ridge that overlooked the woods below. Reynier guided Linden to an ornately carved chair, covered with delicate fay symbols that reminded Linden of her favorite old door at the Valerran Museum. As she turned to sit down, Linden was momentarily overcome at the sight. Spread out before her, across the woods and tumbling onto the stone path, Faymons were waving purple and gold ribbons, which Reynier had explained were the Liege's colors. But more surprising still was a small band of hooded fays materializing near the ridge. They emerged from a mist and added their buzzing voices to the general throng. It was as different as any procession could possibly be from the sedate, yet beautiful Valerran traditions Linden had been raised with—and it was all the more exciting because of the high spirits of the Faymon clans.

The ceremony itself moved quickly, with the high priest chanting a blessing and presenting the crown to Stryker, the tall 'outsider' warrior whom the seers had predicted would crown the new Liege. Stryker lifted the crown high and the crowd roared its approval. As he lowered the crown onto Linden's head, he repeated the high priest's words, "I crown thee Liege Linden Arlyss, head of all the Faymon clans, loyal representative of the fay folk, and protector of Serving magic throughout the realm!"

The crowd jumped to their feet and roared a second time. The women began trilling again while the men stomped and chanted. Reynier waited for the crowd to settle down, and he gave a short speech thanking the fays and council members for attending, and then he recognized each clan present, including each chief. As he called out to them, each clan fluttered their colorful ribbons and cheered again. When he was finished, he returned to Linden's side and escorted her to a small raised platform. He nodded encouragingly and stepped behind her. Linden had been nervously preparing for her first speech as Faymon Liege all week. The crowd quieted down, and Linden cleared her throat. Her side still ached when she took deep breaths, but she inhaled through the pain, knowing she had one chance to get this right. She was determined that everyone would hear her, and so she tried to speak in her most commanding voice.

"Honored fay elders, council members, clan chiefs, and my Faymon brothers and sisters, welcome to this celebration of Faynwood unity!" A cheer went up from the crowd and Reynier led the applause.

"Although you've been without a Liege for five decades, you've been ably led by three brave and strong Faymon Elders during this time—and we are all fortunate to call Reynier Arlyss our Elder!" Linden turned to Reynier and applauded him as another cheer went up.

"I am honored and humbled to be crowned your Liege and will work hard to serve each of you. As you know, I wasn't raised within Faynwood, but in Valerra, where I was the daughter of a Serving Family, and so serving one another, serving the greater good, and ensuring we protect our homes, our families, and our pure Serving magic, has been my calling since I was a child." The fays began buzzing and the Faymon clans applauded, stomping and cheering.

"There's but one thing that mars this perfect day, my brother and sisters." The crowd quieted down. "We still have two clans who are not represented here, two clans we are warring with, two clans of Faymon brothers and sisters who are isolated and cutoff from this celebration. I want to be Liege of all the Faymon clans, to stop the civil war that has lasted far too long and spilled too much Faymon blood. I vow to work with all my strength and all my heart to resolve this civil war. We will have peace in Faynwood!" Linden's heart thudded as she waited for the crowd's reaction. It was the fays who started it—they buzzed loudly and clapped their hands and stomped their feet. Then Reynier began to applaud and stomp his feet, and soon the thunder of applause and stomping echoed throughout the woods.

Reynier helped Linden to step down from her platform. With the ceremony over, everyone began gathering little ones and heading to the marketplace, where the celebration would last well into the next morning. Stryker came over to Linden and squeezed her hand. "You were amazing. Your family would have been so proud."

"I like to think they were cheering me on." She thought of her parents every day, sometimes wondering whether she'd ever see them again. As for the rest—Uncle Alban, Nari, and Matteo—her heart still ached whenever she thought of them.

There was a small commotion near the tip of the ridge, as several of the hooded fays stepped forward and bowed first to Linden and then to Reynier. Reynier's commanding voice asked for silence, and the crowd settled back down, curious to see what was happening. One of the fays, an older man with piercing gray eyes, pushed back his hood to reveal vivid blue hair. He addressed Reynier in his buzzing language. Reynier's eyebrows shot up and he questioned the fay closely. When he was satisfied, Reynier turned to translate for Linden, the clan chiefs, and the council leaders, who had gathered around the small group.

"All of you know Pryl, Chief of the Fay Nation, who speaks for all fays in Faynwood. He says that two of the hooded fays standing with him are in fact Faymons." Reynier paused for emphasis, "They are the clan chiefs of Arrowood and Riverwood."

The chiefs from the other clans erupted in outrage. "What?" "How dare they?" "They weren't invited!"

"Let us listen, please!" Reynier commanded.

Pryl continued in his buzzing language, and Reynier translated. "The chiefs traveled here under fay protection to see and hear the new Liege. They believe she truly wishes for peace, as do the clans of Arrowood and Riverwood. They are here, now, to pledge their allegiance to the Faymon Liege."

The two chiefs stepped forward, pulling back their hoods. Instead of the bright blue hair of the fays, the male chief's brown hair was threaded with blue, and the female leader had a ginger-and-blue braid. They bowed before Linden, exposing their necks in submission. Several Faymon men sitting nearby saw the two rebellious clan chiefs and spat in anger—many Faymons had lost their lives fighting these last two hold-outs. The men unsheathed their swords, shouted an oath, and ran at the two chiefs, prepared to draw blood. While Pryl immediately cast a defensive shield around the two chiefs to protect them from harm, Linden's first instinct was to disarm the men without shedding blood. She shouted an incantation. "Heat those blades until they bake, shift from sword to slithery snake!" The men's swords turned red-hot. Dropping them to the ground, the men cradled their scorched hands, watching in shock as their swords turned into snakes and slithered away into the woods.

Reynier asked for volunteers to take the men to a healer who would see to their wounds, and then he apologized to the chiefs and Pryl, who lowered the shield.

The two chiefs bowed low, stretched out their arms and presented their hands, palms up. Linden knew this was a plea for peace, for a truce among the Faymon clans. Reynier grasped the hands of the two chiefs, and then indicated for Linden to do the same. After Linden, the council members and other clan chiefs also stepped forward, a few grumbling about the need for concessions from their rivals, but in the end they all grasped the outstretched hands of the two chiefs.

Reynier then shouted, "Our new Liege, in her gracious and

moving speech, asked for one thing above all else—unity across the Faymon clans. As you've just witnessed with your own eyes, true unity has come to Faynwood today. Let us welcome Arrowood and Riverwood back into the Faymon fold, and hail Liege Linden for opening our hearts to peace. Peace is an elusive thing, and we must guard it jealously."

A low rumbling roar rose up from the crowd, building into a crescendo that reverberated throughout the forest. Slowly the various clans disbursed, chatting happily as they headed to the celebration meal, while the musicians struck up a lively dance tune in the marketplace. One by one the council members and chiefs left to join their own clans at the celebration, followed by the rest of the procession. Only the chiefs of Arrowood and Riverwood remained behind, with their fay escorts. They bowed again and walked into the traveling mist conjured by Pryl.

Stryker took Linden's hand. "I see you've mastered your shape-shifting spells at last."

She laughed and began to relax. They started to thread their way to the celebration, where there would be a table set aside for the Liege, the Elder, and their companions. Linden was suffused with hope for the first time in many, many months.

"Before you go, there's something else that Chief Pryl told me." Reynier spoke quietly. Stryker and Linden turned to listen, but one look at his furrowed brow told them all they needed to know.

"It's the Glenbarrans again, isn't it?" Stryker asked.

Reynier nodded. "Apparently the Glenbarrans aren't satisfied with occupying Valerra. Pryl's scouts say that King Roi has set his sights on Faynwood."

"Pryl has *fay scouts?*" Linden asked, wondering whether they were small hooded creatures that popped up inside flames, or were actual flesh-and-blood people that spied on the Glenbarran royal family.

Reynier spread his hands. "Of course, they do. How do you think we knew where to meet you when you arrived?" That the fays were keeping a sharp eye out for her had never occurred to Linden. She could see she had a lot to learn about Faymon—and fay—ways.

"How much time do the scouts say we have?" Stryker asked.

"We have a couple of months, at most, to prepare." Turning to Linden he added, "I'm afraid we must ride to Eloway first thing in the morning, as we'll be spending the better part of the next few months holding war councils and drawing battle plans."

She'll finally get to see Eloway, her grandmother's hometown, but she'll be stuck in meetings all day. *Ugh, governing is such hard work! How could Mother and Uncle Alban stand it?*

Linden nodded. "That's fine, but after the battle plans are drawn, don't think I'm staying behind in Eloway." Not that she looked forward to facing the Glenbarrans and their Fallow magic again, but she knew they had to be stopped—for good. Besides, she wasn't about to let Stryker go off to any more battles without her.

Stryker asked, with a hint of a smile, "What exactly do you have in mind, my Liege?"

"Wherever you go, I'll be riding right alongside you. You're not going to escape from me so easily this time." She put her hands on his chest and stood on her tiptoes to plant a kiss on his lips. Stryker drew her into his arms.

"Hmm," he whispered, "I have no intention of escaping."

THE END

Thanks so much for reading *Lady Apprentice*!
I hope you enjoyed it.

Please consider taking a moment to share your thoughts by leaving a review. Reader reviews help other readers discover new books.

Please visit my website to stay tuned for new releases, including the next book in the Serving Magic series, *Lady Mage*, coming in Summer 2021. You can also sign up to receive a free EBook, *Lady Tanglewood*, the exciting prequel to the Serving Magic series:

https://tonicabell.com

~ Thank you, *Toni*

4800355⁶R00194